SPIN
-OF-
FATE

SPIN OF FATE

The Fifth Realm

−BOOK I−

A. A. VORA

putnam

G. P. PUTNAM'S SONS

G. P. PUTNAM'S SONS
An imprint of Penguin Random House LLC, New York

First published in the United States of America by G. P. Putnam's Sons,
an imprint of Penguin Random House LLC, 2024

Copyright © 2024 by Ambika Nagino
Map illustration copyright © 2024 by Sveta Dorosheva

Visit us online at PenguinRandomHouse.com.

Library of Congress Cataloging-in-Publication Data
Names: Vora, A. A., author.
Title: Spin of fate / A. A. Vora.
Description: New York: G. P. Putnam's Sons, 2024. | Series: Fifth realm; book 1 |
Summary: In a universe that segregates beings based on the weight of their souls into upper realms of peace and lower realms of strife, three teenagers join a rebel group defying the powers that be by bringing aid to the inhabitants of the lower realms.
Identifiers: LCCN 2023033490 (print) | LCCN 2023033491 (ebook) |
ISBN 9780593617564 (hardcover) | ISBN 9780593617571 (epub)
Subjects: CYAC: Fantasy. | LCGFT: Fantasy fiction. | Novels.
Classification: LCC PZ7.1.V6796 Sp 2024 (print) | LCC PZ7.1.V6796 (ebook) |
DDC [Fic]—dc23
LC record available at https://lccn.loc.gov/2023033490
LC ebook record available at https://lccn.loc.gov/2023033491

Printed in the United States of America
ISBN 9780593617564 (hardcover)
ISBN 9780593857182 (international edition)
1st Printing
LSCC

Design by Suki Boynton
Text set in ITC Galliard Pro

To maa, without whom
I would be nothing.

CONTENTS

SPIN

-OF-

FATE

Paramos

Mayana

Malin

Narakh

THE FOUR REALMS
AND THEIR BEASTS

The Mayani Institute
of Cartography has not
visited the lower realms.
Thus, the maps of Malin and Narakh
are, at best, an approximation
based on historical account.

PROLOGUE

෧

A Flash of White

A SHARP TWANG PULLED Aina from troubled dreams. She staggered to her feet, ignoring the protest of her muscles as she grabbed her bow and slung a quiver across her back. Razor wire hung across the craggy walls like the web of some monstrous spider. One of the trip wires stretched taut. Aina followed its trembling path out of the cave and into the moonless night.

Her mother whittled a thumb-sized stone by the fire, her back rigid as a blade. "What are you doing up so early?" she barked without looking up from her task.

Aina watched, transfixed, as her mother ran a finger over the stone, caressing away tiny chunks as if they were carved at knife-point. But her mother had never needed a knife. Not when she could shape the world around her through channeling. The stone figure took on the form of a horned monkey with spines that glinted in the firelight.

"Will you give me that once you're done?" Aina asked. "I want to add it to my collection."

"I'll give you a tight slap if you don't go back to sleep. You'll never learn to channel without proper rest."

"Something triggered one of my trip wires—" Aina had barely gotten the words out when her mother sprang to her feet with a curse. "I meant a wild animal, Mama. The wire's intact; it would've snapped under the weight of a human."

"Say that part first, idiot girl," her mother scolded before settling back by the fire.

Aina ignored the withering glare cast her way. The trip wires hardly mattered, given that her mother had channeled a protective shield around their hideout. Kaldrav's stupid soldiers would bounce right off it if they approached, alerting her of their presence. And providing her mother's inexhaustible wrath with another target, for a change.

"And where the blazes do you think you're going?" her mother demanded.

"To get us some food. I'm starving, Mama. *That's* why I can't channel properly."

Her mother made to stand again, but Aina placed a hand on her arm. Under the threadbare cloak, her mother's arm felt brittle as a twig. Shadows ringed her eyes and wrinkles forked across her weathered skin.

"It's probably just a rat," Aina said. "Let me handle it. You get some rest for once."

"You've had it from me if you're not back within ten minutes."

Aina nodded with a glance at the wire. It gave a violent tremor and stretched to the verge of snapping.

Larger than a rat.

Aina set off into the skeletal forest, squinting through the gloom. Fourteen years in Malin had given her excellent night vision. But today was murkier than usual, as if the misery of the realm had condensed into a grim fog that obscured everything beyond a few feet in any direction.

Aina's heart stopped at a gleam of cobalt blue through the haze. *That can't be what I think it is . . .*

But as she inched closer the monstrous form grew clear: a giant nagamor, asleep outside the shimmering dome of her mother's shield. The peacock snake lay in a mound of coils, each as wide as a tree trunk.

Aina crept past the beast and released a tremulous breath. It was just their stinking luck that the one thing in Malin deadlier than enemy soldiers had settled for a nap this close to their hideout. At least it hadn't slithered onto any of her traps. *That* would have thrown it into a rage.

Quiet as a mouse, Aina followed the wire until she came upon her prey. A runt of a fox thrashed in her snare, teeth gnashing and yellow eyes rolled back in fear. The beast's emaciated form carried enough meat to last them three days at most.

Aina's stomach gave a painful rumble. Three days of fox meat would be a luxury after weeks of dried grass and the occasional lizard.

She drew her bow and nocked an arrow. Best kill it before it bit her hand off. The fox's eyes bulged as she neared. Blood stained its fur as it strained against the razor wire.

"Don't look at me like that," Aina muttered.

Had it been born to the blessed realm of Mayana, this fox might have grown powerful and majestic. Instead it was born cursed. Cursed, like her, to live in Malin. At least, unlike Aina, it could die and be spared from its miserable existence by an arrow to the heart.

A soft whimper stopped Aina in her tracks.

She looked down to see a trembling lump of fur, small enough to fit into her palm. A tiny wet nose brushed her ankle. The pup gave a pitiful squeak as it crawled forward on stubby legs. The fox in the wires snarled as she struggled to reach her whimpering newborn.

Aina lowered her bow, chest folding over at the familiarity of the scene: a small creature and its mother trying desperately to survive the fate that had been dumped upon them. How would this fox pup live without its angry, snarling mother to protect it?

"Stop moving," Aina hissed. She unsheathed a short knife and cut through the wires.

The injured fox jerked away from her at once. Aina stepped back, knife raised. But the creature had no interest in attacking. The fox snatched the tiny pup with her teeth and bounded into the darkness.

Hunger clawing at her stomach, Aina trudged back toward the cave. The immense form of the slumbering nagamor came into view.

Then the world flashed around her. For a moment the forest disappeared, and Aina found herself suspended in a vast white nothingness. She'd never seen it before, this eerie blankness. Silent and still, it surrounded her.

Sudden as it had come, the whiteness faded. Aina returned to the same spot in the forest, within her mother's shield, feet away from the nagamor.

What the hell just happened?

Aina had no time to ponder the thought. From beyond the shield came the soft, ragged scrape of scale over stone. Aina's blood ran cold as the beast, awakened by the flash of white, raised its head and turned.

Bulbous eyes gleamed through the murk, the promise of pain in their bloodied depths. Then several tons of scale and sinew lunged forward and slammed against the shield. It held an excruciating second before shattering in an eruption of light.

Aina fled, gaze lowered as she stumbled through the splintered landscape of Malin. Without the shield, locking eyes with the nagamor would induce intense hallucinations—three years of torment packed into three agonizing minutes.

Living in this realm was torment enough. Aina had no need for more.

The stones rattled under the nagamor's advancing bulk. Aina dodged the beast's snapping beak to whip out her bow and fire at its underbelly. A tail swept through the air, batting away her arrows with a plume of rounded feathers. The beast twisted and struck again. Aina's bow sang in desperation as she loosed more arrows.

But the nagamor's serpentine body raged and wrapped around her, an inescapable whirlwind of pain. Aina's quiver poked her back, the contents of her various pouches digging into her hips. The nagamor squeezed tighter and crushed the air from her lungs.

The ground beneath Aina erupted, and a pillar of rock pierced the beast's cobalt blue scales. The nagamor surged upward with the rising rock, screeching as a cascade of blood poured from its flank.

Freed from its hold, Aina leaped to the ground and raised her eyes to meet a pair deadlier than the nagamor's. "Mama—"

"Blasted fool," her mother snarled, lowering her hands and releasing the channeling. The ground stopped rumbling and the rocks froze in place, although the impaled beast continued writhing. "Waking a sleeping nagamor! I'll flay you to the last bit of your soul, if Kaldrav's soldiers don't get to us first!"

"I didn't do anything," Aina wailed. "I was only walking, when a flash of white light came from nowhere!"

Her mother stiffened. Before she could retort, the nagamor broke free of its stony prison and dove toward the ground, sinuous body curving like a scythe.

Swearing, her mother swiped a thumb across her forehead. Mottled energy pulsed from her palms as the fractured earth danced beneath her fingertips. In response, the nagamor loosed a soul-searing cry and swatted away her mother's boulders as if they were flies.

"Run!" Her mother shoved Aina forward. Her dark energy swirled around them in a protective dome, the nagamor's relentless assault eroding it bit by bit.

As they ran, Aina glimpsed something twinkling in the distance: a beacon of light amidst the gloom of Malin. An elegant silver archway and, beyond it, bright fields and a brighter sky. It was one of the torana—a gateway leading to another realm. This silver one led to the upper realm of Mayana.

Which meant Aina and her mother could never get through. They were lowers, with souls steeped in sin. Souls that spun in the wrong direction. The torana would deny them entry as it had all these years. Such was the Law.

Aina's heart shriveled as she neared the torana, the nagamor smashing against her mother's defenses. She pivoted in front of the archway and reached for an arrow.

But her blood-slicked heel slipped in the mud and Aina's left leg slid backward, straight between the silver columns. Soft grass brushed Aina's toes, and she let out a gasp.

Her mother turned to her, inhaling sharply at the sight of Aina's sandaled foot planted in the upper realm while the other remained rooted in the filth of Malin.

"The white flash before," she whispered. "So it's true . . . your soul reversed . . . you're light enough to enter Mayana."

"That—that can't be," Aina said.

None could ascend from Malin to Mayana. It wasn't possible to flip the spin of a soul.

The nagamor clacked its beak, arching its neck to strike. Aina grabbed her mother's bony wrist and tried tugging her through the torana. But the gateway did not yield. An invisible barrier stopped Aina's mother from slipping even a single fingernail into the upper realm.

Aina knew her mother was not a particularly good person. She wasn't as bad as Kaldrav the Cruel, the despotic king of Malin. But she was bad enough, years of violence weighing her down. And if the torana had denied her mother, yet allowed Aina through . . .

"You're Mayani now, foolish girl!" Her mother ripped her wrist from Aina's grip. "Toranic Law has decreed it! Get away from me and stay in your realm!"

"Not without you," Aina declared. Bracing her weight on the foot still in Malin, she made to step back through the torana. "I'll stay here, Mama. I'll—"

Her mother cut her off with a slap that split Aina's lip. "Feather-soul! Counter-spinner!" she growled, shoving Aina fully past the pillars and into Mayana. "I don't want to see your face! If you set foot into this realm, I'll smack you till your skin turns blue!" In the dim light of Malin, her mother's cheeks were wet. "I'll make you suffer worse than a nagamor's glare! I'll—"

Whatever her mother meant to say next was drowned out by the nagamor slamming against the torana. Its fetid breath grazed Aina's cheek, the grimy blue scales an inch from her fingernails.

But for all the ferocity with which it crashed against the archway, the beast could not enter Mayana. Like Aina's mother's, the nagamor's soul spun backward. Toranic Law would not allow it to spill its filth into the upper realm.

Aina watched through the pillars in horror as her mother

clashed with the beast, channeling stone and raising up small mountains against its twisting, thrashing mass.

Aina nocked an arrow and made to race into Malin to assist her. But an enormous slab of stone spurted up on the other side of the torana; her mother's channeling had blocked the path that Toranic Law had let Aina pass.

"Mama!" Aina screamed. "Let me through!" Unlike her mother, Aina could not channel the stone away. So she beat it until her knuckles bled and the nagamor's cries faded. "Please, Mama! Don't do this! Don't leave me here all alone!"

There was no reply, only the shuffle of footsteps away from the torana. Away from Aina.

"Mama . . ." Aina fell to all fours on the sweet-scented grass, tears streaming down her cheeks. "Don't . . . leave me . . ."

Warm sunlight drenched her back, the air crisp and thick with birdsong. Aina paid it no heed as she lay there for hours, pounding weakly at the torana.

For the first time since her birth, Aina was in paradise. Mayana was an idyllic realm, free of Malin's monsters and violence and corruption. Free from the tyranny of Kaldrav's reign, from being hunted by his soldiers.

It was a realm protected by Toranic Law, where only those light of soul and good of heart were permitted to live. A realm that had admitted Aina but would never admit her mother.

Mayana was a heavenly place. Yet to Aina it felt like hell.

PART I

———

When earth was drenched in flesh and blood,
and hate split lives asunder,
when fire and steel surged forth in flood,
the skies lit by fey thunder,
humankind waged a brutal war,
their savagery a blight,
awakening the Beasts of lore
to set their world aright.

And thus the realm was split to four
by will of Beast who made it:
two realms for souls who relished gore,
who sinned and harmed and hated;
two for those proven true and kind,
their realms at peace, united.
And so the balance realigned,
with fair and foul divided.

–SONG OF SALVATION–
Verse V: The Great Toranic Separation

CHAPTER ONE

๏

An Adequate Crime

ONE YEAR LATER

AINA WANDERED THE bustling streets of inner Kirnos, hood pulled low over her forehead.

The marketplace was a vibrant riot of stalls lining a broad street paved with honey-colored stone. Bright-eyed Mayani shouted out their wares without a care in the world, selling embroidered silks and gold-plated pottery amongst an assortment of equally useless things.

Aina wrinkled her nose. *Such abundance,* she thought, recalling the foul-smelling pelts she'd worn in Malin. The wooden straws her mother had carved for them to suck water straight from the ground.

But Kirnos, the largest kingdom in the upper realm of Mayana, was a cesspit of abundance. It oozed from every street and stone, from the lush gardens and tinkling waterfalls, from flowers the size of Aina's face that burst at each corner. Every other doorframe was trimmed with gold, half the shop roofs shingled with

11

gemstones. Even the blasted toilets in Kirnos had seats of jade.

And today, in honor of the crown princess's ascension, Kirnos was at its worst. The marketplace in particular attracted merchants from across the realm, gathered in their most obnoxious display of wealth and frivolity.

Which made it the perfect spot for Aina's next crime.

She stopped by a table draped in cerulean gauze. It boasted a collection of shells from the underwater kingdom of Amaratir, polished to gleam like pearls. Aina glanced around her, then reached out to swipe a shimmering conch.

A hand enclosed her wrist. Aina recoiled, muscles tensing into the familiarity of fight.

"Do not be afraid, child," a kind voice said. An old woman with skin like bark smiled down at her. She plucked the conch from Aina's hands and held out a spiral shell. "Take this instead. It will bring you good luck."

"How so?" Aina asked.

"See the pattern of the swirl? It signifies the forward rotation of the soul. You are meant to have it." The woman pressed the shell into Aina's hand. "May your soul spin straight and swift."

Aina pocketed the seashell and tugged her hood down to obscure her forehead. As if a stupid trinket could hold such powers. Even if it could, this shell was the last thing Aina needed. She wanted to reverse her soul-spin. Load it with sin until the torana sucked her back into Malin.

Back to her mother.

It would have been easier to walk through one of the gateways. But for some hellforsaken reason, they refused to let her through. After ricocheting off the damn pillars for the hundredth time, Aina had lost her patience. So she'd launched a methodical spate of wrongdoing over the past few weeks: pelting unsuspecting Mayani with rotten fruit, flipping off priests, scribbling curse words across the torana, and stealing from Kirnosi teahouses and bakeries.

But today she would not steal food, which was plentiful in this realm. She would steal something of far greater value.

The next stall was piled with Kirnosi goods. Circlets of jasmine and freesia lay in heaps next to emerald-studded miniatures of Sherka the gazarou, the great grass wolf worshipped throughout the realm.

Aina stared at the miniatures, a hand going to the cloth pouch at her waist. She pulled out a piece of shattered rock and ran a finger over its ridges. It had looked like something once. A tusked sea turtle. Her mother had carved it for her many years ago, to keep Aina quiet and out of her hair. Aina never had any playthings in Malin, so her mother had channeled little figurines out of stone: spiked deer and tentacled sharks and elephants with barbed trunks. There was even a broken nagamor somewhere in the pouch, along with the remains of a gazarou.

All her figurines had been crushed during the nagamor attack. But Aina remembered them well, the crude designs of her mother's making. Her gazarou had been a fearsome thing, hackles raised, its tiny teeth on full display. So different from this timid Kirnosi design, gentle-eyed and wrought of gold.

Yet stealing something so extravagant would absolutely burden her soul.

"You are a visitor?" A bearded man peered over the stall. "What luck! To commemorate the crown princess's ascension, I have special gifts for visitors." He produced a jade wolf the size of Aina's thumb and offered it to her.

Aina backed away, fingers tightening around her broken rock. "I don't want that."

"But you must take it," the man insisted. "It is a sacred likeness of Goddess Sherka Herself."

Made from the same stone as the toilet seats? Sacred indeed.

"Accept this gift, child," the man said, "and let Her goodness bless your soul."

A half hour later, Aina found her arms loaded with unnecessary trinkets from across the realm: a lacquer hairpin from the eastern kingdom of Nishaki, useful for poking an eye out; a silken scarf from Tahamur down south, maybe she could strangle someone with it; and an intricately carved wooden bowl from western Samaras that might serve well as a bludgeon.

"Bleeding Mayani," Aina muttered.

How was she supposed to steal anything if they kept gifting her with free samples? She'd considered flinging the wares back at their sellers' faces, but that would only serve to attract the attention of the Kirnosi royal guard.

Aina needed something discreet. If not discreet, at least utterly damning, so Toranic Law would punish her before the guard had the chance.

Her mother had tortured a man once. Ripped off his fingernails after he'd tried to kidnap Aina. While it had seemed acceptable at the time—another bout of her mother's protectiveness—Aina's stomach twinged at the notion of doing that to one of these shallow, softhearted Mayani.

What falls between torture and theft? Aina mused as she jostled through the crowd. A bizarre number of Mayani had flocked to Kirnos for the ascension ceremony, choking the streets with color.

"Word from the palace has it that King Athanken's on edge," said a woman in pink silks. "Spent the past moon at the temple, praying for the princess's successful ascension."

Her companion gave a laugh, his voice airy and unbothered. "Stressing and praying is all the man ever does. Of course Himalia will ascend, her soul's light as a cloud."

Do they have nothing better to do with their lives, Aina wondered, *than watch a pampered princess strut through a pair of pillars?*

An idea stirred in her mind. An adequate crime, more nefarious than stealing, but without the brutality of torture. It wouldn't do permanent damage. But it would do just enough.

Aina approached the chatting pair and addressed them brusquely. "The princess's ascension. What time does it start?"

"An hour from now at the palace gardens," the young man said. He looked to her in surprise as Aina dumped her various souvenirs into his arms. "Wait, why are you—"

Aina dashed off without a word, elbowing her way through the crowd. The palace gardens stood atop the circular plateau that sprouted from the heart of Kirnos. If she hurried, she could still make Princess Himalia's ascension ceremony in time.

I'm coming, Mama. Aina clutched her pouch of broken rocks as she ran. *I'm descending, soon.*

AINA SQUATTED BEHIND the mossy ramparts of the Kirnosi palace. Due to the royal guard's preoccupation with the ascension ceremony, sneaking up had been easy. Aina's vantage point provided her with an excellent view of the garden and the foolish revelry unfolding atop its verdant lawns.

"May your soul spin straight and swift," an onlooker called as Princess Himalia drifted through the crowd, beaming from beneath the flower-studded canopy carried by four of her guard. Himalia's voluminous skirts swirled as she walked, the embedded emeralds sparkling bright as the torana she was to pass.

The golden torana led to Paramos—highest of the four realms and said to be more obscenely beautiful than even Mayana. Himalia's ascension would reflect her own virtue and that of her family, allowing the Kirnosi throne to remain in their bloodline.

If she made it through the torana.

Aina studied the seashell from earlier. She bounced it on her palm, noting its hardness, how it curved to a point: the perfect ammunition. She pulled a slingshot from her pocket. Nerves taut as the coarse band between her thumb and index finger, Aina set the seashell and took aim.

"Let's see if you're as lucky as that old hag claimed," she said, her voice muffled by the clashing cymbals and rhythmic roll of barrel drums.

She had one shot. One chance to shatter the crown princess's ankle. Injury aside, violating the sanctity of an ascension ceremony would be enough to condemn Aina to Malin.

The air grew thick with falling rose petals as Himalia swept across the lawn. The drums picked up pace as she neared the torana, the cymbals rising to a wild crescendo. In stark contrast to the stiffly marching guard, the crowd jumped up and down in wild abandon, waving colored silks and showering Himalia with more petals.

A war might do them good. Aina watched an enthusiastic old man bounce his wig off, then scramble through the crowd to retrieve it. *If this is how they choose to waste their peace.*

She shook her head and readjusted her aim. The entire procession, the dancing uppers, that ludicrous canopy strung with lotus buds—it was all bleeding ridiculous.

"Sherka bless your soul," a voice cried over the clamor as Himalia smiled and waved like the upper-born brat she was.

Sneering, Aina released the band of her slingshot just before the princess reached the torana.

Himalia let out a cry as Aina's shell shot between two of the unsuspecting guards and smashed into her ankle. She fell to her knees by the golden pillars, and her lotus headpiece tumbled to the ground. The startled onlookers froze mid-dance, their praises turning to gasps.

"I'm unworthy!" the young princess wailed. She clutched at her leg in pain. Tears spilled from charcoal-rimmed eyes to send black streaks across her dusky skin.

Himalia retreated behind a curtain of dark hair as the royal guard rushed to her aid. The drumbeats and cymbals faded until only the sound of the crown princess's choked sobs remained. "I'm unworthy. Toranic Law has deemed me unworthy."

Aina's lips curved. That foolish Himalia and her fluff-brained onlookers assumed that Toranic Law had blocked the ascension. Even if they discovered the seashell, they would blame divine intervention or call it the will of Sherka. They wouldn't think to suspect Aina, crouched atop the palace walls.

But Toranic Law was no fool. It was all-seeing, all-knowing, and all-judging. Aina waited for it to judge her for this sin. Drag her toward the nearest torana that led to Malin and cast her through its copper pillars.

But as a cool breeze ruffled Aina's hair, her feet remained firmly planted in Mayana.

Blasted Toranic Law. Aina swallowed the hot lump in her throat. *I failed you, Mama. Yet again, I failed you.*

She stowed her slingshot, climbed down the palace walls, and started for the marketplace, where she could blend into the crowd. Aina had made it halfway across the gardens when she heard the command, followed by the clanking of armor.

"Halt! In the name of Sherka the Benevolent!"

Aina whirled around to see a lone member of the Kirnosi royal guard rushing toward her, grass-knit cape rippling.

So he'd discovered it was her. Given the guard's absolute use-lessness otherwise, Aina couldn't help her surprise. Still, she'd rather face an angry nagamor than this sanctimonious fool in his fancy uniform.

Swiping a finger across her keiza—the swirl of raised skin on her forehead, said to be a window to the soul—Aina darted across trim grass. She felt her chitrons bubbling within her as she ran, pressing against her keiza.

Come on, you little shits, Aina urged. *Hurry up and activate!*

She sprinted through the garden, but the guard gained on her, his strides too fast to be anything but chitronically enhanced. Aina leaped over a hedge, then skidded to a stop at the rounded edge of the plateau overlooking a vertical cliff at least two hundred feet high.

Blast it! Aina took a deep breath and dove off the precipice.

Not a moment too late, her chitrons swarmed to life. Aina funneled them through the soles of her feet and bonded them to the cliff. She shaped the rock face through the bond into ledges that caught her as she fell. Aina hopped from ledge to ledge, keiza thrumming from the effort of the channeling, feet flickering with dim turquoise light.

Chitrons were the tiny spinning particles that made up every living soul and accumulated over the course of a lifetime. While individual chitrons were invisible to the human eye, they appeared as colored light when channeled en masse, responding instinctively to the will of their creator.

Or so they were supposed to work.

Aina was convinced her own chitrons were either stupid or plain unhelpful. Every time she swiped her keiza, the buggers took a full five seconds to activate. Their unruly behavior worsened when she tried to use them for anything, be it enhancing the function of her own organs or channeling the world around her.

Her mother would have sped down the cliff in a flash, sculpting a neat trail of stone behind her. But Aina took longer, the stone slow to mold. More than once, her ledges crumbled under her weight and nearly sent her hurtling to her doom.

"I said halt!" came the cry from behind. "You'll injure some-one, channeling like that."

The Kirnosi guard drew abreast of Aina, his movements swift and precise. She could think of a dozen ways he could have stopped her—collapsing the ledges beneath her feet, summoning a rockslide to knock her out. But a soft-soul like him wouldn't dare risk hurting her. And while Aina held no such compunctions, she was far too engrossed in not falling.

A tangle of gold-leaved trees ringed the plateau base. The guard landed atop one of their ivory branches and waited for Aina to join him.

As if.

Aina severed her chitronic flows and plummeted toward the trees. She crashed onto the guard, sending them both careening down in a flurry of golden leaves and broken branches. Aina rolled over to break her fall, but the guard moved quicker. He pounced, six feet of muscle and armor pinning her to the ground.

"My ribs!" Aina wheezed as her fingers scrabbled across the dirt.

Immediately, the guard lessened the pressure on her back. Smirking at the predictability of it all, Aina grabbed a fallen branch, then twisted in his grip to shove her makeshift weapon into his chest.

The Kirnosi had the most absurd breastplate design Aina had ever seen: four trenches cut across their chests, as if a giant wolf claw had slashed the metal, revealing silken fabric under-neath. The cuts symbolized the "blessing of Sherka," whatever that meant, and provided Aina with a convenient slot to ram her branch into.

The guard heaved, winded, and Aina wriggled out from beneath him. She could hear his labored breaths as she sped through the forest. She was celebrating her escape when a tree root snaked from the ground to wrap around her thighs, holding her in place.

Shit. Gritting her teeth, Aina called once again upon her chitrons. They were slow to respond, and more roots rose to encircle her waist.

"You again?"

Aina jerked her head up at the voice, bright and smooth as the guard's gilded armor. He walked toward her and removed his helm—fashioned in the shape of a wolf's head—to let sleek golden hair spill past his shoulders. Aina's lip curled at the sight of Aranel: youngest member of the Kirnosi royal guard and softer than the rest combined.

"Can't you let me go?" Aina pleaded, squirming against the roots. "Everything hurts!"

Hazel eyes narrowed. "I won't be fooled by that twice."

"Fine. I'm sure Toranic Law will reward you for breaking my bones."

The guard paled, and the pressure around Aina's waist loosened. Like most Mayani she had encountered, Aranel feared nothing more than the prospect of his soul-spin slowing. And terror, she had learned from fourteen years in Malin, made people easy to manipulate.

"You're under arrest," Aranel said. "For sabotaging Crown Princess Himalia's ascension."

His solemn expression made Aina want to punch his stupidly chiseled face in. She would have done it, if he weren't so damn good at channeling. Even now, she suspected Aranel held back so as not to hurt her, which made the entire situation more humiliating.

Without chitrons, Aina would crush him in a fight. But with, she was outmatched. She could neither attack nor break free of his binds, and so she was forced to let him lead her through the golden forest.

AINA FLUMPED ONTO a chair and stared at the familiar earthen walls of the Kirnosi guardhouse. Aranel strode across the room, grass-knit cloak swishing as he locked doors and bolted windows in a vain attempt to make this arrest appear graver than it was.

"I'll have to search you," Aranel said, then swiped a thumb across his keiza.

Aina tensed as tendrils of energy enveloped her, warm and green and nauseatingly bright. There was an unsettling intimacy to being touched by another's chitrons this way, feeling the essence of their soul. Aina had only felt her mother's before, brimming with a cold anger that prickled and pinched. But Aranel's bubbled with sincerity and the freshness of a thousand grass shoots springing from the ground. Aina relaxed once he released the channeling and his chitrons seeped away.

"What's all this?" Aranel opened the pouch he'd confiscated during the search. He removed a smashed figurine and held it up as if it might explode. "More ammunition?"

"Leave them be," Aina snapped. "They're just— They're from my mother."

Aranel set the pouch down. "The commander will arrive soon. If you behave, he may show mercy when deciding your sentence."

The commander would show mercy regardless of how she behaved. Aina turned from Aranel to sweep her gaze across the wall and the scraps of parchment nailed to it: a list of banned items, including unlicensed weaponry, narcotics, and megarya blood; and a wanted notice, showing several names and faces, for a notorious rebel group called the Balancers.

Aina traced her eyes over the portraits, resting on a woman with fiery hair and a gaze that seemed to burn through the parchment. The notice labeled her as Zenyra, leader of the Balancers.

"You'll end up an outlaw like them if you're not careful," a new voice said as a tall man stepped into the room.

Aranel jumped at his commander's appearance, and even Aina was impressed. He'd unlocked the door through channeling, and neither of them had noticed.

Samarel's eyebrows furrowed. "It's your fourth arrest since you arrived, Aina," the commander said. "Are you trying to set a record?"

"Sam—I mean, Commander," Aranel said breathlessly before Aina could get a word in. "She's the one who shot the crown princess! I found her in possession of deadly weaponry"—Aina snorted as Aranel continued—"and her actions have caused grievous harm. As you may know, Her Highness has . . . broken an ankle."

Aina resisted the urge to roll her eyes. Only a Mayani would speak of a broken ankle so grimly. These feather-souled uppers had never spilled blood, never known true pain. Centuries under the authority of Toranic Law had graced Kirnos and the other Mayani kingdoms with a perpetual state of peace.

Aranel reached into his cloak and presented Samarel with the slingshot he'd confiscated from Aina earlier.

"My deadly weaponry," Aina clarified. "I thought a bow would be a bit much, so I went with the smaller stick."

"You own a bow?" Aranel asked, scandalized. He turned to Samarel. "She owns a *bow*. An unlicensed bow! And she admitted to attacking Her Highness!"

The commander remained silent for a long moment before summoning a chair from the corner of the room with a flick of his fingers. Samarel sat down so he was level with Aina.

"Why did you do it?" he asked.

"You should train your guard better." Aina fixed her gaze on the emeralds set into his breastplate. "Aranel found me after I'd already broken through their defenses, and with a single bleeding slingshot at that. They wouldn't last a second in a real battle, especially with such pointless armor." She gestured at the decorative gashes cut into the metal. "Malini soldiers would flay them alive. Hell, even my mother would destroy them in a fight."

At the thought of her mother fighting, Aina's heart gave a twist. Was she all right? Was she in one piece? Her mother was a powerful channeler, but Malin crawled with enemies.

"My guard will never face any soldiers," Samarel assured her, "when Toranic Law protects us from such evil. This is Mayana, Aina. You can stop fighting." Aina did roll her eyes now, and Samarel continued. "I know you didn't mean to injure her badly, or our princess would be sporting far worse than a broken ankle. Which, I might add, she healed promptly thereafter. But you must have known she'd heal herself. So why did you do it?"

Aina picked at a grain of dirt caught under her fingernail and flicked it toward the ceiling.

"Aina," Aranel said, impatience edging his tone. "You might show more respect when the commander is speaking to you."

"Leave it, Aranel," the commander said, but Aranel went on.

"Despite your antics, Samarel's been lenient because of your past—"

"My past?" Aina's eyes flashed. "You mean because I was born into Malin? Because Toranic Law condemned me to a life of suffering before I could even walk?"

Aina's throat grew tight as she recalled her earliest memories, sobbing in front of a silver torana, pounding at it with her fists. *Let me through*, she had wailed. *I didn't do anything bad! Please! Let me through!*

The torana hadn't allowed her to pass then. It functioned on Toranic Law: the absolute and ancient force of nature that had governed the universe for centuries, separating beings into realms based on the spin of their souls.

Toranic Law kept Mayana prosperous and peaceful. It allowed uppers like Aranel to bask in comfort, never knowing the gnaw of hunger, the ache of disease, or the bite of an enemy blade. Such misery was reserved for lowers—sin-steeped beings like Aina and her mother.

Aina could never recall committing any sins. Yet Toranic Law had doomed her the day she was born.

"Regardless of your birth, you're an upper now," Aranel said. "You ascended against all odds, but your petty crimes will burden your soul. Are you not worried about falling back down?"

"I'd prefer walking in over falling, but the bleeding torana won't let me."

Ever since she'd stumbled through the torana a year ago, Aina had tried to return to Malin and reunite with her mother. She'd roamed Mayana—from the floating jungles of Nisharan to the snow-glazed valleys that girdled Samaras to the balmy islands of Tahamur and finally Kirnos—in search of a way back.

"It's like they're all blocked or something," Aina added. "Why won't they work properly?"

Aranel stared at her as if she'd sprouted another head. "The more appropriate question is, why in Sherka's name would you *willingly* descend? Toranic Law has graced you with a better life. You ought to be grateful, rather than squandering this opportunity!"

Aina opened her mouth to retort, but Samarel raised a hand. "Enough, Aranel. It is not upon you to judge Aina's actions." He turned to Aina, softening. "Do be careful, Aina. I'd be sad to see you end up like them."

He motioned at the wanted notice nailed to the wall. Aina found herself once again drawn to Zenyra's searing gaze.

What did she do to land up there?

"That your intent was not to harm may yet extenuate . . ." Samarel prattled on. Aina ignored him in favor of scraping out the dirt from beneath the rest of her fingernails.

"You should preach at the temple," she said once he'd finished. "Even the head priest isn't as passionate as you."

A hint of a frown tugged at Samarel's features. "Toranic Law may have absolved you, Aina. But per the laws of this kingdom, I'm afraid there will be punishment."

"How many nights?" Aina asked.

"Ten."

The pity in Samarel's expression made Aina want to kick something. Specifically Aranel, who watched their exchange with an air of self-righteousness.

She restrained herself and followed the commander out of the guardhouse, Aranel in tow. She didn't know why the royal guard insisted on bringing her to the guardhouse each time, as if they were going to lock her up or properly punish her. In Malin, an attempt to hurt King Kaldrav would result in flogging or torture, at the least. But the Mayani weren't fond of such punishment. And at fifteen, Aina was a minor, which meant the worst Samarel could do was send her to the temple for prayer and repentance.

Aina didn't mind being banished to the temple. The mattresses were plusher than her own, and Aro, the head priest, served delicious sweets. She felt a mixture of contempt and gratitude as she followed the two guards through a field of feathery grass that came up to her waist. Kirnos was a soft kingdom in an equally soft realm.

"I will pray for you, Aina," Samarel said.

"As will I," Aranel added. "I will pray to Sherka for the strength and purity of your soul."

"How virtuous of you," Aina replied, stopping by a pond dotted with tiny lotuses. She peered into its placid waters and pushed back a tangle of dark hair to reveal her keiza. The swirl glowed a healthy turquoise, vivid against her brown skin.

As a window to the soul, a keiza's brightness corresponded directly to soul speed and spin. While not as bright as those of most Mayani she'd met, Aina's keiza glowed brighter than her mother's ever had. Too bright to be forced out of the realm, despite her earlier actions.

Aina stole a glance at Aranel as they walked. The guard's keiza shone like one of the ridiculous emeralds lining his helm.

"I hope this time serves you well," Samarel said. Aina snapped back to her impending confinement. The temple of Kirnos loomed ahead, a sweeping structure of honey-colored stone. The bejeweled dome perched loftily atop its walls reminded Aina of a large, glittering onion.

"May your soul spin straight and swift," Aranel called as Aina swung the temple door open and marched in without a backward glance.

CHAPTER TWO

ⓔ

The Preservation Advisory

Y OU MIGHT HAVE been kinder to Aina," said Samarel. The commander removed his helm and tucked it under his arm. The grass rippled as he walked, long stalks bending at the nudge of his chitrons to clear a path through the pasture.

Aranel followed his older brother, careful to keep his voice even. "I *was* kind. But she's a repeat offender, Sam, one completely lacking remorse. Just last week I caught her flinging horse manure through the torana into Paramos. Do you know what she said to me when I tried reprimanding her?"

Samarel's lips quirked. "Do tell."

"That Toranic Law is a sham for allowing pieces of shit to ascend."

"How inappropriate," said Samarel, although he seemed to be holding back laughter. Aranel glared at his brother, who shrugged. "For Sherka's sake, lighten up, Ran. Aina can't hear us, and Toranic Law won't begrudge you a few laughs."

"That girl is a menace," said Aranel. "A bad influence on society."

"Perhaps, but you don't know her entire story—" Samarel broke off to offer Aranel a sheepish smile. "I'm sorry, Ran. It's our last day together. I shouldn't be wasting it with a lecture."

"I suppose you can't help yourself." It came out snider than Aranel intended, but Samarel only laughed.

"The Preservation aren't expecting me for another couple of hours." His brother motioned to the grove behind him, a labyrinth of gold-toned leaves and sinuous branches. "Would you like to spar?"

Aranel eyed the treetops with longing. Many moons had passed since he and Samarel had last sparred, and there was nothing more thrilling than testing oneself against the best channeler in the kingdom.

Thrilling and humiliating.

"I'd rather not," said Aranel stiffly. *I'd rather not our last memory be of you showing off how great you are.* "I meant I'm a bit tired, what with chasing after Aina."

A small frown flickered across Samarel's face. His brother opened his mouth to say something, then seemed to think the better of it.

They sped through the forest in silence, feet aglow with chitronic energy as they leaped through the treetops. As Aranel took in the scenery around him, he could almost see the phantom images: two young boys wreathed in laughter and sunlight, one shining brighter than his brother.

Come on, Ran, Samarel would say, face split in a dazzling grin as the forest danced around him, branches reshaping beneath his feet. *You can do better than that! Don't try so hard, just go with the flow of your chitrons! Look, it's easy!*

Everything came easy to Samarel, chitronic prodigy and commander of the royal guard. Aranel glanced at his brother. The setting sun fell upon the familiar lines of his profile, gilding him like some otherworldly being.

He may as well be. Aranel's gaze flickered to Samarel's forehead. *He doesn't belong in this realm.*

Although Samarel was five years older, he resembled Aranel with the notable exception of his keiza. While Aranel's keiza sparkled like an emerald, his brother's was radiant as a star. The incandescence of a Paramosi, or one meant to have ascended years ago. Yet Samarel had chosen to remain with him in Mayana, a shining example for Aranel to aspire to.

But Samarel did not simply shine. He blazed like his keiza, casting a shadow upon everything around him. Including Aranel, whose every deed, every achievement, would be but a faded imitation of his brother's.

Curse him to Malin for being so perfect!

A moment later, Aranel shoved the thought into the crevices of his mind. *Pure thoughts,* he admonished himself. He repeated the words his mother had sung to him each night before bed, ever since he'd been old enough to understand. *Pure thoughts and intentions a pure soul doth make, but clouded with malice, that soul doth forsake.* For chitrons were conscious particles—created by each new thought, emotion, intention, and action. Aranel could not afford such small-minded jealousy.

He closed his eyes and dragged a thumb over his palm in a forward circle. Slowly, then faster, as if to counteract his slowing soul-spin.

"You're stressed." Samarel's voice broke Aranel from his trance. They were halfway up the cliff that led to the palace gardens. His brother nodded to Aranel's hands. "Did I say something to upset you? Or do something wrong?"

You never do anything wrong, Aranel wanted to scream at

him, *and that's the blessed problem!* Instead, he circled his thumb over his palm with renewed speed. "I'm fine, Sam. Just . . . sad you're leaving."

Which was likely the first whole truth Aranel had spoken to his brother in moons. Because as much as it stung being in Samarel's constant shadow, the notion of living in Mayana without him cut deeper.

"As am I," said Samarel, and Aranel had to strain to hear him above the tinkling fountains.

They had reached the palace gardens, thick with the scent of honeysuckle and rose. In the distance glinted the torana to Paramos, its alluring golden columns curving to a cusped archway.

The royal guard had wanted to throw Samarel an ascension ceremony, but his brother refused, preferring to keep it a private affair. The torana drew near, and Aranel's every step grew heavier, as if his chitrons were rooting him to the ground.

"I got you something from the marketplace," said Samarel. "A farewell present of sorts. To remember me by."

Aranel stared at him in disbelief. As if he needed something to remember his brother. As if every corner of their home, every tree in the forest, every stone-lined path wasn't already overflowing with memories of him.

"Here." Samarel held out a conical shell with a smile. "You can add it to your collection."

"I didn't think you knew about that." Aranel accepted the shell and traced a thumb over its grooves. It was a foolish thing, his collection: an assortment of snail shells and curling leaves arranged inside his bedside drawer so the spirals faced forward.

"For what it's worth," said Samarel softly, "I don't think you need it, Ran. Any of it. You're fine as you are, no matter what anyone says."

Aranel's chin quivered. He wanted to throw himself at his brother as he had when they were younger, let Samarel pick him up and spin him around. Instead, he clutched the shell, its tiny spines digging into his palm.

Samarel stepped in front of the torana. The ornate columns framed his tall figure, silhouetted against the brightness of Paramos.

"Well, then," he said. "I must go. But I'll be back, I promise. I'll visit you once a moon. More, if I can."

Aranel nodded, refusing to meet his brother's eyes. His parents had promised the same five years past, and his grandparents nearly a decade before. Cousin Taralei had sworn it four moons ago. Aranel hadn't seen any of them since, save his mother, and even she seldom visited.

Lovely as Mayana was, the pulchritude of Paramos was said to extend beyond the limits of imagination. Why would anyone want to return? Why should his brother?

Aranel ran a hand across the torana and traced the verse inscribed into the gleaming metal:

> *Blissful Paramos, the height of perfection,*
> *idyllic, with beauty that sings.*
> *For souls that spin in a forward direction*
> *and swift as a hummingbird's wings.*

He recognized the verse from the Song of Salvation, one of the scriptures he'd memorized as a child, alongside the Chorus of Creation and Aria of Ascension. Aranel had based his life on their teachings. He'd trained in chitronic healing to help those in need. He'd enrolled in the royal guard to help protect the realm against—well, there wasn't much to protect against besides that ruffian, Aina, and Aranel had tolerated plenty of her nonsense. He even donated a quarter of his savings to the temple each moon.

But seventeen years of goodwill hadn't been enough. Aranel's hand slid across the golden column with its flowing scrollwork before thumping against something harder and more unyielding than any physical material.

An invisible wall separating him from Paramos.

"I'll ascend soon," declared Aranel. "I swear on Sherka."

"You needn't swear such a thing," said Samarel. He angled his head, a sheet of hair obscuring his face. "Although I sometimes wonder if you'll be happier without me. If my being here is what holds you back."

"Don't be ridiculous," whispered Aranel. In truth, he often wondered the same. "It's nothing to do with you. I'm simply— I'm not—" His throat closed in on itself, and he forced the words out in sharp, unwilling fragments. "I'm not good enough."

When Samarel looked up, his eyes were brighter than usual. "You've always been good enough." He reached out to brush a finger against Aranel's keiza, then pulled him into a hug.

"I don't want you to leave," Aranel mumbled into Samarel's hair, allowing himself, for a fleeting moment, to clutch at his brother's tunic. "I'd *never* want that."

"I know." Samarel patted his head. "Take care of yourself, Ran." He stepped away and walked through the golden torana.

Aranel watched his retreating back with glassy eyes, then tore his gaze from the archway. He strode across the garden and stopped at its edge.

The Kirnosi palace and its gardens stood atop a cylindrical hill veiled in golden moss that rose from the heart of the kingdom. Unfurled below, the petals of Kirnos glowed fuchsia under the setting sun. True to its name, the Lotus Kingdom of Kirnos was nestled within the curving embrace of twelve immense petals, each softer than velvet and stronger than steel.

The whorl of inner petals—raised higher than the rest—contained a sprawling jungle of gem-studded roofs: the marketplace and its surrounding residences, as well as numerous libraries, eateries, and halls for recreation.

But it was the outermost petal that held Aranel's fondest memories as he traced his eyes across the wheat fields and lakes tucked amidst its gentle slopes. He mapped the winding creek where Samarel had first taught him chitronic control, patient as Aranel floundered atop the water; the knoll by the mango orchard where they'd picnicked and played cards with Cousin Taralei; and the tea stall they'd frequented on the evenings guard duty ended early, sipping cool barley tea as the sun streaked the sky scarlet.

Aranel's gaze settled last on a cluster of yellow thatched huts that dotted the fields like pollen. For seventeen years he and his brother had lived in one of those huts, first with their parents, then as a family of two.

Now Aranel remained alone, with only his collection of shells and dried leaves for company.

ARANEL LEANED AGAINST the brocade wall, stifling a yawn as he listened to various members of the Preservation Advisory drone on about matters of the state: Crown Princess Himalia's flight from Kirnos following her botched ascension, the free-trade agreement with the kingdom of Tahamur, and the location of the annual cloudsurfing championships.

Hardly a day had passed since Samarel's ascension, and several of his duties had already been foisted off on Aranel. A week ago he would have been delighted to take Samarel's place, even as a mere guard and observer. A certain prestige came with attending the Advisories. They were convened by the Preservation, a council of Paramosi elders who oversaw the workings of the universe and descended to Mayana thrice a year to offer guidance.

But four hours into the meeting had Aranel wondering why he'd been so keen to join. He came to the conclusion he'd only wanted what Samarel already had, something that could be said for most things Aranel had strived for. Commander of the royal guard, cloudsurfing champion, elite healer—how much of it had Aranel truly wanted for himself?

Aranel's gaze drifted across the room, taking in the various faces in attendance. The representative of Tahamur, a long-haired woman swathed in richly embroidered crimson fabric, was speaking. Across her forehead lay a strip of bejeweled gold, matching the thick choker at her neck. The Tahamuri, Aranel observed, loved their gold more than the Kirnosi did.

" . . . from Nishaki disappeared a few moons after the young man from Tahamur," said the woman. "They were known to be friends, both in their second decade, and skilled chitronic users, just like the last three who disappeared. Given the timing and their profiles, I suspect Balancer involvement."

Aranel perked at the mention of the Balancers, which meant they had reached their last topic for the day. The rebels were notorious in the realm, their leader Zenyra's face plastered across every guardhouse in Kirnos. The wanted notices listed their crimes in vague terms, such as "disrespecting Toranic Law" and "spreading heresy."

Aranel tried to recall if Samarel had divulged anything about the Balancers. All that came to mind was his brother mentioning how the rebels descended to Malin voluntarily, without a care for their souls. Aranel shuddered. *Why in Sherka's name would anyone do such a thing?*

The Song of Salvation described the lower realm as a teeming cesspit of corruption and disease. A wasteland ravaged by the flames of war, rife with bloodthirsty monsters like the fabled nagamor. The Malini themselves were said to be a diabolic lot, sadists who sought pleasure in the misery of others.

The closest Aranel had been to one was that heathen Aina, but she had ascended to Mayana a year prior. Surely a true lower would be worse. *Although by the Preservation's standards, it's a miracle Aina's face isn't on a wanted notice yet.*

"I suggest the Advisory consider more stringent measures against the Balancers," said the representative of Samaras, a hefty man with hair like straw. "Lest we risk losing our future generation to a rebel cult."

"I strongly concur," said the representative of Amaratir, rising. He wore little clothing, as per was the custom of his people, and had swirling patterns inked onto his glistening skin. When he spoke, the coral beads in his hair clinked together. "Outlawing the Balancers is not enough! If anything, their outlaw status grants them a sense of allure amongst Mayani youth. Nor are the seals on the torana helping, since it seems their leader, Zenyra, is able to unravel them with ease."

A chorus of murmurs followed his words. Aranel leaned forward, intrigued. "Forgive my interruption," he said, "but what are these seals you speak of?"

"Why, the Preservation's seals," exclaimed the Amaratiri man. "Surely you have heard of them. They are on every torana in Mayana that leads to a lower realm."

"Apologies." Aranel lowered his head. "This is my first Advisory. I'm afraid my knowledge is yet insufficient."

Sam would have heard of the seals. Sam wouldn't have asked such an inane question.

"Ah, you must be Samarel's replacement!" The man's tone grew warmer. "An inspiration, your predecessor. The Balancers could learn a thing or two from him." Aranel shuffled his feet, and the representative continued. "I spoke of the chitronic seals. They are unidirectional in nature, placed by the Preservation a few years ago as a precaution against the rebels. The seals cannot circumvent Toranic Law, but they can inhibit voluntary descension from Mayana."

Aranel sat back in shock as the explanation sunk in. Because while Toranic Law blocked the unworthy from ascension—a bitter lesson Aranel learned each time he attempted to pass into Paramos—it placed no barriers on the reverse. The torana were naturally designed to allow free descension between realms. It was how the Preservation could attend Advisories. How Samarel could, if he deigned, visit Aranel in Kirnos.

And why Aina's been behaving like such a miscreant. Aranel's past conversation with her clicked into place. *With the torana sealed, she can only force Toranic Law to expel her.*

Yet the Balancers *could* use the torana to descend. Zenyra had found a way around the seals, which had the Advisory on edge.

"If the seals are ineffectual, we need more concrete actions!" The Amaratiri representative slapped his thigh. "To stop this heretic and her foolish cult from . . ."

He trailed off as another man stood, silver-haired, with a keiza that shone bright as the sun. The man's face was unlined—Aranel suspected chitronic concealment—but his eyes held a depth that bespoke centuries of wisdom. His ivory robes marked him as one of the Preservation.

Despite their status, the Preservation had remained largely silent throughout the Advisory, letting the Mayani decide things for themselves and providing counsel only when called upon. This was the first instance of a Preserver addressing them unprompted.

"What might you suggest?" asked the silver-haired Preserver. "That we descend to Malin and confront the Balancers directly?"

A stunned silence befell the room. There was a reason Toranic Law separated the uppers from the vileness of Malin, why every scripture cautioned against voluntary descension. Mayani wouldn't be able to withstand such darkness. It would gather to their souls like moths to a flame.

"My apologies, Lord Seirem." The man from Amaratir bowed deeply to the Preserver. "I did not mean to imply— Of course the seals were an excellent solution—"

"Stand tall, young man," commanded Seirem. "You need only bow to the gods."

"The gods, old people, and Preservers," said the Amaratiri.

"Watch your language," warned Seirem. The corners of his eyes crinkled. "I like to think I stopped aging a couple centuries ago."

Soft laughter filled the chamber and diffused the tension. Seirem nodded at the Amaratiri representative.

"This fine young man makes a valid point," said Seirem, addressing the room. "The Preservation's strongest seals are unable to withstand Zenyra's extraordinary chitronic prowess, leaving us with no way to prevent Balancer recruitment beyond descending to Malin ourselves, which we all agree is a terrible idea."

Aranel nodded along with the others. He didn't understand the Advisory's obsession with the Balancers. From the sound of it, they rarely bothered with this realm. Apart from recruiting a couple Mayani every few moons, they restricted their activities to Malin.

"There must be something we can do," said the Tahamuri woman, "to set these fools on the right path, as intended by the laws of the universe. Is that not our duty to the Mayani people?"

Seirem spread his arms, silver-hemmed sleeves catching the light. " 'Judge not those who walk astray,' " intoned the Preserver. " 'The will of each shall light their way.' "

The Tahamuri representative blinked in confusion, but Aranel caught on at once. "The Aria of Ascension," he said. "Verse eighteen."

"Precisely!" Seirem clapped his hands together and beamed at Aranel. "It heartens me to see such familiarity with our ancient scriptures in one so young. Now tell me, what do those words mean in the context of the Balancers?"

"That it is not our duty to hold them accountable for their actions," Aranel surmised. "They are answerable to none but Toranic Law."

"Indeed." Seirem turned back to the Advisory. "We have already tried to guide them with the seals, done what we can to deter their folly. Beyond a point, their destinies are their own. If they still wish to flout Toranic Law and descend, we can do naught but pray that Azyaka has mercy upon their souls."

ARANEL LEFT THE palace as soon as the Advisory ended. He hopped down the cliff and onto the golden treetops, their branches twisting beneath his chitrons to form a hidden path. He was halfway through the forest when he sensed another presence draw near.

A gravelly voice cut through the rustle of leaves. "Your channeling has improved considerably since I last saw you, Aranel of Kirnos."

Aranel nearly fell off the branch at the sight of Lord Seirem of the Preservation, ivory robes flapping as he sprinted across the canopy.

"As I recall, your first attempt to cloudsurf was quite the disaster," continued Seirem as he came up to Aranel. "You dropped through the sky like a hailstone. Your brother went running after you and caught you moments before you crashed."

Aranel pressed a fist to his forehead in greeting. "Please pardon my discourtesy. But have we met, Lord Seirem?"

"Why, of course! You were but four at the time, so perhaps you do not remember. I am close with your family, Aranel. Your great-grandfather and I go long back, and I dined with your parents last week. Your mother served up a lovely elderberry pie."

"You've seen my parents? Are they well? And what of my cousin Taralei?"

"Your parents are well as can be. They have built themselves a fine manor with sweeping views of the crater. There is a spare room for Samarel. And one for you."

"Oh," said Aranel, taken aback. "How—how lovely." He trailed his eyes to the sigil emblazoned across Seirem's robes, four interlocking rings in golden thread.

"I will cut to the chase, Aranel," said Seirem. "Your family misses you. They eagerly await your ascension. With Samarel gone, I suspect you do as well."

"I . . ." Aranel felt too ashamed to admit it aloud.

To stay within Mayana, one had to be of generally good character. But Paramosi souls were sinless. Flawless. They spun forward with great speed, fueled by their various virtues and unburdened by vice. Judging by the brightness of his keiza, Aranel had a long way to go.

"There might be a way for you to ascend quickly." Seirem's statement cut into Aranel's bleak thoughts.

Aranel straightened, tempering his excitement. "Is that so?"

"It is not something I would typically advise, but it would fulfill both your need and the Preservation's rather pressing one. Consider it high risk for a high reward."

"High risk for a high reward?" Aranel narrowed his eyes.

Good deeds won't lighten your soul if done solely for reward, echoed a voice, not unlike his mother's, in Aranel's mind.

"A covert mission of sorts." Seirem gave him a wry smile. "One of great importance to the Preservation and to the future of the universe. A delicate undertaking, one I would not even speak of to the Advisory, lest she have ears there."

"She?" asked Aranel. Who was Seirem talking about? And what made Aranel a worthy candidate for this mission over the Mayani representatives of the Advisory?

"You come from a good family, Aranel," said Seirem, as if reading his doubts. "I have watched your progress from afar. You are a skilled channeler."

"Not as skilled as my brother," blurted Aranel.

"Far more skilled than you give yourself credit for." Seirem gave him an indulgent smile that reminded Aranel of his grandfather. "But unlike Samarel, you possess a burning desire to ascend. A desire that might make the risk worth it for you."

"What risk? What are you asking me to do?"

"I need you to descend to Malin. Descend, and infiltrate the Balancers."

Aranel's stomach twisted. "No." The refusal left his mouth more harshly than he'd intended. "That's—that's immoral. Let alone dangerous."

"You would act as the Preservation's spy. You need not do anything immoral, only report back on the rebels' doings."

"You want me to lie!" Aranel's voice pitched higher with every sentence. "Lie and deceive and subject my soul to the darkness of Malin! Do the very things that you—that the Preservation caution against!"

"There are times, Aranel," said Seirem, his voice calm, "when we must look beyond caution and transcend conventional ways of thinking. Situations where the merit outweighs the risk. At least for one with your skill and strength of heart."

Aranel stood rooted to the spot, at a loss for words. What

Seirem was suggesting defied everything he'd been taught to believe in, every rule he'd painstakingly followed. But abiding by those beliefs and rules had not yet lightened his soul. And if all his efforts thus far had been in vain . . .

Perhaps Seirem is right, sounded a small voice in his head. *Perhaps this is what I'm meant to do.*

Seirem bent down and rested a hand on Aranel's shoulder. "You deserve to live in bliss, along with the rest of your family," he said. "The Preservation recognize that, even if Toranic Law does not. It is time you seek another way to ascend."

CHAPTER THREE

<figure>❂</figure>

Last Free Clan

*C*AREFUL AS HE could, Meizan wrapped his fingers around his clanmate's throat and activated his chitrons. They flowed through Taezur's skin and past the muscle of his throat until Meizan felt something hard and rubbery buried amidst the tissue.

"Andraken's balls," Meizan said as his chitrons enfolded the lump. "How the hell were you breathing?"

Taezur didn't reply—couldn't—his watery eyes bulging. Meizan inhaled, concentrating on the flow of energy. He couldn't just yank the tumor out; it was too entrenched in healthy tissue. He'd have to burn it with exactly the right amount of electricity. Lucky for them, the coming thunderstorm had the dank air outside the cave crackling with static.

Channeling the ambient chitrons of Malin always carried a risk. Sometimes they responded well, bent to Meizan's will. Other times . . . not so much.

Meizan shuddered as the surrounding chitrons melded with his own, oozing through his body like sludge. Years of channeling hadn't accustomed him to that sensation, as if the filth of the realm was being injected into him through the bond.

"All right," Meizan said, collecting the static from the air. "Time to electrocute this son of a bitch."

He streamed electricity into the lump in Taezur's throat. Taezur twitched and thrashed, but Meizan held him down by force and focused his energy on the lump. This would work. It had to.

According to that Mayani book on healing they'd found in an abandoned Balancer village a moon ago, destroying tumors through heat or electricity was a proven technique. The upper realm had eradicated various diseases with it.

Meizan bit his lip, keiza burning as his flows trembled. The bond grew volatile as the chitrons of Malin revolted against him. He didn't know if he could control them, hold them steady enough to—

Taezur gave a spasm. Chunks of flesh and blood spilled from his throat and trickled down Meizan's fingers. Swearing, Meizan jerked his hand away and severed the chitronic bond. He grabbed Taezur's bony shoulders and waited for the coughing to die down.

"Can you talk?" Meizan asked. Taezur gurgled more blood, eyes livid as they burned into Meizan's. Meizan wiped his hands, guilt gnawing at his insides. "Don't look at me like that. It's not my fault the flaming chitrons decided to screw shit up."

Taezur's glare didn't lessen as he continued to cough up blood. Unable to bear the sight of him anymore, Meizan released his clanmate and stormed out of the cave.

A wiry woman awaited him outside, her lips twisting at the sight of his dark expression. "What did you expect?" said Kanna, clan chief of Kanjallen. "You're no healer, Meizan. This isn't

Mayana. Burn that book before it puts more absurd ideas into your head."

Meizan nodded and resolved to burn it later. The chief was right. His chitrons were for hurting, not healing. His hands were meant to tear flesh apart. He was a damn fool to expect anything different. Taezur had started off with a tumor. Meizan had shredded the man's throat.

Meizan slumped against the rock, ignoring the way it dug into his spine. He pulled up his scarf to cover his nose and mouth. Even with it, the fumes of the Dead Mountain clogged his throat and made it difficult to breathe.

Not so dead anymore, Meizan thought. *This flaming pile of shit's going to explode, and we don't want to be camped out here when it does.*

They'd have to move soon, if the increasing toxicity of the air served as any indication. Not that Meizan minded. Of all the miserable places in Malin he'd taken refuge in, the crevices at the base of the Dead Mountain of Merumarth were the worst.

They'd fled here to escape Kaldrav's forces, intending to hide out for a day or two until the coast cleared. But whether by design or burning rotten luck, Kaldrav's troops had set up camp in Martharan—the decayed forest that surrounded the volcano— trapping Meizan and his clanmates within.

They'd been here a week, and three men had already developed some sickness in their throats or lungs. Sometimes at night, Meizan felt an itch at the back of his own throat. He dreaded the day he awoke with a lump like Taezur's.

That was part of why he'd tried to heal his clanmate. If Meizan succeeded on Taezur, he'd be able to heal himself. But he'd failed. Which meant that if he did end up with some disease, he'd be stuck with the pain for centuries.

Death did not exist for humans like it did for other living creatures. They were granted no relief, no respite from their misery. Human bodies and souls were cursed with immortality. Doomed to suffer every injury and disease for eternity, or until they ended in erasure, a fate Meizan preferred not to dwell on.

"I've been thinking," Kanna said, pulling Meizan from his thoughts, "and I see no other choice. We have to surrender."

Meizan bristled at the declaration. "Flaming hell, Chief! After all the shit we've been through, you want to surrender to that cockroach?"

"That cockroach controls almost the entirety of Malin. He has troops stationed in Martharan, less than a mile away. If Merumarth explodes, we'll be driven straight into their arms. We're only delaying the inevitable by camping out here."

"We can't surrender," Meizan protested. "We're Kanjallen. The last free clan in the realm. Blessed by the nagamor."

"Last free clan?" Kanna gave a harsh laugh. "We're no clan, Meizan. We stopped being one the day Kaldrav's army stormed the allied villages. And the nagamor haven't favored us in centuries."

Her words nipped at him like mites, stirring up memories from four moons past. The six of them—including Chief Kanna, Meizan, and Taezur—had been off hunting thunderboar deep in the valleys of Raitani. By the time they returned, all seven allied villages had been razed. Nothing remained but smoldering piles of ash and dust, punctured by pikes bearing Kaldrav's banners. The three thousand members of their clan were nowhere to be found. Kanna said they'd probably been captured. Sent to the burning ices of Agakor, where they'd be tortured for days on end.

No one imprisoned in Agakor ever came out in any state worth existing. Meizan had refused to believe such a fate could befall Kanjallen.

Kaldrav's army was vast, but Kanjallen were formidable warriors.

Their clan comprised an alliance between some of the strongest in the realm, united not by blood, but a desire to remain free of Kaldrav's tyranny. The member clans had volunteered to join Kanjallen's ranks decades ago, bringing with them weapons and new tactics for combat. Even without the blessing of the nagamor, Meizan's clanmates were powerful in battle, the weakest fighter worth twenty of Kaldrav's men.

And yet they had disappeared, leaving burned villages and destroyed belongings.

The six survivors had scrounged the ruins for anything of value before fleeing across Malin, taking refuge wherever they could and avoiding Kaldrav's troops at all cost.

Though the chief never mentioned it, Meizan suspected she still clung to hope that the others had miraculously escaped Agakor. That they had regrouped and gone into hiding. He saw it in her eyes when they were on lookout. Kanna wasn't only scanning the bleak horizon for enemies. She was searching for a sign that Kanjallen had pulled through, that their clan existed outside the six of them.

Until today.

Today, Kanna spoke of surrender. Hope had faded from her eyes, leaving emptiness. And if its chief had lost hope, Kanjallen really was dead.

Meizan dug his fingers into his palms and stood abruptly. "We're a clan." He glared at Kanna. "We're six people. Six people is still a clan. So don't you dare give up on us."

Kanna stood too, eyes blazing. "Three of our six are so diseased they can barely breathe, and the other is missing an arm and a leg. If Kaldrav's forces find us, you and I are the only ones left who can fight, Meizan. We're the only ones left who can run."

"What are you suggesting, Chief? That we abandon Taezur and the rest?"

Kanna slapped him across the face, causing Meizan to bite his tongue. He lowered his gaze and spat out a globule of blood.

"Don't accuse me of abandoning anyone," the chief snarled. "I'm just stating the obvious, that the four of them are in no shape to escape, much less fight."

"Then we fix them till they are," Meizan said. "I screwed up once, but I can try healing Taezur again—"

"Don't be ridiculous." Kanna cuffed his neck. "Listen. We'll dig a tunnel under the soldiers' feet to sneak out of Martharan. Raid the nearest Balancer hideout to steal their herbs and supplies. Return to Merumarth and heal the others. Once they are fit to travel, we use the tunnel to escape."

"Solid plan," Meizan said, although she'd left out the most crucial factor. That the success of their plan, their entire survival, was contingent on Merumarth not exploding before they made it out. The notion of trying to outrun boiling lava in a compressed space was terrifying, even to him.

FOOTSTEPS THUDDED OVERHEAD, muffled by the rock. A couple dozen soldiers from the sound of it, camped right above their tunnel.

The flames of Meizan's torch cast shadows upon the chief's face. Kanna gritted her teeth, sweat trailing across her skin as she pressed her palms against the rock, carving through the layers.

Ten hours had passed since they'd left the hideout. Ten hours of continuous channeling and trudging through the earth. Meizan had run along the length of their tunnel and measured out the distance. He estimated they were about a third of the way through the forest. At this rate, it would be another day before they reached the eastern edge of Martharan.

The Dead Forest of Martharan surrounded Merumarth on all

sides, a ring of skeletal trees that encircled the volcano. Kaldrav's troops infested the forest, with even more of them spread along its western fringes. The Balancer hideout lay somewhere to the east, about a half day's walk from Martharan's edge.

Meizan watched the chief, noting the way her eyes fluttered as she channeled. She swayed, and he caught her before she hit the ground.

"You're exhausted, Chief." He set her down. "I can take over while you rest."

"No," Kanna croaked, raising a hand. "Conserve your energy. Just in case."

Meizan opened his mouth to argue, but she shot him a scathing glare. "You are not channeling, Meizan. It's an order."

Meizan crossed his arms and stared at Kanna's limp form, her tawny complexion an ashen gray. Her chitrons would be unusable for a few hours until they recharged, coupled with the physical drain on her body. Meizan didn't envy the chief for digging a tunnel that stretched on for miles. Controlling and molding that much rock required an immense amount of energy and concentration.

"Is it because of Taezur?" Meizan asked. Kanna's eyes glinted like beetles in the firelight as she turned to face him. "That was a lapse in concentration, but I'll focus this time. Let me take over while you rest."

He could see why the chief didn't want him channeling. The chitrons of Malin had a will of their own, a penchant for mischief and destruction. One misstep and Meizan could blow up their tunnel, leaving them exposed to Kaldrav's forces. But he wouldn't screw up. Not again.

"Conserve your energy," Kanna repeated. "In case *I* botch things up. In case we need to fight."

"I'll destroy them if it comes to it," Meizan said, projecting more confidence into his voice than he felt. "Whatever happens, I won't let them capture us."

"Sometimes I wonder what would befall us if they did. Would it burn our sins if they tortured us enough? Would the pain and suffering purge our souls?"

Meizan stared at her. Had the channeling killed her brain cells? The chief never spoke of nonsense like sins and souls.

"The white flash," Kanna went on. "I dream of it, sometimes . . ."

"You're delusional, Chief."

Meizan had never seen the white flash in all his seventeen years. Legend said that when a soul reversed its spin and turned light enough to ascend to Mayana, the world flashed white around them for a brief instant. But Meizan had never heard of anyone ascending. Those who disappeared were usually captured by enemies or devoured by some ravenous beast—Malin teemed with plenty of both.

"I wonder," the chief whispered between breaths, "if I'll ever . . . be able to ascend . . ."

Meizan snorted. "A vicious hag like you? I doubt it."

Kanna cracked a smile, her eyelids drooping. "You're right. Toranic Law . . . would never . . . let me . . ."

MEIZAN JERKED AWAKE at a sharp rap on the side of his head. He scrambled up to the sight of the chief shaking her fist. "Worthless brat. You were supposed to remain on guard, not take a nap!"

"I was bored," Meizan grumbled. He'd already set trip wires at the mouth of the tunnel to warn of any intruders. But their enemy was aboveground, not under.

Still, Kanna's fiery temper meant she had returned to normal.

Meizan didn't have to listen to her exhausted blathering about white flashes and Toranic Law.

He stretched, then leaned against the rocky wall as the chief channeled. He drew his sword from its wooden scabbard. Its pommel was forged in the shape of a nagamor's head, with braided cord wrapping around its grip in an imitation of the beast's coiled body. The pattern was echoed in the circular guard and extended across the curved blade, where a feathered tail was etched into the steel. The clan maxim, inscribed between the feathers, read:

Thy grief is a weapon; let tears temper the blade,
which, wielded with vengeance, sees enemies unmade.

Meizan ran a finger over the steel, then used a flat piece of rock to sharpen its edge. That blade had been a weapon of honor once, wielded only by Kanjallen's second-in-command. Kanna had recovered it from the rubble of their destroyed village and tossed it to Meizan as a replacement for his broken sword, rather than a gift of any significance.

Meizan knew it meant nothing with Kanjallen all but gone.

Clan chiefs and their seconds-in-command were picked by trial through combat. Kanna had earned her title nine moons ago, when she'd stormed up to her predecessor in the middle of a clan meeting and demanded a duel. Meizan remembered laughing out loud at the sight of yet another blustering fool rising from obscurity to challenge their mighty chief. The last challenger had lasted three whole minutes. This strange, small woman would last no more than two.

He'd been silenced when Kanna yanked her fallen opponent's eyeballs from his skull with a squelch and tossed them at Meizan's head. She was pronounced chief then and there—the first to hail from one of the assimilated clans rather than the original Kanjallen bloodline.

Meizan had earned no similar victories despite being of old Kanjallen blood. He'd done nothing to deserve the second-in-command's sword. Yet he couldn't help but trace the winding form of the nagamor with his finger and polish the steel at every chance.

As he worked, something dripped onto the back of his neck. A cold liquid that sizzled as it seeped into his skin. Meizan looked up, and another splashed onto his forehead.

Raindrops, laden with volcanic fumes, had percolated through the ground. The storm had arrived. The rain would soften the rock, making it less resistant, which meant Kanna needed to reduce the force of her channeling or else she risked blasting the ceiling apart.

"Chief!" Meizan sheathed his sword and jumped to his feet, grabbing Kanna's arm to get her attention. "It's raining, you have to—"

The tunnel burst open, rocks and wet dirt shooting into the sky.

Meizan found himself thrust upward by the force of the explosion. Swiping his forehead, he erected a quick chitronic shield to protect himself from the falling rock. He landed upright, eyes darting through the rubble for a sign of the chief.

He found her clambering out of a small crater where the ground had blown open to expose the end of their tunnel.

"Blasted rain," Kanna cursed, dusting herself off. "Blasted rock. Blasted chitrons."

Meizan looked at the crater in despair. All that channeling, wasted. Even the chief couldn't repack so much dirt and stone and make it look natural. He watched her collapse the tunnel with a flick of fingers.

Kanna turned to him, face grim. "It would have led them straight to our hideout."

She had done the one thing she could to stop Kaldrav's soldiers from discovering their clanmates. But it also left the two of them with no escape route as they stood exposed in Martharan.

The toxic rain pelted down in a fury, biting Meizan's skin like a swarm of angry wasps. And beneath the steady patter came the ominous rumble of footsteps.

Meizan and Kanna made to flee, but in moments they were surrounded by Kaldrav's soldiers: more than two dozen mismatched brutes clad in dark armor, their breastplates stamped with a single white circle. Amongst the jeering men Meizan glimpsed a young boy, wide-eyed and quaking under his chain mail.

"Kanjallen worms," a soldier growled, taking in Meizan's and Kanna's garb, their boiled-leather vests painted with twin streaks of blue.

Meizan drew his sword with his right hand and trailed a finger across his keiza with his left. His chitrons quivered with excitement. He'd grown sick of all the fleeing and hiding over the past few moons. It had been a while since his last battle. And from the ropy red scars that maimed the soldiers' faces, it was clear this lot hailed from clan Chiren.

"I've always wanted to fight a mangler," Meizan said to Kanna, spinning the hilt of his sword into a reverse grip.

"Be careful," she warned. Her back pressed against his. "If anything happens to me, take over as chief. Do not let our clan die."

"Not much of a clan, with just six people."

"Six people is still a clan." Kanna unsheathed her sword with an enticing scrape, the promise of imminent bloodshed. "Our enemies unmade."

"Our enemies unmade."

The next few moments passed in a whirl of metal, blood, and

chitrons. The chief opened a chasm in the ground that swallowed the first line of soldiers. The earth groaned as she channeled and caved it in beneath the second group. Meizan leaped back to avoid being buried.

She's more tired than she's letting on, he realized as he watched Kanna throw up her arms. Branches rained down in a careless volley, spearing several soldiers and forcing Meizan to retreat farther.

If the chief wanted to use wide-range attacks, that was fine by him. Meizan preferred fighting solo. And he couldn't afford to worry about Kanna with close to a dozen soldiers bearing down upon him.

Meizan ducked under a swinging axe to slide his sword through a gap in the nearest soldier's armor, then stabbed him in the thigh.

He felt the chitrons of Malin at his fingertips, yearning for chaos, lusting for a fight. Directing the chitrons with his own, Meizan gathered the toxic rainwater, shaping it into throwing stars he launched at the soldier's eyes. The man clutched at his face, screaming, and Meizan channeled again, harnessing the static in the air. Lightning burst from his palm and wrapped around the throat of a second soldier. The mangler spasmed, then collapsed, the spiked club he'd been about to smash into Meizan's head thudding to the ground.

This was easy. Much easier than healing Taezur had been.

The chitrons of Malin rushed through him like a river, exhilarating, intoxicating, sending Meizan's own chitrons trembling with unfettered joy. His mind grew hazy as he fought, as if he'd drunk one too many shots of that foul rum his clanmates were so fond of.

But even in his haze, the universe responded to his every whim. Meizan sent out successive bolts of lightning, using the raindrops to conduct their path.

A diagonal slice to a soldier's neck before Meizan sheathed his sword with a spin. He didn't need a steel barrier. He wanted to use his hands, wanted to feel the chitronic streams beneath his skin.

A seventh soldier fell to his knees screaming, his blood pooling at Meizan's feet. And then an eighth, contorting as electric currents forked through his flesh.

Meizan was facing less resistance than expected. These soldiers weren't trained fighters or experienced channelers. Kaldrav's recruitment strategy had always favored quantity over quality.

A small figure rushed at him, rusty axe flailing in desperation. Underneath the soldier's helmet, Meizan spied the terror-struck eyes of the boy he'd seen before. His young flesh was marred by the skin-carving rituals of his clan.

A cold shock pierced Meizan's battle haze. He was reminded of himself a couple years ago—scared and alone after an enemy clan ambushed him outside the village. His own clanmates had rescued him and pulverized his attackers.

But this boy was not part of Kanjallen. Meizan spun away from the axe to aim a swift kick at the mangler's neck, knocking him out clean.

He had no time for mercy. No time for pity.

Only two soldiers remained. Cowards who'd hung back and waited for the others to tire him out. Meizan sank back into the frenetic delirium of his chitrons. He lunged at the manglers with a feral grin. They would not die, but they would break, and he broke them repeatedly until they were but a misshapen heap, their shattered bones and quivering flesh smashed into the dirt.

The fight ended almost as soon as it had begun. Meizan surveyed the carnage around him, blood singing, chitrons clamoring for more. The chief and her opponents were no longer in sight, but she had left a trail of destruction in her wake that he could follow easily enough.

Meizan released the bond, and the chitrons of Malin sloughed off like a layer of dead skin. He blinked, once again scanning the fallen bodies. Two of them were mutilated beyond recognition.

They would not die of these injuries. Their bodies were immune but slow to repair. Instead they would suffer decades of agony, unless one of those soft-souled Balancers found them and healed them.

I did that. Guilt curled in Meizan's gut as he stared at the bodies. *But how?*

He remembered kicking the boy and knocking him out cold, but the rest of the fight blurred in his mind.

It would have been enough to knock out the other soldiers for a few hours, but he'd done so much more. Too much. And the rushing in his veins and the tingling of his chitrons told Meizan that he'd enjoyed it.

Maybe now the damn manglers would learn not to attack anyone bearing the sigil of Kanjallen.

What's done is done. Not like I can heal them or try to change it.

Shoving away the remorse, Meizan stalked through the trees in search of his chief.

CHAPTER FOUR

☙

The High Priest

O N THE THIRD day of her imprisonment, Aina decided to visit the shrine. She wasn't particularly religious. No, she'd cursed the gods more than she'd ever prayed to them. But a group of Tahamuri pilgrims had shown up that morning with offerings for the gods—in the form of chewy coconut fudge sprinkled with pistachio bits and those delectable yellow milk balls of saffron and sugar.

They didn't make such sweets in Malin, where Aina had gone weeks without proper food, scavenging for scraps and starving until her stomach bled. Aro fed her well during the imprisonment, but he'd refused her the Tahamuri sweets, insisting they first needed to be "enjoyed by the gods." As if a bunch of stinking statues could enjoy anything.

Aina sidled into the shrine and was smothered at once with the scents of fresh marigolds and wisteria incense. The room itself was less offensive than its smell, consisting of a square chamber of white limestone with a statue at each corner. The statues represented the four seitarius: the Planetary Beasts worshipped across the realms. The seitarius were gods and goddesses, said to have used their chitronic powers to create the universe from the emptiness of the Void. And at the center of the room, more sacred than any statue, lay the pyramid of white and yellow sweets.

Aina's mouth watered as she eyed the treats and plotted her next step. She couldn't just run in and grab them. Half a dozen priests circled the room, chanting in unison as they showered the statues with dried rice and marigold petals.

She considered flying a milk ball across the room and straight into her mouth. But the priests could channel too, and Aina always lost when it came to chitronic showdowns. Her only option was waiting until the priests finished their rites so she could nab the sweets right after.

One of the priests shot her a suspicious look. Aina darted to the nearest statue, clasped her hands together, and gave a perfunctory bow.

The statue depicted Sherka the gazarou, great grass wolf of Mayana, seated atop an emerald pillar veined with jade. Reminded of the Kirnosi royal guard and that blasted Aranel, Aina twisted her clasped fingers into a crude gesture before turning to her right.

An amethyst pillar supported a majestic statue of Sorken the megarya, the winged dolphin of Paramos. Aina shifted her gaze across the room, where the two lower realm deities stood.

Unlike their upper counterparts, the statues of these two seitarius were demonic, their countenances as vicious as the realms under their domains. Across from Sherka on a sapphire column rose Azyaka the nagamor, peacock snake of Malin. The hundreds of smaller nagamor inhabiting the realm were supposedly her offspring.

Aina turned from Azyaka to the fourth statue: Andraken the

vandraghor, the colossal roach said to rule Narakh. Narakh was the lowest, basest, and vilest of all the realms, reserved for those with souls just as iniquitous. Aina's mother had told her tales of the rare Malini who descended to Narakh, sucked through the torana after a particularly ghastly string of crimes. None returned that she knew of. Not once they fell to Andraken's realm.

Carved in jet-black marble, the vandraghor cut a terrifying image: a mass of squirming legs and protruding eyeballs, each eye rimmed with razor-sharp teeth. Aina averted her gaze from Andraken's grotesque form to the ceiling, where a verse was inscribed in the white stone.

And thus the realm was split to four
by will of Beast who made it:
two realms for souls who relished gore,
who sinned and harmed and hated;
two for those proven true and kind,
their realms at peace, united.
And so the balance realigned,
with fair and foul divided.

She'd seen the words before. They came from the Song of Salvation, an old Mayani scripture whose verses were plastered across the realm—on storefronts and teahouses, even bathroom stalls. Once, Aina had found great use for that holy parchment, specifically verse six, when she'd run out of toilet paper.

The Song of Salvation spoke of four Beasts who stopped the great war by splitting the realms and balancing the universe—whatever the hell all that meant. Aina didn't bother herself with the nuances of the wording, although its intentions were clear. The scripture painted the four Planetary Beasts as valiant deities whose divine intervention had saved the universe from destruction.

The same way the Mayani belief system painted Toranic Law as egalitarian and just.

But they'd gotten it all wrong. Aina remembered the nagamor that nearly gored her in Malin and triggered the chain of events that had separated her from her mother. If Azyaka existed, she'd be the furthest thing from a savior.

Not that it matters, since the seitarius aren't real.

Unlike Toranic Law, which was a hard, unfortunate truth, the Planetary Beasts were nothing but a symbolic construct created for weak-willed uppers who needed something to pray to.

Even so, their statues made for decent back support. Aina leaned against Sherka the gazarou as the priests' rhythmic chanting lulled her to sleep.

It was in this decidedly irreverent position that the high priest Aro found Aina a few hours later and awakened her with a tap on the shoulder.

"I was praying," Aina lied, scrambling to her feet. She grabbed a clump of fallen marigold petals and tossed them haphazardly at Sherka's head.

"An unconventional position for prayer," Aro observed.

"Well, I was deeply absorbed in it." Aina's eyes darted around the room.

"The priests took the sweets out after the ritual," Aro said. "I am afraid they have already been distributed." Aina cursed under her breath, and Aro smiled. "You are an interesting one, Aina. If you craved the sweets so, you could have simply asked, and waited. But you never ask, do you? I studied your records in detail. You always steal. Steal, and shoot princesses, it would seem." The priest fixed her with a stern look. "Would you care to explain why?"

Aina leaned against Sherka, the marble cool against her back. "I already told the twits who brought me in. I want to descend." Aro lifted an eyebrow at that, and Aina plowed on. "I'd take a torana, but none of them bleeding work. Toranic Law is only supposed to keep evil out of Mayana. Why won't it let me into Malin?"

"I have seen those desperate to ascend from Malin to Mayana," Aro remarked, "but never the contrary. What draws you to the lower realm?"

When Aina didn't respond, he reached behind him and produced a fat yellow milk ball.

"I only want to understand you, Aina. Is there anything you can tell me that might make it possible to reduce your sentence?"

"My—my mother's in Malin." Aina grabbed the offering and shoved it into her mouth. Even the burst of saffron sweetness could not mask the bitterness that welled within her. "I need to find her."

"Your mother," the priest repeated. "Of course. You were born there, after all, yet here you are in Mayana." Aro reached forward, pushing up Aina's bangs to reveal her keiza. "How did you ascend, may I ask? What happened, in the moment?"

"I don't remember." Aina shifted away and tugged her bangs back down. "There was a lot going on. We were attacked by a nagamor."

"Did you see anything odd at the time? A flash of white, in the days or hours before you ascended?"

"I don't know," Aina said. Her mother's face materialized in her mind, eyes blazing and wet with tears. "Maybe. I don't like thinking about it."

"Forgive me." Aro offered her another sweet. This time, Aina didn't take it. "I have a profound interest in ascension between Malin and Mayana, and I let my curiosity get the better of me. It must have been a difficult time for you." The priest paused. "Even so, that you would voluntarily return to Malin, despite knowing full well the horrors that dwell there and the peril to your soul . . ."

"I don't care about my soul," Aina snapped. "My mother's been condemned by Toranic Law! If I'm not with her, she might—"

Aina clamped her mouth shut, not daring to voice the thought. That her mother might commit a crime heinous enough to get her thrown into Narakh.

Aina wasn't sure what the soul-spin limits between Malin and the lowest realm were. But sometimes after a vicious battle, her mother's keiza appeared dangerously faded, close to disappearing altogether. Her mother was a talented channeler with the power to obliterate enemies with a snap of her finger. But she didn't always know when to stop. And without Aina's tears and tantrums, begging her, *Let them be, I'm safe, you've won . . .* her mother's anger might push her over the edge.

It was said the Narakhi could not walk upright. They were so burdened by their amassed evils that their souls weighed them down like boulders and forced them to crawl. Aina could not let her mother become one of them.

"So you would descend to a lower realm out of love?" Aro asked.

"Not love," Aina mumbled. "Only necessity."

The woman had raised her, after all, and fed her when she could. Maybe, beneath the slaps and harsh words, she had cared something for Aina. Or maybe she'd hoped looking after a child would land her own soul in Mayana one day.

Regardless of her reasons, she had ensured Aina's survival. Aina felt bound to her, like a moon to its planet, their fates entwined.

"She's the only family I have." Aina's hand dropped to the pouch at her waist. Her fingers curled around the rock fragments, the pain a small comfort as they dug into her flesh. "After all she's done for me, I can't leave her to decay in that monster-infested hell." She continued with a recklessness, voicing thoughts she had left unspoken upon ascending. "It's not just her. There are thousands trapped in the lower realms, caught in a vicious cycle of suffering. We could help them if we weren't so busy wasting away in our good fortune, sparing nothing but pity and *prayer* for their souls."

She spat the word *prayer* as if it were a curse, her words bordering on blasphemy. Aina fully expected a furious sermon to follow.

But Aro did not lecture her. Instead, he asked, "How would you have us help?"

Aina hadn't considered how to help her mother, much less anyone else. She only knew it had to be done.

"Maybe we could provide food and medicine, to relieve hunger and disease," Aina suggested. "Small acts of kindness to curb at least some of the suffering."

"Perhaps," Aro said. "But as the Preservation say, there is a reason the universe imposes such trials upon the lower realms. Those people are there because they sinned, Aina. Suffering is the quickest way to burn their sins and reverse the spin of their souls. Curbing it would go against Toranic Law, against the natural order of things."

"To hell with the natural order of things!" Aina shouted, losing her patience. "I don't care for a tyrannical law that blesses some and curses others! You say the lowers suffer for their sins? Then answer me this: What sins did I commit when I was born to Malin? What sins does a newborn carry, unless you count their birth?"

Bitter memories churned within her. Of beating at the silver torana. Crying amidst the desolation of Malin.

"Why me?" Aina had screamed into the darkness. "Why was I born here? Why does the universe hate me so? It's not fair!"

"The universe is not fair," her mother had told her. "Toranic Law is not fair." And yet, despite the unfairness, Aina had made it up to Mayana. But she didn't want to be the only one.

"I do not have answers to all your questions," Aro said. "But I can tell you why the torana do not let you pass. It is not a misfunction of Toranic Law, but rather the unidirectional seals placed by the Preservation that inhibit voluntary descension. Were those seals to be deactivated, one could enter Malin at will."

Hot anger reared in Aina's chest. "Those meddling fishbrains! If Toranic Law doesn't restrict descension, who the hell are they to? How craven, how bleeding selfish!"

"Self-preservation is not selfishness," Aro said patiently. "The lower realms are dangerous. If the darkness taints your soul, you will forever remain in its grasp."

"So you're saying it's better to stay here, rotting in the light?"

Aina's entire body shook with anger. Aro gazed at her long and hard, as if he could see through her keiza into the depths of her soul. The priest brought a hand to his temple. His tone shifted when he spoke next, growing low and rich.

"You hold unorthodox convictions, Aina. Unorthodox, but interesting."

"What do you . . ." Aina's mouth fell open as Aro's fingers slid to the center of his forehead.

The priest's face rippled, then peeled off like a mask, dispelling the illusion. He—or rather, she—grew taller, hair lengthening, chest and hips swelling out.

All traces of Aro the priest disappeared. In his place stood a beautiful woman with deep bronze skin, her hair a cascade of flames.

"I saw you at the ascension ceremony and wanted to understand your motivations," the woman said, piercing eyes fixed on

Aina. "Disguising myself as your priest seemed the best way for honest conversation." She brushed a lock of hair from her forehead to reveal a keiza that sparkled like the sun. Aina stared at it, drinking in the brightness. "My name is—"

"Zenyra," Aina breathed. She recognized her from the notice in the guardhouse. "The leader of the Balancers."

"Leader and founder," Zenyra corrected, with a smile at Aina's stunned expression.

"You're wanted in this realm." Aina's eyes flicked toward the door. "The royal guard's searching for you. They have a notice with your face on it."

"Several guards have searched for several years, but our base is too well hidden." Zenyra's smile widened. "You have heard of us, Aina, but do you know our purpose?" Aina shook her head, and Zenyra continued. "We are a group of uppers endeavoring to aid those trapped in Malin. We descend with the intention of alleviating their suffering as best as we can."

"But you said—" Aina spluttered. "You said yourself—that's against the natural order of things."

"To hell with the natural order of things." Zenyra winked, then leaned down so she was at eye level with Aina. "Not quite the Balancer maxim, but close enough."

"I don't follow," Aina said. "Why are you here? What do you want with *me*?"

"Your actions at the ascension ceremony piqued my interest. I heard rumors about your crimes, so I decided to meet you in person. It would seem I was right about you, Aina. You are worthy."

"Worthy of what, exactly?"

Zenyra's eyes sparkled, and Aina shivered at the intensity of her gaze. "Why, of joining the Balancers, of course."

CHAPTER FIVE

@

Unfortunate Destiny

*T*HE MOON HUNG low in the sky when Aranel made
it out of Kirnos. He gazed upon the Lotus Kingdom
and committed it to memory. Its petals, glazed silver in
the moonlight, dewdrops adorning their edges like giant pearls.
The swirls of cloud around its base, parted in places to reveal the
glittering waters of Mir Amaratis, the Honeyed Sea, far below.

Aranel tore his gaze from Kirnos to the cloudy path ahead.
It snaked across the sky for hundreds of miles, traversing the
diamond-studded peaks of the Meruhirs before melding into the
fluttering lights of the Karaeni—the skybound river known more
commonly as the Aurora Rapids.

The torana Seirem had instructed him to take was situated
westward, in the Diamond Mountains, between Kirnos and the
mouth of the Karaeni. The Preservation did not know the location of the Balancer hideout, but Zenyra had been sighted near
that specific torana on a number of occasions.

Swiping a thumb across his keiza, Aranel drew a longsword from the scabbard belted to his waist. Due to the secrecy of his mission, he had opted against taking a flying chariot out of Kirnos, relying instead on his preferred mode of transport: cloudsurfing.

Aranel streamed chitrons across the sword's surface so it hovered above the cloud. He hopped aboard, feet pressed against the flat of the blade. The sword dipped but stayed horizontal. Aranel funneled more chitrons through his feet to propel the longsword forward until he was scudding across the cloud.

Cloudsurfing required precision, balance, and delicacy; to Aranel, after years spent chasing his brother across the skies of Kirnos, it came as easy and natural as breathing. Most cloudsurfers, including Samarel, used broader mounts such as shields. But Aranel preferred the sleekness and swiftness of his blade.

He skimmed the clouds past dawn, spraying frothy white chunks in his wake. The sun rose as he crested the prismatic ridges of the Meruhirs. In its light, Aranel's chitrons recharged quicker than they had through the night. He hastened his pace till he found the torana wedged between two immense diamonds, its mottled surface a blight upon the scintillating mountainside.

Seirem stood by the copper pillars, sipping from an engraved hip flask. The Preserver's face broke into a benign smile as Aranel approached.

"I trusted you would come," said Seirem. He stowed his drink and raised a fist to his forehead in greeting.

Aranel responded in kind as he dismounted his sword and sheathed it. "I'm not sure why I did. I still don't quite see how such an ill-fated mission could lighten my soul."

"And yet here you stand, which means you have some hope. How much do you know about the Balancers' activities, Aranel?"

"I've heard the rumors. That they fraternize with the Malini, *live* with them." Aranel shuddered, bringing a hand to his forehead. "I don't think I can do this after all, Lord Seirem. The lowers will torture me, find ways to taint my soul."

"The Malini are not all as bad as you believe," said Seirem gently. "There is evil in the lower realm, yes, but the majority of its denizens are miserable souls attempting to make the most of their wretched existence. I suspect this is why the Balancers take pity on them, and what motivates their well-meaning but hopeless quest to help. By providing the Malini with food, medicine, and other non-chitronic assistance, the Balancers are trying to assuage their suffering."

"Is that why you want me to descend?" asked Aranel. He'd been taught that the Malini were wicked, their suffering the judgment of Toranic Law. By helping them, the Balancers were undermining its authority. "So you can find a way to halt their charity mission?"

"The Balancers descend to Malin under the guise of charity," said Seirem. "But I believe there is more to it than that. Their leader is a cunning woman. It is just a hunch, Aranel. But certain members of the Preservation, including His Supremacy Lord Kyrian, suspect that Zenyra is up to something. Something that extends beyond helping the Malini."

"What is it you think she's doing?"

Zenyra's name was notorious in the realm. Yet, for all her notoriety, her keiza was said to burn brightly as a Paramosi's. Someone Toranic Law had deemed so pure couldn't possibly be doing anything wrong. Yet when Seirem spoke of her, his voice grew wary, concern lining his smooth forehead.

"We know naught of her true purpose. All I can tell you now is that we have detected disturbances in the chitronic system." At Aranel's confused expression, Seirem clarified: "The Preservation have access to a cosmic system of sorts that allows us to monitor chitronic activity across the four realms."

"All four?" exclaimed Aranel. "Where is this system? Is it in Paramos? How can you monitor the lower realms without entering them?"

"Back to the disturbances," prompted Seirem, and Aranel fell silent. He couldn't have the Preserver think him some mannerless brat who asked insolent questions.

"Imagine, now, each realm as a sphere composed of still water," said Seirem. "Standard chitronic activity manifests in the system as ripples across the spheres, the strongest channelings as waves. But certain disturbances originating in Malin present as explosions tearing across the surface. We suspect these are connected to Zenyra's activities."

"I thought Malin is plagued by war," said Aranel, unconvinced. "Could it not be the fighting that's causing the explosions?"

"The timing of the disturbances is suspicious. Furthermore, Zenyra has been sighted in Paramos several times—not far from the Preservation headquarters in Ashkator. She never made it past our defenses, but she is up to something, Aranel. I feel it in my bones." Seirem reached down and gripped Aranel's shoulders. "Whatever it is, I fear it may endanger Toranic Law."

Aranel nearly choked on his own spit. "How is that possible?"

Toranic Law couldn't be endangered, as if it were a rare species of bird. It was an absolute force of nature, unmovable as bedrock. When Aranel was younger, he'd asked his brother why the Preservation didn't simply change Toranic Law and make it so the lower realms were less horrible. Samarel had explained that Toranic Law was no council or legislation that could be reasoned with. The Preservation could not control its workings any more than they could stop the moon's orbit or dim the light of the sun.

If the Preservation could do nothing to change Toranic Law,

how could a single Paramosi rebel and her cult following endanger it?

"I cannot provide more details at this time," said Seirem. "All I can say is this: Zenyra's mission—her true mission, not the charity she is running—could pose a danger to our universe. Protecting it is the noblest thing one could do, and you are our best hope, Aranel."

Aranel felt a swell of pride at the Preserver's words. He'd never been the best anything with his brother around. That the Preservation would entrust this task to *him*, over any other, over perfect, pure Samarel . . .

Aranel stared at the copper torana and the bleak expanse that lay beyond. His gaze shifted to the inscription carved into the pillars, a stanza from the Song of Salvation:

> *Wicked Malin, where fell men and their prey*
> *both suffer a harrowing fate.*
> *Here souls spin backward, so drenched in decay,*
> *their chitrons afire with hate.*

Fear seized him at the words. "What if I end up tainting myself, Lord Seirem? What if I'm condemned to live in Malin for eternity?"

Seirem leaned down, the Preserver's eyes bright. "You will not be punished for merely watching and reporting, Aranel. You need only inform us of the Balancers' identities, their activities, and Zenyra's every move. I'll monitor the nearby torana so you can request to meet with me when convenient. If you do that, I promise your soul shall spin swifter for it and you will be permitted entry into Paramos."

"But I'd have to lie to the Balancers." Aranel's index finger circled frantically over his palm. "Even the Aria of Ascension says honesty is a virtue."

"'Check thine intentions: nefarious or nice, may turn vice a virtue and virtue a vice,'" said Seirem, closing a hand over Aranel's palm. "Also from the Aria of Ascension. Verse twelve, as I am sure you are aware." He squeezed Aranel's hand. "You are taking this mission with the best of intentions, and your success will ensure the future of humankind. Worry not over such trivialities, and focus on what is truly at stake. If you do that, the universe *will* reward you."

"V-very well, then," said Aranel, swallowing his fear. "Teach me how to unseal the torana."

"Sorken bless you, my boy," said Seirem. "Sorken bless your soul."

ARANEL'S KNEES WOULD buckle under the heaviness of this realm.

Malin was laden with melancholy. It hung from the air and draped thickly over the trees. Aranel felt it with each ponderous step, as if whatever misery permeated the realm was creeping into his bones and settling at the pit of his stomach. He plodded through a maze of rotting trees, their branches bare and their bark peeling.

It was a far cry from Aran Kirenkar, the Dappled Forest at the heart of Kirnos, with its vibrant golden leaves and sun-streaked paths. No sunlight graced this part of Malin. Between roiling black storm clouds, the sky appeared a dreary, washed-out gray—the same color as the trees and the hard, grassless ground.

Mere hours in the realm, and Aranel was already sick of it all—the heaviness and the grayness and the perpetual sense of dread.

How can anything live in such a horrid place?

Aranel shivered, pulling his cloak around him. On second thought, he supposed he ought to count his blessings; he hadn't run into the mythical nagamor or any of the other beasts said to lurk in Malin. But he also had no concept of where he was or how to find the Balancer hideout. Every inch of this forest looked disturbingly similar, with its endless rows of dying trees.

After another hour of traipsing about mindlessly, Aranel came upon something different: an area of the forest littered with craters and broken branches, where an enormous rift split the ground. Pained groans echoed from the fissure, the soil around it stained crimson. Aranel stumbled back in surprise.

Sherka protect me! There are people trapped in there!

Whoever lay inside must be heavily injured. Aranel swiped his keiza to activate his chitrons and pushed them toward the broken rock.

A prickle of something cold and sinister seeped through the chitronic bond, filling him with unease. In Mayana, bonding with the chitrons of the environment felt calming. Aranel loved the warmth that infused him when they enveloped his soul, thrumming through his body and responding to his every request. But in Malin the chitrons felt wrong. Unnatural. *Dirty.*

An ear-piercing screech rent the air and distracted Aranel from the bond. It went on for a full minute, shattering into echoed screams that assaulted his ears like shards of glass.

A trio of monkeys with twisted horns swung through the branches. Their beady eyes glinted with malevolence, and their razor-sharp teeth were bared in horrifying grins.

Aranel took a step back and nearly tripped into the fissure.

The monkeys of Mayana were a friendly lot, with curling tails and soft, gleaming fur. They were nothing like these creatures, with their spiny fur and spiteful little faces.

Without warning, the largest monkey lunged, arching its back to shoot off a volley of spines. Aranel pushed out with a blast of chitronic energy that swept the spines away. But something stinking and sodden hit his chest, sliding down his tunic to fall onto the dirt with a plop. Aranel looked down to see an unmistakable brown smear against his gray silks.

That little demon!

The monkey beat its chest and emitted another shriek as it swung through the branches.

Aranel drew his sword and mounted it, injecting chitrons into the blade. He sped across the fissure, but his sword began to sink, the very air of Malin dragging it down. He'd made it halfway across when his chitronic flows gave a shudder and snapped.

Aranel leaped off his blade just as it plummeted into the rift, his trusty companion lost to him. But he had no time to lament. Just as he landed on solid ground, the monkeys swung overhead to cut off his path. They pelted him with feces and rocks, hooting and cackling as they sprayed the air with urine.

Why are they so bent on attacking me? Aranel snatched a fallen tree branch and battered away a second volley of spines, quickly pulling his hood over his head to shield himself from the rest. *Is this the nature of creatures in Malin, to harm without reason?*

Forcing down hysteria, Aranel crouched into a defensive position and gripped the branch like a sword. He had undergone extensive training in hand-to-hand combat as part of the Kirnosi royal guard. He could defeat these monkeys even without chitrons, by hurling a sharpened branch at them or hitting their necks.

But they were no training targets. They were living creatures with no armor to protect them.

The monkeys seemed to sense that Aranel posed no real threat. They descended upon him in a tornado of gnashing teeth and swiping claws. Aranel fended them off, careful to ensure he didn't accidentally poke one of the beasts' eyes out—or end up gored by their horns. But he was outnumbered and his foes incessant in their assault.

Aranel bonded to a nearby tree, then directed its branches to wrap around his attackers and bind their movements. The chitrons of Malin responded at once, skeletal branches twisting through the air. But instead of immobilizing the monkeys, the branches pierced their chests and skewered the two smaller beasts in a splatter of blood.

"No," gasped Aranel. The monkeys screamed in pain, thrashing against the branch as torrents of blood spurted from their chests. "No—I didn't mean—"

The chitrons of Malin seemed to vibrate with glee. Aranel snapped the bond in horror and pressed a hand against his forehead. How could he hurt a living creature? Why had his channeling gone so terribly wrong?

Aranel dropped his branch and ran toward the monkeys, soul curdling at their pained shrieks. He had to fix this. He had to heal them.

A moment later, he stumbled backward. His cheek burned with three lines of pain where the largest monkey had scratched him. The creature snarled and lunged again.

"I'm sorry!" cried Aranel, ducking the swiping claws. "I never meant to hurt you!"

He turned and fled through the forest, the monkey in fierce pursuit. He wouldn't be able to outrun it on the ground. Aranel bonded to a tree once again, then sprinted up its trunk and leaped across the branches in a well-practiced motion.

But the chitrons of Malin were treacherous, and a branch snapped beneath his feet. Aranel pitched backward with a yelp, fingers scrabbling against the tree trunk. Its chitrons refused him and he hurtled toward the ground—

Until a dark blur sped past him and someone grabbed onto his ankle, yanking hard. Aranel hung there, upside down, all the blood rushing to his head as his heart drummed up a frenzy.

He crunched upward to meet his savior's eyes, black as the storm clouds overhead. A boy who looked to be his age crouched on the branch, holding Aranel by the ankle like a fish on display. In his other hand the boy held the remaining monkey by its tail. The creature twitched once before going limp.

"Running from a kapizer," the boy scoffed. His lip curled as he flung the limp monkey aside. "You uppers are pathetic."

"Thank—you." Aranel's breaths came out in short, staccato bursts. "For—saving me."

"Saving you?" The boy cocked his head. "Aren't you optimistic?"

Without warning, he loosed his grip. Aranel flailed, managed to roll himself upright midair, and landed messily on his feet.

The boy dropped beside him and shoved Aranel face-first into the ground. Digging a knee into his neck, he yanked Aranel's arms behind his back. Panic flared through Aranel as he struggled against the boy's hold. A tight pressure circled his wrists and lashed them together.

"Wait, what are you—" Aranel choked as he attempted to free his wrists. But they were in a chitronic bind of sorts, and Aranel dared not channel again. "Release me! At once!"

Instead, the boy grabbed Aranel by the collar and pulled him to his feet. "Don't waste your energy trying to break loose," he said, voice dripping with disdain. "You're useless without chitrons, and we both know you're too damn scared to channel again."

Aranel turned to him. "You saw that? With the monkeys?" His captor nodded, and Aranel's cheeks grew hot. That hadn't been his finest moment. "Do you think we could heal—" he began, but the boy silenced him with a glare.

"This isn't one of your charity cases," he snapped. "Now let's get out of this dump so you can take me to your hideout."

"My hideout?"

"Your bleeding Balancer hideout. Stop acting like you don't know."

"R-right," said Aranel. "So you're joining the Balancers as well?"

The boy regarded him with disgust. "I'm trading you for medicine so I can heal my clanmate." At Aranel's stunned expression, he added, "My *sick*, *suffering* clanmate, one of the Malini you uppers claim you want to help."

Aranel stared at his captor in shock, allowing himself to be dragged through the forest. He'd assumed the boy to be one of the Balancers, a grave mistake. This boy was a Malini. A born-and-bred lower.

Suddenly, Aranel found it hard to breathe.

He tried to calm himself and make sense of the situation. The lower looked quite ordinary, apart from having clearly not bathed in weeks. His pale face was caked with dried blood and grime. Twin smears of blue paint extended from below each eye and across his hollow cheeks. The Malini were said to be monstrous beasts. Aranel had expected horns like the monkeys'. Perhaps claws and sharp teeth. But the lower's teeth appeared straight and his grubby fingernails otherwise unoffensive. Aranel wondered if he was concealing his true form with chitrons.

"Walk faster!" barked the lower, kneeing Aranel in the back. "Kaldrav's soldiers are swarming the forest like roaches, and you'll be no good in a fight."

Who's Kaldrav? Aranel almost asked, before clamping his mouth shut. This lower seemed to think him a Balancer. Aranel couldn't risk his lack of knowledge giving him away. The moment his captor realized Aranel wasn't tradeable for medicine, he would likely lose all incentive to not maim him.

"Perhaps not fighting, but I *am* fairly good with chitrons," said Aranel, eager to get on the lower's good side. If he had one. "What you saw earlier was merely a—a lapse of control."

The lower snorted, and Aranel continued, vaguely recalling a past chitronic lesson about the perils of channeling in a lower realm. "I presume it has something to do with the First Principle of Chitronic Equilibrium. You know, the transfer of opposite-spinning energies . . ."

He looked at the lower expectantly, but the boy continued to regard him as if he were something nasty.

Do I smell bad? wondered Aranel, before remembering with a burst of mortification what he was covered with. *How can he stand to be near me?*

But the lower seemed not to take notice of the various excreta staining Aranel's clothing, which he supposed was a small mercy.

"The First Principle," repeated Aranel, forcing a smile. "Living in Malin, you would be more familiar with it than I am, I expect." No response. "Do they not teach fundamental chitronic theory here?" Still no response. "But without basic theory, however did you learn to channel?"

"By fighting." The lower kneed him again. "Try it next time you're attacked, instead of yammering about *theory*."

The minutes dragged by as they trudged through the forest, and his captor seemed in no mood to continue conversing.

"May I know your name?" asked Aranel out of a desire to break the silence. He added, undeterred by the lower's flat stare, "Mine's Aranel, and I'm originally from Kirnos."

The lower said nothing, and Aranel tried again. "What brings you to this forest? It's rather . . . barren, wouldn't you agree?"

The lower's face twisted into a scowl. "I'm looking for my clan chief. Have you seen anyone wearing a vest like mine?"

"Sorry, I haven't." Aranel ran his eyes over the boy's tattered leather vest. It was marked with two lines of peeling blue paint that echoed the pattern on his cheeks. "What clan is this?"

"Kanjallen. The last free clan in the realm."

Kanjallen. Of course. Aranel had come across the name in the ancient scriptures. It meant "eternal tears." A morbid nomenclature, although it explained that unsightly face paint.

"It would be nice to know your name as well," he said, and the lower shot him a murderous glare. Aranel returned it with another smile, pleasant as he could manage.

"Meizan," said the lower at last. It took a moment for the meaning to sink in.

Unfortunate destiny, thought Aranel. *Fitting, I suppose. Meizan of Kanjallen. What a morbid name indeed.*

"So, um, Meizan," said Aranel, still not quite used to how the name rolled off his tongue. "If you didn't truly mean to save me, why *did* you stop that monkey from harming me earlier? You could've let it—"

"Put you to sleep?" Meizan yanked on the binds, forcing Aranel to walk faster. "Little use you'd be then." His dark eyes narrowed. "You don't know what kapizer venom does. Are you a new recruit?"

"I—I've not been here very long."

Aranel hadn't even known those monkeys, those *kapizer*, were venomous. It was a miracle he'd gotten away unscathed. And it would be an even greater miracle if he survived Meizan's wrath once they made it out of the forest and it became evident that Aranel hadn't the faintest clue where the Balancer hideout was.

Because even if Meizan looked all right, his soul spun backward. He would hurt Aranel like he'd hurt that kapizer. *But I'd deserve it,* thought Aranel, gut clenching. Even if by mistake, he had harmed two living beings. Possibly killed them.

Aranel wanted nothing more than to wrench himself free of his binds, flee this accursed forest, and return to Kirnos for a steaming bath. But he couldn't risk calling upon his chitrons again.

And as his eyes traced over his captor's muscled form, Aranel had an inkling he wouldn't fare well if it came to a physical fight. They were similarly built, Meizan perhaps half an inch taller. But a curved sword hung from his hip and several knives were strapped to his calves, while Aranel carried nothing to defend himself with.

Surely he wouldn't think to use those knives on me, Aranel reassured himself. *They're likely for chopping firewood. And I suppose he cloudsurfs on that sword.*

His optimism faded as the hours dragged by.

Aranel hated this realm. It was a strong emotion, hatred, one he had seldom experienced in Mayana. But Malin was insufferable and Meizan no better.

Aranel swallowed his spit in hopes it would soothe his parched throat. It felt as if someone had run sandpaper along the length, and the spit didn't help in the slightest. His shoulders throbbed from the unnatural position Meizan had forced them into.

"Can we—take a break—" Aranel wheezed. He ignored Meizan's hostile glare, which seemed to be a permanent fixture on his face. It had been unnerving at first, but after five hours of putting up with him, Aranel was growing immune. "I need water. I need—"

"What you need," said Meizan, "is to stop your damn whining. If this is too much, you should've crawled back to your realm when you had the chance."

I'm happy to crawl back now, thought Aranel. But the Preservation had entrusted him with the future of the universe. If he wanted to ascend like his brother, he had to endure. So Aranel bit back his complaints and followed Meizan without another word.

There wasn't much of a sunset in Malin. No vibrant splash of gold and scarlet across the sky, only a gradual darkening from gray to black. Aranel nearly cried out with relief when Meizan decided to stop for the night. He was beginning to think lowers required no sleep.

"I'm not going to run away," grumbled Aranel, as Meizan tied him to a tree. The Malini ignored him, as he did about half the time Aranel spoke, and settled against the tree trunk opposite.

Meizan swiped his forehead, hands glowing with mottled blue energy. His chitrons flowed forth in thin lines that spread across the trees like giant spiderwebs.

"Are those a precaution against the kapizer?" asked Aranel.

"Them, and worse."

Once Meizan completed the webs, he flicked a finger at a nearby tree. Several branches splintered off and fell into a neat stack on the ground. Another flick and Meizan had sparked a fire. Aranel couldn't help but feel impressed by the ease with which he channeled.

Because he's evil, reminded a voice in his head. *As evil and corrupt as the chitrons of this realm. Of course they'll submit to his will.*

Aranel studied his captor across the flames. Meizan's brows knit together as he removed his sword and examined it under the firelight. His coarse hair was a mess, leaving Meizan's keiza scarcely visible underneath unkempt bangs. And yet if he just brushed his hair and wiped the grime from his face . . .

He looks Nishakian.

With his inky black hair and angular features, Meizan could have passed for a native of Nishaki. Perhaps his ancestors had been Nishakian, centuries ago. Perhaps Meizan had Mayani blood in him still. *Although a true Mayani would never manhandle me as he did.*

"What are you staring at?" Meizan glowered.

"Your face." Aranel flushed at how that sounded. "I meant that you've got blood. On your face. Quite a lot of it."

"Better the blood of my enemies than their shit."

So he *had* noticed. Aranel wriggled in his binds, wishing he had a wet towel.

"I don't normally look like this," he said, earning himself another unblinking glare before Meizan returned to scrutinizing his weapon: a single-edged blade with what appeared to be a nagamor looped around its hilt. "That's an interesting sword," offered Aranel. "Personally, I prefer a straight blade, but some might favor the angle of attack afforded by the slight curve."

Meizan looked up. "*You* can wield a sword?"

"Of course. As part of the Kirnosi royal guard, I've trained in both swordplay and hand-to-hand combat."

"And yet you couldn't hold your own against three flaming monkeys."

"I was trying not to harm them! I'd never fought a living being before."

"How the hell did you train? Why learn swordplay if you're too scared to harm anything?"

"We have exhibitions where we showcase our techniques," said Aranel. "On chitronically powered training dummies, or sometimes fruit. Who can carve pumpkins fastest, or slice the most watermelons."

"You learned swordplay so you could slice *fruit*?" Meizan's expression was torn between horror and incredulity. "Your realm is a travesty."

"Better we carve fruits than humans."

"Is it?" Meizan had a strange gleam in his eyes. "The feeling of slicing down an enemy . . . it's unlike anything else."

He drew a long knife and slid it across the ground. Aranel jerked his foot away with a yelp as the blade spun dangerously close to his toes.

"Fight me," drawled the lower. He stood, raised his own blade with a flourish, then sent out a pulse of chitrons to unravel the ropes around Aranel.

"What? No! Why?" Aranel scrambled to his feet and backed against the tree as Meizan approached.

"Because I'm bored." Meizan flexed his shoulders, lips pulling into a smirk. "You can pretend I'm fruit, if it helps. Although *you'll* be the one getting cut into."

"But I don't want to fight you!" cried Aranel. "And violence is wrong; you can't cut into people simply because you're bored! That's precisely the sort of thing that'll weigh on your soul."

"Hell, you uppers are wimps." Meizan swung his sword in a series of circles. "Who cares about souls, when . . ."

He trailed off, bolting to the edge of the campsite. Aranel followed, picking up the fallen knife on the way. He didn't intend to use it himself, but it would be entirely foolish to provide potential enemies with a spare weapon.

Meizan was examining the chitronic web he'd set up earlier. One of the lines trembled, then snapped in half.

The lower lunged forward, blade flashing. Aranel threw himself to the ground as a flurry of arrows whistled overhead. He heard a thump, followed by a high-pitched yelp, and looked up to see Meizan wrestling a petite figure in an oversized blouse and baggy pants.

The figure put up a good fight, kicking and punching, hollering a barrage of expletives that made Aranel's ears burn. There was something familiar about that high, grating voice and ill-fitting burlap smock. About that intractable dark brown hair and vivid turquoise keiza.

"Stop!" Aranel ran to Meizan and yanked him off the intruder. "Don't hurt her!"

Meizan elbowed him in the face. Aranel staggered back, nursing a bruised cheek.

The intruder jumped to her feet, her pointed face a snarl. Her amber eyes burned with an unearthly fire as she drew her bow and aimed it at Meizan's chest. Meizan's blade was at her neck, cutting a thin line of blood across her brown skin.

Aranel pushed past Meizan to grab the hilt of his sword and pull it away from the girl's neck with great effort. The intruder snapped her gaze to his, her grip around her bow slackening.

"Aranel." Aina gawked before wrinkling her nose. "Why are you covered in shit?"

CHAPTER SIX

๑

The Dead Mountain

Y OU *JOINED THE* Balancers?" the upper girl asked, voice heavy with contempt. "I saw you in Kirnos just three days ago. Besides, aren't you scared about tainting your precious, shining soul?"

"M-my recruitment was rather recent," Aranel stammered, sending a nervous glance Meizan's way. What was his damn problem? He kept acting like Meizan was going to bite him or something.

The girl sniffed. "After all that drivel you gave *me* for wanting to descend."

"I—I was wrong," Aranel said. "About everything. In fact, um, you inspired me, Aina. You made me realize how wrong I was. That's, ah, that's why I decided to join."

Aina's eyes grew wide, and she stared at the ground.

"How did you get here?" Aranel continued. "Should you not be at the temple, repenting your sins?"

"Where better to repent than Malin itself?" Aina muttered. "I took a flying chariot from Kirnos, then passed through the torana a few hours ago." She turned to Meizan. "Are you a Balancer too?"

"No, but this one's my hostage," Meizan said. "My clanmates are sick. I'm going to trade him for medical supplies once we reach your hideout."

Aina considered that for a moment, then shrugged. "I doubt a flake like him will fetch much, but do what you must."

Aranel let out a strangled yell. "How is that acceptable? Are you not going to help me?"

"Why would I?" Aina asked. "He clearly needs the supplies, and while you may be a Balancer, you're still a jerk."

Meizan bit back a smirk at Aranel's outraged expression. This Aina didn't seem so bad for an upper. She was less annoying than Aranel—with his stupidly glossy hair and stupid self-righteousness—and strong for someone who just about reached his chin.

"I'm headed for the hideout too," Aina continued, pulling out a piece of crumpled parchment. "But this way's blocked. An entire contingent of Kaldrav's soldiers have gathered along here." She smoothed the map and pointed at the eastern edge of Martharan.

Meizan frowned. That wasn't far from where he'd lost the chief. His attempts to find her had been unsuccessful. If more of Kaldrav's soldiers had gathered in the area, there was a high chance she'd been captured.

If anything happens to me, take over as chief. Her words echoed through his mind. *Do not let our clan die.*

Meizan ripped the map from Aina's hand. He'd headed southward in search of the chief but hadn't risked going west in case more of Kaldrav's troops remained stationed there. It had been reckless trekking through the forest with Aranel, but

Meizan couldn't return to the tunnel. The explosion would have attracted more soldiers, and the area would be swarming with enemies. The northern fringes of Martharan could also be occupied. Meizan had no way to know unless he looked upon it from above.

"Here's what we'll do," Meizan said. "We'll climb Merumarth so we can see the position of Kaldrav's troops. We'll probably have to cut across the mountain and circle around them if we want to reach the Balancer hideout here." He jabbed the spot on the map that had been marked with a red circle. "Then you two can piss off and do whatever charity you're here for, and I can get my medicine and return to my clan."

"Why are you deciding everything, when you're not even a Balancer?" Aranel grumbled, at which Meizan promptly whacked his head.

"WE'RE CLIMBING *THAT*?" Aranel gaped as Merumarth came into view.

Meizan had become so used to staring up at the mountain from its base, he'd forgotten how much uglier it looked from afar: a grotesque pile of rock shaped like some old sod's gnarly fist, with a single finger pointed up in eternal damnation. Or an eternal flip-off, depending on the angle.

"What's that coming out of it?" Aranel motioned to the soot belching from Merumarth's peak, where the sky glowed an angry vermilion.

"You don't have volcanoes in your realm?" Meizan demanded.

"We do. But Mayani volcanoes pour forth holy nectar. Or flowers."

Meizan snorted, and was surprised to see Aina roll her eyes. Mayana was ridiculous. Then again, what better to expect from the realm that had spawned a preening pain in the ass like Aranel? Aina looked much more human, her clothes frayed and patched like Meizan's own.

"How are we getting up?" Aina asked, once they'd reached the southern foothills of the Dead Mountain.

Her eyes watered, and she was constantly sniffling due to the fumes. Beside her, Aranel was a sniveling mess. Neither carried a scarf, and Meizan was tempted to throttle them with his own. How had these boneheads come to Malin so unprepared?

"We're going to climb chitronically," Meizan said. He felt a stab of annoyance at Aranel's stiff expression.

"It's unsafe to channel here," Aranel began. "You *saw* what happened with the kapizer earlier. I'm already stained with enough sin—"

"And shit," Aina chimed in.

"And piss," Meizan felt compelled to add.

"What I am saying"—Aranel raised his voice above theirs— "is that the chitrons here are unnatural. It's as per the First Principle."

"Get over yourself," Meizan said. "There's nothing unnatural about Malin's chitrons. You're just incompetent."

Aranel raised his chin. "I'll have you know I won *medals* in Mayana for my abilities."

"What do you mean by Malin's chitrons?" Aina asked before Meizan could retort. He stared at her in disbelief, and she glared back. "It's not as if the realm has a soul!"

"He's talking about the ambient chitrons," Aranel explained. "The ones that make up the environment. Stop looking so shocked, Aina, you've channeled them before."

"I have? When?"

"When you ran down the cliff in Kirnos. You bonded to the chitrons in the rock."

Aina scrunched her face. "I thought I was channeling particles of the rock."

"Conscious particles," Aranel corrected. "Therefore chitrons."

"How can rocks have chitrons when they don't have souls?"

"This isn't time to debate chitronic theory," Meizan interrupted, swiping his keiza and bonding to the mountainside.

To his relief, the chitrons complied as he strode up the slaggy rock, though he'd have to be careful not to trigger a landslide. A grumbling Aranel followed in Meizan's wake, but Aina stood rooted at the base, scowling as she pressed a finger against her keiza.

Aranel sighed as Aina began her shaky climb. "Her fundamentals could use some work."

Aina's control was abysmal. She took too long shaping the rock. Once she did, several of the steps crumbled under her weight, and she fell down and had to start over.

"Is your keiza broken or something?" Meizan asked. "Aranel, carry her up."

"No!" Aina yelled from below, going red. "I can climb myself!"

"Your chitronic bond with the rock seems unstable," Aranel said. He hopped down and proceeded to instruct Aina on the basics of channeling. "Try activating your chitrons again. And this time, say the incantation."

"I'm not saying the damn incantation," Aina seethed. "Nobody says the damn incantation."

"Either say it," Meizan gritted out, "or let Aranel carry you."

Aina huffed but pressed a finger to her keiza. "Fine. What was it again? I think it went like, beloved Sherka, please lend me your— Wait, no, that's wrong."

"We're in Malin," Aranel said. "This is Azyaka's realm, not Sherka's."

"I know whose bleeding realm it is," Aina groused, once again swiping her keiza. "Revered Azyaka, please lend me your strength."

Still no change. Aina wobbled up the mountain, chunks of rock skittering in her wake until Meizan was sure she'd be the one triggering a landslide.

"Burn it," he said, leaping down to her level. Ignoring her protests, Meizan grabbed Aina around the waist and hoisted her over his back like a sack of wood before sprinting up the slope of Merumarth.

It was a damn miracle they made the climb without incident. Meizan thought his head would explode, what with Aina's screeching—*Let me down, you lout, I can channel just fine*—and Aranel's whining—*There is something amiss with the chitrons of this realm, they are a blight upon my soul.* Meizan had come dangerously close to drop-kicking them both off the side of the mountain. The acrid fumes made it all worse, stabbing Meizan's nostrils through his scarf.

Meizan dumped Aina on the rock once they'd scaled Merumarth's middle finger and peered over the inner edge. It was like staring down the throat of a fire-spewing beast. The hollow mountain oozed a ropy expanse of lava pricked with enormous bubbles. Every few seconds, a bubble would pop and send up sizzling orange droplets. Even Meizan's scarf couldn't block the oppressive heat that pressed upon his face like a branding iron.

"You call this a volcano?" Aranel asked weakly, keeping a safe distance from the edge.

Meizan turned from the lava pit and surveyed the forest below. Kaldrav's troops scurried around Martharan like cockroaches. They had surrounded the forest on all sides but the north, where the sludgy waters of the Muzireni and its tributaries crawled across the land like a giant, ugly centipede. Meizan mapped out one path that would sneak them past the soldiers to the Balancer hideout and another that would lead him back to his clanmates.

They'd have to be quick, since the soldiers appeared to also be heading northward. Meizan could only hope the cockroaches cleared out before Taezur and the others were ready to travel, because there was no way in hell he was digging another tunnel.

"We're crossing over and then climbing down the north side," he said, scowling at the sight of Aranel collapsed on the ground. "Oi." Meizan kicked his leg. "Get up."

"I'm exhausted," Aranel said, amidst a fit of coughing. "It's been hours since my last meal. I need sustenance if I'm to channel my way back down."

"You should've kept your skewered kapizer from earlier and cooked them over the fire. Your hair's loaded with enough oil to fry a couple monkeys."

Aina snickered at that, and Aranel glowered at them both. He flipped his hair over his shoulder with a long-suffering sigh. "I've had about enough of the two of you. If we're not stopping for food, let's get the hell off this wretched mountain."

"Careful, Aranel," Aina said with a sly grin. "Such filthy speech will burden your soul."

Meizan yanked Aranel up by the collar before he could respond and led the idiot and Aina around the western rim of the crater.

"Don't channel," he warned, jerking his head at the lava. "Even the slightest mistake, and this all blows to shit."

As it stood, the Dead Mountain seemed calm enough to go another few weeks without erupting.

We're going to make it, Meizan told himself, nails digging into his palms. The northern periphery grew closer by the minute. *I'm going to get Kanjallen out of this dump so we can search for Chief Kanna.*

Chilling screams fractured Meizan's calm like stones smashing a thin layer of glass.

Dozens of kapizer swarmed up the western slope and cut off their path. The monkey he'd electrocuted earlier led the pack, its eyes twin balls of fury.

That little scumbag! I should have ground its bones to dust!

Meizan drew his sword as Aina readied her bow. He reached for his knives and tossed two to Aranel. The blades were shorter than ideal but better than nothing. The flea-brain carried no weapons of his own, only an empty scabbard strapped to his waist.

"We can't risk channeling," Meizan said at Aranel's startled look. The upper held the knives as if they were coated in kapizer venom. "Do what you have to do. Chop them up like fruits. And for Azyaka's sake, make sure nothing disturbs the lava."

The first wave of kapizer leaped forth amidst a shower of spines. Meizan batted away the projectiles and pivoted on his heel, spinning and slashing his way through the mob. Any kapizer he cut down, he flung over the outer edge of the volcano.

Next to him, Aina whipped up a fury of arrows, directing her shots away from the lava. Her aim was true and she fell into step next to him, shooting down the kapizer he missed while avoiding the whirling path of his sword.

They cleaved a passage through the horde, and Meizan felt a swell of relief, one that quickly turned to rage when he spied Aranel behind them.

The feckless upper had wrapped the knives with strips of his tunic and was gripping them by their blades. Meizan had never seen anything so absurd in his life. Aranel's movements, while elegant and swift, were entirely impractical. He wasn't attempting to attack the monkeys, only defending against their spines. Occasionally, he'd knock one out using the hilt, then carefully slide its body away from the lava pit with his foot.

"You piss-brained idiot!" Meizan shouted over the kapizer's screeches. He brought his sword down in an arc and neatly beheaded the kapizer Aranel was fending off.

Aranel turned to him, wide-eyed. "How could you—"

"Shut it," Meizan snarled, lunging forward to cut another beast.

Aranel kicked it out of the way, flipping the knife in his wrist to smash its cloth-covered blade against Meizan's own.

"They're not immortal, and they can't heal themselves," Aranel cried. "Knocking them out is enough. There's no need to cut them up!"

"That's what knives are for, you spineless, sinless moron!" Meizan shoved Aranel aside to stab an incoming kapizer. "I'm trying to get *us* out of this in one piece."

"At what cost?" Aranel's eyes fell to his forehead.

"Don't you dare judge me."

"I would never presume to, but Toranic Law—"

"Should understand the meaning of self-defense," Meizan growled. "Even if it doesn't, I don't give a shit because there's no burning way in hell I'd ever ascend!"

The next wave of kapizer descended on them in a whirlwind of spines and shrieks and snapping teeth. But for every kapizer Meizan and Aina felled, another three leaped to take its place, their beady eyes bright with malice, raucous screeches threatening to burst his eardrums.

"Meizan . . ." Aina's voice grew faint. "I know . . . s'bad timing . . . m'sleepy . . ."

Meizan swore as Aranel rushed to catch her tottering form. A gleaming spine was buried in Aina's shoulder.

Aranel wrenched it out and examined the wound. "It's shallow, thank Sherka."

But even with a shallow wound, Aina would be knocked out for the next couple minutes. Meizan couldn't handle so many beasts alone until she awoke. Not without chitrons.

"I'm going to channel." Meizan clenched his jaw. "Pray to your grassy bitch goddess I don't screw up."

He swiped his thumb against his keiza just as the kapizer sent a volley of spines whistling toward them.

The chitrons of Malin slithered over his own like a coat of tar. Meizan compressed the air around him so it was dense as stone, to form a protective dome that encapsulated him, Aranel, and Aina. The kapizer spines clattered off harmlessly, and even as the creatures pounded it with their fists, the air dome did not give way.

"This is our chance," Meizan called. He forced his way through the mob, and Aranel followed closely behind with Aina.

They were halfway to the northern rim when the dome gave a violent shudder. Meizan ground his teeth as his chitrons strained against the bond, forcing the air particles to keep their shape. But the will of Malin's chitrons prevailed, and Meizan lost control.

The dome exploded and swept an entire line of screaming kapizer into the lava.

"No," Meizan groaned, as the lava began to rise, spluttering and bubbling with a fury.

He had to stop it. Merumarth couldn't erupt now. If it did . . .

Meizan looked toward the eastern rim of the crater, cold fear clawing at his heart. His clanmates were down there, hiding in a cave at Merumarth's base. The four surviving members of Kanjallen whom Meizan had sworn to protect.

Meizan barely had time to register the guilt as lava surged forth like a tsunami. Towers of fiery liquid spurted skyward. Then, with a shattering crash, the eastern wall of Merumarth blew open. Lava poured through the new vent and down the mountainside in torrents.

Numbness spread through Meizan's bones, freezing him in place as he watched the lavafall. In seconds the Kanjallen hideout would be flooded. His clanmates buried alive.

They wouldn't die but live on in scorching, suffocating darkness . . . until they lost the will to exist and ended in erasure, the most terrifying fate to befall one's soul. Erasure marked the ultimate end of a being. An irreversible destruction of their soul that left not a single chitron intact.

Meizan heard it happened most often in Narakh, when a Narakhi, unable to endure even a moment more of their trauma, gave up on existing. But erasure was rare in Malin. Almost unheard of.

And now Taezur and the others would face that grisly fate, and it was Meizan's plan to cross Merumarth that had caused it.

"We need to get out of here." Aranel shook his shoulder. "Meizan?"

Meizan tore his gaze away from the lavafall. Aranel studied him with an odd expression. "Are you all right?" the upper asked. Meizan didn't know how to answer that. "The mountain's unsteady," Aranel continued.

Beside him, Aina rubbed her eyes. "What . . . the bleeding . . . hell . . ."

Merumarth rumbled below their feet, large cracks forking across the stone. The explosion had relieved some of the pressure, but more lava bubbled up. The kapizer fled down the western slope, their revenge utterly forgotten.

"We could try climbing down," Aranel said. "But I'm worried the other side will blow. I think it might be best to—"

A deafening crack cut him off as the rock beneath Meizan's feet split apart.

"Come *on*!" Aranel yelled over the uproar, yanking Meizan to safety.

Lava trickled from the newly opened fissure. In a few minutes the entire mountain would explode. They'd be buried. Buried and forgotten like the rest of Kanjallen.

"Hurry!" Aranel tugged on Meizan's arm, dragging him toward the lava pit.

Meizan stared at the gushing river of fire. It swept away from them and spilled over the eastern edge of Merumarth. Amidst its flows, Meizan spotted the corpses of several kapizer, some burned to death and others crushed between floating chunks of rock.

"You can't be serious," Meizan heard Aina say.

"It's our only option," Aranel replied. "The lava will clear a path through the army and carry us straight to the hideout. But if we wait any longer, it'll be too late."

"Fine," Aina said. "But you go first. I need proof the damn rock won't sink."

Aranel turned to Meizan. "Could you trust me on this?"

Meizan stared at him blankly. Trust? What was he on about?

"You can thank me after," Aranel said, then jabbed the base of Meizan's skull. Meizan stumbled, black spots swimming in his vision. An arm wrapped around his shoulders and he pitched forward, right into the lava river.

Meizan reached for his chitrons in a panic, but his feet hit something hard. He found himself atop one of the floating rocks with Aranel crouched beside him.

"Son of a bitch," Meizan hissed once he'd realized what Aranel had done.

"You blanked out," Aranel snapped. "I had no choice."

The rock gave a horrible lurch as Aina landed next to them, her arms spread to keep balance. "You've lost your senses, Aranel!"

"As have you," Aranel shot back, shifting his weight until the rock steadied. "You might've chosen another rock!"

Their makeshift raft rushed forward with the tide and neared the brink of the lavafall.

"Meizan." Aranel nudged him. "Help me channel, or we'll capsize."

"Burn this," Meizan muttered.

He couldn't believe the situation they'd gotten themselves into. But Aranel's deranged plan was their best chance at survival. Meizan drew upon his chitrons as their rock pitched over the precipice, gathering speed as it plunged down the mountainside. Hot air whipped Meizan's face, lava splashing against his hastily erected chitronic shield. Behind them, Merumarth exploded with an earth-shattering roar.

The lava river slowed once they reached flat land, mowing through the trees of Martharan. Meizan pressed himself horizontal against the rock to avoid a low branch. The lava had cleared a straight path through the forest. Whatever trees remained standing were wreathed in orange flame, the most color Meizan had ever seen on them.

"I can't believe that worked!" Aina crowed. "The lava will boil Kaldrav's soldiers alive, and— Wait! What about the hideout?"

"With luck, the lava won't reach that far," Aranel said. "Even if it does, at this pace, the Balancers ought to have time to evacuate." He nudged Meizan's shoulder. "What's the matter with you?"

"Why did you help me?" Meizan asked hollowly. "You could've left me there, to a burning burial. You probably think I deserve it for killing those kapizer."

"I considered it," Aranel admitted. "But I couldn't do that to another person."

"It's what I would've done to you."

"Perhaps." Aranel gave him a tight smile. "But I'd like to believe I'm better than you."

"Don't flatter yourself," Aina sniped from Aranel's other side. "You only did it for the soul benefit. The same reason you joined the Balancers."

"About that . . ." Aranel rubbed a palm across his forehead. "I lied. To the both of you. I'm not a Balancer yet. I wasn't even recruited. I entered Malin in the hope they'd accept me, but then Meizan found me and took me hostage."

"I *knew* it," Aina said. "I knew Zenyra wouldn't recruit a moralistic prig like you."

"I'm here, in Malin!" Aranel said hotly. "I'm still planning on joining." He looked at Meizan again. "I'm afraid you won't be able to trade me for anything useful."

"You can trade me," Aina piped up. "Or better yet, I'll talk to Zenyra and she'll give you what you need. You want medical supplies to help your clanmates, right?"

"No." Meizan reached up to touch his cheekbones, where the fading marks of his clan rested below his eyes. "Not anymore."

Even in the unlikely situation that Taezur and the others endured the lava for a few days, there was no way Meizan could find them and dig them out in time. Kanjallen had been three thousand strong once, then six. Now only Meizan remained.

Grief is a weapon, he told himself. *Tears temper the blade.*

But Meizan felt no grief, only emptiness. He had no tears to shed.

"Do you—" Aranel started, then seemed to think better of it and shut his mouth.

They lapsed into silence and lay on the rock as it bobbed along the fiery river. The lava grew sluggish as it cut through the forest, thickened by the slurry of dead trees and ash. It flowed lazily past

Martharan's fringe and coasted across barren wasteland before curving to the right.

"It appears we've found the Balancer hideout." Aranel pointed at the bend of the river. An invisible dome seemed to push it back, forcing the lava around it.

"That must be the chitronic shield," Aina said. "Zenyra mentioned that it encircles the hideout, and only she controls who enters."

"Quite a powerful shield, to redirect a river," Aranel said. "I expect it's been layered with a concealment of sorts to render the hideout invisible." He frowned. "Little good that will do now that its location has been revealed to all of Malin."

"Maybe they already knew. Maybe that's why Kaldrav's soldiers were camped out here. We should warn Zenyra." Aina turned to Meizan. "Are you sure you don't need supplies? The Balancers probably have plenty to spare."

When Meizan didn't reply, Aina leaned over to look at him. "Your home was destroyed by the eruption, wasn't it? Where will you go next?"

A sharp, burning sensation rose at the back of Meizan's throat.

"I don't . . ." He swallowed, his voice a hoarse whisper. "I don't have anywhere to go."

Aina's eyes softened. She reached out to wrap thin fingers around his wrist.

"Yes, you do."

CHAPTER SEVEN

❦

The Balancers

INA KNEW THE look in Meizan's eyes. The tempest of rage and despair that gave way to empty acceptance. She knew the aching loneliness hidden behind halfhearted glares and desultory scowls.

She didn't know what he'd lost, but she knew his pain.

Ignoring Aranel's skeptical look, she dragged Meizan into the hideout. The air rippled as they crossed the boundary of the chitronic shield.

It almost felt as if they had stepped into another realm. The suffocating heat of the lava evaporated, leaving the air dank and heavy, but clean. A flattened mountain stood before them, about a quarter as high as Merumarth and crowned with a ring of leafless trees.

"Not another volcano," Aranel groaned, although he was too tired to complain further as they scaled its rugged slopes.

They passed through the trees to find themselves overlooking a caldera with walls of dark granite that curved in protectively. Instead of lava, the depression was filled with clear water, a small island at its very center.

As they descended into the crater, Aina noticed rough staircases and entryways hewn into the rock, along with orifices she guessed were windows looking upon the lake below.

"My keiza," Aranel said, staring at his reflection in horror.

Aina peered at her own. Unlike Aranel's keiza, which had gotten a shade duller, Aina's remained unchanged.

"You're in Malin. It doesn't matter anymore," Aina said, looking around the crater.

It was crude and primitive, this hideout. Bare of the frills and finery she'd gotten accustomed to in Mayana. Aina took a liking to it at once.

One thing stood out in jarring contrast to the rest of the dwelling: a massive banyan tree on the islet at the lake's center. Its trunk rose from the ground like a pillar of solid gold, ribbons of blue flowers dripping from its branches.

"I grew it from a sapling I brought over from Mayana." A rich voice caught them off guard as Zenyra emerged from an entrance behind them.

Her copper hair was tied in a thick braid. She wore a knee-length linen tunic over dark breeches, and a simple necklace of colored beads. Her muted garments did little to cover up the air of nobility and power she exuded. "I wanted to prove that beautiful things could thrive in Malin too, if given the chance."

She smiled at Aina before looking to Aranel. "I expected one new recruit, not three. But Mayani are always welcome here, and I must confess . . ." Her gaze rested on Meizan, and she inclined her head slightly. "I have long thought of enlisting a Malini to our cause."

"So you'll let them join?" Aina asked, relieved. She'd dragged Meizan in here, but a part of her worried Zenyra might turn him away.

"Of course," Zenyra replied. "They certainly possess the chitronic skill, if what I witnessed on Merumarth serves as any indication."

"You saw that?" Aranel asked. "How?"

"I was monitoring your progress from afar," Zenyra said, "planning to intervene if things looked too dangerous."

"Why didn't you?" Meizan asked hoarsely. "You could've stopped— You could've saved—" He broke off, sounding more lost than angry.

"His clan," Aranel said. "I think they were nearby. Got caught in the lavafall."

Zenyra's smile faded in an instant. "No . . . how terrible . . ." She closed her eyes, lips moving in a silent prayer. "I shall search for them myself," she told Meizan once she was finished. "If they still exist, I *will* find them."

If they still exist. Aina shuddered to think of the alternative.

"Tragic as it is about your clan," Zenyra continued, "there is little I can do to help them until the lava cools, and even less I could have done to stop that explosion. An explosion the three of you did a commendable job surviving on your own. You have what it takes, which is why I permitted you into Incaraz."

She gestured around the crater. "This is the main Balancer hideout, where we train new recruits in preparation for missions. We have about a dozen villages as well, scattered across the realm. They house Malini children and those injured in the war. Much as I would like to keep it all in one place, the smaller size is easier to conceal. Too large a chitronic shield would become weak and unstable."

"That's an incredible shield," Aranel said. "To keep out all the low—the enemies."

Aina glared at Aranel for his slip. "Kaldrav's soldiers were here a few hours ago," she said. "Do they know about the hideout?"

"They are not a threat," Zenyra said. "The soldiers prefer not to linger under the fumes of Merumarth and only pass through this area on occasion. The shield protects us from them, as well as from the volcano."

Aina gave a dubious nod. She couldn't imagine any shield would be enough to hide from the sadistic king, but Incaraz had remained standing all this time. She glanced at Meizan, but he didn't seem to be paying attention as he stared listlessly at the golden banyan.

"What happens now that we're here?" Aranel asked. "When might we take these missions you spoke of? And visit the villages?"

"While I commend your enthusiasm, you have a few moons of training before I can allow you outside Incaraz," Zenyra said.

Aranel bristled, and Aina felt a similar spike of outrage.

"A few moons!" she cried, thinking of her mother. "I don't have that much time." She looked to Zenyra in dismay. Though the Balancer leader had made no promises, Aina had assumed she would help search Malin for her mother.

"You are not ready," a male voice cut in. A trio of uppers, all clad in cream tunics similar to Zenyra's, approached from the lake. They walked across its surface as if it were firm ground.

"For a group of aspirational Balancers, you entirely destroyed the stability of Merumarth," said a strapping young man with hair like shards of diamond. Flowing patterns inked his dark skin in a tapestry of waves, fish, and seashells. "Your overreliance on chitrons endangers you and those around you. You must adapt your channeling methods before you're permitted to leave Incaraz."

"Don't be so hard on them, Hiraval," his companion said. She had crescent eyes and delicate features, her keiza a swirl of ruby. "If I recall, you and Taralei set fire to Martharan less than an hour after you entered."

"I had nothing to do with that," Hiraval said primly. "Taralei was acting the fool, per usual."

"I needed light!" protested the third arrival, an apple-cheeked young woman with hair that rippled to her waist. "So as not to drown some poor insect while I relieved myself."

"So instead you burned down their homes," said Hiraval.

"It was an accident, for Sherka's sake!" Taralei waved him off. "Reimi, *you* saw what happened."

"Reimi and I saw nothing but a foolish attempt to control the will of Azyaka's chitrons," Hiraval replied.

Aina watched them bicker with interest. Hiraval's tattoos suggested he was from Amaratir, while Reimi's wooden sandals and the hairpin peeking from her topknot both looked unmistakably Nishakian. Taralei spoke with the lilting accent of Kirnos, but Aina couldn't be too sure, since the Lotus Kingdom attracted a wide variety of people from across the realm. Aina hadn't interacted with many young Mayani, with the exception of Aranel, who always tried to act older, smarter, and more important than he was. At least these three seemed normal.

Taralei turned to Aranel with a cheeky grin. "Well, if it isn't Kirnos's finest. I'm shocked to see you in Malin, Ran, looking and smelling like a toilet. Whatever would your brother think?"

"He would think you flippant as ever, cousin," Aranel shot back.

Cousin? Aina looked between Aranel and Taralei. They both had tan skin, golden hair, and the same long, straight nose. She could see the resemblance.

"Why are you here?" Aranel asked. "I thought you ascended to Paramos!"

"I meant to," Taralei said. "But I met Zenyra near the torana, and she convinced me to join. Paramos will be ever open to me, but how many chances does one have to visit a lower realm? I'm surprised *you* followed me here, little Ran. Never imagined you'd leave Sam's side."

"Don't call me that," Aranel muttered. "I'm here of my own choice. I certainly didn't follow you or even expect you to be a Balancer . . ."

"What did you mean before, when you said Azyaka's chitrons?" Meizan addressed Hiraval. "Malin is called her realm, but what do the chitrons have to do with it?"

"An excellent question," Hiraval began, and Taralei and Reimi exchanged a dark look.

"Hiraval was training to be a priest before he joined the Balancers," Taralei said. "Never ask him about the seitarius or you're in for one of his sermons."

"They're long, and he can be very enthusiastic," Reimi added.

"Or as enthusiastic as Hiraval can be," Taralei amended.

"You already know that chitrons arise from living consciousness," Hiraval said, ignoring the other two, "and exist bound to their creators' souls. But grains of sand and drops of water possess neither consciousness nor soul. Whose soul, then, are the chitrons of the universe bonded to? The chitrons of rock and river, of land and sky?"

Meizan remained silent, though Reimi and Taralei were shaking their heads.

"The incantation you say before channeling," Hiraval prompted. "Can anyone repeat it?"

"Beloved Sherka, please lend me your strength," Aranel supplied.

"No one says it much anymore, but the deity to whom you appeal differs across realms."

"That is only half the incantation," Hiraval said. "The full verse goes, 'Beloved Sherka, please lend me your strength and light my consciousness with your soul.'"

"That's just a prayer," Aina dismissed. "It doesn't actually mean anything."

Hiraval tensed, and Taralei gave a chuckle. "Careful, Aina," she warned. "Don't blaspheme in front of the almost-priest."

"What is a prayer," Hiraval asked, "if not a request to the ruling deity of your realm? In this case, to share a tiny, insignificant portion of their chitrons. A portion of their soul."

A silence followed Hiraval's statement, and Aina could not believe her ears. "Are you saying the seitarius are . . . real?"

"As real as anything else that exists in our universe." Hiraval's dark eyes glittered. "Sorken the Majestic. Sherka the Benevolent. Azyaka the Fierce. Andraken the Undaunted. For centuries, they have lain dormant within the core of our realms. That is why they are known as the seitarius—the Planetary Beasts. Their souls comprise what we refer to as the consciousness of the universe. It is their chitrons you harness when you channel the environment."

His words sent a frisson down Aina's spine. She'd always dismissed the Planetary Beasts as fictitious beings, alternate forms of worship since Toranic Law was too abstract. The verse inscribed in the temple of Kirnos came to mind: *and thus the realm was split to four by will of Beast who made it.*

Was that meant to be taken literally? Aina felt another frisson as she imagined Azyaka the nagamor, deity of Malin, a colossal snake slumbering deep within the earth. Her thoughts then turned to Andraken, the roach of Narakh, with thousands of eyes and countless legs, each the size of a tree. Something of such terror, at such scale, could not be real.

"It's a religious sermon," Taralei said. "Don't take it as truth, you three. Hiraval's not even an ordained priest."

"I was two days from anointment," Hiraval objected.

"Consider yourself an ordained Balancer," Zenyra said lightly. "Enough talk of the seitarius. Hiraval, Taralei, Reimi, show our new recruits around Incaraz and to their quarters. Once everyone is settled, and bathed"—she cast a look at Aranel—"you are to commence their training."

She then turned to Meizan, whose face had resumed its blank facade. "Let us speak before that. I would like to know more about your clan and their whereabouts. I promise, I will do everything in my power to help you."

"I need your help too," Aina reminded her. Meizan's situation was more dire, but she had waited over a year to reunite with her mother.

Zenyra offered her a smile. "Join the training for now, Aina. I will find you at sundown."

AN HOUR LATER saw them bathed, changed, and gathered by the edge of the lake for their first training session, the granite walls of Incaraz looming above. Aina, like Aranel, had been grateful for the new clothes. Meizan still wore his blood-splattered old vest, though he'd traded his ratty blue tunic underneath for the Balancer one.

"You want us to *what?*" Aranel asked once Hiraval had explained the first exercise.

"Run up the wall to the top of the crater," Hiraval repeated. "If you do it to our liking, we might let you skip this part of training."

"I've been running up bleeding walls since I was four," Meizan said.

"I can fly across *clouds*," Aranel said at the same time. "I was junior cloudsurfing champion."

"Runner-up to champion," Taralei reminded him. "Prince Mirya of Tahamur beat your time by half a second."

"By cheating." Aranel sniffed. "This is preposterous. I did not come all the way to Malin to waste my time on rudimentary chitronic techniques."

Aina resisted the urge to bash his teeth in. Aranel was more bearable with his mouth shut. Maybe once she learned to channel properly, she could find a way to muffle his voice. He had a nice face, after all. Removing the sound would be a vast improvement.

Though he did say he was inspired to join the Balancers because of me.

"I expected Zenyra would be teaching us something a bit more sophisticated," Aranel went on. "Neutralization, immuno-therapy, perhaps even psychosomatic stimulation."

Aina had no clue what any of that meant. Unlike Aranel and Meizan, she was thrilled at the simplicity of their training. No one had coached her thoroughly on chitronic basics. Her mother had given up when she realized Aina wasn't a natural like her, focusing instead on physical combat.

"Zenyra's too busy to oversee new recruits," Taralei said. "You're stuck with us for the next couple moons, till you're at a level worthy of her time."

"We'll move on to advanced techniques once we see you've mastered the basics." Reimi pointed to the caldera wall. "Now then, up you go."

Aranel and Meizan swiped their keiza and raced one another up, leaving twin trails of evenly spaced indentations in their wake. Aina ground her teeth as she waited for her chitrons, painfully slow to activate.

By the time she started climbing, the other two had already reached the top. Aina ignored their scrutinizing gazes as she scrambled up, clumsily shaping the rock underfoot.

"You fail," Hiraval barked once Aina had finished. "All three of you. Try it again."

Aranel dropped to the ground and crossed his arms. "Is this some sort of prank?"

"I'm leaving," Meizan said. "This is a waste of time."

"What did we do wrong?" Aina asked. "Rather, what did *they* do wrong?"

Hiraval gave Aina an appraising nod. "At least one of you is willing to acknowledge your issues. Watch now. I'll demonstrate how Balancers climb."

Hiraval swiped his keiza and darted up the caldera wall on his toes. The rock remained smooth, without shaping itself to support him.

"How did you do that?" Aranel demanded. "Are you even channeling?"

"Of course I am." Hiraval sped back down the cliff, leaving no mark upon its surface. "But instead of maintaining the bond throughout, I created it for only the split seconds during which I touched the rock. And rather than releasing chitrons through my entire foot, I used only my toes, channeling a tiny portion of the rock's chitrons to thrust myself up."

"What's the point of that, beyond showing off?" Meizan asked. "Your way isn't any faster. And all that extra control seems mentally exhausting."

"Mentally *and* physically exhausting," Taralei said. "Since precision channeling relies more on your natural speed and strength to compensate for the reduced chitronic thrust. But don't worry, we'll toughen you up. Your training schedule includes running laps, lifting stones—"

"Running laps with stones strapped to your calves." Reimi grinned. "That one's my favorite."

"But why bother?" Aina asked. She could hardly manage a normal channeling without misshaping her surroundings. This precision nonsense sounded unnecessarily difficult.

"Can you repeat the First Principle of Chitronic Equilibrium?" Hiraval asked.

Aina stared at him blankly, while Aranel shot up a hand. "The First Principle," Aranel recited, "states that when chitrons interact, they transfer their energy until it is evenly spread out and all chitrons are rotating in the same direction at the same speed. This is referred to as a soul's average chitronic spin."

Upon finishing, he glanced at Meizan with something akin to triumph, only for the other to turn promptly away.

"Well said, Aranel." Hiraval looked impressed. "Now consider the ambient chitrons of Malin, which spin opposite to those of Mayana. Opposite to your own. Whenever you bond to them, their energy interferes with and counteracts your own, slowing your chitrons and burdening your souls."

"Zenyra invented precision channeling as a method to minimize interaction with the chitrons of Malin," Reimi said, "thus reducing this risk."

A stark silence followed, until Meizan said, "My soul spins the same direction as the chitrons of Malin. There's no reason for me to learn your method."

"Actually, there is," Reimi replied. "Experience tells us the chitrons here are less malleable than those of Mayana and have a propensity to sow chaos. Given you've lived here longer than we have, you'd know better."

Meizan nodded after a long moment. "There were instances in the past. When the chitrons didn't always do what I wanted."

"Ha!" Aranel said. "So it wasn't just me who struggled."

"I didn't *struggle*, you pestilential—"

"Here are your Balancer checklists." Taralei raised her voice over their bickering and handed Aina a scroll wrapped in white ribbon before tossing the remaining two at Aranel's and Meizan's heads. "Also includes your shifts for lookout duty."

Aina unfurled her scroll and read over the techniques. Precision climbing, running, and shielding; concealment; stun beams; and something marked as classified.

"How are we expected to train," Aranel grumbled, "with lookout duty every couple nights? At least eight hours of uninterrupted sleep is required for optimal channeling performance."

"You'll do what you're told," Taralei said, while Meizan cracked his knuckles, glaring mutinously at Aranel. "Mastering this list is a prerequisite for taking missions outside. You can channel safely within Incaraz because the shield largely protects us from the influence of Malin."

"But it'll take ages to learn all this," Aina exclaimed.

"Four to six moons is the average," Reimi said. "But it'll be worth it."

There's no way I'm sticking around here that long, Aina thought, scanning the list once more. Some of the techniques, like concealment and shielding, did sound useful. *Mama wouldn't have to protect me all the time if I could do some of this.*

"Let's begin," Taralei chirped. "You've plenty to learn and seem impatient to learn it."

THREE HOURS LATER, Aina was soaked to the bone. Her keiza throbbed from the exertion, and her foot felt ready to fall off. Next to her, Aranel and Meizan were conspicuously, annoyingly dry.

This is a useless exercise.

They were at the lake, each atop a narrow wooden pole over

ten feet tall. Aina stood on one foot, the other pressed against her knee, arms flailing to keep her balance—a posture Hiraval claimed was the first step to mastering precision channeling.

Yet all Aina had mastered was the art of falling gracefully into the lake. Meizan's pole wobbled on occasion, though he hadn't fallen off yet. Only Aranel stood perfectly still, tossing back his hair as if the entire training were beneath him.

"You're moving too much," Aranel said to Aina. "You're using your hips and arms to maintain balance, which defeats the point of this exercise. You're supposed to focus your chitrons to a single point of contact—"

"It would be easier to focus if you'd shut up," Aina snapped, "and stop buzzing in my ears like a bleeding mosquito."

Meizan gave a huff of what might have been laughter, and his pole tilted a fraction to the left. Aranel looked between them, affronted. "I'm merely offering some much-needed advice. You two make this look far more difficult than it ought to be!"

"Aranel." Meizan lifted an arm to steady himself. "While you're probably used to living with a ten-foot pole lodged up your ass, the rest of us aren't as accustomed to these flaming things."

Aina cackled, waving her arms to stop herself from falling in again. Aranel twitched, then leaned forward and shoved Meizan off his pole. Meizan kicked Aranel's pole as he fell and sent them both careening into the water with a splash.

"Yes!" Aina pumped a fist, only for her own pole to sway in the waves.

A second later, she hit the icy water. Aina spluttered out a curse once she surfaced, pushing sopping curls from her face. Aranel and Meizan spared her a glance from where they stood atop the water, before returning to glaring daggers at one another.

"Three down at once," Hiraval noted, choosing that moment to come check on their training. "One might call that teamwork."

Muttering under her breath, Aina steadied her pole and climbed back onto it. Aranel was right. The physical element of precision channeling was secondary; the main part was the blasted precision. While Aranel and Meizan stood with their arms pressed to their sides as instructed, Aina continued to windmill about, unable to stay on her pole for more than a couple minutes at a time.

The other Balancers released them from their training at sundown. "A soak in the hot springs before dinner might do you well," Hiraval said. "Precision channeling takes a toll on the muscles."

Aina dismounted with trembling legs. The water sloshed about her ankles as she followed the others across the lake, then doubled back to the pole once they had left. She preferred speaking to Zenyra in private, and getting in more practice while she waited.

An hour passed, and Zenyra did not show. Aina made little progress aside from angry blisters on her foot and a new bruise on her elbow from when she'd banged it against the pole.

Cursing, Aina made her way to dry land. She collapsed and stared up at the starless sky of Malin, a hand going instinctively to her pouch of rocks.

Her mother was somewhere in this realm, underneath the same sky. They were closer than they had been in a year, yet Aina felt farther away than ever. What had she expected—for the torana to lead her straight into her mother's brittle arms? Instead, it had brought her to an unfamiliar part of Malin. Even if Toranic Law no longer stood between them, there were soldiers and exploding volcanoes and hundreds of angry kapizer separating her from her mother.

A round object entered her line of vision. Aina sat up to see Hiraval holding a plate piled with food. "While I admire your dedication, you're going to need sustenance," the Balancer said kindly.

"I'm fine," Aina gritted out. "I don't need your charity."

"I once fasted for three days, during my time at the monastery," Hiraval said.

Aina scowled. She had gone weeks without food in Malin. What did she care about his voluntary, superficial starvation?

Hiraval held the plate closer. "Nearly fell through a cloud on my way back home. Channeling takes energy, Aina, and our training is rigorous. You must take care of yourself if you want to succeed."

"I don't care about your stinking training!" Aina grabbed the plate and tossed it aside. It shattered to pieces, bread and skewers of meat rolling across the hard ground. "I just want to get out of this damn hideout!"

The Balancers were supposed to help her find her mother. Instead, she was stuck in Incaraz, slogging away at a technique her chitrons were clearly unsuited for.

I could run away. Zenyra was my way around the Preservation's seals. I don't need her anymore, or the Balancers.

But even if Aina did leave, how would she find her mother? She didn't know where she was or where to start looking.

"I will take over from here." Aina looked up to see Zenyra walking over. "Thank you for looking after Aina, Hiraval," Zenyra said. "But it is late, and I expect you are tired."

Hiraval picked up the shattered plate and excused himself. Aina exhaled, twisting the hem of her tunic between her fingers as Zenyra sat down beside her.

"I understand your frustration," Zenyra said in a low voice. "It seems a waste, to spend time on such trivial matters, when an entire realm suffers outside the walls of this hideout. I often wish I could do more myself. Speed it all up. Engender a more drastic change. But things take time, Aina. You must learn patience as I have." She looked at Aina, her gaze bright. "We *will* find your mother. But until then, you must stay here and work on your chitronic control."

"What's the point? How will precision channeling help my mother?"

"The stronger you are, the more you can channel in your mother's stead. She will no longer need to rely on her own chitrons to remove you from perilous situations. She will be able to rely on you."

"She's powerful enough on her own." Aina remembered how her mother had called forth landslides to crush violent nagamor, summoned whips of flame to bind her enemies.

"So she may be," Zenyra said, "but that power is what encumbers her soul. You are familiar with the First Principle of Chitronic Equilibrium, are you not? How chitrons spread their energies until they are all spinning at the same speed, in the same direction?"

"I learned about it today."

"Then you can understand how it affects a soul such as your mother's," Zenyra said. "With their proclivity for violence, the chitrons of Malin tend to cause more harm than their channeler intended. The more your mother harnesses them, the further she gets from ascension."

Aina's head pounded as she tried to make sense of Zenyra's words. Thinking back, she could remember few times when her mother's channeling hadn't inflicted violence or suffering.

It's no wonder she was so skilled, Aina thought bitterly. *Her attacks were as twisted as this realm.*

"You can help her, Aina," Zenyra said. "By mastering the Balancer techniques, you can take the burden off your mother. You could even teach her some tricks yourself."

Teach her myself! Aina recalled the Balancer checklist, all the skills she'd never known existed. How many battles could she and her mother have avoided by use of concealment? How many skirmishes could they have fled had Aina been able to climb mountains quicker?

"*If* I ever master them." Aina stared at her feet. "It's only been a day, but I'm already behind Aranel and Meizan. They're probably wondering why you recruited me. Them, and the other Balancers."

"I assure you no one is thinking any such thing."

"I am." Aina failed to keep the dejection from her tone. "I'd heard rumors, back in Mayana. About how the Balancers only enlist the best and the brightest in the realm. Did you make a mistake, taking me?"

"I made no mistake, Aina. In fact, I—"

"You're regretting it now, aren't you? You didn't know I'd be this bad. If you'd known, you would've picked someone more like Aranel."

"I did not recruit you for your skill."

"Or even Meizan, if you wanted someone who'd lived in Malin."

"Aina." Zenyra leaned forward and rested her hands on Aina's shoulders. "Listen to me, child. I did not recruit you for your chitronic prowess or your life in Malin. There are thousands living in Mayana and Malin who could easily take the roles of Aranel and Meizan. But you have something neither of them do. Something that makes you unique."

"You can save the empty compliments. I know you're only being nice because you pity me."

"Pity you?" Zenyra's grip on her shoulders tightened. "You think I pity you? You think that is how the other Balancers would feel, if they learned of your past?"

"I know Aranel already does. Compared with the two of you, I've led a miserable life."

Zenyra shook her head. "I do not pity you, Aina. I admire you." Her words sounded genuine, but Aina couldn't bring herself to believe them. "For those born to Mayana, it is a matter of time and good deeds until their chitrons spin faster, allowing them to enter Paramos. But you were not born so blessed. Yet you accomplished something no other Balancer could."

She paused, smiling. "You alone changed the rotational direction of your chitrons. You alone changed the spin of your soul."

"But I'm still hopeless at channeling," Aina said, unsure why Zenyra spoke as if she possessed some rare gift. "Does it make a difference how I ascended?"

"Oh, it does, sweet child." Zenyra brushed a hand atop Aina's hair. "It makes all the difference in the universe."

PART II

———

In an age before time and life and thought
stretched an endless Void that was filled with naught.
In this blankness, two chitrons came to be
and spun through the Void, unhindered and free.
The pair were equal in all but their spin,
for one whirled contrary to its own twin.
Gathering speed, for long eons they spun,
till each held the power of countless suns.

As fate would have it, the pair did collide,
their massive explosion felt far and wide.
Mighty energy forever destroyed,
leaving but a fraction yet in the Void.
The lingering chitrons combined in new form,
and from these remnants the seitarius were born.
Planetary Beasts, such creatures of glory,
and with their origin unfolds our story.

–CHORUS OF CREATION–
Verse I: The Coming of the Seitarius

CHAPTER EIGHT

@

The Necessity of Violence

*A*RANEL LEAPED BACKWARD through the treetops, parrying Meizan's blows. The Malini fought with his usual viciousness, cyclonic in his attacks. Meizan rained down hits in an unrelenting sequence that forced Aranel deeper into the forest.

Aranel let out a growl of frustration as Meizan's blade slammed against his own, a longsword he'd borrowed from the Balancers' stash. They were sparring in the forest that crowned the crater of Incaraz, little more than a thicket of dying trees. But it was still a forest, which meant as a Kirnosi, Aranel ought to have a natural advantage.

As they exchanged blows, Aranel recalled sunlit days spent racing across the treetops of Kirnos's Dappled Forest. Samarel had trained with him, teaching Aranel how to find hidden paths through the canopy and tell, from sight, whether a branch would support his weight.

That's it!

Light-footed as he may be, Meizan was not weightless. Aranel allowed the Malini to drive him back before slashing upward and severing several branches. They came crashing down, and Meizan sprang aside to dodge. As Aranel predicted, the branch he landed on gave way, sending Meizan hurtling toward the ground.

"Got you!" Aranel leaped after him, sword raised.

He could picture his brother observing their spar with an encouraging smile. Aranel's sword whistled through the air, and Samarel's expression shifted, eyebrows jutting together in disappointment.

An image of a golden torana flashed through Aranel's mind. His arms trembled, sword halting for the briefest of moments. What if he missed and hit Meizan's arm? What if he split his flesh or broke a bone? What if—

"Too slow," said Meizan from below.

Aranel snapped out of his thoughts to see Meizan flip over midair. Teeth bared, the Malini slammed his sword against Aranel's. The impact of the blow knocked the blade from Aranel's fingers as the two of them landed on the ground.

Aranel reached for his falling blade, but his opponent moved quicker. Meizan spun into a sharp crescent kick that landed neatly on the pommel and sent Aranel's sword sailing across the clearing to bury itself hilt-deep into a tree.

Sweet Sherka!

Aranel stared between his trapped sword and his opponent, overcome with begrudging awe. Meizan was good. *Unfairly* good. On instinct, Aranel reached for his keiza.

"No, you don't," said Meizan, shoving him backward.

He hurled two throwing stars at Aranel in rapid succession. The tiny blades pinned the sleeves of Aranel's tunic firmly against the tree, an inch below his buried sword.

Then Meizan was in front of him, his breath warm on Aranel's skin, the edge of his blade grazing Aranel's neck.

"What was it you said before?" taunted Meizan. "That your kind had an affinity for trees?"

"Shut it." Aranel's face flamed as he tried to wriggle free. "We agreed on one weapon each. You cheated with the throwing stars."

"Says the person who was about to call upon his chitrons. So much for being part of the royal guard." Meizan pressed his blade in harder until Aranel felt a prick at his neck.

"What are you doing? The spar's over!"

"It's just blood." Meizan held the blade up between Aranel's eyes. A single drop of red clung to its tip before rolling down Aranel's nose. "Get used to it. On yourself. On others."

"You're sick."

"And you're weak," said Meizan. His blade dragged lightly down Aranel's cheek. "I could carve you up, and you wouldn't bother fighting back. That's not noble—it's pathetic."

Aranel's grudging admiration vanished, giving way to an urge to punch Meizan's smirking face in. He ripped his sleeves free of the throwing stars.

Pure thoughts, Aranel told himself, closing his eyes. Almost as a reflex, his fingers began tracing circles against the rough bark. *I can't let my soul-spin slow under his influence.*

"I think that's enough." Taralei pulled Meizan away from Aranel. She held out a hand to Reimi, who shoved a glinting something into her palm.

"What was that?" demanded Aranel. He rubbed his neck, then sent a few chitrons to stem the trickle of blood.

"What does it look like?" asked Reimi as Taralei flipped her coin in the air.

Aranel rounded on his cousin, struggling to keep his voice

down. "You bet against me? Where is your loyalty? To Kirnos? To family?"

"It faded sometime during your fifth loss," said Taralei with a shrug. "I'm lucky Reimi was fool enough to bet against Meizan."

"You gave me fantastic odds," grumbled Reimi. "I couldn't resist. Was it too much to expect that Aranel would—"

"Last more than three minutes in a one-on-one duel?" Taralei gave an airy laugh. "Ran's been losing to Meizan since he got here, let alone that he's useless without chitrons."

"This is a waste of time," said Meizan, sheathing his sword with a spin. "Where's Aina? I want an actual fight."

"Aina's got remedial chitronic training," answered Reimi. "She still hasn't mastered concealment, so you'd best let her focus. But I'll fight you. Unlike the Kirnosi, we Nishakian are not afraid of a little blood." She shook back her sleeve to display a thin scar stretched across her pale forearm and grinned at Aranel's dour expression. "Courtesy of dear Hiraval. He healed it after, but I told him to leave the scar. Tells a story, you know?"

"No, I do not." Aranel wrenched his sword from the tree and tossed it to the ground. He stalked from the clearing, the sounds of Meizan and Reimi's sparring fading away.

The Balancer training regime incorporated non-chitronic combat, claimed to be essential for survival in Malin. But Aranel hadn't come here to become a fighter. He certainly didn't want to become anything like Meizan.

A week had passed since Merumarth's explosion, and any pity Aranel had felt for the Malini had dissipated. Meizan was cocky and sadistic, and took great pleasure in beating Aranel to the ground. It didn't help that his chitronic abilities were almost on par with Aranel's own. And his fighting style—Aranel had expected something rough, crude, vulgar. But Meizan fought as if it were an art form. He moved with a fluid grace that rivaled even Samarel's, although his showboating was far worse.

At least Sam can hold a sword properly. Who even uses an inverted grip? Does he think it makes him look sophisticated?

Aranel climbed down the crater, his frustration mounting. He was to make his first report to Seirem later that night, but amidst the rigorous training regime, he hadn't managed to gather anything of import.

Twice he'd scoured the hideout, to find only medical supplies, spare weapons, and cans of the same unappetizing slop they ate at every meal. While Incaraz had enough rooms to house dozens of Balancers, most of them sat empty. According to Taralei, recruitment numbers were dwindling, and the other members had all been deployed to the villages. Aranel had confirmed a couple of their names with his cousin, but nothing beyond.

Why am I still here?

Aranel pushed open the door to his room and flopped onto the lumpy mattress. Even his modest hut in Kirnos seemed grand compared to this hole. He glared at the cavern-like walls before reaching toward his dresser. His hand curled around the conical shell Samarel had given him, the only memento of his previous life Aranel had permitted himself to bring. He traced a finger over the spiral, another coming to touch his keiza.

He needed to find *something* for the Preservation. Uncover some secret that would allow him to ascend and see his brother again.

I'll be sure to get Sam a souvenir before I go, thought Aranel, getting to his feet. *A kapizer spine, perhaps. There will be plenty lying around outside Incaraz, and I expect they could have interesting medicinal applications . . .*

He exited his room and padded across the hallway. One of the doors was ajar, and a flash of blue caught his eye. Aranel peered inside to see a dark vest with twin lines of blue paint. Meizan had stopped wearing his clan attire a few days after they arrived at Incaraz, but the gleam of the leather suggested it had been polished recently.

Meizan was busy training, as were the others. He was also the most unsavory person in this crater, along with possibly Aina. If Aranel took a few moments to search both their rooms, ensure nothing was awry . . .

Aranel wasn't sure what he expected to find once he stepped inside—bones or kapizer carcasses or an assortment of brutal weaponry. But Meizan's room was identical to Aranel's: sparsely furnished and with a circular window overlooking the lake. His pillow sat upright, the blankets folded into a tight square, and Meizan's meager belongings were stored in the dresser. Without the vest hanging from the wall, it could have passed as Aranel's own room.

Contrary to Meizan's, Aina's room looked as if a horde of kapizer had stormed it. Aranel wrinkled his nose at the unmade bed. He stepped over a mud-stained blouse to survey the wreckage of broken rocks scattered across her dresser. He'd seen her carrying them around back at the Kirnosi guardhouse.

On closer inspection, they appeared to be figurines of sorts. Aranel picked up a broken wolf head, its features disfigured by an unsightly snarl.

Is this supposed to be a gazarou? Such a frightful countenance, nothing like the original.

"Why the hell are you in my room?"

Aranel whirled around to see Aina at the doorway, poised to fight.

He thrust the rock at her, concocting a lie. "I—ah—I found this by the lake. You must have dropped it when you got here. I didn't want to disturb your training, so I thought to leave it in your room."

Aina snatched it from him like the ill-mannered wretch she

was and cradled it to her chest. She seemed rather fond of the ugly thing.

"Those are from your mother, are they not?" asked Aranel, watching Aina place the rock into a discolored cloth pouch. "A pity they're all smashed up. One of the Balancers could fix them for you. It would involve a fairly precise bit of channeling, but—"

"No need," Aina cut him off. She swept the rest of the rocks into her pouch and secured it carefully to her waist. She paused, crossing and uncrossing her arms. "Thanks. For bringing it to me."

"Of course."

Aranel had turned to leave when Aina said, "You should stop holding back so much, if you want to beat Meizan."

"Meizan," enunciated Aranel, "is a ruthless barbarian who takes pleasure in violen—"

"He's not cruel. You wouldn't understand since you've never lived here, but fighting's probably the only way he knows how to communicate."

"Well, I have no interest in *communicating* with someone who so freely spills blood—"

"Get over yourself," she cut him off again, and Aranel felt a flare of anger. "A few drops of blood is nothing. I've seen your spars, Aranel. In terms of raw skill, you're nearly as good as he is. But *every* time you come close to landing a winning blow, you hesitate. You *let* him win—"

"I don't let—"

"—all because somewhere in your soft, fast-spinning soul, you think not striking makes you better than he is in the eyes of Toranic Law."

"Violence against another human being is wrong," said Aranel, rankled by her warped arguments. "There's a reason Toranic Law keeps Mayana peaceful and free of war. Is it so wrong for me to respect that?"

Aina let out a derisive laugh. "You don't respect Toranic Law, Aranel. You fear it. You live your life in fear of how it will judge your soul and let that fear control your every action."

"You know nothing of my life," cried Aranel. How dare she imply he did not respect Toranic Law? How dare she imply his morality was built on fear?

"We both know you want to beat him," said Aina. "If you could get over this obsession with your soul, maybe you'd stand a chance. Maybe you'd become a decent Balancer and do some good for this realm. You have *so* much talent, Aranel, but you're wasting it by holding back." She looked at Aranel as if his refusal to fight Meizan offended her personally.

"I don't want to become a decent Balancer," said Aranel, "if it means bending my morals to accommodate some wretched training regime."

He turned on his heel and marched away, leaving Aina fuming behind him.

THE HOT SPRINGS were located in a firelit cavern at the bottom of Incaraz, with the men's and women's pools separated by a stone wall. Zenyra insisted they soak for at least a half hour each day to ensure they were properly rejuvenated. Aranel saw no need for her insistence. The springs were the one thing that made Incaraz bearable. He would gladly spend half a day here if his training regimen allowed for it.

As Aranel sank into the water's silken embrace, his earlier anger at Meizan and Aina eddied away. He swirled a finger across the surface, marveling at its lustrous texture and the way it coruscated in the firelight.

There was something magical about this water. Aranel had trained under the most gifted healers in Mayana, yet none had refreshed him the way the springs of Incaraz did. Every droplet thrummed with an intoxicating energy that soaked through his skin and seeped into his soul, filling him with lightness.

"Nice, isn't it?" a deep voice interrupted his musings. Aranel squinted at Hiraval's form through the steam as the Balancer settled at the far side of the springs. "Even the bathhouses of Nishaki do not have such invigorating water. I was surprised to find it within a crater in Malin."

"Perhaps Zenyra cast some Paramosi enchantment upon it," said Aranel.

"Perhaps." Hiraval chuckled, leaning against the rock. "How fares your training, Aranel? Taralei mentioned you've been facing some challenges with non-chitronic combat."

"Not so much challenges as moral disagreements on the necessity of violence."

"Ah. I see."

Aranel waited for Hiraval to say more, but he remained silent. "Were you not training to be a priest in Mayana before joining the Balancers?" asked Aranel. "Which means you preached Toranic Law and are well-versed in our holy scriptures. The Aria of Ascension and such."

"Correct," answered Hiraval. "Go on."

"How do you bring yourself to do it? I heard you injured Reimi's arm during a spar. How can you wield a sword against another person, knowing it bears such risk—not only to their bodies, but also to your soul?"

Hiraval paused, considering the question. "There is one lesson I learned during my time at a monastery in Ashkator," he began, and Aranel nearly jumped out of the water at the name.

A monastery within the Preservation's domain? So he's a Paramosi like Sam!

Hiraval had only ever mentioned his birthplace, Amaratir,

giving no indication that he'd ascended to the highest realm.

"You know how it's spoken of," Hiraval went on as Aranel leaned forward in anticipation. "Souls spin this way or that. Actions can be good or bad. It paints Toranic Law as black and white, as a dichotomy. In reality, it is much more nuanced, placing great emphasis on intention."

"What does that have to do with our spars?" asked Aranel.

"Those spars are meant to strengthen us so we can better survive Malin and help those in need. We must be able to fight—to protect and defend—to fulfill our duty as Balancers. Shirking that means shirking our duty, which I believe is worse in the eyes of Toranic Law."

At his words, Aranel remembered Meizan atop Merumarth, eyes filled with rage as he sliced down the kapizer.

Toranic Law should understand the meaning of self-defense, Meizan had shouted at the time. Had he been right? Had Aranel been the fool, trying to stop him? *What would Samarel have done?*

As he thought of his brother, Aranel raised a hand to his forehead. A drop of steaming water hit his keiza, making it throb uncontrollably. Aranel's head grew light.

"Why did you join?" he asked in a daze. "You were in Ashkator, and the Preservation caution against descending."

"I used to dive in Mir Amaratis often," said Hiraval. "The currents are quite strong beyond a certain depth. They flow in one direction, year-round, and are near impossible to navigate."

Aranel nodded in bemusement, and Hiraval continued. "I once saw a seahorse struggling in the current, too weak to swim against it. I was thinking of helping when a manikai appeared and rode the current till it reached the seahorse."

A manikai! The jeweled sea turtles were a rare sight even in Mayana. Aranel had never seen one in his life.

"Unlike the seahorse, the manikai *could* swim against the current. It let the seahorse ride on its back till they were both safely in the shallows." Hiraval stopped speaking, and Aranel realized that he had, in some abstruse way, answered the question.

Aranel stumbled out of the hot springs, his mind in disarray. Hiraval's story, coupled with the spring water, had jumbled his thoughts.

He smacked his cheeks before pulling on his clothes. He needed to focus. He was meeting Seirem tonight to deliver his first report since joining the Balancers, for which he needed to slip away from lookout duty. It was convenient he was paired with Meizan. The Malini wouldn't seek him out the way Taralei did, nor would he find it odd if Aranel avoided him.

Aranel settled at the southern rim of Incaraz that night while Meizan took the north. The shield glistened in front of him like a sheet of transparent silk pulled across the sky. Aranel could sense Zenyra's chitrons, powerful and pure, thrumming against its barriers. The feel of her energy made his soul sing, not unlike how the spring water had.

For such a strong shield to hold even when its caster is away . . . truly, the Paramosi are remarkable.

Inside the crater Aranel spied Aina practicing on the lake. She floundered atop her wooden pole with the chitronic control of a toddler. To his surprise, she was accompanied by Zenyra herself.

For the past week, the leader had left mentoring to Taralei and the others while she visited the villages. Aranel had never gotten the chance to exchange more than a greeting with her. The woman flitted in and out of Incaraz faster than he could keep track. Yet here she was—and with free time on hand— training Aina, of all people, while he was stuck on lookout duty.

I suppose Aina does need the added supervision, Aranel thought, feeling rather miffed as he set his sights on the tenebrous hell- scape outside the crater.

In the distance twinkled a point of gold, like a lone star in a clouded sky. A torana to Paramos, less than half a mile from Incaraz.

Aranel had discovered it during his first lookout and decided it would be the perfect place to meet with Seirem. He'd snuck to the torana and tossed through a pebble—onto which he'd engraved the lotus of Kirnos, a date, and a time.

It was almost that time now. Seirem had promised to monitor the torana, though Aranel had no assurance the Preserver had received his message. Seeing that Zenyra was occupied with Aina and Meizan remained on his side of the crater, Aranel climbed down the outer cliff. He smoothed the rock as he did, removing all traces of his descent.

His journey across the barren wasteland was uneventful, with the exception of putrid fumes that crawled up his nose and threatened him with a slow suffocation.

For the love of Sherka, this better be worth it. Aranel's nervousness mounted with each shallow breath. *What if he never found my pebble? Or what if he's too busy attending to other business?*

Aranel coughed as he reached the torana. The moonlight streaming in through Paramos was a sight for his sore eyes. He sagged with relief as Seirem appeared between the golden columns and tossed a small bottle at him. Aranel caught it, the mild sweetness sifting from within a poignant reminder of home—of that mellow breeze when Kirnos coasted low over the sea.

"Honeyed wine from Mir Amaratis," said Seirem. "The least you deserve for your efforts. That pebble was quite clever, I must say."

He produced his own flask, toasting Aranel from across the torana. Aranel unscrewed the bottle and dumped the golden liquid down his throat, thankful for something flavorful at last.

"So," said Seirem. "How was your first week? What do you have to report?"

"Well, the training is barbaric," answered Aranel, "and the hideout is cold and miserable, although I suppose Zenyra's shield protects us from the worst of it . . ." He launched into a breathless explanation of everything he knew—about Incaraz, its protections, their training, and the villages. He spoke even of the hot springs and the luminous water that flowed through them.

To his disappointment, Seirem did not seem impressed by any of it, although the Preserver frowned at Taralei's name.

"Your cousin was meant to ascend to Paramos a few moons ago," said Seirem. "When she did not, we assumed she had chosen to stay in Mayana, like Samarel at the time. The other two—Hiraval of Amaratir and Reimi of Nishaki—are not surprises. They were on our list of suspected recruits, along with various others from Kirnos, Tahamur, and Samaras."

Seirem pulled a piece of parchment from his robes and held it through the torana.

Aranel took it, scanning the list of names. "What is this?"

"You mentioned three Balancers currently at Incaraz." Seirem uncorked his flask and took a gulp. Shining liquid dribbled down his chin, and he wiped it with a silver-trimmed sleeve. "All three went missing within the last few moons, but the group's operations have been going on for years. This lists all the unaccounted disappearances, all suspected recruits to the Balancers' cause."

"Eniya of Tahamur, Namyra of Amaratir, Tenshir of Nishaki, Soranil of Samaras," Aranel read aloud. "Taralei mentioned Eniya and Namyra, but there must be over forty names here. Are you certain all of them joined? I heard recruitment has been slow recently, so perhaps some are off adventuring in Mayana."

Their realm was packed with wonders to explore, and Mayani lifetimes spanned centuries. A couple years without contact was nothing out of the ordinary.

"Their profiles match those of the confirmed recruits," said Seirem. "Young, idealistic, skilled at channeling. I expect a majority, if not all, descended on Zenyra's invitation. Look into them, Aranel. Find out where they are now."

"I'd imagine they're in the Balancer villages. Zenyra mentioned there are a dozen across the realm. Whoever finishes their training is sent to live in one to look after the sick Malini."

"Confirm that is the case. And find out more about Zenyra's activities. You said she leaves the hideout often. I want to know where she goes and what she does, along with what exactly happens in these villages."

"Following her would only arouse suspicion. I have to abide by their ridiculous training regime if I'm to blend in."

"Then find another way to get close to Zenyra," said Seirem. "A way to gain her trust. There must be a Balancer she entrusts with important tasks. With recruitment or running the hideout."

"We all split lookout duty and chores amongst ourselves, and she hardly speaks to any—" Aranel paused, thinking back to earlier that night. "On second thought, there may be someone. A girl I saw her training earlier, whom she personally invited to join."

"Oh?" Seirem leaned forward with interest. "Where does this girl hail from? Does she display any exemplary chitronic abilities?"

"She's entirely unremarkable. Her chitronic prowess can be equated to a seven-year-old's, and she lived in Malin before ascending. I believe Zenyra has simply taken pity upon her."

"Nonetheless, you must get close to that girl, Aranel. She may know something or become privy to it in the future. If you cannot get to Zenyra directly, befriend those she keeps by her side."

"It'll be an utter waste of time," said Aranel at once. "I doubt Zenyra would trust Aina with anything. I knew her back in Kirnos, Lord Seirem. She holds a criminal record there. Even Samarel couldn't quite handle her."

"But you are not Samarel," replied Seirem. "Perhaps it is as you say, and Zenyra merely pities Aina. But given we have no other leads at the moment, I request that you pursue this one. And for Sorken's sake, find a way into one of those villages."

Aranel gave a disgruntled nod, and the Preserver reached through the torana to rest a single hand on his shoulder.

"There is something happening in Malin, Aranel," said Seirem, voice low and steeped with urgency. "Something Zenyra is doing that is disrupting the chitronic system. For the future of the universe, I need you to find out what."

CHAPTER NINE

❂

A Soldier's Delusion

*T*WO WEEKS INTO the Balancer training, and even Meizan had to admit these uppers knew damn well what
they were doing when it came to channeling.

He streamed chitrons to his sole, funneling them to a point.
The top of Meizan's pole had been whittled down until it was
fine as the tip of his sword. It should have pierced his foot. But
it didn't, his newfound control allowing him to stand on it for
hours on end.

A pebble thwacked the side of his head and threw Meizan off
balance. He righted himself, then glared across the lake, where
Reimi and Taralei sat firing pebbles with the speed of arrows. Next
to him, Aina and Aranel bore an assortment of cuts and bruises.

"Is this ethical?" Aranel groused, deflecting a pebble with a
flash of green light.

"It's well intentioned," Reimi said. She flicked a pebble at
Meizan, who lashed out with his chitrons.

They materialized in a blue shimmer the size of his palm—
a chitronic shield, much smaller than he was used to. Normal
shields involved compressing air or sand particles into encompass-
ing domes that could reflect all types of attacks. But precision
shields restricted their surface area only to points of incoming
contact—thereby reducing interaction with Malin's chitrons,
which in turn made the shields more stable.

This would've been useful in bleeding Merumarth, Meizan
thought, as Taralei sent a pebble slamming into his shin with the
force of a sledgehammer.

"I suppose Zenyra has these techniques taught to the Malini
in the villages as well," Aranel said. "That reminds me, exactly
how many Balancers are stationed at each village?"

"I'm not sure," Taralei replied as she launched another round
of pebbles. "At least two or three, since every team that comes
into Incaraz is sent to a village together."

"Every team," Aranel repeated. "Do you mean if we complete
our training, I'd be stuck living in some village with these two?"
He gestured at Meizan and Aina, who exchanged an exasperated
look and sent their next round of pebbles ricocheting in Aranel's
direction.

"Aina can't channel properly, and Meizan would terrorize
the children," Aranel continued, deflecting all the pebbles in an
infuriating show of chitronic prowess. "What even would we be
doing? What goes on in these villages? I'd like more information
if I'm expected to one day—"

"Aranel, you gnat," Meizan snapped. "The bleeding mission
is moons away. Do you have to start whining about it now?"

"But I—" Aranel paused, his expression shifting to indig-
nance. "I'm not a *gnat*!"

"Yes, you're more of a leech," Aina agreed. "Sucking the fun
out of every conversation."

"Sapping our motivation to train," Meizan added.

"Draining our souls with every word you say," Aina said.

Meizan watched with mild amusement as Aranel struggled to mask his outrage. "You ought to thank me," the upper said flintily, looking from Aina to Meizan, "for having found a way to finally lighten your souls."

"*Ran*," Taralei scolded. "That's crossing a line."

"It doesn't matter," Meizan said. "Zenyra won't allow a weakling like him to leave this crater, much less handle a village. He can't even wield a sword properly."

He turned his back to Aranel and left him to stew in silence.

Unlike the upper, Meizan didn't give a damn what happened after their training was complete. He wasn't sure how long he'd be here. Incaraz was not his home, nor the Balancers his clan. They were nothing more than a convenience. A place to sleep and eat until Kaldrav was no longer a threat or Meizan decided what the hell he wanted to do with the rest of his life, whichever came first.

THE NEXT AFTERNOON during training, Aranel fought like one taken over by the spirit of Azyaka herself. He attacked Meizan with a single-minded intensity, hazel eyes empty of their usual hesitation. His blows came fast and sure, his form unwavering. Meizan's arms began to ache as Aranel backed him against a tree.

Meizan aimed a roundhouse kick at Aranel's leg, but the upper jumped up and somersaulted through the air to bring a heel crashing down on Meizan's head.

Meizan swore as he stumbled forward. Pain ripped across his skull. Something sharp pressed against his pulse, and Aranel glared at him through sweat-drenched locks.

"What the hell happened to you?" Meizan breathed.

"Do not underestimate the Mayani," Aranel said quietly. "Choosing to not engage in violence does not make us weak."

Meizan shoved him off, feeling a mixture of loathing and exhilaration. Beneath the shiny hair and silken clothes, the upper was sharp as a nagamor's beak. Meizan didn't know what had spurred the change, but this ruthless Aranel was much better than the simpering coward from a day ago.

"Another round," Meizan demanded, rotating his wrists. It had been a while since he'd encountered a worthy opponent.

"No, thank you." Aranel sheathed his blade and stalked off.

Meizan watched him go in murderous indignation. He was about to attack him from behind when Taralei placed a hand on his shoulder.

"I've never seen him so fired up." Taralei sounded amazed. "He probably gave you a concussion."

"I'll give him a concussion," Reimi fumed from beside her. "The *one* day I decide to bet against him. Wretched Kirnosi."

"Pure thoughts, Reimi, pure thoughts." Taralei reached over and pushed up Meizan's bangs. He flinched at the touch, stepping away. "We need to heal this," Taralei said, undeterred.

"It's a damn scratch," Meizan said. "I'll break his neck tomorrow."

"I'd rather you didn't," Taralei said firmly. "Now, I can risk healing this with chitrons or get you some ice. You decide."

"I don't need—" Meizan began, but then Hiraval came to his side and pressed something rough against Meizan's forehead. The throbbing where Aranel had kicked him subsided at once. "What did you do? Did you channel?"

"Gazarou fur," Hiraval said. He held out his palm to reveal a small bundle of grass tied together with a satin ribbon. "It can heal almost any nature of injury in mere seconds. Keep this. It will come in use."

"Where the hell did you get it?" Meizan asked, taken aback.

The great grass wolf was a mythical creature said to be descended from the Planetary Beast Sherka. Why would Hiraval offer him a clump of its fur as if it were a piece of rock?

"I brought it from Mayana," Hiraval said. "It's the last of my stock, so take care of it."

"Why—" Meizan's throat went dry. "Why give it to *me*?"

"You're a fellow Balancer. We must look after one another."

"No." Meizan backed away from him. "No, we must not."

"Meizan, listen." Taralei exchanged a look with Reimi and Hiraval. "Aranel told us what happened with Kanjallen."

At the mention of Kanjallen, Meizan's hand dropped instinctively to his sword. His thumb ghosted over the carved nagamor head at its hilt. Zenyra's efforts to find his clanmates had been unsuccessful, which meant they'd either miraculously escaped despite their various handicaps . . . or ended in erasure. Meizan wasn't fool enough to hope for the former.

How long did they suffer? How long did they hold on, unable to move or breathe, before giving up?

If only he'd been able to heal them properly. Meizan clutched the bundle of gazarou fur, trying not to picture how his clanmates' fates might have played out had he gotten his hands on it a few weeks earlier.

"We can't imagine what it's like to lose everyone you care about," Reimi said. "Just as we can't imagine how much you suffered growing up in this realm."

Meizan looked away. When Reimi spoke again, her whispered words shattered through his skull like the screams of a kapizer. "The Balancers can be your new clan," she said, and Meizan wanted to rip her tongue off.

"I don't need a new clan," he bit out. "What I need is—I need you to teach me how to heal. Without chitrons."

MEIZAN RETURNED TO his room at sundown, arms loaded with medicinal herbs and head bursting with new information. Fireflower oil to reduce inflammation. A paste made of silverbark to accelerate bone growth. Tigerfruit seeds, swallowed to prevent infection.

So easy. It would have been so bleeding easy to save them if he'd had the right supplies. Supplies that Mayana had in abundance yet did not grow in Malin, where the air itself caused leaves to crumble and bark to rot.

Meizan's bitter mood continued even as he focused his energy on training and healing, learning ways to survive his realm without relying on its treacherous chitrons. He thought of Kanjallen often, each time with a pang of longing and regret.

But as days rolled by, Meizan found himself thinking of them less. It was hard to dwell on past miseries when he was finally breathing clean air and drinking pure water and eating three full meals a day. The itch in Meizan's throat disappeared, the last visceral reminder of his clanmates fading away.

Meizan thought of them only during his lookouts, as he kept vigil atop the crater and gazed at the river of hardened lava that twisted across Malin.

"Do you miss your clan?"

Aranel appeared from the thicket and settled cross-legged on the hard dirt. Reimi had lookout duty tonight, so Meizan had no clue what this freak was doing here.

"You have this look on your face," Aranel continued, unaffected by Meizan's glare. "The same look you had when Merumarth exploded."

"Burn in Narakh," Meizan said, his preferred greeting for Aranel in most situations.

"That's cruel of you." Aranel sounded sulky.

Was he still bitter about their earlier spar? Now that Aranel had stopped dithering about, they were almost evenly matched, though Meizan scraped a win two out of three times.

"I was *going* to offer to teach you," Aranel went on.

"Teach me what?" Meizan asked, vaguely horrified. "I don't want to memorize your stupid Dirge of Descension."

"It's called the *Aria* of *Ascension*! And I meant healing. I hear you've been learning from Taralei and the others. I can't imagine why, given your disturbing enjoyment for all things painful."

"I don't enjoy pain!" What kind of masochist did Aranel take him for? "I'm just used to it, unlike you."

"Well then, you ought to be glad to have me teach you." Aranel lifted his chin. "I happen to be quite adept at chitronic healing. Far better than my cousin."

"We're using plants, not chitrons."

The upper fell silent. Meizan wondered if he'd imagined the shadow of disappointment on his face. But then Aranel started babbling again about something Meizan didn't care to understand.

"The shape of the lava reminds me of the Karaeni," Aranel said. "It's a river of light that cuts across the sky of Mayana. The chitronic energies in the area are volatile, making it nearly impossible to channel. Even the lotus of Kirnos never strays too close."

Meizan said nothing, staring at the dreary horizon as Aranel rambled on. He couldn't tell if Aranel was conversing with him or reminiscing to himself. Either way, Meizan had no interest in hearing about a realm he would never enter.

Meizan was about to interrupt when Aranel addressed him. "What's Malin like outside this hideout? I've only seen Merumarth and Martharan, but where did the rest of your clan live? And what of your kingdoms, and your—"

"We don't have kingdoms, you blabbering twit." Meizan scowled at Aranel's look of surprise. "Our largest settlements crumbled under war and disease, and those lucky enough to survive were ripped apart by the great earthquake. All that's left is the fortress of Kaufgar, but that's controlled by Kaldrav and his bleeding army."

Aranel didn't seem to know how to respond, and Meizan hoped he would go away. Instead, Aranel asked, "Who's Kaldrav? And why is he raising an army?"

"Kaldrav," Meizan spat, "is a cockroach who would call himself king of Malin. All the other clans are packed with flaming fools who have aligned themselves to his cause. He's assimilated them into his armies, sucking the realm dry."

"What *is* his cause?" Aranel pressed. "Who is he fighting against?"

"Burn me if I know. All the clans—starting with Chiren, damn manglers—began flocking to him years ago. He promised them some great war, though I don't know who he thinks he'll be fighting, given he's trying to unite everyone, which is a flea-brained idea. The clans live on violence. If he deprives them of it long enough, his soldiers will tear each other apart."

"Is that what you're waiting for, the day Kaldrav's army implodes?" Aranel asked shrewdly. Meizan refused to answer, but Aranel persisted like the nuisance he was. "Are the clans truly loyal to him? I've only ever met two Malini, but you and Aina both seem to hate him with a passion."

"Aina's a Malini?" Meizan exclaimed.

"Not anymore, given she ascended over a year ago." Aranel looked at him, alarmed. "Don't tell me you thought she was born-and-bred Mayani?"

Meizan hadn't given it any thought at all. Aina acted different from Aranel, who made Meizan feel like he'd swallowed a slug each time they spoke. She didn't grind his nerves with overbearing niceties like the rest of the Balancers, but to think she was lower-born!

How the burning hell had she ascended?

Something shifted on the horizon and interrupted Meizan's deliberation, a flicker of movement amidst the expanse of hardened lava.

He peered into the gloom and tensed as a dozen of Kaldrav's soldiers came into view. They trudged toward Incaraz, their black armor blending into the rock. As they drew near, Meizan could make out voices filtering across the stillness.

" . . . hate this pissing road," one of the soldiers was saying. "Should've taken a damn boat."

"And become saberfin food?" his companion replied. "Did you *see* what they did to the last ship that tried sailing Mir Tamasa?"

"Still better than what happened to those sods camped in Martharan a couple weeks back."

A round of harsh laughter followed, then the first soldier asked, "What d'you think happened to that Balancer hideout? Isn't it around here somewhere?"

Aranel let out a soft gasp, and Meizan grasped the hilt of his sword.

"Buried in lava's my guess," came a guttural reply. "Though it's worth raiding if it's intact. I hear they've got clean water. And *food*, actual bleeding food."

"I'll alert Zenyra and the others," Aranel whispered, but Meizan shook his head.

"They can't see us behind the shield. Even if they attack, two is enough to take them out."

The soldiers shuffled closer, unaware they were being watched. "If I starve a day longer, my stomach's going to crawl out of my belly," one of them grunted. "Kaldrav's a stingy maggot, can't even feed his own damn troops properly."

"Where's the bleeding meat I was promised?" another added.

"Forget meat, where's our stinking war? I'm sick of lying low. Pissing commanders, acting as if waiting around will make the torana explode."

Aranel stiffened beside him. Meizan leaned forward, streaming chitrons to his ears to enhance his hearing.

"Screw it," a soldier said. "I say we raid the hideout today and butcher ourselves some uppers. I'll bet *their* meat tastes good. Plump and juicy, not hard and dry like a starved-out Malini."

Aranel looked ready to vomit. Meizan gripped his wrist to stop him from making any sudden movements. One of the soldiers, probably their leader, slammed an elbow into the head of the man who had just spoken.

"One more word about raiding anything and your skull will break faster than Toranic Law," the leader rasped. "Then I'll fill your head with ice from Agakor before stitching you back up and dumping your body in the frostlands. How does that sound, you little maggot?"

The soldier swore at his leader's threat but said nothing more. The group trundled past the shield but made no move to attack. Meizan watched them continue northward and fade into the distance, releasing a breath he didn't realize he'd been holding.

"What was that about?" Aranel sounded strained. "About breaking Toranic Law and exploding the torana? They don't truly think they can do that, do they?"

"They're soldiers," Meizan said. "They talk shit. It's all they have to do."

"But it's not possible to break Toranic Law. It's unyielding and absolute."

"I *know* it's bleeding absolute. You think those soldiers are the first idiots to think of blowing up the torana? A bunch of kids in Kanjallen tried it too, years ago, blasting them with explosives and chitronic attacks."

"And?"

"And nothing. Not a scratch, though they triggered a small landslide. Your precious torana won't break even if Kaldrav slams against them with the might of his entire army."

Aranel didn't look especially reassured, but Meizan couldn't be bothered by a soldier's delusion about breaking Toranic Law. It did bother him that they'd known the location of the hideout. They'd known and considered attacking, yet walked away.

From Meizan's experience, Kaldrav's soldiers were an impulsive lot who reveled in fighting whatever appeared before them. That their leader had stopped them was both unusual and unsettling.

Was Kaldrav preparing some sort of coordinated attack on the Balancer villages and Incaraz? Meizan would have to get the hell out of here if that happened. Strong as the Balancers were with their precision channeling, Kaldrav's army numbered hundreds of thousands. If even a small fraction attacked, the Balancers would be crushed like ants.

Crushed like Kanjallen.

CHAPTER TEN

๏

An Irregularity

HERE IT WAS again. A hint of movement in the darkness, not ten feet away.

Aina crouched behind an outcrop of rock and stilled her breath. Her chitrons quivered, one lapse in concentration away from breaking the concealment.

Maybe sneaking out in the middle of the night hadn't been the brightest decision. But she'd finally mastered the art of concealment under Hiraval's watchful eye. The thin covering of chitrons would render her invisible—at least to other humans.

Please don't be a nagamor . . . Aina's fingers tightened around her bow, and she glanced over her shoulder. Even though she couldn't see it, Incaraz stood less than half a mile away, behind the safety of Zenyra's chitronic shield.

What was I thinking, leaving the hideout?

But an entire moon had lapsed since she'd joined the Balancers, and Aina's patience wore thin as a frayed bowstring. Being able to pull off a decent concealment seemed as good of an opportunity as any to at least scout the surroundings for a trace of her mother.

I could make a run for it. Aina's eyes darted between the Balancer hideout and the advancing form, half obscured in the shadows. *Or I could stay and fight.*

Run, her mother's voice echoed in her mind, a command she had heard at least a thousand times. *Run, Aina! I'll deal with them!*

But you're not here to deal with them, Mama, Aina thought as a familiar face flashed across her mind, lines of fear and fury cutting across her mother's skin.

Aina's chitrons wavered at the memory. Her concealment flickered, and the shadowy figure tensed.

Aina had barely nocked an arrow to her bow when someone barreled into her, strong hands grabbing her wrists and twisting them behind her back. A hardness pressed against her throat. Aina looked down to see a blade covered in strips of thick white cloth.

"Aranel?"

Her panic dissipated in an instant, for no one else would be brainless enough to wrap their weapons.

"Aina?" Aranel released her, voice laced with confusion. "What in Sherka's name are you doing out here?"

"I could ask you the same." Aina turned to face him. Aranel's keiza gleamed, the only light apart from the golden glint of a distant torana. "Aren't you supposed to be on lookout?"

"I—I *was* on lookout. That's how I noticed you creeping about. I thought you were an enemy."

"So you decided to come down here and attack me? How noble."

"Well, I do what I can to protect Incaraz." Aranel gripped her arm. "Come on, then. Let's get you back."

Aina sighed but allowed herself to be steered in the direction of the hideout. "Could you avoid mentioning to Zenyra that you caught me out here?"

"Of course," Aranel said. Aina was surprised at how readily he agreed but decided not to question her luck. "If I might ask, what *were* you doing, Aina?"

"I . . ." Aina kicked a stray pebble. "I was looking for my mother."

"Ah." Aranel's grip loosened. "Did you ask Zenyra for help? You seem close to her."

"Zenyra wants me to wait until I finish my training. I've already waited more than a year. I'm bleeding sick of waiting." Aina stopped abruptly, chewing her lip. Why the hell was she telling Aranel all this?

But Aranel let out a soft laugh and said, "I know what that's like. My parents ascended to Paramos when I was twelve. I haven't seen my father since, and the last time my mother deigned to visit was over nine moons ago."

"That's hardly the same . . ."

"I know it's not! I simply meant I understand how it feels to be helpless. To wait for something you have no control over."

Aina remained silent, unsure how to respond. Aranel struck her as someone who always got what he wanted when he wanted it. She couldn't imagine him feeling helpless or having to wait for anything.

The air rippled as they neared Incaraz, the shield allowing them through as if it were made of water. Aranel slowed his pace to climb alongside Aina as she stumbled up the outer wall.

"Careful," Aranel murmured. He reached out to steady her, his hands warm on her shoulders. "You know, you really ought to use your chitrons more efficiently. I noticed you've a bad habit of squandering energy—"

"I don't do it on purpose!"

"—and there's a visualization technique my brother taught me that might improve your chitronic control. You start by focusing your thoughts on a singular image."

Aina wondered if she'd misheard him. "Are you actually trying to help me?"

"Why do you sound so surprised?"

"You've only ever tried to arrest me before—" Aina tripped over a rock and grabbed Aranel's arm for balance.

"I was trying to help you then as well," Aranel said. "I know you didn't see it that way, but I was worried about your soul."

"Sure you were," Aina mumbled, releasing him. "So. Um. How does this visualization thing work?"

"You envision your soul as an object. A lotus, or another flower might do. Then imagine your chitrons as, say, dewdrops that gather on its surface. Draw them into the flower's core—" Aranel stopped abruptly as Aina dissolved into giggles. "What?"

"My soul is a lotus and my chitrons are dewdrops." Aina snorted. "That's quaint."

They reached the top of the crater, suffused in pale light from the banyan below. It cast the fine lines of Aranel's face into sharp relief. Aina found herself staring, a moment too long, at the slope of his nose and the way Aranel's golden locks framed his square jaw. He'd stopped applying that ridiculous hair oil, which, to Aina's dismay, only improved the appeal.

The Mayani was blessed in more ways than one. A part of Aina hated him for it.

"Has Zenyra given you any tips on chitronic control?" Aranel asked as they passed the thicket and began their descent. "I noticed you're often with her. What is it you talk about?"

"She—um—she helps me train on occasion," Aina replied, tearing her gaze from his face. "We talk about my life in Malin. My mother. Nothing you'd want to hear about."

"I didn't mean to pry." Aranel sounded disappointed, though Aina couldn't imagine why he'd care. "I understand if you don't want to tell me."

"I—I don't *not* want to tell you."

"Really?" Aranel looked to the side. "Well then—did you ever discuss the Balancer villages? Who's assigned to them and what they do?"

"No." Aina suppressed an eye roll. Sometimes Aranel could be *so* transparent. "Are you still worried about being stuck with us for the mission? If it helps, I don't think Meizan's going to stick around here that long."

And neither am I.

At the mention of Meizan, Aranel's brow twisted into a frown. "I'm not the slightest bit bothered what that fiend does or doesn't do. Although he seems to detest me."

"What makes you say that?" Aina asked, amused by how dramatic he sounded.

"Every time I've tried having a civil conversation with him, he's done nothing but insult or ignore me."

"That doesn't mean he hates you. Meizan hates Kaldrav, Kaldrav's soldiers, and enemy clans like Chiren. If he ignores you, he probably just finds you irrelevant."

She meant it to cheer him up, but Aranel deflated further.

"On the bright side, I don't—" Aina clamped her mouth shut, heat creeping up her neck.

I don't hate you. What a pointless thing to say.

She hoped Aranel hadn't noticed her slipup. He seemed rather preoccupied, staring straight ahead as if he'd seen a nagamor.

Meizan sauntered toward them, spinning his sword in aimless circles.

"Why aren't you on lookout?" he asked Aranel, who jumped at being addressed.

"Y-you! How long have you been here? And why are you not in bed?"

"I was training." Meizan shot him his most scornful look. "Not everyone needs eight hours of sleep, you ass."

"Well, *I* was talking with Aina," Aranel retorted. "Not everyone shirks pleasant human conversation."

"Whatever. You're in for it if Zenyra catches you ditching."

"Zenyra's back?" Aranel brightened. "Since when? Where did you see her last?"

"A few minutes ago," Meizan said, gesturing vaguely across the lake. "She went that way."

"Come on." Aranel turned to Aina with a manic sort of gleam in his eye. "Let's find her."

"Um. Sure?" Aina looked at Meizan, who shrugged and returned to practicing motions with his sword.

Aina followed Aranel across the lake, bemused by his sudden enthusiasm. They found Zenyra in a stone passageway, accompanied by a small girl who looked no older than three or four. The girl cradled a musty boot in her arms as if it were made of glass. She gave a startled squeak at their appearance and darted behind Zenyra's legs.

Zenyra chuckled, addressing the girl. "You need not fear them, dear. They are friends."

The girl edged forward to peek at them out of wide blue eyes. To Aina's surprise, Aranel knelt down and offered her his hand.

"Hello there." He flashed the little girl a smile. "How are you today?"

What a charmer.

The girl blinked in confusion before reaching out and poking the center of Aranel's palm with a tiny finger. "H'llo."

"That's a nice boot you have," Aranel said.

"S'not a boot." The girl held it toward them, and Aina saw

the boot was filled with twigs, its stained leather covered in chalk scribbles of windows and a door. "A house. For the twig people."

"You made that for them?" Aranel asked. "How clever of you."

"I *had* to," the girl whispered. "It keeps them safe." She hugged the boot to her chest before dashing back behind Zenyra.

"Ummi is rather shy," Zenyra said. She flattened the girl's dark bangs and lowered her voice. "Her home was razed. I rescued her from a band of Kaldrav's men on the way here. I will take her to one of the villages tomorrow, once she is fed and rested."

"That's good of you," Aranel said, eyes fixed on Ummi, who was now playing with the ends of Zenyra's long braid.

"It is only humane," Zenyra said with a sad smile. "You two ought to rest so you are fresh for your morning training session."

She led Ummi down a passageway. As they left, the little girl turned and waved at them wildly. "See you later!" she hollered, then disappeared with Zenyra.

"Lucky Zenyra rescued her from those men," Aranel said once they were gone.

"Lucky those men didn't do anything before Zenyra found them," Aina replied darkly. That little girl, alone with those monsters. She had been lucky, indeed, to escape unharmed.

"She seemed so sweet," Aranel said. "I wonder what she did to land in Malin?"

Any goodwill Aina had felt toward him swiftly evaporated. "She was born here, Aranel. She didn't *do* anything." Before Aranel could argue, she added, "I'm tired, and Hiraval said we're starting stun beams tomorrow morning. Good night."

"Come on now, Aina," Hiraval said a week later at training. "You know the drill. Clear your mind. Empty your heart. Summon your soul."

Aina closed her eyes and exhaled. She felt her chitrons vibrating within her and began gathering them. Not like dewdrops—she wasn't as weird as Aranel—but more like the lava flows of Merumarth converging into a blazing stream. She opened her eyes to see her fingertips glowing with turquoise light.

"Don't lose focus," Hiraval encouraged. "Concentrate on the flows. Keep them packed together. Good. Now release just one beam of energy."

Aina thrust her chitrons out with a rush of exhilaration. Turquoise light flashed, then dissipated. Across from her, Hiraval stumbled and held up a hand.

"That was progress," the Balancer said, flexing his fingers. "You could improve your aim, but for a second there, I think you froze my fingers."

"Stop pretending." Aina's shoulders slumped. "It didn't work. I'm no good."

She looked around the clearing at the others' practice. Aranel seemed reluctant to attack Reimi, who was hopping on one foot and yelling, "Just get this over with and hit my forehead, Aranel! Your aim can't possibly be that bad."

Aranel gave her a sheepish smile. The next beam of light hit Reimi's shoulder and paralyzed her arm. Even if his stun beams were not hitting the mark, they were powerful.

Not far from Aranel, Meizan leaned against a tree with a bored expression. Taralei lay at his feet, stiff as stone. Meizan's stun beam had hit her straight in the keiza. He had all but mastered the Balancer's preferred chitronic technique—concentrated blasts of energy that could knock out an opponent for up to an hour.

While Aina could see the appeal in a technique that caused minimal physical damage, she had once again fallen behind. Most of the time, her chitrons broke loose of the beam to scatter all over the place—singeing the grass and warming the air, but doing little in terms of stunning her opponent.

"Shall we try again?" Hiraval suggested.

Aina nodded, readying her chitrons. A couple weeks ago, she might have snapped at him. But Hiraval's calm rivaled one of the manikai, and Aina found it exhausting to lash out.

Yet even Hiraval's tenacity could not improve Aina's volatile control. At the end of the lesson, she had barely managed to paralyze his right hand, and the ground around her was a smoking, pitted mess.

"You have power," Hiraval said, surveying the ring of wreckage around Aina's feet. "Too much, at times. To harness it efficiently, we must work on your control. A hand is good progress, Aina. Tomorrow, you will stun my arm. Next week, an arm and a leg. By the end of the moon, you will knock me out in one shot."

"If that's the goal, I could just bash your head with a rock, save us both the trouble."

Hiraval gave a small smile, sparing Aina the usual lecture—*The Balancer methods are aimed at reducing the injury suffered by our opponents*—and turned to leave for dinner. He paused to look over his shoulder.

"I'll be late," Aina said. "Save me some stew."

Hiraval nodded and walked over to the others. Taralei was passing Reimi a gold coin while Aranel and Meizan bickered about stun beams—"Must be embarrassing, *Kirnos's finest* bested by a mere lower." "I was being careful! I didn't want to risk harming her keiza!"—and Aina was overcome by a sudden urge to join them.

Idiot girl, a voice not unlike her mother's echoed in her mind. *Why waste time with these fools when you should be training?*

Aina skipped dinner and trained into the night with little progress. She took a break only to recharge her chitrons and sprawled on the lone patch of grass she hadn't accidentally ruined. She lay there, bouncing a broken rock figurine on her palm—she'd tried fixing it to no avail—when Zenyra stepped into the clearing, her keiza a beacon in the darkness.

"How's Ummi doing?" Aina asked, rolling upright. She hadn't seen Zenyra for the past week but had often wondered about the little girl. "Did she make it to the village all right? Kaldrav's men won't find her, will they?"

"Worry not, Aina," Zenyra said. "Kaldrav's men will never touch that sweet girl again. Now, Hiraval told me of your trouble with stun beams." She sat Aina on a log and knelt in front of her. "I wanted to have a closer look at your keiza. May I?"

Aina nodded, unsure where this was going.

Zenyra shook back her sleeves, threads of golden energy trickling from her palms. Aina shivered as they wrapped around her head.

"Forgive my intrusion," Zenyra said before sending a stream straight through Aina's forehead. Aina squirmed at the contact and dug her fingers into the log.

"That cannot be," Zenyra muttered as she probed Aina's keiza. "But of course . . . that would explain . . . never seen anything like it."

Aina shifted on the log. "Anything like what? Is something wrong?"

Zenyra sat back and withdrew her chitrons. "Not quite *wrong*," she said delicately. "Although I should have thought to inspect your keiza closer, given your trouble with channeling. I merely assumed it was a lack of practice, but . . ."

"But what?"

"Do not be alarmed now, Aina. It appears there is an . . . irregularity in your keiza."

"An irregularity," Aina repeated, heart sinking.

"There is a cleft in the swirl," Zenyra clarified. "It is minute, scarcely noticeable to the naked eye, but it seems to be affecting your chitronic flows."

"I don't understand! How could that happen?"

"I suspect you were born with it," Zenyra said. "I have never encountered a cleft like yours, but it would explain why you find it so hard to channel. The keiza is used both to activate chitrons and to link them to the outside world. With yours split the way it is, it is a miracle you have progressed this far. You should be proud."

Aina felt numb. She failed to see what there was to be proud about.

Zenyra's pretty words didn't hide the fact that her keiza was deformed. Defective. Which meant no matter how hard she practiced, she would never be able to channel the way Aranel and Meizan could. Her mother would be forced to continue risking her own soul to protect her.

It was yet another injustice the universe had thrust upon them.

"I mean it, Aina," Zenyra said. "For Aranel and Meizan, even for myself, chitronic control comes naturally. You have to fight for what we take for granted." She paused, her eyes softening. "But you are used to having to fight for things, are you not?" She raised a hand and brushed away Aina's bangs. "You have fought against adversity since the day you were born."

Aina gripped the sides of the log, knuckles whitening. She wanted to speak, but her throat was tight and she couldn't get out a single word.

"I am sure it is difficult," Zenyra continued, "but you must not lose hope, Aina. The irregularity in your keiza may come with certain . . . advantages." Aina looked at her in disbelief, and Zenyra smiled. "Do you remember what I told you when you first arrived here? How you are the only one of us who reversed the spin of your soul?"

"Yes." Aina shrugged. "So?"

"I reckon that too is because of your keiza. The irregularity protected you from the influence of Malin's chitrons and enabled you to ascend."

"I don't understand."

"We bond to the chitrons of the universe through our keiza," Zenyra said. "That bond allows us to channel effectively but also exposes our souls to Malin's negative energy. In your case, your keiza prevents you from bonding properly. And while that dilutes the control you have over your channeling—"

"It also lessens the influence on my chitrons," Aina finished.

"Exactly!" Zenyra's smile widened. "For Hiraval or Aranel, even for myself, a few hours of continuous channeling outside the walls of Incaraz would substantially slow the spin of our souls. But for you, I suspect the effect would be far more gradual."

She leaned forward, eyes glittering. "Aina, I apologize if this is too forthright, but could you tell me about the day you ascended to Mayana? Did you see a flash of white around the time it happened?"

"I did," Aina admitted. "But it was less of a flash, and more like—like I'd been transported to another dimension. This unending whiteness that stretched in all directions."

"I see," Zenyra said, intrigued. "How long were you in this space? What happened after?"

"A few seconds, I guess? It disappeared soon after it came, and I was back in Malin. A nagamor attacked us, and my foot slipped through a torana—"

Aina stopped as memories of her mother's tearstained face flashed through her mind.

"A few seconds," Zenyra murmured, fixated on Aina's keiza. "Interesting . . . very interesting."

"What does it mean?" Aina asked. "What was the whiteness? And what does it have to do with my keiza?"

"Perhaps everything . . . perhaps nothing at all."

"You're not making any sense!"

Zenyra snapped out of her strange trance. "My apologies. I might have mentioned it before, but I have a deep academic interest in the process of ascension between Malin and Mayana. But that is not important right now. Are you feeling all right?"

"I'm fine," Aina said. "This is nothing." She reached up to touch her forehead. "Do you think— Could you fix it? Could you fix *me*?"

"Oh, Aina," Zenyra said sadly. "My dear child. If only I could. But I have never seen a keiza like yours in my life. I would be terrified of making things worse."

"You won't even try?" Aina deflated. If Zenyra couldn't heal her, it was futile staying in Incaraz, trying to learn techniques her body would never let her use.

"I cannot promise it will work," Zenyra said after a moment, "but I will try. Prior to that, I will need to practice, and to study your keiza in depth. If you can give me some time, Aina, stick with me for a while longer before running off in search of your mother again."

"H-how did you know?" Aina stammered.

Did Aranel tell her? That rat!

"Because I understand your impatience." Zenyra touched a hand to her chest, where Aina noticed a six-petaled flower embroidered into the fabric. "I, too, have been waiting, *longing* for something. Something that seems tantalizingly close, yet just a hair's breadth out of reach." She hooked a finger under Aina's chin and forced her to look up. "Stay here for a few more moons, Aina, and I promise you we will both get what we desire."

CHAPTER ELEVEN

@

Respect and Fear

*T*HANK YOU FOR the report," said Seirem from across the golden torana. He studied the parchment Aranel handed him. "In the future, I would refrain from writing things down. You are a spy, Aranel. You must be discreet."

"My apologies, Lord Seirem. I was worried I'd forgotten something."

"Not much here to forget," replied Seirem, a slight strain to his smile.

Aranel hung his head. This was his sixth weekly report to the Preserver, and he had yet to uncover anything suspicious about Zenyra or the villages. He hadn't even tracked down the names of all the Balancers stationed in them.

Sam would have figured it out by now. Perhaps Lord Seirem was mistaken putting his trust in me and he's realizing it now.

Seirem took a swig from his hipflask and returned to Aranel's notes. "So Zenyra has each new batch of recruits train for a period of four to six moons in Incaraz prior to dispatching them on missions to villages. And your cousin told you the most recent mission was dispatched when?"

"A couple days before I joined," answered Aranel. "Around the time of the Preservation Advisory."

"Indeed. The missions coincide not only with the timing and frequency of the Advisory, but also with the disturbances I noticed in the chitronic system. When is the next mission scheduled for?"

"Zenyra hasn't announced it officially, but I expect a couple moons from now, once Taralei and the rest complete their training." Aranel straightened, an idea coming to mind. "What if you convened the Advisory early?"

"And see if Zenyra moved up the mission?" Seirem tapped his chin. "Not a bad idea."

"It would confirm that Zenyra's timing the missions according to the Advisories, rather than the actual training."

"So it would," agreed Seirem, "although that would tell me little I did not already suspect. The week of the Advisory is when the Preservation are at our busiest, with several members visiting Mayana. It is no surprise Zenyra would schedule missions then, to avoid detection. The question is, what is she so desperate to hide? And how does it relate to the disturbances?"

Aranel shuffled his feet as the Preserver took another drink from his flask. "Have you learned anything of value from the girl, Aina?" asked Seirem.

"It's a waste trying to get information from her. Aina knows nothing, nor does she care to find out."

"Then you must make her care, Aranel. You know the saying: a kind act or word, each night and day, to win a heart is the surest way."

Aranel frowned. "That's not from any of the holy scriptures."

"No." Seirem's eyes twinkled. "But it's how I got my wife to marry me."

"Well then, I certainly won't be using it on Aina," said Aranel, revolted.

"I am not asking you to do much, Aranel. Merely a small act of kindness to move her heart and make her want to help you in return."

Aranel crossed his arms. He had already lied through his teeth for this forsaken mission, but what Seirem suggested seemed downright manipulative.

What would Sam have done? His brother had a talent for drawing people to him, men and women alike. *Forget Aina, Sam would've won over Meizan too by now . . .*

"I still believe Kaldrav is the bigger threat," said Aranel. "I overheard his soldiers talk of breaking the torana. Surely *that's* what is causing any disturbances you've detected."

"Worry not about a lower king and the empty words of his soldiers," dismissed Seirem. "They can ram against the torana with their full might and Toranic Law will stand strong."

Even Meizan had said something similar. Aranel nodded, his unease not wholly abated.

"Focus on your task, Aranel." Seirem waved the parchment of notes. "The dates of past missions are useful, but what I need is information on Zenyra and her villages. There must be *something* she is hiding there, outside the walls of Incaraz."

Seirem had raised his hipflask once more when a gust of wind swept through Paramos and pulled the parchment from his grasp.

The Preserver lunged and caught the parchment between long fingers. As he did, a few drops sloshed over the side of his flask—the same shining liquid Aranel had seen him drink weeks ago. Seirem wiped it away, but not before Aranel noted the familiar pearly consistency.

That cannot be . . .

"What are you drinking, Lord Seirem?" asked Aranel, struggling to keep his voice even. "If it is more of the Amaratisian wine, I would love to have a sip."

"I shall bring you a whole bottle next time," said Seirem, screwing his flask shut with a smile. "But today, I drink only to an old man's vanity. I may not look it, but I have walked these realms for centuries." He lowered his voice to a conspiratorial whisper. "Some slather themselves with chitronic illusions, but I myself find the constant channeling a chore. Why squander your chitrons when a simple tonic can do the trick?" He gave the flask a small shake and stowed it in his robes.

Aranel nodded, at a loss for words. He'd always suspected there was something not entirely natural about the man's face. And yet that liquid . . .

It means nothing, Aranel told himself. *It's a harmless youth tonic, just as he said. It was rude of me to pry. Surely even Paramosi are allowed a few vices.*

Aranel said nothing more of it and left the torana shortly after to return to Incaraz. He was surprised to find Meizan in the thicket atop the crater, not far from the spot where Aranel was supposed to be on lookout.

Did he see me? Aranel began inventing excuses in preparation for the inevitable confrontation: he'd been studying the chitronic shield up close, he'd seen a group of soldiers nearby and thought to spy on them, he'd dropped his sword and had gone to fetch it.

But Meizan appeared to not have noticed Aranel's return. He stretched his legs and sprinted down the cliff, leaving Aranel staring after him. Aranel noted how Meizan's ledges were scarcely visible in the rock, a far cry from a week earlier.

I can't let him surpass me!

But what with sneaking about Incaraz and reporting to

Seirem, Aranel had little time to get in additional practice for himself. His eyes fell to the lake, where Aina teetered across the surface like a newborn deer. Seirem's words played in his mind—*make her want to help you*—as he walked toward her.

"I see my visualization technique isn't helping much," said Aranel.

With a shriek, Aina slipped ankle-deep into the water. Aranel extended his chitrons, and tendrils of green light pulled her back onto the surface.

"You dolt!" cried Aina, flushing. "You broke my concentration!"

"Sorry," said Aranel. "Where's Zenyra? Is she not training you today?"

Aina shrugged and spread her arms as she shifted atop the water. "It does help. Your visualization technique, I mean. Except, instead of a flower and dewdrops, I imagine my soul as, well, a kind of lava pit, or a volcano. And the chitrons are lava flows and I'm trying to stop the explosion—what?" she asked, indignant, as Aranel pressed his lips together, trying to stifle laughter. "What's your problem?"

"It's nothing." Aranel grinned in spite of himself. "I simply thought it fitting. That you'd have a volcanic soul."

"What's that supposed to mean?" Aina splashed at him with her foot, nearly falling into the water from the effort. "Why are you here? Are you ditching lookout duty *again*?"

"Hiraval's got that covered. I thought I'd help you train."

Aina blinked several times. "Are you doing this for some kind of chitronic benefit? Because I'm not a charity case."

"Of course not! I want to help you, Aina. I may not be Zenyra or Hiraval, but I was trained by one of the best—"

"Best channelers in Mayana, three-time cloudsurfing champion, elite healer, youngest-ever commander of the Kirnosi guard, your precious brother," recited Aina. Aranel was taken aback. He didn't speak of Samarel that often, did he?

"It's nice of you to offer," continued Aina, "but there's nothing you can do. Meizan was right, back at Merumarth. My keiza *is* broken." She recounted what Zenyra had discovered about her keiza, her voice a monotone, amber eyes fixed to the ground.

"That explains a lot," said Aranel once Aina was finished. He couldn't conceive how she lived with knowing she'd never be able to channel properly. "You've done really well, Aina. Dealing with all of that, on top of everything with your mother." He cracked a smile. "Although, as a former member of the Kirnosi guard, I shudder to imagine how we would have handled you with a properly functioning keiza."

"You would have suffered."

"And Zenyra's agreed to fix this for you? Did she know about it when she recruited you?"

"She only realized a couple weeks ago."

It struck Aranel odd that Zenyra would go out of her way to recruit someone as untalented as Aina. He'd assumed she'd done it out of pity, since Aina wanted to descend, but now that he'd learned about her keiza . . .

Aranel wasn't sure of the connection, but it seemed a crucial bit of information. *Or it's nothing, and I'm desperate to find anything remotely suspicious to report back to Seirem.*

Aranel coached Aina on chitronic fundamentals until sunrise. During their breaks, he grilled her about Zenyra and the villages. Half the time, Aina gave noncommittal, one-word answers. The other half, she stared at him with an odd, vacant expression that made Aranel want to tear his hair out. Only his newfound appreciation for her perseverance made him stay.

Aina knows nothing, concluded Aranel at the end of their session. *My only option is to visit a village myself. But I haven't a clue*

where they are, and it's too dangerous to go looking alone. Does that
mean I'm stuck in this hovel till Zenyra dispatches us herself?

That would mean no answers until they completed their training, another four moons, at the least. Seirem would not be amenable to waiting that long. And neither would Aranel.

ARANEL VISITED THE hot springs that evening, allowing the velvety water to wrap him in its embrace. He leaned against the slick rock and raised a calf to flick at the water with his toes.

As he watched the pearly droplets, an image of Seirem drinking from his flask came to mind.

It was the same blessed liquid. Aranel flicked at the water again. *I'm fairly certain he's been drinking it since my first report. Is that why he was so quick to dismiss the springs when I first told him about them?*

When he kicked the water a third time, the steam parted to reveal a pair of eyes, charcoal dark. Aranel lowered his leg with a splash, hugging his knees to his chest.

"What are you doing here?" he spluttered, all thoughts of Seirem wiped from his mind.

"*Trying* to unwind," said Meizan.

"I—I thought I was alone." Aranel sank deeper into the water. What would Meizan think, seeing him splashing about like a child?

A silence fell over them, broken only by the gentle ripple of the spring. Aranel glanced at Meizan through the rising steam. His pale face was clean of dirt and his hair no longer a matted mess. Perhaps it was a trick of the candlelight, but was his keiza brighter than before? The blue swirl turned in the opposite direction to Aranel's own, but if he brushed aside that little detail, Aranel realized his initial judgment about Meizan had been correct—he resembled a Nishakian. A Mayani.

And it might have been the same spring water addling his head, but Aranel found himself craving a simple, friendly conversation.

He opened his mouth, closed it, then opened it again, finally managing, "What does one do, in Malin? For leisure, I mean." He could almost feel Meizan's glare through the steam. "I don't suppose you've much time for it, but surely you've got a hobby. Beyond polishing your sword and slicing things to pieces with it?"

Meizan didn't reply, and Aranel ducked his face into the water under the pretense of washing it. He should have expected to be ignored.

He surfaced, pushing wet strands from his face, when Meizan said, "Books."

Aranel blinked. "Sorry, what?"

"I like books."

"You mean you *read*?"

"What else would I do with them?" Meizan sounded very much as if he regretted joining the conversation.

"Bludgeon enemies on the head, target practice, firewood," listed Aranel.

From behind the steam, he thought he saw Meizan's lips curl.

"One of my clanmates found a Mayani book near an abandoned Balancer village," said Meizan. "It had a bunch of healing techniques, but they didn't work . . ." He trailed off with a scowl.

"I like reading too," said Aranel eagerly. "The royal library of Kirnos has one of the best collections in Mayana. I'd spend hours there when I was on guard duty. You know, since there was never much to guard against." Meizan gave a derisive huff as Aranel continued. "Are you not curious at all? As to what Mayani do in their free time?"

"Beyond brushing your hair and amassing good deeds to lighten your soul?" quipped Meizan, and Aranel bit back a smile.

"That too, but we also have competitive sports. Have you ever heard of cloudsurfing?"

Meizan rolled his eyes. "Have you ever heard yourself speak?"

"I might've mentioned it a couple times."

"A couple dozen, when no one asked."

"It's quite fun, though challenging at first," said Aranel. "You'd be good at it, I'm sure."

"How . . . does it work?"

Aranel felt a victorious thrill at the grudging question. He rattled off the mechanics of cloudsurfing, recounting his races and the various medals he'd won.

"It sounds interesting," said Meizan. "But it wouldn't work in Malin. That level of precision. You'd never get the chitrons to comply."

"You could try it when you—" Aranel broke off, and another silence befell them. He had no idea whether Meizan would ever be able to ascend, or if he even wanted to.

Meizan shifted against the stone wall and stretched toned arms behind him. "Why are you really here, Aranel?"

"What do you mean?" asked Aranel, quickly averting his gaze.

"We both know whatever you told Aina about her inspiring you is a lie. You pretended to be a Balancer when I took you hostage to save your own ass. But why did you join? What were you even doing in Malin?"

"I always intended to join! The Balancers are famous in Mayana, and I genuinely believe in Zenyra's mission of helping your realm."

"Do you?" Meizan's eyes cut through the steam, and the springs felt uncomfortably hot. "Aina may be a fool, but I'm not. I saw you sneaking around last night when you were supposed to be on lookout."

The blood drained from Aranel's face as he scrambled for words. "I wasn't— I don't—"

"Save the lies," said Meizan. "I know your loyalties aren't with the Balancers. At first, I wondered if you were secretly aligned with Kaldrav."

"What?" yelped Aranel, stung by the accusation. "I'm not. I would *never.*"

"I know." Meizan tilted his head, sending damp bangs falling over his eyes. "You're too terrified for your own flaming soul to ally with that cockroach. As long as it's not him, I don't care. I won't even tell Zenyra."

"You won't?" asked Aranel, still trying to wrap his head around the fact that Meizan had figured him out. "Why not?"

"We all have our loyalties. Some run deeper than others." Meizan stood abruptly, spring water sluicing down his chest. Aranel followed suit and tensed for a fight as Meizan drew near.

"Do what you want outside Incaraz, Aranel." A dangerous edge crept into Meizan's voice. "But right now this crater is the only place in Malin where I'm free of Kaldrav and his soldiers." Meizan slammed a hand on the wall behind them. His glare pierced straight into Aranel's soul.

Aranel shrank back against the wet rock, lips moving wordlessly.

"If you do anything to screw that up," continued Meizan, barely audible above the thudding of Aranel's heart, "I will destroy you."

"I won't," said Aranel after a long moment. He angled his head to retreat behind a curtain of hair. "It's as you say, Meizan.

I won't do anything that might risk hurting someone. Anything that might . . . taint my soul." The words left a bitter aftertaste in his mouth.

"Good." Meizan stepped back. "At least your debilitating fear of Toranic Law has some use."

The statement felt like a punch to his gut. Aina's accusation from five weeks ago rang in Aranel's mind: *You don't respect Toranic Law. You fear it. You live your life in fear of how it will judge your soul and let that fear control your every action.*

Was he truly as selfish as Meizan and Aina saw him?

Aranel released a breath as Meizan turned and stalked out of the cavern. "They're wrong," he whispered to himself. His fingers curled against the rock. "They don't know the difference between respect and fear."

Besides, Aranel had a will of his own. Sometimes, he did things simply because he wanted to, such as when . . .

Aranel froze as he tried to recall a time when his actions hadn't been influenced by a desire to lighten his soul. He'd been more carefree in his childhood, but ever since their parents had ascended, ever since Aranel had noticed how Samarel's keiza shone brighter than his own . . .

Aranel stared down at his fingers, the forward circles they were unconsciously drawing over the cavern wall. He'd acquired the habit at thirteen, after a Kirnosi priest mentioned that his brother might be close to ascension.

"They're wrong," repeated Aranel, stilling his fingers.

He had a will of his own, even if Meizan and Aina couldn't see it.

CHAPTER TWELVE

๑

A Forbidden Technique

*I*F MEIZAN SQUINTED hard enough, he could pretend he was out hunting for Kanjallen again. The isolation surrounding Incaraz was not so different from the arid gray slopes of Raitani. Flatter, maybe, but just as ugly. Though none of its game shone as brightly as Aranel's stupid head. It would have been a lot easier to track them if they had.

Spinning a throwing star on the tip of his index finger, Meizan watched Aranel as he skulked along the rim of the crater. Two weeks had passed since their encounter in the hot springs, and the upper had been infuriatingly polite to Meizan throughout, refusing to rise to his taunts and smiling through all the teasing. It convinced Meizan more than ever that the shiny-haired freak was up to something.

Aranel swiped his forehead, and his form gave a ripple before disappearing.

Burn him! Meizan cursed. The throwing star wobbled, cutting his fingertip.

Meizan shoved it into his holster, then sucked on the wound. Aranel's concealment was bleeding flawless. Streaming chitrons to his ears, Meizan strained in the dark and tried to make out the telling footfalls. But Aranel moved silent as a shadow. Meizan had no way of tracking him.

If he's meeting someone, where would he go? Meizan stared into the darkness until a glint of gold caught his eye. *Is that a torana?*

Meizan crept down the slopes of Incaraz. The torana to Paramos twinkled against the gloom. As Meizan neared it, he spied someone behind the pillars: a long-haired man clad in white robes marked with four overlapping circles. He looked like an older, stuffier Aranel.

Is that his brother?

Meizan's suspicions were confirmed when Aranel removed his concealment and appeared in front of the torana. "Sam!" Aranel yelped. "What the— Why are you here? And wearing those robes?"

"I thought you'd be happier to see me," his brother said. "The robes are, well, a recent appointment."

A long pause followed. Then Aranel said, "I suppose I ought to congratulate you, *Lord* Samarel. You're the youngest Preserver in what, decades? Centuries?"

Preserver? Meizan perked. *Is this about that upper organization Aina keeps griping about?*

"Forget about me, Ran," Samarel said. "I found your correspondence with Lord Seirem." He tossed a white pebble through the torana. "And decided to meet you in his stead."

Aranel's shoulders stiffened, and his brother continued. "I thought it odd when the last three times I visited Kirnos you were nowhere to be found."

"You . . . actually visited?"

"Of course I did," Samarel said. "I promised, remember?"
Aranel was silent, a rare feat for him. Meizan inched closer under
his own concealment, careful to muffle his breathing.

"I assumed you were traveling the realm," Samarel continued.
"It wasn't until I overheard Lord Seirem speaking to another Preserver about a covert mission to Malin that I grew suspicious."

Aha! Meizan straightened. Aranel, that slippery little snail
was here on a mission. Under orders from some Preserver, by the
sound of it.

"I trailed Lord Seirem as he monitored the torana and found
your message before he did," Samarel said. "I recognized your
handwriting at once."

"Well done," Aranel said, his tone acerbic. "I imagine you're
here now to offer your help? Take over my mission?"

His brother drew back. "Take over? Aranel, I'm here to tell
you to cease this foolishness and return to Mayana."

There was a long pause. Then: "No." Aranel sounded petu-
lant. "I won't."

"Ran . . ." His brother sighed. "Please listen to me. I don't
know the details about this mission of yours, although I can
guess it involves the Balancers. Lord Seirem was, dare I say it,
irresponsible to approach you. You are too young to be involved
in matters of the Preservation."

"Don't patronize me! Just because Lord Seirem chose not to
tell *you* about it."

"It's not just me. Even His Supremacy Lord Kyrian has not
authorized this mission."

"How do you know that?"

"Trust me on this, Ran," Samarel said earnestly. "Lord Seirem
is using you for his own benefit. There are politics within the
Preservation that you are unaware of, and—"

Aranel cut him off. "Have you not considered that it's *you* who's unaware? I suppose it's difficult for you to accept. The Preservation entrusting me over you. Choosing me over you."

"That's not what this is about." His brother sounded stung.

"Yes, it is!" Aranel stormed. "You're used to being the best. Fastest cloudsurfer, strongest channeler, youngest Preserver. But this time, it's not about you. Lord Seirem specifically picked *me* for this mission, and if he's not told you about it, perhaps he thinks you don't deserve to know."

Aranel blustered on, and Meizan could only listen, amused by his pettiness. "I'm not a fool. I know the Preservation have factions and you're clearly not as high-ranked as Lord Seirem. For one thing, your sleeves are unlined."

Samarel raised an arm to display the pure white sleeve of his robes. "You mean this?" he asked, shocked. "Ran, did Lord Seirem tell you what the silver lining represents? Because it's not what you think."

"Then what is it?"

Samarel hesitated. "It's classified."

Meizan didn't know why they were so fixated on bleeding sleeves, but Aranel let out a harsh laugh. "Classified, is it?" he asked, injecting a surprising amount of venom into his voice. "Well, brother, my mission is classified too! So you can try ratting me out to Lord Kyrian if you'd like."

"I would never," Samarel said at once. "I don't want to get you into trouble, Ran. I'm only worried about your well-being. Your time in Malin has clouded your judgment."

"My time in Malin is nothing you could ever understand, given how desperate you were to run away from even Mayana!"

Damn, Meizan thought. *He really does have a stick up his ass.*

"That's not fair," Samarel said. "Ran, you know that's not fair,

I—" He made to step out of the torana, then stopped. "Forget it. It's your life. I've no right to intervene."

Even Meizan could sense the hurt in his voice, but Aranel seemed unaffected. "So you'll leave me alone, then? And stop meddling in my communications with Lord Seirem?"

"I hope you succeed," Samarel said. "Truly, I do. May your soul spin straight and swift, Aranel."

He turned around and disappeared. Aranel stood there, frozen. When he made no move to leave, Meizan returned to Incaraz, mind bursting with questions about what he'd just witnessed.

He found Aina, Taralei, and Reimi seated under the banyan tree. A pack of cards lay spread before them.

"Meizan!" Taralei greeted as she shuffled the cards. "Come, join us. Have you ever played Spin of Our Souls?"

Meizan shook his head. Judging by the name, it sounded ridiculous.

"I want to know about the Preservation," he said, and Aina made a disgusted noise. "Who they are, and what they do."

"The Preservation are a bunch of decrepit fish-brains," Aina supplied, "who like to meddle in things that don't concern them."

"They're the ruling council of the upper realms," Taralei said, lips twitching. "The Preservation are based in Paramos but advise the Mayani on certain matters of governance. They tend to be rather conservative when it comes to matters of the lower realms."

"Meaning they prefer not to get involved at all," Reimi added. "They've outlawed the Balancers, so Zenyra's not much of a fan."

"Oh, but you know who is?" Taralei leaned forward, eyes glinting. "When Ran was six, he made himself a white cloak out of a pillowcase and drew four little circles on it."

"Typical." Aina smacked her forehead.

"He'd wear it everywhere," Taralei continued, "acting like a snotty little Preserver in training, till Sam begged him to stop."

"Did he now?" Meizan's eyes narrowed.

Taralei's words confirmed everything he'd just witnessed. Aranel, that duplicitous snake, was spying on the Balancers for the Preservation. It explained why he'd been in Martharan that day, and why he constantly pestered everyone for information about Zenyra and the Balancer villages.

For a brief moment, Meizan debated reporting him. If this were Kanjallen, he would've done it in a heartbeat. But Zenyra wasn't Kanna, and Meizan owed the Balancers no loyalty.

Besides, a soft-souled bunch of Paramosi posed no threat to his future. Whatever business Aranel had with them was not Meizan's damn problem.

"Why the sudden interest?" Taralei asked, offering Meizan a set of four cards.

Meizan ignored her question and studied the cards. Each was marked with a number of spirals, some facing forward and others backward. "Don't tell me this is what I think it is . . ."

"It's worse," Aina said. "Spin of Our Souls is the most didactic game ever invented. The entire goal is to lighten your deck so you can ascend."

"Azyaka's burning beak." Meizan tossed his cards down. "You uppers aren't subtle at all. I bet Aranel loves this shit."

"He has a special edition," Taralei said with a sheepish smile, "with verses from the Aria of Ascension written all over it."

Aina snorted at that. Meizan turned to her and lowered his voice. "Speaking of ascension, I wanted to ask you something."

Aina quirked an eyebrow and followed him as he set off across the lake. "You're awfully curious today."

Meizan wheeled around to face her. "Aranel told me a few weeks ago that you were born to Malin. How did you ascend? I didn't think it was possible."

"Ah." Aina touched her forehead. Her keiza glowed turquoise, brighter than any lower-born Meizan had ever seen. "I don't know myself. One moment my mother and I were being attacked by a rabid nagamor. The next, my foot had slipped through the torana."

"Slipped through." Meizan shoved his hands into his pockets. "Did you see the white flash? Like a flash of lightning just before you ascend?"

"I think I did," Aina said, scrunching her eyes. "But it was less of a flash and more like I was in a sea of white, and—" She stopped abruptly and looked down.

"You don't have to talk about it." Meizan had plenty of memories he preferred not to dig up. He kept them locked away in the darkest corners of his mind.

"What clan were you in?" he asked instead, a hand dropping to the hilt of his sword. Much as he tolerated Aina, if he found out she was from Chiren, he'd be honor bound to fight her.

"None." Aina eyed his sword warily. "My mother and I were always on our own. She never spoke about a clan. All I know is she ran away from her village not long after I was born. My father used to go into drunken rages where he'd . . . well, you know . . . and she was scared that . . ."

Aina trailed off, and Meizan retracted his hand from the hilt. He'd met his fair share of people like Aina's father. "Good you escaped," he said. "What's Mayana like?"

All he'd heard was the sugary nonsense that spouted from Aranel's mouth. For the first time, Meizan found himself curious as to what lay beyond those silver torana.

"It's mostly as Aranel describes it," Aina said. "But underneath all the beauty, it's rotting with abundance bestowed upon it by that bleeding law."

"Toranic Law, you mean," Meizan said. "You really hate it."

"As should you," Aina replied. At his blank expression, hers grew heated. "It's a twisted system! One that places undue suffering on one realm for the safety and prosperity of another." Meizan shrugged, and Aina grabbed his wrists. "It's wronged you, Meizan, worse than it wronged me! How *don't* you resent it?"

"It's been a while since you last lived in Malin, Aina." Meizan tugged his wrists free. "Outside the walls of this hideout, Kaldrav's army is growing. His soldiers constantly raid the villages and steal what little food they have. The nagamor have multiplied, and even the seas are infested with sharks."

"Yes, but—"

"I was trying to survive all that. I was too busy fighting actual enemies to waste my energy hating on a flaming system. A force of nature that can't be changed no matter what we throw at it."

"But you're not even angry," Aina said in a small voice. "How? How aren't you even the slightest bit angry at Toranic Law? I know I am, for everything it put me through."

"You're wasting your anger, Aina. Toranic Law is our reality. All we can do is try to live the best we can within its constraints."

ARANEL ARRIVED LATE to training the next morning, eyes swollen and rimmed with red. He forwent his usual greeting—giving Aina unsolicited pointers, being a general annoyance to Meizan—and sat cross-legged on the ground.

"Is something wrong?" Aina approached him, looking rather nervous. "You don't look well."

"Missing dear Mayana?" Meizan couldn't help but add, "Missing your precious brother?"

Aranel leaped up in a flash, sword drawn and pointed at Meizan's throat. "One day," he fumed. "You could go one blessed day without being a complete prick."

"Why would I do that?" Meizan backstepped and drew his own blade. "You're more fun when you're riled up."

"Oh, leave him alone," Aina said. "Can't you see he's upset?"

Aranel and Meizan froze, staring at her. She ducked her head and fidgeted with the stray fibers of her tunic. "I—I meant. It would be nice not to fight. Once in a while."

What's gotten into her? Along with Taralei, Meizan could usually count on Aina when it came to goading Aranel.

"Have you ever cared for someone," Aranel asked suddenly, sheathing his sword, "but also hated them at the same time?"

"No," Meizan said, baffled by the question. Aina, who had turned red, said nothing as she began practicing stun beams.

"You never had siblings?" Aranel pried. "Cousins? Family members who—"

"No," Meizan said shortly. His parents had fled Kanjallen after he'd been born, and while there had been a few clan members near his age, none shared his bloodline.

"Right." Aranel looked rather awkward. "But then, I don't suppose either of you have ever felt like—felt like you weren't enough."

"You're really going to ask *me* that?" Aina muttered, as her stun beam fizzled away the moment she released it.

"Not enough?" Meizan asked. "You're in one piece, and you can fight. What more do you want?"

He expected Aranel to attack him again, but the idiot's dour expression brightened. Aranel began bossing Aina on some method to promote efficient chitronic usage, and it was only when Zenyra stepped into the clearing unannounced that he shut up.

Why is she here? Meizan's hand went to his sword at once. *Did she find out about Aranel? Is she here to punish him?* Then: *Is she here to punish me for withholding information?*

In Kanjallen, traitors were stabbed in both eyes. Or one—if the chief was feeling generous.

"I shall be supervising your training today," Zenyra said, and Meizan felt a rush of relief. "Your seniors need to focus on their own preparations, for they leave on their mission soon."

"To one of the Balancer villages?" Aranel asked at once. "Where? What are they going to do?"

Meizan resisted the urge to laugh. Wasn't Aranel supposed to be a spy? How desperate had the Preservation been?

"The details are yet to be decided," Zenyra said. "But rest that thought. Today, I plan to teach something I expect will be of far more interest to you than the villages."

"Oh?" Aranel asked. "What would that be?"

"Why, a new technique." Zenyra's eyes crinkled. "Complete soul projection."

The words didn't mean much to Meizan, but Aranel had begun circling his thumbs over his index fingers in that weird, obsessive habit of his.

"That's a forbidden technique," Aranel said. "The Preservation outlawed it centuries ago."

Zenyra gave a short laugh. "You must have realized, Aranel, that we Balancers do not concern ourselves much with what the Preservation forbid and outlaw."

She turned to Meizan and Aina and said, "You are used to partial soul projection—casting a portion of your chitrons outside your body each time you bond to and channel the environment. Complete projection takes this a step further. It involves casting the entirety of your soul, with every last chitron, outside your body and into, for instance, the sky. Or a rock. A successful complete projection will render your body comatose, but you will regain consciousness and normal bodily function immediately upon your soul's return."

"And why," Meizan asked, "are you teaching us to stuff our souls into rocks?"

While the rest of the Balancer techniques had been useful, he couldn't wrap his head around this one.

At his question, Zenyra flicked her hand. One of Meizan's knives flew from its scabbard and hovered in front of his eyes for a split second before impaling his keiza.

Searing pain ripped through Meizan's skull. He turned to Zenyra in anger. "What the hell was that for?"

To his right, both Aina and Aranel collapsed to their knees, knives piercing each of their keiza. "Is this strictly necessary?" Aranel gasped.

"Try to channel," Zenyra said. "Call upon your chitrons. Use them to heal yourself, hurt me, do whatever you must to escape this situation."

Still not understanding the purpose of this exercise, Meizan gritted his teeth through the pain and reached for his chitrons.

Nothing.

He tried again, repeating the words Hiraval had taught them. *Clear your mind. Empty your heart. Summon your soul.*

Still nothing. Every time Meizan tried to activate his chitrons, the pain knocked him back with angry spikes of agony that lanced through his skull. It subsided slightly when Zenyra placed a warm palm on his forehead, wrenched the knife free, and stitched together his broken skin.

But even as the pain faded, Meizan's chitrons slipped from his grasp, any attempt to draw upon them like sucking water from an empty well.

"What have you done?" Aranel croaked.

"I have suppressed your chitrons," Zenyra said. She waved her hands, and the knives fell from Aranel's and Aina's foreheads. "Piercing the keiza will inhibit its function. Even once the obstruction is removed, it will take a couple hours before you regain full chitronic control. In that time, should you be captured—by a hostile clan, or worse, one of Kaldrav's soldiers . . ." She lowered her voice. "They have methods, those soldiers. Methods designed to chip away at your sanity, turn your every thought dark. Methods that could crush even the purest Balancer."

Meizan felt a shiver at these words. He thought of Kaldrav's torture pools in Agakor, with cold that scorched worse than fire. An hour inside those pools was said to make one's skin blister until it bled pus, which would then freeze over into a shroud.

Is that what befell Chief Kanna? What will befall everyone in this hideout if his army decides to attack?

"Projection is your last resort to protect your soul," Zenyra said. "If all other methods fail, if you find yourself trapped and with no way to channel . . . projection is the one method that will get you, or at least your soul, temporarily out of danger. Your powers will be limited outside your body. But you will be able to flee, call for help, or at least escape whatever trauma your captor decides to inflict."

"Would that not directly expose our chitrons to those of Malin?" Aranel asked, wiping the blood from his forehead. "Our bodies shield us from their influence. Without them we would corrupt within hours, if not sooner!"

For once, the nagging upper had a point. Based on what Meizan had learned the past two moons about that First Principle of whatever they called it, projecting into Malin would be more dangerous than channeling—at least for a flake like Aranel, with his featherlight soul. Meizan's own soul wasn't at risk, and projection sounded like the single most useful technique invented.

I could sweep the realm for the chief, he thought, fingers drumming against the hilt of his sword. *With her channeling abilities, she could have escaped the lavafall, though there's a high chance she's been captured. But I could find her. I could send my soul to Agakor. To Kaufgar. Search every one of Kaldrav's bleeding prison cells.* Hope swelled in his chest. *I could even search for the rest of Kanjallen!*

Beside him, Aina rocked on her heels, face set with determination.

"Most Balancers have gone years in Malin without having to rely on projection," Zenyra said. "But even knowing the risk it carries, I must teach it to you. Although I hope you are never in a situation where you have to use it."

Burn that, Meizan thought. He would project the hell out of his body the second he figured out how. This technique alone made the past two moons in Incaraz worth it.

THE SKY HAD darkened to a smoky gray when Meizan sagged to the ground. He had regained function of his keiza a few minutes ago, for all the bleeding good it did.

Projection wasn't exactly a channeling technique. While it required intense control over the movement of one's chitrons, it didn't involve bonding them or manipulating their form. It wasn't even a physical technique, though it had left Meizan feeling as if he'd run up and down Merumarth a hundred times over while an army of termites gnawed at his skull.

All projection involved was shoving his soul out of his keiza, which in practice was a lot tougher than it sounded.

"It's unnatural," Aranel complained, rubbing at his temples. "Tearing my soul from my body. It's not right. It's not meant to happen."

"I almost got it out," Aina said. "But at the end, I felt something pulling me back, anchoring my soul to my body."

"That is your chitronic core," Zenyra informed her. "Like the nucleus of an atom, it binds together your chitrons. Breaking it is the most difficult part of projection, and the sensation can be unpleasant."

"Unpleasant?" Aina shuddered. "It felt as if I were cutting myself open from the inside."

"I can see why the Preservation outlawed this," Aranel said. "Something so painful ought to be illegal."

Zenyra pursed her lips. "Their reservations are less with projection itself and more with its potential for exploitation. Abuse of the technique occurred widely during Kal Ekana."

Kal Ekana?

The words stirred memories of old tales swapped over the Kanjallen campfire. Of Kal Ekana, the glorious One Realm Era that existed before the Great Toranic Separation. A single realm containing souls of all spins, each granted an equal chance at life.

Human death existed during Kal Ekana. It was a wondrous thing—killing one's body but never one's soul. Legend said that after death, a soul could reincarnate and life could continue in a new body with fresh memories. But death had ceased after the Great Toranic Separation. Kal Ekana remained nothing more than a myth. Their reality was Kal Charana, a universe split into four.

"What was projection used for during Kal Ekana?" Aranel asked.

"The less spoken of that, the better," Zenyra replied.

"Then why are you teaching us? If it's so horrid and vile?"

"Aranel," Meizan snapped. "If you don't want to learn, go surf on a cloud or something." He turned to Zenyra. "How long does it take to figure this out?"

"It will come with time," Zenyra said. "Projection is one of the most difficult techniques you will ever attempt. But until you master it, I am afraid I cannot permit you to leave Incaraz."

"What?" Aina and Aranel exclaimed at the same time.

"Worry not," Zenyra said. "Even your seniors only managed it recently, and you have many moons of training ahead."

Many moons. Would they have that long? It was a matter of time until Kaldrav decided to attack Incaraz. Meizan needed to make the most of every last minute, perfecting this technique under Zenyra's tutelage before shit came crumbling down.

The three of them practiced late into the night, long after Zenyra had left them. Hiraval stopped by to drop off a basket of food. Meizan lay on his back, munching a bar of sugar and nuts wrapped in waxed paper, too exhausted to eat anything more.

"What do you think Zenyra was referring to earlier?" Aina asked. "When she mentioned potentially dangerous uses of projection?"

"I can think of plenty," Aranel said. "Eavesdropping on Preservation Advisories. Smuggling your soul into private residences. Spying on someone in the bathhouse."

"Interesting how your mind works," Aina said. "Pervert."

"I'm not— I wouldn't—" Aranel spluttered. "I'd never do any of that *myself*!"

"There's worse that could happen with projection," Meizan said. "Like souls swapping bodies."

"Is it possible to project into other living things?" Aina asked, to which Meizan shrugged. "Even so, how is that worse than spying?"

"Imagine being stuck as Aranel for a day," Meizan said. He polished off his bar and folded the wrapper into the shape of a throwing star. "I'd rather stuff my soul into a kapizer."

"I might not mind," Aina mused. "It'd be nice to experience that level of chitronic control, and he does have nice—" She stopped, eyes going wide, and shoved the remainder of her bar into her mouth.

Aranel propped himself up on his elbows and turned to Meizan in indignation. "Why, for the love of Sherka, would you prefer being one of those wretched monkeys over me?"

"At least their spines are useful. What can your hair do beyond smacking your opponent in the middle of a spar?"

Aranel's eyebrow twitched. "You're just upset I won last night! And I'll have you know, my victory was—oh, curse you!" He broke off angrily as Meizan flung the paper throwing star in his face.

Meizan cracked his neck, rolling to his feet. He would master this technique, even if it tore him apart.

Once he did, he would have all the pieces—precision channeling, healing, and projection—to survive Malin on his own and rescue his chief.

CHAPTER THIRTEEN

❦

Under the Banyan

INA HAD HARDLY slept the past two weeks since Zenyra had taught them soul projection. More than one morning she'd woken up in the clearing next to her dozing teammates, to realize they'd all passed out from exhaustion.

She closed her eyes now and pinched her wrist to stay awake.

"Come on, Aina," Zenyra said. "Visualize your chitrons. Feel them within you."

Aina nodded, taking note of the various flows and pushing them through her throbbing keiza. She forced out the first few waves of chitrons, but the resistance increased sharply at the three-quarters point until it felt as if she were trying to shove a mountain out of her skull.

The remaining quarter of Aina's chitrons refused to budge. They stuck to her body as if they were extensions of her skeleton, their rage at being forced out manifesting in an excruciating ache directly under her keiza.

"You have reached your chitronic core." Zenyra's voice sounded faint to Aina's ears. "Do not give up now. Push a bit harder."

Aina clenched her fists, the pain in her skull increasing tenfold and spreading to every nerve ending. She was afire, her body immolating from within.

Come on, Aina screamed at her soul. She forced it through her keiza, breaking past the invisible barrier that bound it to her body. *Bleeding, good-for-nothing keiza! Let me through, damn it!*

She recalled a time, over a year past, when she had pounded against the stone slabs that trapped her behind a silver torana. *Let me through!* Aina had screamed back then, but her mother had ignored her pleas, left her all alone in Mayana. Aina could find her, if only she mastered projection, if only she got her soul through this blasted barrier—

Aina let out a voiceless cry as she barreled toward Aranel. He seemed too exhausted to react. Aina flailed, bracing herself for the impact.

It never came.

She passed straight through Aranel, and the tree behind him, to find herself surrounded by a ring of knotted brown. Panic flooded her until Aina realized what had just happened.

I did it! I projected!

Aina floated through the trees in the thicket. She had made it a couple of feet when she felt a tug directing her back to the training ground. She saw Zenyra holding her limp body while both Aranel and Meizan looked around in confusion.

It was a surreal sort of feeling, watching them—watching herself—and Aina drifted closer to her own body.

"Did she really do it?" Aranel asked. "Aina? Can you hear us? Where are you?"

"She is close," Zenyra said. "Aina is not yet advanced enough to project more than a few feet, nor can she contact us with her soul. Nonetheless, she pulled off a successful projection."

"How the hell . . ." Meizan shook his head in disbelief. "Are you sure she didn't just pass out?"

"I heard that!" Aina cried as she snapped back into her body.

She didn't know how it happened. It was as if something magnetic had pulled her soul through her keiza until it was firmly lodged in its rightful place.

Aina sat up and flexed her shoulders. Her body felt fine. *She* felt fine—although lightheaded—from the exertion of projecting, and also from the stunned looks on Aranel's and Meizan's faces.

Neither of them had projected yet, despite practicing as much as her. For the first time since coming to Incaraz, she had beaten her teammates hollow.

"Aina, I am amazed." Zenyra clapped her on the shoulder. "We have never, in the history of the Balancers, had anyone manage a successful projection only ten weeks into their training."

"How?" Aranel asked. "How can she be so good at this, and so—so—"

"Useless," Meizan said. "So useless at other techniques."

"Perhaps it was luck?"

"Maybe her keiza's stopped working again."

"Or maybe," Aina cut in with a grin, "I'm more talented than the both of you losers combined."

The training lesson ended shortly after, once Meizan declared he wanted to spar and dragged Aranel with him.

Sore losers, Aina thought, watching them leave.

"Seems like this keiza of yours is a blessing in disguise," Zenyra said with a smile.

"That's why I could project?" Aina asked. "Because I'm defective?"

"Unique," Zenyra corrected, leaning forward. Aina held up her bangs so Zenyra could examine her keiza. "And yes, that is precisely why, although I beseech you to not project out of Incaraz just yet. There are many things I have left to teach you."

"Like what?"

"Like how to extend the range of your projection. You will need that in order to find your mother. And how to channel remotely when outside your body."

"I could do that?" Aina exclaimed.

Long-range projection. Remote channeling. The possibilities were endless. *I could find Mama and drag her all the way to Incaraz.*

"There is also the matter of fixing your keiza," Zenyra continued. "I require more time to figure out the precise amount of concentration needed. It must be precise, you see, for everything to work. I do not want to risk harming you in the process."

"Couldn't you do that after I found my mother?"

"I could," Zenyra said. "But were you to project outside Incaraz, it would change your chitronic spin, and even a slight change would force me to recalculate everything."

"Right," Aina said. Zenyra had been spending a couple hours each week observing her keiza at length, occasionally probing it with her chitrons and jotting down notes. It seemed wrong to let that all go to waste. "But if you fix my keiza, won't that make it harder for me to project?"

"Harder, but not impossible. The other Balancers have done it, and the first projection is always the most difficult." Before Aina could protest further, Zenyra added, "You need only project once to find your mother, Aina. But you will channel for the rest of your life."

"All right, then," Aina relented. "When will you teach me long-range projection?"

"Not today," Zenyra said with a laugh. "Do not overexert yourself, Aina. Your mother has waited over a year to meet you. She can wait a few weeks more. Perhaps a dip in the springs might refresh you."

AINA RETURNED FROM the hot springs that evening to find Aranel outside her room, fidgeting with something behind his back.

"I guess you want tips on projection," Aina said. She tried not to appear too pleased he'd sought her out. "There's not much I can help you with, as it turns out I'm a natural." She pointed at her keiza.

"Ah," Aranel said. "That's both a blessing and a curse, I suppose. But that's not why I'm here, Aina. I needed a favor."

"From *me*?"

"Yes." Aranel licked his lips. "But before that . . ."

He held out her pouch of smashed rock. Aina grabbed it, hugging it to her. "Where did you find this? I didn't realize I'd lost it!"

Aranel hesitated, then gestured at the pouch. "Open it."

"Why?"

"Just open it."

Aina did, peering inside. She pulled out one of the rocks and her stomach clenched uncomfortably. A little gazarou figurine sat on her palm, perfectly pieced together. It had been exquisitely channeled, each strand of fur curling gracefully at the tip and its fangs barely visible underneath a benign smile.

Aina tossed it back in and pulled out another piece. A nagamor, deadly eyes lidded, its tail feathers fanned out in a striking display. She threw it back in, then fished out a third figurine. A manikai, the sea turtle's once-serrated shell now smoothed to a gentle bump, its sharp tusks whittled down.

Hot anger flared within Aina. *How dare he! How dare he lay his hands upon them, that presumptuous, meddling—*

"Do you like them?"

Aina raised her head at the tentative question and blinked back tears.

Aranel looked at her hopefully, his eyes bright as a sunlit forest. "They were broken, so I thought I'd . . ." He stopped once he caught her expression. "What's wrong, Aina?"

"You—" Aina swallowed, the words dying at the tip of her tongue.

You useless jerk! Don't try to fix things you don't understand!

Because he'd *ruined* them, every last one. He'd remade them into something they were never meant to be. Removed all traces of her mother's channeling with his bleeding Mayani sensibilities.

But she couldn't bring herself to say any of that. Not with Aranel regarding her the way he was, tender and expectant, as if nothing mattered more to him than her liking his gift.

"You don't seem happy." Aranel's face fell. "I messed up. I should never have touched them."

"They look different," Aina managed. "Different from how my mother made them."

"I'm so sorry, Aina." Aranel took a step toward her. "I'm such a fool."

Yes, you are! Aina wanted to scream. She wanted to throw the rocks in his face. If it were anyone else she would have. But it was Aranel, and he'd tried to do something nice for her, and he was looking at her so *softly.*

And as Aina peered inside the pouch, taking in the prettily carved figures—so elegant, so refined, so like Aranel himself—

her anger melted, leaving nothing but a strange fluttery warmth in her stomach.

"I like them." Aina forced herself to smile. "They'll take some getting used to. But they're better whole than broken, and I couldn't have mended them myself."

"You don't mean that, Aina . . ."

"Yes, I do. I like them, and I'm glad you fixed them." If she said it enough, maybe she could convince herself. "You needed a favor from me?" she added, remembering. "What is it?"

"Ah. That . . ." Aranel's brow wrinkled. "I was, ah, going to ask if you'd join us for dinner under the banyan tonight. Taralei was grumbling about how we're so busy practicing that we never eat with them anymore."

"Oh." Aina felt a wave of affection toward Aranel and his cousin. "Yes. Yes, I will."

She followed Aranel across the lake. Taralei greeted them cheerily and pulled Aina over to sit next to her.

"I believe congratulations are in order," Hiraval said, eyes twinkling as he ladled a liberal helping of canned fishbone stew into Aina's bowl. "You completed your first soul projection."

"And broke the Balancer record at that!" Reimi clapped her on the shoulder. "Well done!"

"From now on, I shall place my bets on you," Taralei declared, then held out a hand. "But before that, pay up, Aina. Your teammates sparred today. No surprises who won."

"You bet on *Aranel*," Meizan scoffed. "Have you learned nothing since coming here?"

Aina flushed, digging out a coin from her pocket and pressing it into Taralei's hand. Across the table, Aranel shot her a tiny smile that sent her stomach swooping.

This is getting ridiculous, she told herself, taking a gulp of cool water.

She hadn't come to Malin to get flustered by a boy or pulled into a betting ring. Yet, as Aina watched the other Balancers—a beet-red Aranel yelling something at Meizan amidst Taralei's teasing and Reimi's laughter, while Hiraval observed them all with detached amusement—something tugged at her chest, rooting her to this spot and to this crowded wooden table under the banyan.

She was comfortable here. Comfortable and content in a way she'd never felt running through the realm with her mother.

I could stay, Aina thought, watching Meizan pull Aranel into a headlock that caused the latter to spit out his stew. *Once I master long-range projection and find Mama, we can come back and live here together. Here, or in one of the Balancer villages, since that's where the rest of them will be going.*

Taralei produced her pack of cards and began dealing as Hiraval and Reimi separated the two brawling idiots. Aina joined the game but paid the cards no notice, her mind painting a vivid future she'd never dared to dream of.

We'll have our own hut in the village, Aina decided. *Nothing fancy. A small hut made of stone by a stream filled with fish. They could be skunkfish for all I care, as long as they're edible and we don't have to starve.*

Aina's hand found the stone nagamor in her pouch, its form so unfamiliar, so different from how she'd known it, yet undeniably whole.

We won't have to run anymore, Mama. We'll have a home.

CHAPTER FOURTEEN

@

The Sunken Barrier

*I*T WAS A well-known phenomenon in Mayana that the petals of Kirnos's great lotus changed color with each passing
season. The white of winter blushed into the pink of spring
before brightening to scarlet in the last days of summer.

Aranel thought of those petals now, letting the image of his
beloved kingdom fill his mind. He imagined he *was* the lotus—
his body its ever-changing petals . . . and his chitrons what lay
within: the rivers, the pastures, and the cluster of thatched yellow huts.

Aranel exhaled and began emptying the lotus. First to go were
the rivers, draining in a great surge of water. Next went the pastures, blades of grass ripping from their roots.

He was close to pulling off a projection. He could feel it. He
had to do it, if he wanted to search for the Balancer villages.

Aranel's original plan had been to seek Aina's help. But after his
attempt to fix her rock figures had ended in disaster, he couldn't

bring himself to ask Aina for anything. And his other teammate would likelier insult Aranel than ever agree to help him.

Come on, pleaded Aranel to his chitrons. *Out with you!*

The lotus was near empty now, but the huts were always the hardest to remove. Aranel's chitrons tugged at his consciousness, twittering and chittering their disapproval.

Be quiet, he told them. *Get out.*

He was down to his core. The last few chitrons. The last thatched hut. One with square windows and a raised veranda all around.

That's my hut. Mother's wicker blinds hanging from the windows. And Sam's favorite swing on the veranda, the one we always fought over as children.

How wrong it felt to uproot this hut from the lotus. It was a part of him, after all. It was home.

But it's an empty hut now, Aranel reminded himself. His parents and brother were in Paramos. And if Aranel didn't give Seirem what he needed, he'd never live with them again.

There was a bond between his soul and his body, but Aranel could break it if he tried. He shaped his chitrons into a blade and hacked at the hut's foundations. It felt deeply and instinctively wrong, but Aranel had no choice. He hacked away, until the clay walls cracked—

And then he lurched forward until he was floating in thin air. Below, his own form slumped against the base of the gold-trunked banyan tree on the islet at the center of Incaraz's lake.

It worked!

Aranel felt the pull of his soul trying to return to its proper container. He resisted and forced himself to float downward through the islet. What a surreal experience it was, not being attached to his body. Aranel drifted through the rock as if it were water.

He felt something hard, a part of the rock even his soul could not enter.

How was that possible? He was intangible. No physical obstacle should stop him.

And yet it did. For it was no physical barrier but a chitronic one, similar to the shield around Incaraz. If he looked carefully, he could see it: a diaphanous film stretched beneath the lake's surface. Try as he might, Aranel's soul could not pass.

That's odd.

The shield around Incaraz made sense, but what purpose did this second, sunken barrier serve? Zenyra had never mentioned it before. And while the first shield had been designed to let him through, this one remained unyielding as the torana to Paramos.

Someone's sealed off the bottom of the crater, realized Aranel with a jolt. Most likely Zenyra, since none other had the skill to create such a barrier. *But why? Could she be hiding something?*

The sound of voices above distracted Aranel from his observations. He drifted up to find Taralei and Aina standing over his limp body.

"He did it," said Taralei. "And in just over a moon. Guess Sam's not the only one in our family with talent."

"Meizan is going to be pissed," said Aina. "I practiced with him this morning, and he hasn't even come close."

Aranel listened to the exchange with glee and followed Taralei and Aina as they wandered across the lake. The pair sat down by its crenulated shoreline, and Taralei caught Aina's limp body as she completed a projection. Aranel watched, entranced, as wobbly lines began carving themselves onto the ground. Aina returned to her body a few moments later, breathing heavily.

"Wonderful, Aina!" gushed Taralei. "Although I haven't the slightest idea what you were trying to write."

Aina's already learned remote channeling? Aranel stared at the carvings and discerned something that could have passed as the letter *A*. And a line next to it that might be an *I*.

It was a pity about Aina's keiza. Without the irregularity, Aranel surmised, her chitronic abilities might even surpass his own.

A tug at his soul dragged Aranel back to the banyan.

Not yet, he admonished, resisting the inexorable pull of his body.

Aranel floated back underwater. Once again, he pressed against the mysterious chitronic barrier. This time he followed it through the lake, into a stone passageway. The water around him took on a familiar shimmer, and Aranel realized this passageway led to the hot springs.

A dizzying energy pulsed through Aranel as he flowed with the current. It trickled into his chitrons and shook them so hard he feared they'd burst free of his soul.

Strange, thought Aranel giddily as he floated back toward the banyan tree. Perhaps it was a coincidence, but the chitronic barrier below the lake extended to the springs. Aranel still hadn't figured out the mysterious substance in the spring water.

But there was *something* in there that had triggered a strong reaction in his soul. The same thing he'd observed Seirem sipping from his flask over a moon ago, although the Preserver had been careful with his drinking habits since.

Aranel snapped back into his body and opened his eyes to see Taralei leaning over him.

"It's about time you returned," she said. "I was worried you'd forgotten where you kept your body . . ." She trailed off, her expression turning to wonder.

"What is it?" asked Aranel. He stood and stretched his limbs.

Taralei gave him a small smile. "It's just, I never noticed how bright your keiza had gotten. For a second, I thought you were your brother."

ARANEL WAS DISTRACTED later that night as he made his report to Seirem at the golden torana. The question of the spring water remained at the tip of his tongue, but it seemed rather rude to bring it up again.

"When did you say the next mission is scheduled for?" asked Seirem.

"In two days," answered Aranel, taken aback at the realization. He'd been so occupied with trying to master projection that he'd forgotten about the seniors' mission.

"That coincides with the preponed dates of the Advisory, as we suspected," said Seirem. "I shall monitor the system myself over the next week. If we sense another disturbance soon, we can confirm it has something to do with the missions." The Preserver's expression turned grim, creases lining his forehead. "On that note, I have a theory regarding the disturbances."

Aranel nodded, and Seirem lowered his voice. "I believe they are being caused by erasures."

"Erasures?" The word sent a tremor through Aranel's chitrons. "Why would you say that?"

"There is an enormous amount of energy holding together the chitrons of one's soul and binding the chitronic core," said Seirem. "During erasure, this energy is released all at once, registering as a small explosion in the chitronic system. I have been monitoring the system for decades, and I first noticed these explosions originating in Narakh. But recently, I observed similar disturbances in Malin as well, which leads me to believe—"

"That the Balancer missions are triggering erasures?" Aranel crossed his arms, fingers digging into his elbows.

Erasures only occurred when a soul lost its own will to exist. If subjected to enough violence and pain over a prolonged period, a soul might give up. Aranel found it impossible to imagine Zenyra or any of the other Balancers engaging in something so odious.

"Malin's at war, Lord Seirem," said Aranel. "Meizan told me Kaldrav's soldiers spent the last few years terrorizing the villages and torturing those who resisted them. I don't know about—the lowest realm." He couldn't bring himself to utter the name aloud. "But is it not natural to assume that, rather than any Balancer activities, Kaldrav's crimes are causing the erasures?"

"It is possible, although the timing still concerns me. I need you to monitor those villages, Aranel." Seirem lowered his voice to a whisper. "Have you mastered *that* technique yet?"

"You mean complete soul projection?" asked Aranel, and Seirem winced. The Preserver would never mention the name aloud, but Aranel had no interest in his attempt at plausible deniability. "I managed it for the first time today, but I can't travel too far from my body yet."

"I am sure that will come with practice. Soon, Aranel, you will be able to search Malin unhindered."

Aranel clenched his fists. The idea of projecting outside Incaraz terrified him. How long would his soul last before reversing its spin?

"Fear not, my boy," said Seirem. "Three moons in Malin, and your keiza has yet to dim. On the contrary, it shines brighter than ever. By searching the villages and discerning the cause of these erasures, you will be doing the universe a great service." He spread his arms, invoking the Aria of Ascension: "'Amongst many a good and generous deed, naught else is nobler than helping souls in need.'"

"Right," muttered Aranel. *Then instead of reciting blessed poetry all the time, why don't you come down here and search for the villages yourself? Learn an illegal technique or two while you're at it.*

He recalled his brother's warnings—that Seirem was using him and of Preservation politics—then briefly considered confronting the man. But Seirem was Paramosi and had been for longer than Samarel.

Just a couple more moons. Both Seirem and Taralei had commented on his keiza getting brighter. *Whatever I'm doing here is lightening my soul. Soon I'll ascend, and Sam will realize I was right all along.*

His eyes fell on Seirem's hands, empty of his usual hipflask. He still needed to report the presence of the sunken barrier, but something held him back.

Aranel gave a stiff bow. "If I may take my leave, Lord Seirem. We have a feast of sorts, to celebrate the upcoming mission. I need to hide the wine, lest my cousin drink herself into oblivion."

"As expected of Taralei," said Seirem with a fond smile. "Always a delight at parties, that girl. Do try to enjoy yourself as well, Aranel. Toranic Law would not object to a drink or two." He reached through the torana and patted Aranel's shoulder. "May your soul spin straight and swift."

THE NEXT EVENING, Aranel found his cousin under the banyan tree sorting through a large wooden crate. Hiraval and Aina were with Taralei, stacking glasses into a large pyramid.

"Ran," greeted Taralei. "Come, we're finalizing the refreshments for tonight." She held out a bottle filled with a clear gold liquid. "Would you like to sample some in advance? It's Amaratisian wine, courtesy of Hiraval."

She began pouring a glass without waiting for his response. Aranel accepted it, and Aina held out an eager hand.

"She's not of age," said Aranel, but Taralei ignored him and poured a second glass of the glistening drink.

Aina lifted it to take a tentative sip. "This is divine!" she declared. "What's this sweetness?"

"A single drop of holy nectar from the depths of Mir Amaratis," said Hiraval. "It is the finest wine in all of Mayana, and you mustn't let Reimi tell you any different."

"I didn't know priests were allowed to drink," said Aranel. He'd seen Taralei and Reimi sipping plum wine some evenings, but Hiraval never indulged with them.

"I am no priest, but a Balancer," replied Hiraval. "And tonight is a special occasion."

"Are you nervous about your mission?" asked Aina.

"There is nothing to be nervous about, Aina. We have mastered the skills necessary for survival, and Zenyra believes us ready."

"And you trust her?" asked Aranel, ignoring Aina's scandalized look.

"Why of course," said Hiraval. "I trust Zenyra with my soul. She is a Paramosi after all, and purer than even the Preservation."

"How do you know that?" pressed Aranel. "Have you compared the brightness of their keiza?"

"Have you not heard the stories?" Hiraval dropped his voice. "Of Zenyra's youth? How she befriended one of the megarya, a descendant of Sorken Himself?"

"What?" Aranel dropped his wineglass, catching it with a tendril of energy just before it shattered against the ground.

"Are you drunk already?" asked Taralei. "There is something called pacing yourself, Aranel. Not that I'd expect you to understand, given how you drained your chitrons during the first leg of the junior cloudsurfing qualifiers."

"I was nine," said Aranel, then turned to Hiraval. "But a megarya? Truly?"

He could not believe his ears. Native to Paramos, the winged dolphins were noble beasts. Very few were said to have survived Kal Ekana, and those who would approach a human were even rarer. A megarya's presence was a blessing in itself, given only to those with the purest of souls.

"I never asked Zenyra about it. But word in Amaratir is that they became dear friends," said Hiraval in a hushed voice. "The beast even accompanied Zenyra on some of her travels."

"That's amazing," said Aranel.

The revelation, if true, cast doubt onto the Preservation's claims that Zenyra was dangerous. The megarya were intelligent and could not be fooled like humans. Perhaps Zenyra had been young back then, but who were they to doubt a megarya's judgment?

Besides, Zenyra was not the only one with secrets. Seirem's hipflask had been noticeably absent their past few meetings. The Preserver claimed it contained youth tonic yet now refused to drink from it in Aranel's presence. And he'd spoken of erasures—erasures!—implying they were linked to the Balancers, all the while ignoring Aranel's warnings about Kaldrav.

Frustrated, Aranel lifted his wineglass and downed the contents in one gulp. A moment later, Taralei snatched it away, pouring him a refill with a saccharine smile.

Aranel lost track of how many glasses he drank over the next hour. The glowing flowers of the banyan flickered like dancing fireflies.

Aranel reached out to grab at the blossoms, his fingers slipping through the cool air as he stumbled forward. He hit something hard and straightened to meet Meizan's unimpressed gaze.

"Lightweight," drawled Meizan. "Why am I not surprised?"

Aranel stepped back, cheeks burning. "I don't drink often, but that incorrigible cousin of mine . . ." He shook his head and gestured at Meizan's empty glass. "You liked the wine?"

"It's weak," said Meizan. "And too damn sweet."

"Stop complaining." Aina sidled up to them. "I bet Malini liquor tastes like piss. I wouldn't know because I've never drunk it. But this stuff, this stuff is magical." She emptied her wine in three large gulps and grinned widely.

"How much have you had?" Aranel tried to look stern. "Are you sixteen yet, Aina? When's your birthday?"

"I don't know." Aina's smile faded. "Mama—she never—we never had time for birthdays."

"If you're fifteen, that makes you underage," said Aranel. "It's against Kirnosi law to—"

"Oh, will you shut it already!" Aina groaned. "Kirnosi law, Toranic Law, all you ever do is talk about the bleeding law. You're lucky you're so pretty, Aranel, or no one would listen to a word that comes out of your priggish, prissy mouth."

Aranel's retort was cut off by Hiraval, ever the peacemaker. "For all we know, Aina could already be sixteen," said Hiraval. "I know you mean well, Aranel, but for tonight you could take a break from all your well-meaning and lighten up a bit."

"See, Aranel." Aina snickered. "Even the ex-priest finds you a prude." She turned to Hiraval, sobering. "Be careful once you leave. You're a good channeler, but some of the Malini . . ." Aina chewed her lip and seemed to struggle for words. "Just be careful. Prayers won't help you here."

"I am stronger than you think, Aina." Hiraval reached down to pat her head. "And not so naive as to rely on prayer in Azyaka's realm."

"May your soul spin straight and swift," said Aina. It was the first time Aranel had heard her utter the phrase.

"Do stop," entreated Taralei, pushing herself between Hiraval and Aina. "The night is still young! Let us speak of more compelling subjects!"

"Such as?" asked Aina as Hiraval wandered off to talk with Reimi.

"Well, it's my last night here." Taralei's eyes twinkled as she raised her glass. "I thought it best to speak freely so I can leave Incaraz with no regrets."

"I think *I* shall regret whatever it is you're about to say," said Aranel.

"It's not for you, Ran, but your teammate." Taralei turned to Meizan. "I don't suppose you've been told this much in Malin, but you realize you're rather handsome?"

Aranel nearly choked on his wine. Taralei thumped him on the back, then carried on. "Reimi and I were wondering, did you have a lover before you joined? Do Malini take lovers? Does the concept of marriage exist in this realm? Surely your clan must have had a wedding now and then."

Aranel continued to splutter and choke while Meizan looked bored. "Not that I know of," he said.

"No romance, then," noted Taralei. "But what about, you know—even Malini must have basic needs? Or does procreation work differently in this realm?"

Aina burst into giggles, and Meizan shot Taralei a look of undiluted scorn.

"Taralei," exploded Aranel, regaining control of his voice. "You're embarrassing yourself!"

"How sweet of you to care, but I'm not in the least bit embarrassed," said Taralei, but she allowed Aranel to drag her away.

"Has another soul taken over your body?" he demanded, once they were a safe distance from Meizan and Aina. "What were you thinking, throwing yourself on him like that?"

"I wasn't throwing myself on him." Taralei rolled her eyes. "He *is* nice looking now that he's been taking regular baths. And

Reimi and I were talking earlier about whether or not the concept of love exists in Malin. Because if the Malini are capable of feeling love, it means they ought to be able to ascend, don't you think?"

"A-as if I'd ever think about—about Malini like that!" cried Aranel, his face aflame. "We're here to help the Malini, Taralei, not speculate on their love lives. Have some shame, will you?"

"Prude. Just because *you've* never had a lover . . ."

Aranel raked a hand through his hair in frustration. Everyone, from Aina to Hiraval to his own cousin, seemed to think him a prude these days. He struggled for clarity amidst his alcohol-induced haze and forced himself to focus on more important matters.

"Listen, Taralei." Aranel grasped her shoulders. "Aina was right. Malin is dangerous. You may have mastered the Balancer techniques, but Kaldrav's army is still out there. There were nearly forty previous Balancers, but it worries me we've never heard from any of them."

"Oh, calm down." Taralei waved him off. "Zenyra's in regular contact with the villages. Besides, I won't be alone. I don't know about Hiraval and Reimi, but the village I'm going to is being run by Eniya. You remember him, Ran? He's Sam's old friend from Tahamur."

"What do you mean you don't know about Hiraval and Reimi?" Aranel's grip on her shoulder tightened. "Are the three of you not going to be together?"

"Not at first. Zenyra wants us to stay with more experienced Balancers until we get the hang of things, so they're being sent to a village south of mine."

Everything Taralei was saying made logical sense. Yet with every word, Aranel's stomach turned until he felt queasy with fear.

"That's the wine," said Taralei once Aranel told her. "It's

going to be *fine*, Ran. I knew what I was getting into when I joined the Balancers."

"If you'd like to return to Kirnos, I could sneak you out. Or forget Mayana, there's a torana to Paramos nearby. It's perfectly reasonable, and I'm sure Hiraval and Reimi would understand."

"Aranel." Taralei sounded uncharacteristically serious. "I appreciate your concern, but I *want* to do this. I *want* to help, to do something meaningful with my life. That's why I joined the Balancers instead of ascending in the first place."

She extricated herself from his grip to pull him into a hug.

"I'm worried for you," said Aranel as he thought about Seirem and his veiled warnings: *unaccounted disappearances, disturbances in the chitronic system, erasures.* "I don't know why, but I'm worried, and confused, and—"

He bit his tongue. For a moment, Aranel considered spilling the truth about his mission. But even if Taralei was his cousin, she'd been a Balancer longer than he had. She could very well take his secret and run straight to Zenyra.

And so Aranel said nothing and returned Taralei's hug with a heavy heart.

"Seems you'll be missing me a lot more than I expected," said Taralei with a grin.

"Seems so," said Aranel as he followed her back to the banyan.

The tree glowed bright as the Mayani moon, casting an ethereal light about the crater. The Balancers gathered in a circle around Zenyra, their leader's face luminous under the blue blossoms.

"This is our last night with three of our number," said Zenyra. "Hiraval, Reimi, and Taralei will leave Incaraz shortly to fulfill their part in our legacy. Let us toast them by repeating the maxim of the Balancers."

"We have a maxim?" whispered Aina to Aranel. "Since when?"

Aranel shrugged, watching Zenyra raise a glass and nod to the three seniors in turn. "May these words give you power and conviction," she said, "even when times are troubled."

Aranel picked up his own glass as Zenyra began reciting. Her voice rang through the air like a gong, rich and unwavering.

"We lived in fear of Toranic Law, our lives bound within its shackles. We feared corruption from the darkness, so we chose to rot in the light. But remember"—Zenyra's voice rose—"those are selfish fears. And we, the Balancers, do not fear."

She clinked her glass against Taralei's, then Reimi's, and finally Hiraval's.

"We descend to help those whom Toranic Law has forsaken," proclaimed Zenyra. "We shall give them light where the universe gives them naught but darkness!"

"Hear! Hear!" said Hiraval. His eyes brimmed with resolve. Next to him, Taralei's face was set as she held her glass to Zenyra's.

"Our minds shall endure," said the three seniors in unison, repeating after their leader. "Our hearts shall stay pure. Our souls shall not tarnish."

Across from Aranel, Meizan's eyebrows had all but disappeared into his bangs. Aina, on the other hand, watched in a dazed rapture—although whether from Zenyra's words or the indecent amount of wine she had consumed, Aranel could not tell.

Aranel's gaze then fell on Zenyra's fierce countenance. She truly believed in what she was saying. And though her words could have been perceived as a slight against Toranic Law, her keiza glowed brighter than the blossoms of the banyan.

Ruled by selfish fears. Bound within the shackles of Toranic Law. Was that how Aranel had lived all this time? Was that how the Preservation lived? Zenyra lived so differently, and yet Toranic Law had not punished her. It had not dimmed her keiza or slowed the spin of her soul.

Could they both be right? The Preservation and Zenyra? Could they both be good, in their own distinct ways?

Seirem had been drinking the very liquid that flowed through the crater of Incaraz. But he'd hidden it from Aranel, just as Zenyra had with her sunken barrier.

Or could it be . . . that they're both dangerous?

He stared again at Zenyra's keiza, brilliant as Seirem's had been. Two beings with keiza so bright could not be guilty of much wrong. The more Aranel pondered it, the more his head spun, until he concluded Taralei was right: He was drunk. He would think more on this another time.

Taralei, Hiraval, and Reimi took their leave at the first light of dawn.

Aranel stood with Meizan and Aina at the rim of the crater and watched Zenyra lead the other three across the scabrous terrain. He clasped his palms on instinct, drawing forward circles over the back of his left hand with his thumb.

I'll see you once you finish your training, Taralei had said to him before she left. Yet those words sounded like a lie, or a portent of impending calamity. As Aranel watched his cousin disappear, he felt the onset of sudden dread—as if this were the last time he'd ever see her.

PART III

Blissful Paramos, the height of perfection,
idyllic, with beauty that sings.
For souls that spin in a forward direction
and swift as a hummingbird's wings.

Virtuous Mayana, of light and love,
a land rich in wealth and learning.
While not quite as swift as the realm above,
their soul-spins are rightly turning.

Wicked Malin, where fell men and their prey
both suffer a harrowing fate.
Here souls spin backward, so drenched in decay,
their chitrons afire with hate.

Accursed Narakh, damnedest of all,
obscured in darkness, steeped in sin.
Whence souls seldom rise after they fall,
iniquity fueling their spin.

-SONG OF SALVATION-
Verse VII: The Four Realms

CHAPTER FIFTEEN

◎

Sinless Lives

*F*OUR MOONS BREATHING the clean air of Incaraz, and Meizan had almost forgotten what being in Malin was like. Each ragged breath felt like the scraping of kapizer claws against his throat, each blink as if his retinas were on fire.

Was it always this bad, Meizan wondered as they cut across the craggy landscape, *or have I become spoiled in the company of uppers?*

Zenyra had interrupted their earlier training session to announce they would be visiting a Balancer village for an emergency healing mission, something Aranel seemed especially excited about. They left at night, with Zenyra setting a punishing pace through the darkness. Meizan was convinced they'd run into Kaldrav's soldiers. The Balancer leader claimed she had scouted the route earlier, but Meizan stayed on high alert.

Soldiers weren't the only enemies that lurked in the realm. Even as they moved, keeping their steps silent and forms concealed, Meizan spotted burning eyes amidst the shadows. Prowling forms more hideous than the jagged ruins of rock.

Aranel nearly jumped out of his skin when Zenyra motioned to the silhouette of a sleeping nagamor. He wedged himself between Meizan and Aina for the rest of the journey, and no number of whispered insults would make him go away.

They crossed the Muzireni on foot, using their enhanced chitronic control to walk its turbid waters, with Zenyra supporting Aina so she wouldn't slip in. Three days' travel saw them at the slopes of Ish'shai, the Gloomstone, bone tired but otherwise unscathed.

The Balancer village was just to Ish'shai's east, crammed within an enormous rift in the ground. It consisted of a network of subterranean caves that overlooked the deep fissure. According to Zenyra, the top floors contained living and healing quarters and those farther down served as storage for spare supplies.

The entire rift was suffocatingly warm and grungier than Incaraz had been. Flimsy structures extended from the caves and spilled onto the side of the cliff—canvas tents and shacks made of corrugated iron. They perched precariously at the edge like a pack of tottering drunks, looking as though the slightest disturbance would send them tumbling into the abyss.

"We are over capacity," Zenyra said. "The caves can accommodate around one hundred, but the recent violence has put us at nearly double that." She led them down the side of the rift, warning them to use precision channeling as they descended. "Disrupting the rock here would be inconvenient."

They followed Zenyra into one of the larger caves, which contained a circle of ramshackle tents around a large firepit.

"Those are the healer's quarters for this level." She gestured toward the largest tent. "There are crates inside with basic medical supplies. Get to work while I find the village heads." She turned to Aranel. "Your cousin tells me you are well-versed in healing. Take over for now, and I will be with you shortly. And take note of the brightness of their keiza."

She disappeared into a dark passageway, and the trio warily entered the tent.

Meizan didn't know what he was expecting inside, but it wasn't this: a motley group of a dozen or so children huddled on a thin mattress. They bore an assortment of injuries, from raw red burns to broken bones.

Beside him, Aranel had gone white, bringing a hand against his mouth. "What . . . how . . . who would . . ."

"Kaldrav," Meizan and Aina said at the same time.

"The soldiers must've raided their villages," Meizan said.

He refrained from adding more because Aranel looked ready to pass out.

But Meizan knew the drill. The soldiers had taken the adults and left the children. From the appearance of the injuries, Meizan didn't think the soldiers had deliberately harmed any of them—he had seen what deliberate harm in Malin was like, and these children were still in one piece. No, they had just been in the wrong place at the wrong time, their injuries an unfortunate byproduct of whatever violence had ripped apart their homes.

Most of the children were silent, except a bawling toddler who couldn't have been older than two. A couple of them played with sullen expressions, stacking together towers of twigs and fish bones. A girl in the corner was threading together bits of frayed rope into a necklace of sorts.

His fingers glowing with green energy, Aranel started for the crying toddler. Meizan grabbed Aranel's wrist and stopped him in his tracks.

"Not with chitrons." Meizan nodded to the crate. "It's too risky. I would know."

Aranel ripped open the crate and pulled out various healing ointments and supplies before picking up the tiny child. Meizan couldn't tell who was shaking more, Aranel or the toddler.

"Come on." Aina nudged Meizan. She grabbed a roll of bandages and knelt in front of a little girl with a battered leg.

"Have you seen my mama?" the little girl asked, clutching a ragged bundle of cloth to her chest. Its ends had been tied to resemble rabbit ears, and it had two round pebbles for eyes. "I want my mama."

Aina's lower lip quivered. "I'm sorry," she whispered, taking the girl's leg. "I haven't."

Meizan scanned the remaining children to figure out whose injuries were the worst. He settled on a boy with red-rimmed eyes who was prodding the ground with a thin branch.

Without a word, Meizan packed the boy's wounds with silver-bark paste, then wrapped and splinted his arm.

"When can I fight again?" the boy asked. "This is my sword arm, y'know." He brandished the branch weakly, hissing in pain.

"Not for a while, it isn't." Meizan took the branch and placed it in the boy's good hand. "Ambidexterity is useful. Learn it."

He moved on to the next victim, one of the older boys who looked to be around twelve.

As Meizan cleaned and sterilized his wound, he thought of the scared mangler he'd taken down the day he'd been separated from the chief.

He wasn't much older than this kid. Meizan glanced over at Aranel, who was tending to a girl with a stomach wound. The upper's hands shook as he dressed her injuries, his countenance wide-eyed and distraught.

Idiot. With a face like that, Aranel would only scare the children more.

How would Aranel react if he knew Meizan had knocked out that young soldier, then left him on the ground in a heap? Aina might have accepted it, but not Aranel.

Is that why he's a Mayani, and I'm stuck in Malin?

Even now, seeing the injured children, Meizan didn't feel much inside. But witnessing Aranel's reaction, Meizan wondered if there was something wrong with him. Some sort of basic human empathy that Aranel had but Meizan lacked.

Is it because his soul is lighter than mine? So he can feel things I can't?

Meizan had felt pain too once. Pain, horror, and even remorse in the face of suffering. But eighteen years of living in Malin had numbed him to it all. Expression blank and heart devoid of emotion, Meizan tended to the next child.

Aranel joined him, the toddler from before now asleep and strapped to his back in a sling.

"Do you plan to carry him around all day?" Meizan asked.

"He's a baby." Aranel sounded pained. "He needs the warmth of another human. He needs his parents. He needs . . ." Aranel shook his head. "How can this happen? How can he be left all alone, to fend for himself in this cruel world? It's not fair. It's not—"

"It's Malin," Meizan told him. He left out the part where that had been Meizan himself, abandoned before he could walk. "He'll survive. He doesn't have a choice."

"I was such a fool," Aranel whispered as he dressed another child's wounds. "My parents and brother ascended to Paramos, and I felt like the loneliest person in the universe. But now that I've seen this . . ."

This is nothing, Meizan almost said. But Aranel's eyes were wet and he looked ready to break. Meizan held his tongue and concentrated on healing the child in front of him as best he could with their limited supplies.

"I wish I could use my chitrons," Aranel said, stitching together a gash on a little girl's chin. "Chitronic healing would be far quicker, neater, less invasive than these substitute techniques. Were we in Mayana, I could have healed these children in seconds."

"Were you in Mayana, I doubt there would be children to heal."

ZENYRA AWAITED THEM outside the tent, accompanied by Taralei.

Aranel gave a cry at the sight of his cousin, though Meizan wasn't sure why he seemed so relieved. Taralei looked much worse since they'd last seen her a moon ago. Her hair was thin and lank, her skin coated in the omnipresent crud that seemed to exude from every pore of the realm. Only her keiza shone as brilliant as before.

"It is good to see you all," Taralei said with a strained smile. "I was busy in one of the eastern caves. We have fifteen more tents of injured children scattered across the village. We're short on staff; it's just Eniya and me here. Some of the older children help out, but they're not much good at healing, and we haven't had time to train them properly, what with the inrush of new casualties—" She paused, creasing her brow. "Never mind that. Just know your help is much appreciated."

"Did you check their keiza, Aranel?" Zenyra asked. "Did any of the children look as if they could ascend?"

"I didn't look closely," Aranel said. "But yes, some of their keiza did seem bright."

He rotated the sling around his back so the sleeping toddler was in his arms. Zenyra leaned down and pushed aside the child's curls. His keiza gleamed. Not as brightly as Aranel's or Aina's, but brighter than those of most Malini that Meizan had seen.

"He has hope for ascension," Zenyra said. She took the toddler from Aranel. "If I can find a torana, he might be able to make it, given time."

"Is that what you're trying to do here?" Aina asked. "Help these children ascend?"

"One of the many things," Zenyra said. "What you see here is the crux of our mission as Balancers. While a part of it is medical aid and food, there is a larger hope that it could contribute toward their ascension. That is the Balancers' core belief and why I founded this organization."

She cradled the baby in her arms, smiling as he gripped her finger with a tiny hand. "I do not believe people are inherently good or evil, but rather a byproduct of their circumstances. It would be impossible for even the gentlest souls to live sinless lives when they are surrounded by constant famine, violence, and war."

Zenyra looked straight at Meizan as she spoke, and he felt as if all the air was being squeezed from his lungs.

"If we elevate the Malini's quality of life, I believe they will have greater opportunities to lighten their souls and ascend," Zenyra said. "None of the children in this village are evil. They are only unfortunate—unfortunate to have been born to such circumstances. The Balancers cannot change Toranic Law, but we can change their circumstances. We can show them love and kindness, and give them hope for a better life."

A hotness rose at the back of Meizan's throat. His eyes stung as if from the fumes of Merumarth.

Love, kindness, and hope for a better life?

As if that would work. As if that would be enough to reverse a soul's spin. He glanced at Aina and traced his eyes across her bright turquoise keiza. Aina was living proof that souls *could* change spin. Meizan turned his gaze back at the baby clutching Zenyra's finger.

I am years too late.

Meizan knew how he'd fought. How he'd reveled in the fights, reveled in winning and in violence. He wasn't like Aina or the helpless toddler or the injured children inside the tent. He wasn't innocent. There might be hope for them, but not for him. Not anymore.

Zenyra took the toddler, along with a boy and a girl with bright foreheads, and left the village shortly after.

Taralei guided Meizan, Aranel, and Aina to another tent, where they spent the evening healing more children. A pair of rambunctious twins, whom Meizan and Aranel were helping, seemed cheerier than the rest while they compared their various burns.

"Mine's bigger," said the girl with the broken tooth. She shot her twin a lopsided grin. "Yours is shinier, but mine's *way* bigger."

"Yours is bleedin' ugly!" her twin retorted. "Mine's shaped like a nagamor!"

"D'you have rocks for eyes? That's nothin' like how a nagamor looks."

"Is too! I *saw* it!"

"You saw a nagamor?" Aranel asked. "That's terribly brave of you. I think I might pass out from shock if I saw one."

"I think you might too," the girl told him seriously. "Though your hair's nice."

"*I* didn't pass out." Her twin puffed her chest. "It flew *this* close"—she pinched her fingers together—"and I stared right at it."

"Lucky it didn't stare back," Meizan said, ignoring Aranel's glare.

"You know you're not supposed to meet a nagamor's eyes, don't you?" Aranel said. "You'll be in a world of pain, a thousand times worse than these burns, if you do."

"I can handle it," the little girl assured him. "Last year, I went fishin' with my pa and got bit by a saberfin shark." She pulled up her skirt to reveal a ring of shallow incisions around her ankle. "That hurt a thousand times worse'n this."

"That looks nothing like a saberfin bite," Meizan began. He fell silent at Aranel's look and resumed working on the girl's bandages with a shake of his head.

" 'Sides, the nagamor wasn' even the coolest part," she went on. "There was this angry old lady, breakin' rocks with her fingers. She'd go like this"—the girl wiggled her fingers with a flourish that looked nothing like actual channeling—"and then boom! A huge rockslide."

There was a loud clatter as the instrument tray Aina was holding dropped to the ground. Cursing, she ducked to pick it up.

"Sorry," Aina muttered as she surfaced. "Whereabouts did all this happen? The nagamor and the—the angry rock lady?"

"Up north, by the Muzireni," the girl replied. "We were camped by the banks and got caught in all the fightin'. There's a big battle goin' on between the king's army and the weepers."

Meizan squeezed the tube of ointment he was holding so hard it spurted all over his fingers. Either he'd misheard her, or this little girl had no idea what she was talking about.

"What are the weepers?" Aranel asked, casting an odd look Meizan's way as he handed him a spare tissue. "Some sort of monster?"

"No, you dummy," her twin said derisively. "The weepers are

the rebels who ran away from the king's ice dungeons. There's thousands of 'em, and they all got ugly blue lines down their faces that make it look like they're cryin' all the time."

Meizan's heart hammered. Blood rushed to his ears and blocked out all other noise.

They had escaped. The three thousand disappeared members of Kanjallen had escaped Kaldrav's clutches. His clanmates had survived. And they had regrouped and were fighting Kaldrav's army not far from this village.

MEIZAN VOLUNTEERED FOR lookout once they'd finished healing the children. With Zenyra away in search of a torana, they'd be staying a night in the rift before returning to Incaraz. Or at least Aina and Aranel would.

Meizan snuck out as soon as he could and crept past the chitronic shield. He wasn't familiar with this part of Malin, but they'd crossed the Muzireni a couple days back. All he had to do was retrace their steps back to the Noxious River, then follow it northward until he reached the battlefield.

He would be reunited with his clan soon. He would be able to fight alongside Kanjallen.

"Good. You're here."

Meizan whirled around to see Aranel, face grim, hood drawn low over his forehead to hide his keiza. "I figured you'd go after her as well."

"Why aren't you in the village?" Meizan demanded.

"Same as you, I'd hope," Aranel said. "To stop Aina before she does something incredibly daft. I know she wants to find her mother, but for Sherka's sake."

Meizan narrowed his eyes. So Aina had slunk off too? The

girl could barely channel. What the hell was she thinking, trying to sneak into a war zone by herself? Meizan cursed under his breath and turned to Aranel. "Did you see what direction she went in?"

From her reaction earlier, he hazarded a guess that Aina was headed to the Muzireni too. Her mother was probably fighting for Kaldrav's army. A lot of clan runaways ended up captured and forced to join his ranks.

"I saw her heading that way." Aranel pointed into the gloom. "But it's too dark to see far."

Meizan nodded and set off without another word. To his surprise and annoyance, Aranel decided to tag along. The meddling upper was the last thing Meizan needed to worry about in this situation.

"Go back," he told Aranel. "I'll deal with Aina."

"I'm coming too," Aranel protested. "The both of us have a better chance of convincing her than you do alone."

"I'm not going to convince her. I'm going to beat some sense into her stupid, thick head."

"And I'll heal her after so you don't cause permanent damage."

Meizan spun around, eyes blazing. "You realize we're headed to a flaming war zone, Aranel. Full of fighting and violence, your two least favorite things."

"I know that."

"Then you know there's no way you could survive with your precious soul untainted. It's not worth the risk. Not for you."

"Yes, it is," Aranel said, and it took every bit of Meizan's patience not to garrote him with his own hair.

"You'll get in the way," he growled. "This is not the time for your charity."

"This has nothing to do with my soul. I'm coming because

Aina is my friend, but she's also a foolish girl who can't channel properly. I can't abandon her to—to whatever happens in this realm to girls who can't channel properly."

Meizan glared at him, and Aranel stared defiantly back. Either the idiot was telling the truth, or he was utterly delusional.

"This better not be like Merumarth with the bleeding kapizer," Meizan warned. "If we come across Kaldrav's soldiers, you *will* hurt them, your soul-spin be damned."

"Incapacitate. I will incapacitate them and hurt *only* if I deem it absolutely necessary."

Fine. Meizan could deal with that. "Come on. If we're quick, we can stop her before she reaches the war zone."

And then Meizan would send Aina back with Aranel and reunite with his clan.

CHAPTER SIXTEEN

֍

The Rebel Army

A BATTLE RAGED ACROSS the broken plains of Malin, staining the Noxious River red with blood. From where Aina stood atop the plateau, she could make out two factions.

The first bore the sigil of Kaldrav the Cruel, tattered black flags with a single white circle. They chased a second faction, smaller in number, that carried unfamiliar blue banners marked with a crying eye. The majority of the blue-bannered soldiers seemed to be retreating from the battle while a quarter of their ranks stayed behind to fend off the pursuers.

Is Mama a part of this chaos?

Aina scanned the mass of fighters, but they were too numerous and distant for her to make out anything. Even if her mother were here, Aina had no idea which side she was on. Was she one of the rebels fleeing Kaldrav's army? Or had she been captured and forced to fight for the sadistic king himself?

As Aina watched the skirmishes unfold, another thought struck her—one she had never bothered to contemplate during her own days of running from Kaldrav's soldiers. Why the hell *did* the king want to unite the clans into a single army? Once united, they'd have no one to fight against.

Even Kaldrav can't be idiotic enough to try for peace.

Or could he? The idea of a peaceful, united Malin was too strange to comprehend. Outside of Incaraz, Aina hadn't lived in the realm for over a year. But she'd heard enough about the clan wars—the bitter blood feuds between Kanjallen and Chiren, Virator and Razamir—to know that whatever their king's plans, the Malini needed to fight *something*.

Regardless, Aina's priority remained finding out which side her mother fought for. And while she had an excellent vantage point from atop this plateau, she needed to get closer to the actual battle.

Checking that her chitronic concealment was in place, Aina crept down the cliffside, scanning the chaos below for broken earth or falling rocks—telltale signs of her mother's channeling.

Hers, and possibly hundreds of other Malini who can channel the rock of the realm, said a fussy voice in her head. Aina ignored the voice—not unlike Aranel's—as it chastised her recklessness. Because even if the odds of it being her mother were low, it was the only lead Aina had.

Halfway down the cliff, she spotted a deep recess a dozen or so feet to her right. It looked big enough for her to squeeze through and would provide a good hiding spot for her body once she projected her soul into the battlefield.

Channeling chitrons to her sweaty palms, Aina inched sideways toward the recess.

A haunting wail rent the sky. It shattered Aina's concentration and nearly sent her falling off the cliff. She clung on by her fingertips, twisting around to see Kaldrav's soldiers look up toward the sound.

Morons.

A wave rippled through the army as hundreds of Kaldrav's soldiers threw up their weapons in despair and crumpled to the ground.

Keeping their eyes shielded, the rearguard of the rebel forces charged. They cut through their immobilized foes with the ease of felling bushes and uttered an ululating war cry in imitation of the wailing creature overhead.

Aina squinted upward, careful not to look directly at the serpentine shadow that dove through the clouds. The nagamor twisted through the vermilion sky, skimming over the armies of Kaldrav. The beast must have measured at least one hundred feet long. Its feathered tail beat like an enormous fan to propel it through the air.

Sections of Kaldrav's soldiers—the ones with the presence of mind not to look directly at the new arrival—remained standing. These troops aimed their offense upward. A flurry of weapons and ropes of chitronic energy exploded from their ranks in the general direction of the nagamor.

Darkness burst from above the beast's neck and blasted the attacks to the ground.

That can't be. Aina squinted as the nagamor grew closer.

A single figure stood atop the cobalt blue scales, its outstretched hand swirling with crackling energy. With the other hand it held a pair of reins. Spikes of metal lodged in the nagamor's neck, and a length of barbed wire encircled its beak.

To control a nagamor, even by inflicting pain, was something Aina had never heard of.

Still, if the rebels had a nagamor . . . Aina found herself hoping that her mother had not been captured by Kaldrav and was part of this fleeing resistance. It would only make sense. Her mother loathed Kaldrav with a passion. She would sooner let her bones be smashed to dust than fight for his army.

Aina watched the nagamor sweep across the battlefield. Chitrons descended from its rider's palm like black lightning to smite line after line of Kaldrav's soldiers. The rebels took advantage of the new arrival to put more distance between themselves and their pursuers.

The nagamor swooped past Aina's cliff with another hair-raising shriek, dangerously close to smashing her against the rock with its tail. As it passed, Aina glimpsed its rider's blue cape and a helm lined with twin streaks of paint.

That's the same pattern as Meizan's old vest!

Could the rebel army be a part of his clan? Before Aina could think on it more, the nagamor turned sharply. Its tail slammed against the cliff.

Aina lashed out her chitrons as the rock crumbled around her, but she was too slow to make the bond. With a yelp, she skidded down the cliffside, curling into a tight ball to reduce the impact of the collision. She rolled out of the fall to find herself standing a few feet away from a battalion of Kaldrav's soldiers.

"Blast it," Aina said under her breath. She was lucky the soldiers were too distracted by the nagamor passing overhead to notice her, their eyes shielded and their weapons aimed skyward.

I need to get the hell out of here!

Aina looked up at the destroyed cliff. The recess she had found earlier was mercifully intact. She could try climbing while the soldiers remained distracted and stick to her original plan of soul projection. Or she could attempt a concealment to sneak past the soldiers and get to the rebels, which was stupider than Aranel trying to fight a bunch of kapizer with the hilt of his knife.

Up it is, then.

Aina bounced on the balls of her feet, then sprinted up the cliff. Her legs burned, but it was easier now that the rock was broken, providing her with plenty of footholds to maneuver herself.

She'd made it nearly a quarter of the way up when something yanked at her cloak. Aina tumbled down, the back of her head slamming against the ground. She reached for her bow to find two splinters of wood—her only weapon broken by the fall.

Eyes watering, Aina lurched to her feet.

One of Kaldrav's soldiers leered at her, crooked teeth bared in a grin. "Think you could run away again, Kanjallen brat?"

Aina perked at the name. So the rebels *were* from Meizan's clan.

"I'm not a rebel," she said. "I'm a Balancer."

Kaldrav's soldier didn't seem to care what she was or wasn't. Brandishing a spiked axe, he lunged toward her with a roar. Aina ducked easily—the man was slow and clunky in his armor, and she had trained with Hiraval, who was twice as fast—and swept his legs out from under him.

The soldier stumbled to the ground. Aina rolled into a somersault, grabbing the dagger attached to his waist and slicing it across his neck in one clean motion. She felt a curl of guilt as the soldier went limp.

I should have used a chitronic stun beam, Aina thought as she wiped the dagger clean.

Still, one enemy down, and she had a weapon now, even if it wasn't her bow.

"You scrawny little bitch," a voice rasped.

Nearly a dozen of Kaldrav's soldiers advanced toward her. Even if Aina could move faster, a single dagger wouldn't do much against their varied weapons.

Come on, you damn chitrons, she pleaded as she drew on her reserves. *Bleeding keiza! I don't care if you're broken, you have to do something right! Or I'm leaving you and this body, and projecting the hell out of here.*

Fingers glowing, Aina released her energy.

The ground split open to swallow the first line of the soldiers. Arrows of green light shot overhead, and the remaining soldiers keeled over, stunned. Aina stared at her hands in awe.

I couldn't have . . .

"You think that was you?" a familiar voice scoffed from behind her.

"What in Sherka's name were you thinking?" added another, dripping with disapproval.

Aina whirled around. Her mouth dropped as Aranel and Meizan sprung down from the cliff.

"That's not a Balancer technique." Aranel frowned as he surveyed the chasm Meizan had opened.

"I know." Meizan smirked. "But I've seen it so many times, I wanted to try for myself."

"What are you two doing here?" Aina demanded, before turning to Meizan. "The rebels are from—"

"We're saving your stupid ass," Meizan cut her off, with a near-imperceptible shake of his head. "Aranel's right, what the hell were you thinking, charging into a war zone all by yourself?"

"We know you want to find your mother, Aina," Aranel chided. "But of all your ill-advised schemes, this is by far the most foolish."

"I didn't *charge* into the war zone," Aina said. "I was on the cliff, trying to find a spot to project, but a nagamor smashed the rock and I fell—" She broke off and crossed her arms at Aranel's and Meizan's unimpressed faces. "Whatever happened, it's none of your concern! And Aranel, why are *you* even here? This is a war zone. It's full of violence."

"So I've been told," Aranel said sourly. "I saw you sneak out and knew you'd land yourself in trouble."

"But it's dangerous to step outside the chitronic shield," Aina said. "What about the risk to your soul?"

"You're one to talk about risk," Aranel shot back. "Do you have any idea how worried I was? We ought to get back to the village at once."

"You—you were worried about me?" Aina's heart stuttered at his words.

"Is that so hard to believe?"

"We don't have time for this shit," Meizan said. "You two go on ahead. I'll stay back to make sure we're not followed."

Aina turned to him in confusion, and Meizan gave a slight nod.

Oh. He intended to stay. Aina wasn't surprised. Meizan was a part of Kanjallen. The clan was his identity. He'd only joined the Balancers because he had nowhere left to go, so it was natural that he'd leave now.

"My mother might have joined the rebels," Aina said to him, ignoring Aranel's questioning gaze as he looked between her and Meizan. "It's only a hunch. But I think I'll go with y—"

She was cut off by the nagamor's soul-curdling scream.

"Don't look up!" Aina shouted. She pulled Aranel and Meizan down as the beast wheeled overhead to circle the remnants of Kaldrav's army.

"What in Sherka's name," Aranel asked, "was that?"

The earth exploded before Aina could reply, knocking her off her feet. A chitronic attack, far stronger than Meizan's. Far stronger than even her mother's had ever been.

Aina shielded her face as she was flung upward, along with a large part of Kaldrav's soldiers. Panicked shouts filled the air as entire battalions hurtled through the sky like debris.

A stream of emerald light snaked through the raining chaos.

Aina recognized Aranel's energy as it wrapped around her waist and yanked her toward him.

She landed jerkily on the ground next to Meizan, who erected a chitronic shield, deep blue energy swirling around the three of them. Aina poured her own chitrons into the shield, wincing as the falling rocks and soldiers thudded against it.

The shield held, and they avoided being crushed. But it was a flashy technique, and the combined light of their chitrons drew the attention of every fallen soldier in the vicinity. As the naga-mor sped across the battlefield in search of another section of the army to ravage, the battered soldiers turned their vengeful eyes upon the three of them.

"Bleeding snake," Meizan muttered. He dusted himself off and unsheathed his sword, hesitating a moment before he tossed it to Aina. "It's better than that dagger," he told her. "Don't use ambient channeling. We can't afford you screwing up."

Aina nodded, then gripped the hilt between sweaty fingers. Beside her, Aranel and Meizan swiped their foreheads, hands glowing.

The first wave of Kaldrav's soldiers descended upon them in a wave of spiked clubs and jagged axes.

Aina drew on her own chitrons, streaming them to her fore-arms and shins until the skin hardened to a bone-like density. She met the blows with her enhanced limbs and used Meizan's blade to cut through as many soldiers as she could.

Next to her, Aranel and Meizan sent out stun beams in all directions until Aina was surrounded by a tornado of green and blue light. She didn't know how they could aim amidst the chaos and not accidentally hit one another or her. But their stunners worked, and the ring of collapsed soldiers around them grew larger with every passing minute.

But for every soldier they stunned or cut down, twice as

many came in their place, attracted by the flashing lights. Aina could only be grateful most of these soldiers weren't experienced channelers. She dodged the few chitronic attacks hurled at her easily.

But as the battle dragged on, Aina's breaths grew sharp and labored. Her arms trembled under the weight of constant blocks and blows.

Meizan had all but discarded the Balancer techniques to fire throwing stars at whatever exposed flesh he could find. Once his projectiles ran out, he began sending large rocks flying through the air in an attack that reminded Aina painfully of her mother. One of the boulders, more brutal and efficient than a stun beam, crushed four soldiers at once.

But Meizan lacked her mother's chitronic reserves. And as the scant sunlight rapidly faded, it would take him even longer to recharge. With time, the flying boulders grew smaller and fewer. Aina took in Meizan's shaking shoulders and fluttering eyelids. He would pass out from sheer chitronic exhaustion if he kept this up much longer.

"Aranel," she called, and the Mayani looked over his shoulder. Aina jabbed a thumb at Meizan. "You have to channel properly! He can't do it alone, and if I do, I might—" Aina swore, hating her chitrons and her stupid, defective keiza more than ever.

Aranel hesitated, shooting another pair of stunners that knocked out two advancing soldiers.

Beside Aina, Meizan swayed.

"You upper-born idiot!" Aina shrieked. "Just attack them properly!"

There was a flash of emerald light, and for the second time that day, the ground blasted apart beneath Aina. She fell at least twenty feet but somehow landed upright amidst the crashing rocks.

She turned to find Aranel helping up Meizan, who was on

the verge of collapse. Aranel looked at Aina, his face contorted in horror.

"I tried, Aina," he moaned. "I tried manipulating the rock, but when I channeled, the chitrons—the wretched chitrons—"

Of course. Aranel's weak-willed channeling was as dangerous as Aina's own volatile bond.

Aina took in their surroundings, aghast. Aranel's botched attempt had opened up some sort of a pit. They were trapped.

His breath recovered, Meizan looked up and let out a string of curses. Aina followed his gaze to see a line of soldiers gathered at the edge of the pit, their silhouettes juxtaposed against the vermilion sky. Aina had no time to think before the soldiers surged forth, weapons raised, and poured down the sides of the pit like a monstrous landslide.

AINA WOKE TO find herself behind bars. Something stabbed at her forehead. She tried to reach up and touch it, but heavy chains jerked at her wrist. Across from her and chained as she was, Aranel and Meizan sat slumped against a wall of obsidian. Metal shards stuck out from their keiza, their faces streaked with blood.

That explains the pain. Aina reached for her chitrons. As expected, she couldn't feel them with her keiza obstructed.

She turned back to her teammates. Meizan remained unconscious, but Aranel stirred, hazel eyes cracking open. Stricken, he looked around the cramped cell. "Where are we? What happened?"

Aina tried to recollect the last moments of the battle amidst the maelstrom of flashing weapons and pain and blood. She'd passed out after a point, so her memory remained fuzzy, but there was only one possible explanation for their incarceration.

"I think we're in Kaufgar," Aina said.

"Kaufgar," Aranel repeated. "Kaldrav's fortress?"

"I can't be sure. But if we've been captured by his soldiers, they'd bring us to either Agakor or Kaufgar. Agakor's supposed to be made of ice, which means—"

"We're in Kaufgar." Meizan's eyes snapped open. He sat up straight and observed his chained wrists. "I pass out for one flaming minute, and you two boneheads get us captured."

"I'm more concerned as to why they'd bring us *here*," Aina said. "If they wanted to torture us, they'd send us to Agakor, right?" At the word *torture*, Aranel flinched in his chains. "Maybe things changed from when I was in Malin, but only important people get taken to Kaufgar. We should've been sent to Agakor or left on the battlefield."

Meizan swore. He looked down at his waist, absent of its usual wooden scabbard, then back at Aina. "Where's my sword?" he barked.

"I don't know," Aina said. "They must have confiscated it when they chained us up." Meizan swore again, and Aina felt a flash of irritation. "I'm sorry I lost it, but don't we have more pressing things to worry about right now?"

"That weapon," Meizan said through gritted teeth, "along with its scabbard, was only ever carried by the Kanjallen chief's right hand."

"You're Kanjallen second-in-command?" Aina gawked at him. "I didn't know you were important!"

"I'm not, exactly," Meizan said. "My chief found the blade in the rubble of our old village and gave it to me when I needed a new weapon. But if the soldiers took it, that means they think—"

"Look what we have here," a raspy voice interrupted. A pair of soldiers trundled toward the cell. Their leather jerkins bore the white circle of Kaldrav. Jagged scars crisscrossed their faces and arms. "Three little worms, awake at last."

Meizan's eyes narrowed in anger. "Chiren scum . . ."

"Is he the one, Raxaz?" asked the shorter of the Chiren soldiers, a woman with close-cropped hair. "He had the scabbard, but she was wielding the weapon."

"The description says male," her companion, Raxaz, said. He limped up to the cell and pressed up against the bars. "Does this runt look like a man to you?" His eyes roved over Aina before settling on Meizan. "It's definitely him, Raxazi. I remember his face from Martharan. Do you remember mine, weeper?"

Meizan stiffened but fixed the man with a flat stare. "What's to remember? All you scarfaces look the same."

"Son of a worm!" Raxaz bared his teeth. The scar above his lip cracked open to bead blood down his chin. "You smashed two of my chums to pulp! And you stabbed my leg with this blasted piece of metal!"

He produced the nagamor-patterned sword from behind his back and slid it through the bars to press against Meizan's chest, drawing a trickle of red.

Aina winced, but Meizan did not bat an eyelid even as the tip of the blade dragged across his skin to open a thin line of blood.

"Do you know how it feels?" Raxaz asked. "To lie in the mud, your body reduced to pieces of burning agony. Unable to move or breathe or think beyond the pain."

"Don't you manglers like carving yourselves up—"

"Silence!" Raxaz roared, pressing the blade in deeper. "I stitched them together, piece by bleeding piece. But they still lie unmoving. Their eyes red with unending tears. And for that, I shall scourge you to the last bit of your wormy soul."

"Leave him be, Rax," Raxazi said. "The terms of the trade demand he be returned in one piece."

"Trade?" asked Aranel, who had remained uncharacteristically silent throughout the exchange.

"Your worm of a chief's agreed to give herself up for him,"

Raxazi replied. "One worm for another. Give it another day, tops, and she'll come crawling to our door."

"Weepers and their bleeding loyalty." Raxaz sniggered. "More like stupidity, if you ask me—trading a chief for her brat-in-command. Still, if she wants to be in chains, I'm not going to stop her."

His gaze fell on Aina then, lips curving into a predatory grin. A cold dread snatched at Aina's chest, and she shrank against the wall.

Mama. The plea sprang to her mind, unbidden. *Mama . . . help . . . don't let him hurt me . . .*

"I can't harm you," Raxaz said to Meizan. He angled his sword toward Aina, then Aranel. "So how about you watch me do to your clanmates what you did to mine?"

"They're not my clanmates!" Meizan's calm shattered. "They had nothing to do with what happened in Martharan, so leave them out of it!"

"You think I'll believe that, you filthy worm-worshipper?"

"He's telling the truth," Raxazi interjected. "Look at their keiza. The long-haired one's is so bright, just looking at it makes me want to puke."

"An upper, eh?" Raxaz gave another snicker, leering at Aranel. "Probably a Balancer, then. And what the hell's a bleeding Balancer doing with Kanjallen's second-in-command? Are you allies?"

"We're not," Meizan said before Aranel could reply. "The Balancers aren't allied with any of the clans. They operate independently. You should know this."

"Don't lecture me, weeper." Raxaz spat in Meizan's face and returned his leer to Aranel. "I've been itching to fight an upper. They say your souls are pure, but what about your blood? Must be the same scummy shit flowing through your veins as ours."

He shoved Meizan's blade through the bars again, but Raxazi yanked his arm back.

"Stop tormenting prisoners, brother," she reproached, snatching the weapon from her clanmate. "You'll fall to Narakh if you keep it up. Besides, you'll have enough chances to spill upper blood once Toranic Law breaks and we invade their realms."

Aina heard a sharp intake of breath from Aranel as the woman hauled her clanmate away.

"*If* Toranic Law breaks." Raxaz's voice echoed through the halls. "I'm beginning to doubt Kaldrav's even capable of such a thing. Miserable leech should stop wasting his time and use it for something useful. Like teaching the bleeding troops how to properly channel."

Meizan sank against the stone once their voices faded and brought a hand to his chest.

"Are you all right?" Aranel asked in alarm, chains clinking as he scooted closer. "That monster! I have gazarou fur on me somewhere, if I can just reach it."

"Don't bother," Meizan said. "It's a shallow cut. The least of what I deserve."

Aranel froze. "You don't mean you actually—"

"Do you think your chief's really coming for you?" Aina cut in before Aranel could start expounding about nonviolence. "It seems like a big risk to free a not-exactly-second-in-command."

"She'll come." Meizan's eyes flickered with emotion. "Only she won't trust those vermin to keep their end of the bargain. Knowing Chief, she'll bring all of Kanjallen with her and try freeing the other prisoners too."

"But this is Kaldrav's stronghold. He's got to have thousands of soldiers here," Aina said. "Trying to break everyone out would be insanity!"

"It would. And Kaldrav's soldiers are probably expecting it too. I think they're using me to lure Kanjallen so they can try and recapture them."

"And your chief would fall for such an obvious trap?"

"Only if she thinks she can break out of it with Kanjallen unharmed."

"Did neither of you hear what else they said?" Aranel asked, his voice pitched higher than normal. "About Toranic Law? They talked about breaking Toranic Law! Invading the upper realms! You heard them, did you not?"

"We did, but no one cares." Meizan brushed him off. "It's just mangler talk, it's never going to happen."

"I say let it break," Aina said vindictively. "Bringing down that twisted system will be the one good thing Kaldrav does for the realm."

"You don't mean that!" Aranel stared at her in horror.

"Yes, I do." Aina glared back. "You were there at the Balancer village, Aranel! You *saw* those children! After having seen the state Toranic Law has put them in, how can you still hold it in such high regard?"

"I . . ." Aranel faltered. "I admit, the system has its—well, its flaws. But the idea of it *breaking* . . ."

"That's all it is," Meizan dismissed. "An idea. Even the mangler said it, Aranel, that whatever Kaldrav's trying with Toranic Law is a waste. Because it's not going to break and we're stuck with it for eternity. So stop worrying your damn head over it and start worrying about how you're going to get out of this dump."

Aranel said nothing more and chose to sulk in silence. The stillness that overtook their cell left Aina with no distraction from the splintering pain in her keiza. She reached for her chitrons in vain, wishing she could do something to numb the ache.

But she was helpless as she had been as a child, when she had to rely on her mother to get them out of dangerous situations. If only her mother were here now, or better yet, Zenyra—

"I got it," Aina whispered, and if her hands weren't chained she would have smacked herself for not coming up with it sooner. "Projection. I can project my soul to alert Zenyra of our situation. If anyone can get us out of this mess, it's her."

"You think?" Meizan asked. "Zenyra's powerful, but she can't single-handedly storm Kaufgar. It's as you said before, there are thousands of soldiers here."

"But she won't be alone, right?" Aina felt a flutter of hope. "Your clan will be attacking the fortress soon. Zenyra can take advantage of the chaos to help break us out!"

"I already thought of projection, and it won't work," Aranel said. "We have no idea where we are in relation to Zenyra. It could take hours to search the realm, and you know what she said about the risk of chitronic taint. Meizan can't project yet, so it would have to be one of us. Most Mayani wouldn't last more than a few minutes of direct exposure before the chitrons of Malin began to corrupt their soul."

"I know," Aina said. "But I'm not most Mayani." She closed her eyes and tried to ignore the throbbing of her keiza. Her weak, defective keiza.

Zenyra had said Aina's keiza was the reason her soul was affected more gradually by the chitrons of Malin. She wasn't sure whether this would apply once her soul was outside her body, but Aina was willing to take the chance.

"Stop and think, Aina," Aranel said. "This is dangerous! What about the spin of your soul?"

Aina smiled, reminded of the time he'd arrested her and taken her to the guardhouse of Kirnos. It had been over four moons since, but some things never changed.

"I'll let you worry about that," she told him, pushing out her chitrons.

Aina watched her own body go limp in the chains. She saw Aranel's distraught expression and Meizan's mildly impressed one. Noting the location of their cell, Aina fled Kaufgar and sped across the realm.

CHAPTER SEVENTEEN

@

The Walls of Kaufgar

*A*RANEL LOST TRACK of how long he and Meizan spent trapped in that narrow cell with Aina's unconscious body in chains by their feet. Meizan sat with his knees drawn to his chest, staring blankly at the corroded bars. Aranel watched him out of the corner of his eye, a dozen questions at the tip of his tongue. Even if Meizan deigned to respond, Aranel wasn't sure he wanted to know the answers.

To his surprise, Meizan addressed him first. "What?"

"What do you mean, what?" asked Aranel.

"Stop flapping your mouth like a gutted fish and say whatever it is you want to say."

Aranel's lips pressed into a tight line. "It might annoy you if I do."

"Everything about you annoys me."

"I caught you when you collapsed," said Aranel, aggrieved. "Earlier, on the battlefield."

"I wouldn't have collapsed if you'd been channeling properly."

"It seems we differ on what constitutes *channeling properly.* What that Raxaz fellow said about Martharan— Did you— Was that—" The words stumbled in his mouth, and Aranel blurted instead, "Was that why you were covered in blood when we first met? Because you'd been fighting Chiren?"

"You were covered in worse," said Meizan. Aranel's face burned at the memory. "And yes. My chief had been digging a tunnel to get us out of Martharan. It collapsed with the rain, and a couple dozen manglers ambushed us."

So they'd been trying to escape when Chiren attacked them first.

Somehow, that little fact filled Aranel with relief. Perhaps Raxaz had been exaggerating. Perhaps Meizan showed more mercy to other humans than he did to kapizer.

"I thought Kanjallen and Chiren were allies," said Aranel. "The scriptures say they fought together during Kal Ekana."

"That was centuries ago. I doubt whoever wrote your stupid texts has been down here since the split."

"That's true," conceded Aranel, curiosity piqued. "What do the Malini say about the Great Toranic Separation?"

"What's there to say? One day, the war stopped. Thousands of people disappeared, and no one knew where. The ones who remained were stuck in this dump, unable to die."

"You say that as if death's a good thing." He frowned at his teammate's incredulous look. "Does it not scare you, Meizan? The notion of your soul leaving your body for eternity? Like projection, but you can never return, and your body is left to decay."

"There are hundreds of Malini who'd do anything to die. The Kanjallen elders once spoke of how—" Meizan paused. It was rare for him to volunteer information about his clan.

"You may as well tell me," said Aranel. "We're stuck here

together with nothing better to do. Unless you'd like me to try healing that wound for you."

Meizan shot him a disgruntled look but obliged. "Just after the split, when no one knew about the torana, some clan members thought they were the gates to death. But they'd never seen anyone ascend through the gold or silver ones. They'd only seen others dragged through the black torana after committing unspeakable acts. So they concluded the key to dying was to inflict as much pain and suffering as humanly possible."

"How terrible." Aranel shuddered, wrapping his arms around his knees. "When did they realize what truly awaited them?"

"When a person who'd descended returned from the dead." Meizan's lips twisted. "Most never made it back, not even the fools who walked in. They either erased or they're still rotting in Narakh. Maybe they think it's a purgatory. Or the afterlife."

"What about the upper realms?" asked Aranel, eager to talk about something less upsetting. "How did they find out about Mayana and Paramos?"

"I don't know—" Meizan stopped abruptly as Aina stirred by their feet.

Her amber eyes fluttered open, and she sat up in a clatter of chains.

"They're on—their way," panted Aina. "Couldn't find Zenyra. Found Taralei instead. Did the thing. You know. Carving letters using my chitrons. I *think* she understood. Said she'd get Zenyra—"

She broke off, breathing heavily. It was hard to tell through all the blood and the metal stabbing her forehead, but Aina's keiza appeared to have dimmed only slightly, nowhere near as much as Aranel would have expected.

"You did well," he said. "Thank you, Aina." He nudged Meizan, who had returned to staring at the bars. "When do you think your clan's getting here?"

Meizan shrugged, and it took all of Aranel's self-control to not ask the one question that had been bothering him the most. The thing he'd suspected from the moment he'd caught sight of his teammate's face after the little girl mentioned the weepers.

Meizan was leaving the Balancers. Aranel just hadn't expected Aina to leave first.

"What now?" asked Aina, finally catching her breath.

"Now we wait," said Meizan.

ARANEL JOLTED FROM his stupor to an unearthly, wavering wail. Meizan shot up beside him, eyes bright in the candlelight.

Streams of dark energy slithered across the walls like vines. The obsidian began to ripple as if it were made of satin.

"These chitrons," gasped Aina. "They feel . . ."

"Wrong," murmured Meizan, more to himself than to Aina. "Her chitrons feel wrong. Foul and full of hatred."

"Her?" asked Aranel.

"My chief," said Meizan. "There's something off about the energy, but I recognize her channeling."

Aranel watched the stone, entranced. Tiny flakes of it fluttered to the ground, as if being rubbed by sandpaper, until the dark surface was smooth enough that Aranel could see his own blood-soaked reflection. Around him, every stone wall, even the ceiling, had been polished until it shone.

It was an impressive feat of channeling, although Aranel could not fathom how slicking the walls of Kaufgar would get them out of the fortress.

"Shut your eyes!" shouted Aina. Aranel heeded her out of instinct.

Pained screams filled Kaufgar, echoing off the walls and raising goose bumps across Aranel's skin. Never had he heard a sound so raw, so agonized.

As the screaming continued, other sounds rose above it—the thundering of feet and clashing of metal as hundreds of soldiers stormed the fortress. Their war cries mimicked the wail from before.

"What's happening?" yelled Aranel over the commotion. "Is it Kanjallen? Have they broken in?"

"They have," said Meizan. "Keep your eyes fixed to the floor. The chief—I can't believe her—she's turned the stone into mirrors!"

The unearthly cry sounded again. It reverberated through the fortress, followed by another chorus of pain.

Sweet Sherka . . . they've got the nagamor with them!

It took Aranel a moment to fully appreciate the genius of Meizan's chief and her plan. By turning the stone smooth enough to reflect the nagamor's glare throughout the fortress, the Kanjallen chief had wiped out the majority of Kaldrav's troops within in one fell swoop. They'd be thrashing for three minutes in utter, debilitating pain. Even once the effects of the nagamor's glare wore off, they'd be too traumatized to fight properly.

Kanjallen's rampage resounded through the fortress. As the screams died down, Aranel could only assume that Kaldrav's soldiers had been knocked out or worse.

"How do we get out?" asked Aina.

"We wait," said Meizan. "They'll free all the prisoners."

Soon enough, Aranel felt the stone wall rumble behind him as its foundations weakened. He tugged on his chains until they clattered to the ground, still attached to his wrists but no longer to the stone. While he was not entirely free, at least he could move his arms.

Aranel wrenched the metal rod from his keiza and nearly

passed out from the pain. He looked over at Meizan's and Aina's feet, where their bloodied rods had been tossed to the ground.

"Let's get out of here," said Aranel, still not daring to look up.

They raced through the destroyed passageway, which was packed with escaped prisoners. The few soldiers Aranel presumed were from Kanjallen—it was difficult to tell when he could only see their legs—were slicing apart the remains of Kaldrav's writhing army, seemingly unbothered with rounding up the prisoners.

Aranel flinched as warm blood sprayed his cheek. He kept his head down as he ran, eyes fixed on Meizan's heels. If the jerk was going to ditch them for his clan, he'd better not do it while they were still inside Kaufgar.

Only once Aranel's foot hit dirt did he look up, feeling relief for the first time to face the ruinous sky of Malin.

They had made it out.

But still they were surrounded. Even if Kanjallen had neutralized the forces within Kaufgar, Kaldrav had plenty of backup outside. The base of the fortress was a storm of chaos, swarming with soldiers and escaped prisoners. Arrows whizzed overhead, along with the occasional body and bursts of dark energy that threw up chunks of rock.

Aranel, Meizan, and Aina forced their way through the throng. Aranel ducked as Aina's chain swung through the air, smashing one of Kaldrav's men in the skull. Meizan had used his own chain to strangle another. It was far messier, far rougher than Aranel would have liked, but they were otherwise weaponless and had no access to their chitrons.

They finally extracted themselves from the horde and scrambled to higher ground. Aranel stopped to catch his breath once they'd crested a small hill, a safe distance from the battle that raged around Kaufgar.

The fortress cut an imposing sight. It rose from the ground like the half-buried blade of a scythe, its windowless obsidian walls tapered to a cruel point. Save a splintered portcullis at its base, Kaufgar had little in way of fenestration. Unlike the Mayani, the Malini appeared not to be great architects and had chosen to work with what the realm had given them.

It looks like a beak, thought Aranel, with a shiver as he remembered Hiraval's tale of the seitarius. A colossal beak belonging to Azyaka the nagamor, who, according to Hiraval, slumbered deep below their feet. *Why am I thinking of that now?*

He glanced at Meizan, who was watching the clashing armies with something akin to longing. With all the prisoners freed, Kanjallen had begun their retreat. The nagamor circled overhead, and Meizan squinted at it, shielding his eyes with a hand.

There was someone riding the beast. Someone wearing a rippling blue cloak and whose hands glowed with dark energy.

That's her. Aranel's heart sank at Meizan's reverent expression. *That's his chief.*

He turned to Aina. Her gaze followed Meizan's as she picked at the metal cuffs around her wrist. "Where's Zenyra?" asked Aranel.

"I don't know," said Aina absently. "Taralei said they'd come as soon as they could."

"We should get away from here," said Aranel. A blur of black bled over the horizon and crawled toward Kaufgar. Kanjallen had their nagamor, but it seemed Kaldrav's reinforcements would arrive soon. He took a step toward Meizan. "Come on. We need to return to Incaraz."

Meizan turned to him with the faintest of half smiles.

"You're truly leaving?" asked Aranel. "I thought you might . . ."

It was why he had followed Meizan out of the Balancer village in the first place, though he could not explain the logic to himself. Meizan was Malini. A sadist who had held Aranel hostage when they'd first met and goaded him at every chance he'd gotten since.

Yet, over the past four moons, Aranel had begun to wonder if there was something more beneath Meizan's rough exterior. Some latent affection—or at least acknowledgment—behind the taunts and sneers and repeated challenges to spar. And despite every chitron in his soul telling Aranel he'd be better off without Meizan around, the idea of him leaving made Aranel's stomach turn.

"They're your clan," said Aranel. "You're loyal to them, you always have been. We all have our loyalties, and some run deeper than others." He prayed his next words didn't land him with a fist to his face.

"Loyalties can change, you know? Just because you grew up thinking something doesn't make it true. You could—you could stay. With the Balancers. I know you like to pretend you're an emotionless prick with no chance of ascension, but Aina did it. You could as well, if you stayed."

Meizan tilted his head. His dark eyes flickered with something unreadable. He opened his mouth a fraction, and Aranel waited, chest thumping, for Meizan's next words.

But his teammate turned away, and at that silent dismissal, something inside Aranel broke. He stumbled forward and grabbed Meizan's sleeve, the words tumbling unbidden from his lips. "If you go, you'll be sucked back into the violence! You'll be surrounded by these soldiers, by these *brutes* who revel in war."

"In your eyes," said Meizan. "They're brutes in your eyes, and in the eyes of Toranic Law. But to me, they're my clan. They've been good to me, Aranel, and protected me from harm."

The Balancers will be good to you, Aranel wanted to shout. *The Mayani will protect you from harm.*

But he'd already said too much. His arguments shriveled and died in his throat as Meizan pulled his sleeve away and turned around a second time. Aranel's arm dropped to his side.

As he watched Meizan's retreating back, Aranel was overcome by a helplessness similar to what he had felt as Samarel had walked away. But this time, the sting felt different. Keener.

"Aranel!" called a familiar voice.

Taralei ran toward him and clutched his arms, her green eyes glistening. "Oh, thank Sherka I found you!" The bands around Aranel's wrists came undone and fell to the ground. "What were you thinking, Ran, sneaking out like that? And *you*!"

She turned to Aina and shook her shoulders before undoing her shackles as well. "I didn't have time to scold you when you projected, but how could you run away? And where's Meizan, that brooding wretch?"

"Meizan's not coming," said Aina, her gaze fixed to the sky. "Where's Zenyra?"

"Fighting to get you lot free," answered a male voice. A bearded young man joined them. Aranel recognized him as Eniya, one of Samarel's old friends. "We should alert her that you no longer require assistance."

Eniya gestured at the swarm of soldiers. A shockwave of mottled golden light pulsed through their ranks and threw them back to reveal Zenyra in their midst.

Her copper hair billowed like a cape as she turned this way and that, sending out pulses of chitrons to clear a path toward Kaufgar's entrance. Zenyra's desperation made her indiscriminate in her attacks. She blasted away any who stood in her way, both Kaldrav's men and those of Kanjallen.

What is she doing?

Aranel's heart lodged in his throat as he searched for Meizan amidst the crowd. He made to run down the hill, but Taralei stopped him. "Just where do you think you're going?"

"Some of those soldiers she's attacking are from Meizan's clan!" cried Aranel. They're the ones who freed us! They're fighting *against* Kaldrav!"

"Zenyra doesn't know that! Or she's too overwhelmed to care—" Taralei broke off to raise a shaky finger at the sky, where a shadow had burst from the swollen clouds. "Ran, don't tell me that's what I think it is . . ."

Aranel groaned as the nagamor and its rider skimmed over the soldiers and flew, straight as a spear, at Zenyra.

She should have been more careful. She shouldn't have let her attacks hit Kanjallen. And now she's upset their chief.

But even as the nagamor dove toward her, Zenyra did not falter. Golden light swelled from her palms, and rock crumbled to dirt at the flick of her fingers. The dirt swarmed the nagamor's head to wrap around its beak and eyes before solidifying into a rocky helmet of sorts.

She neutralized its glare! Aranel's relief gave way to dread as the nagamor landed with a heavy thud. The beast was Kanjallen's greatest weapon. By incapacitating it, Zenyra had inadvertently helped Kaldrav's soldiers.

Screeching, the nagamor slammed its head against the rock in an attempt to break open the helmet. The Kanjallen chief slid off her thrashing mount, chitronic energy pouring from her in waves. A streak of it shot skyward to lance the bulging clouds and bring forth a deluge of rain. The rain and chitrons twisted together, then ripped toward Zenyra in a black hurricane.

Zenyra countered with more golden light; thousands of tendrils spiraled around the hurricane, slowing its rotation until it dissipated entirely.

"Someone needs to stop them," yelled Aranel to Taralei. "This is a misunderstanding. They have a common enemy. They ought to be fighting for the same side!"

But none could stop them or even dared approach, the power of the two women's attacks overwhelming in its intensity. Both sets of soldiers had backed away, unwilling to get caught in the crossfire. Kanjallen took advantage of the mayhem to hasten their retreat, although a few of their number remained to observe the duel from afar.

So this is what a battle between two seasoned chitronic users looks like . . .

Aranel watched in awed trepidation as Zenyra faced Meizan's chief. While the Balancer leader was clearly stronger, the Kanjallen chief had an advantage channeling in her own realm. Her attacks were violent, meant to cause harm, while Zenyra focused on neutralizing and preventing damage.

With pulses of light, Zenyra doused fires and unraveled tornadoes, steadied earthquakes and subdued tsunamis, smote missiles of rock and crushed them to dust. No matter what the Kanjallen chief did, Zenyra countered, her face tight with concentration, her keiza blazing like a dying star.

What will this do to her chitrons? Aranel's stomach lurched.

Zenyra's soul could take more than most on account of being Paramosi, but even she was not immune to so much expansive channeling. She needed to end this battle soon.

"We have to stop her," cried Aina. Eniya held her by the arms to keep her from running to Zenyra. "She can't attack! That woman on the nagamor is—"

Hands crackling with black lightning, the Kanjallen chief leaped forth with a shout. Zenyra flipped backward to dodge her before leaping high into the air and bringing her foot down on her foe's head.

The Kanjallen chief's blue-streaked helm cracked and slipped to the ground, revealing a shock of graying curls and yellowed teeth bared in a snarl.

Beside Aranel, Aina went limp in Eniya's grip. Her chin trembled, and a single broken word fell from her lips.

"Mama."

CHAPTER EIGHTEEN

❧

Loyalty

EIZAN HAD KNOWN it was his chief long before Zenyra unmasked her. He recognized her channeling; the way she whipped her arms about her, fingers curled into claws. But she was much more powerful than Meizan remembered, and her chitrons felt darker. Like an entirely different person. For a moment, it had made him doubt.

He sighed in relief at the sight of her face and that familiar withering glare. Chief Kanna was stronger than ever. Kanjallen was free.

Meizan should have been happy. Yet something pulled his gaze back to the hill where Aranel and Aina stood.

They never mattered, Meizan told himself, tightening his hold on the iron grille. Unseen amidst the chaos, he'd climbed the smashed portcullis at Kaufgar's entrance. His position gave him a clear view of the duel at hand.

It was Zenyra's flaming fault for starting it by not aiming her attacks properly. The chief had been forced to engage and protect Kanjallen from harm.

Misunderstandings aside, Meizan wasn't stupid enough to put himself in the middle of a fight between two chitronic users of such skill. So he watched with bated breath, waiting for an opportunity to reveal himself so he and Kanna could retreat with the rest of their clan.

Zenyra had, Meizan noted with reluctant admiration, completely wrecked the chief's nagamor. When the hell had Kanna gotten herself a nagamor, and tamed it at that? The beast thrashed against the ground, unable to break free of its rocky helmet.

The chief leaped a few paces back, dark energy streaming from her arms. She was preparing one of her hard-hitters. Across from her, Zenyra summoned a ball of light. Zenyra's chitrons glowed golden, but their brightness was tinged with shadowy specks where the corruption of Malin had seeped into her channeling.

The Balancer leader made to launch an attack when a figure dashed in front of her and barreled into the chief, forcing Zenyra to redirect her chitrons. The ball of light landed a few feet away and stirred up a cloud of dust, which settled to reveal the figure at Chief Kanna's side: Aina, her small face slick with tears.

"Mama!" Aina sobbed, clutching at the chief's tunic. "Mama! It's me! It's Aina!"

Meizan felt as though the breath had been knocked from his lungs.

The chief was Aina's mother? He hadn't been aware Kanna had a daughter, and they didn't look much alike. But as he recalled the chief's talk about white flashes and ascension, and Aina's past mentions of her mother, it all clicked into place.

Meizan had first met Kanna over a year ago, when she made chief. The Kanjallen elders often criticized her prolonged absence from the clan, but Kanna had never revealed the reason behind it.

She must have run away shortly after Aina was born, to return only once her daughter ascended.

As Meizan watched the reunited pair, he wondered if he should make his presence known. The chief had come to save him, after all.

"Mama, I've been looking all over for you," Aina wept. "I tried to descend but the torana were sealed, and nothing I did was enough to reverse my soul-spin."

The resulting slap echoed through the realm. Aina stumbled back, clutching at her bruised cheek.

"I think I told you," Kanna said coldly, "to stay in your blasted realm."

"But—but I'm a Balancer now! We're based in Malin—"

Another slap. "I told you not to set foot into this realm!" the chief snarled. She grabbed Aina by the shoulders and shook her hard. "I told you I didn't want to see your face ever again!"

She couldn't mean it. It wasn't anger that made the chief's form rigid, but fear. She wore the same expression as on the day they'd returned to their village in Raitani and discovered nothing but ash and rubble. But Aina didn't seem to perceive what Meizan had. She rounded on her mother, hurt but not yet deterred.

"How can you say that to me?" Aina wailed. "I tried burdening my soul just so we could be together again!"

"Together? After I was finally rid of you? Do you know what a relief it was when you ascended? That I'd no longer have to drag around a useless child."

"I'm your only family, Mama! I'm your *daughter*!"

"My daughter?" Kanna gave a cruel laugh. "Look at your keiza. The way it shines. You were always weak and now your soul has grown soft. You are no daughter of mine."

Aina gave a whimper, and Meizan had to look away. The sight

was too pitiful. Too pathetic. The chief had always been heartless when it came to those she wanted to protect.

Still, better a heartless mother than none at all.

"Enough," Zenyra's voice cut in. She strode toward Kanna and Aina. "If you truly are Aina's birth mother, I do not intend to fight you any longer."

"You're one of those Balancers?" the chief asked. "I have heard of your little gang. Seems you're running some sort of charity in this realm."

"I am their leader," Zenyra replied. "And Aina is one of my dearest comrades."

"And some of those soldiers you blasted aside were mine." Kanna drew herself up to full height, a head shorter than Zenyra. "Not so charitable of you, Balancer, to attack the very men resisting Kaldrav's."

"An honest mistake." Zenyra inclined her head and pressed a fist to her keiza. "All I wish is to take Aina to safety. Or would you begrudge her even that?"

"Take her," Kanna said. "Take her, and do with her what you will."

Turning on her heel, she marched toward the thrashing naga-mor and snapped her fingers. The rocky helmet crumbled, and the chief hopped onto the beast's back. The nagamor's body rippled as it shot into the sky, soaring over the army of Kanjallen.

Zenyra placed an arm around Aina's shoulders and steered her to the hilltop where Aranel stood. Meizan watched them disappear into the distance, then turned and raced toward his clan.

JUST AS MEIZAN had expected, it wasn't long before Chief Kanna withdrew from the battle. The fight against Zenyra had exhausted her. She would need a nap to recharge her chitrons.

Kanjallen retreated with their chief, and Kaldrav's soldiers seemed too terrified of the nagamor to give pursuit. Meizan snuck away from his clan's ranks—he spotted a few familiar faces, but he wanted to speak with Kanna first—and followed the nagamor's trail.

Clearly spent, the beast drifted toward a pinnacle of rock. It took Meizan considerable effort to scale the cliff, a task made harder by the damn chains attached to his wrists. His keiza still throbbed, and he hadn't entirely recovered the use of his chitrons, but he reached the ledge a few feet under the sleeping nagamor where the chief was hiding.

"You definitely unmade our enemies," Meizan said, dropping by her side. Kanna reached out with a shaky hand.

"Meizan . . . is that you?"

"Though you didn't have to send Aina away like that," Meizan continued. "She's been desperate to find you. It's why she joined the Balancers."

"It really *is* you." The chief sat up slowly and studied Meizan's face. "When I learned those rats had possession of your blade, I could only hope. But their trade offer sounded so absurd, I thought it was a trap."

"It *was* a trap. And bringing Kanjallen with you into it was risky as hell."

"We made it out, didn't we?" Kanna said. "The troops at Kaufgar weren't prepared for a nagamor attack. It was a good chance to catch them off guard and impair Kaldrav's main stronghold. Some of the prisoners we freed could prove worthy allies in the future, and most importantly, I was able to find you." A ghost of a smile flitted across her face. "You look well, Meizan."

"And you look miserable," Meizan replied, to which the chief gave a snort.

"I'm glad to see you escaped Merumarth. I dug Taezur and the others from the lava. They'd drained their chitrons trying to shield themselves, and it took weeks for them to regain consciousness. When I couldn't find your body, I feared you might have . . ."

Meizan gripped her sleeve, relief flooding him at her words. They had survived. All of them.

"How's Taezur doing?" Meizan asked. "Does he still have that tumor in his throat?"

"The tumor is the least of his worries. The fires of Merumarth burn deep. It will be decades before he recovers from the pain."

Meizan nodded, trying not to think too much about that. Taezur had been a grumpy asshole who complained about every flaming thing. Sometimes he made Meizan want to break his teeth and give him something worth complaining about. It would seem he now had that something.

"How do you know my daughter?" Kanna asked. "Did you join that Balancer group too? What are they like? Is the hideout safe?"

"I didn't even know Aina was your bleeding daughter, I just bumped into her in Martharan," Meizan said. "I joined the Balancers after Merumarth exploded because I thought everyone in Kanjallen had been captured or erased. The hideout is safe, for now. We have clean water and beds and good food. But I think Kaldrav is going to attack it one day. His soldiers know the location, but they haven't tried anything yet. Maybe they're scared of Zenyra."

"Zenyra's the woman I fought? She's an upper?"

"A Paramosi, I think. And abnormally powerful, as you've seen. But she's not around much." Meizan paused. "Aren't you going to ask about Aina?"

"There's nothing to ask. I saw her keiza." Kanna reached up to push Meizan's hair back from his forehead. "Yours is brighter too. In all these years, I have never seen it this bright."

"Who cares about shit like that?" Meizan shoved her hand away. "Aina's going to be a mess after what you did."

"So let her cry and curse at me from the warmth of her bed. She'll get over it after a few good meals." At his surly expression, the chief gave a sharp laugh. "There are a hundred different ways I've failed Aina as a mother. But the one thing I have never failed at is keeping her safe."

"And you think she's safer with the Balancers?"

"If the Balancers fall, Aina can always ascend to Mayana. She stays in Malin for me. Because she is a disobedient brat who never listens to her mother." She looked at Meizan and patted his cheek. "You're not like her, Meizan. You're a good kid who always heeds my commands."

Meizan stiffened. "What are you getting at?"

"Kanjallen is no longer safe for you."

"What?" Meizan cried, outraged. "It's my clan! My home! Our clanmates are finally free—"

"After great efforts on *my* part to break them out of Agakor," Kanna said. "In the weeks since, Kaldrav's troops have pursued us across the realm. We've evaded capture so far due to a combination of the nagamor and our enemies being more disorganized than usual. But once the beast loses its element of surprise, we'll be at a disadvantage, and those maggots won't rest till every one of us is back in chains."

"Why run when we can fight?" Meizan protested. "Every one of our members is worth at least twenty of Kaldrav's. And even without the element of surprise, that nagamor's got to be worth more than a quarter of his weak-ass army."

"We *are* fighting when it makes strategic sense. But with Kaldrav's numbers continuing to grow, I doubt that will be enough."

"But we have *you* too, Chief! How did you get so powerful? And how are you controlling the beast? Did you bond with it—

like the bestial warriors of Kal Ekana? Did you restore our alliance with the nagamor? You could overthrow Kaldrav yourself if the bleeding roach dared to show his face in a fight!"

"I do not think I will remain in Malin that long," the chief said gravely.

Meizan's eyes widened. "You don't mean . . ."

"You asked how I got so powerful? How I can control that nagamor?" Kanna shook her head. "I did not bond with it, Meizan. I could not. I am not so blessed, to be favored by that beast."

"Then how?"

"There are some things you're better off not knowing. My only hope is to wipe out as much of Kaldrav's army as I can before I fall."

"No," Meizan said vehemently. He would not accept it. The chief could not fall to Narakh. She was ruthless at times, but whatever she did was for their protection.

But then he remembered the feeling of her chitrons at Kaufgar. So vile and full of hate.

"I don't know what you're doing for your power," Meizan said. "And with that nagamor. But whatever it is, it's not worth it."

"I am the chief," she said softly. "For the future of Kanjallen, everything is worth it."

"All the more reason I should stay. Kaldrav's soldiers took my sword, but I want to be your second-in-command. I'll take the trial and defeat whomever I have to."

"There's no need for a trial. I already think of you as my second-in-command, Meizan. Ever since that day in Martharan when I entrusted you with the future of our clan."

"But I . . ." Meizan found himself at a loss for words. He should have felt proud—elated—that his chief thought of him so highly. But all he felt was a creeping sense of shame.

I failed her. She trusted me back then, and I failed her.

"I'm not . . ." Meizan tried again. *Deserving. Worthy.* "I want a chance to prove myself."

"Then prove yourself." Chief Kanna rose. "By fulfilling my final command."

She reached for her hip and unbuckled her own sword—a curved blade with a gem-encrusted hilt—along with its leather scabbard.

"Return to the Balancers, Meizan. Return and stay with them. Regardless of what Toranic Law may indicate, you have a good soul. One day, you may even ascend yourself."

"I don't want that." Meizan jumped to his feet. "I want to stay here and fight for Kanjallen. For you."

"Return to the Balancers, Meizan," Kanna repeated, her tone firm as she secured her scabbard to Meizan's belt. It was heavier than his old one and felt wrong at his waist.

Meizan made to protest, and she added, "As your chief, I command it."

She put a hand on his shoulder, squeezing hard. "You have served me and Kanjallen well, but it's time you took care of yourself. And . . ." Her voice wavered. "My daughter. Please, Meizan. Take care of Aina."

THE CHIEF'S FINAL command echoed through Meizan's mind as he journeyed back to Incaraz, along with her ominous implications that she might fall to Narakh. Kaldrav hadn't even fallen to Narakh yet. What the flaming hell had Kanna done?

Meizan stepped through the chitronic shield three days later, surprised when it let him in without trouble. He scaled the crater and peered over its inner edge, relieved to see the candles were lit in Aina's room. Through the window, he could see her silhouette curled in bed.

Take care of Aina, the chief had said.

Meizan wasn't sure what that entailed, but Aina being safe in Incaraz seemed good enough for now. Scanning the others' windows, he noticed Aranel's was dark.

It's probably his turn for lookout.

He searched the thicket and found Aranel leaning against a tree with his nose buried in a book. Meizan wasn't sure how he could read in this gloom. Or how this constituted as lookout in any way.

Unable to resist, Meizan picked up a fallen tree branch and lunged at the upper. With reflexes quick as lightning, Aranel dropped his book and whirled around, palms glowing with green energy. Hazel eyes widened, and Meizan took advantage of his momentary confusion to pin Aranel against the tree, bringing the branch to his neck.

"Still too slow," Meizan said with a smirk.

"Meizan . . ." Aranel breathed. "What are you doing here?"

Meizan raised an eyebrow. "Thought you'd be more excited, given how hard you tried to convince me to stay."

Aranel shoved him away, flushing. "Th-that was just— I was just concerned about your soul, is all."

"That's what everything's about with you, isn't it?"

"But what of Kanjallen?" Aranel asked, fighting down a smile. "Why are you here?"

Meizan considered that carefully, before replying, "Loyalty."

"Loyalty?" Aranel's face lit up.

"Loyalty," Meizan repeated, flicking his keiza. "Why are you smiling like an idiot?"

"It's nothing," Aranel said, but the grin he gave Meizan was the happiest he'd ever seen on anyone. "I'm just— I really— It's nothing."

Liar.

It definitely wasn't nothing. Aranel wasn't loyal to the Balancers himself, so why did it matter to him that Meizan had returned? But Meizan was in no mood to ask or analyze that eccentric Mayani brain. He tossed the branch aside and began climbing the tree Aranel had been leaning against.

"What are you doing?" Aranel asked, still grinning.

"Lookout," Meizan said. He swung his legs over the bough, then settled against the trunk. "Since you're bleeding useless at it. I got through, and you didn't even realize."

"That's because the chitronic shield is supposed to let you pass." Aranel sat on the grass below Meizan and picked up his book. "You belong here."

CHAPTER NINETEEN

❦

The Second Principle

Y OU ARE NO *daughter of mine.*
The words replayed through Aina's mind in cold, punctuated syllables that raked at her like claws. She burrowed into the bedcovers and stared out her window. A day had passed since their return to Incaraz. Aina hadn't left her bed since.

You are no daughter of mine.

A shadow appeared over the rim of the crater. Aina vaguely registered it to be Meizan. So he was back. She couldn't bring herself to care.

You are no daughter of mine.

Squeezing her eyes shut, Aina curled into a ball. She tried to drown out her mother's icy voice.

You are no daughter of mine.

"Liar!" Aina shrieked, tearing at her hair. "She didn't mean— She wouldn't—"

Aina dug her fingers into her scalp and screamed in frustration. Maybe if she dug deep enough, she could uproot the memories and toss them away, pretend none if it ever happened, pretend she hadn't just been rejected by a mother she had spent over a year trying to find.

"Aina." The mattress dipped and soft fingers gripped her wrists. Sorrow lined Zenyra's lovely face. "Aina, I am so sorry, child. I am so incredibly sorry."

Zenyra blurred before her, and then Aina was sobbing loudly. Tears dripped down her cheeks and soaked Zenyra's tunic. The older woman wrapped an arm around Aina and held her as she cried.

"It hurts, does it not?" Zenyra whispered against Aina's hair. "I know, child. I know the pain. The pain of separation. Of being torn from the one you love most."

"I don't love her!" Aina pulled away with a snarl. "I never *loved* her! But she was the only family I had. Even if she treated me like a nuisance, I thought somewhere in her stinking heart she might actually—" She hiccuped, and Zenyra patted her on the back. "I made a mess of things, didn't I? I broke the rules and endangered everyone. I even forced you to channel in Malin. I'm the one who should be sorry."

"You need not apologize," Zenyra said. Her kind eyes held no judgment. "You did a foolish and reckless thing, running away from the village. But we are all permitted some amount of folly and recklessness in our lifetimes. It is only natural." She gave Aina a small smile. "There was no lasting harm done. My soul remains light, and even Meizan has returned to us. The universe was on our side, I think."

"More like you were on our side." Aina sniffled, eyes flickering to Zenyra's keiza. It had dimmed, but not considerably so.

"No one's been able to fight her like that before. She always protected me from enemies and was the strongest person I knew. She did everything in her power to keep us away from the war. And now . . . she's leader of a rebel clan and rides a nagamor."

Aina gave a harsh laugh. "A part of me suspected she enjoyed violence, but I made excuses for her in my mind. I was stupid to think she needed saving from it all. Stupid to think she *wanted* to be saved, stupid to walk into Malin for her."

"For what it is worth, *I* am glad you entered this realm," Zenyra said. "You may have lost your purpose, Aina, but you can always find a new one. The Balancers' purpose remains."

Aina looked at her in confusion. "You're letting me stay? You're not throwing me out?"

"Why would I do something like that?"

"I broke the rules! I snuck out and put Aranel and Meizan in danger."

"I suspect Meizan would have left regardless of what you did," Zenyra said. "But he is back now. And Aranel needed to see what the world is truly like. He does not realize it, but this may be the best thing for him, in the long run."

"So you're not going to punish me?" Aina asked. A glimmer of hope broke through the dread. "You'll let me continue training as a Balancer?"

"You are clearly distraught at your own folly, which you summarized nicely yourself." Zenyra's eyes twinkled. "I trust you will obey my instructions and never run away like this again."

"Never," Aina said fervently. "I swear it. From now on, I'll listen to every word you say."

"Good. While I would do it again in a heartbeat, I would prefer you not put me in a situation where I must risk my soul to protect you, Aina."

"There was only ever one person"—Aina's lower lip trembled—"who risked their soul to protect me. Though when I think about it, my mother—no, *Kanna*—wasn't risking anything at all when she channeled. Her soul was dark to begin with."

She looked at Zenyra, a burning question consuming her thoughts. "Why would you go so far for me? Is it because it's part of your mission to help those in need?"

"It is because you are important to me, Aina! Surely you realize that."

You are important to me.

The words wrapped around Aina like a quilt. Warm and soft, they soothed the wounds Kanna had opened. She gazed at Zenyra, affection stirring in her chest.

Bronze skin unlined, the Paramosi woman appeared far younger than Aina suspected she was. Like a woman in her third or fourth decade—around the same age Kanna had been when she'd given birth.

Aina didn't know who her father was. According to Kanna, he had been a waste of a human. Sometimes Aina liked to think it was his fault Kanna cursed at her so much. Because Aina reminded her of him. Not because she found her own daughter a burden.

Yet, for whatever reason, maybe to lighten her own soul, Kanna had never abandoned her. She'd dragged Aina with her, and Aina had followed. The woman had been the least diabolical thing in a land teeming with evil and had kept Aina safe from the rest.

In a matter of a few hours, Zenyra had protected Aina in the same way Kanna always had, risking her soul in ways Kanna never could have.

"I wish I'd been born to *you* instead," Aina blurted.

Zenyra gave a musical laugh, eyes crinkling. "Just as well. I like to think of Incaraz as my home and the Balancers as my . . . not quite my children. But an integral part of my life. Without the Balancers, there would be little purpose to my existence, and you, in particular, are very special to me." She smiled, and Aina wondered if Zenyra might hug her again.

Instead, she moved Aina's bangs to examine her keiza.

"Amazing," Zenyra murmured. "Even after a prolonged projection exposed to the chitrons of Malin, your soul has not changed its spin as quickly as I would have expected."

"That's great," Aina said, unable to find it in herself to match Zenyra's enthusiasm. "You know, we wouldn't have found ourselves in that situation if I could channel properly. Have you made any progress as to my kei—"

She stopped herself, mortified. Zenyra had risked her soul for her, and here Aina was demanding that the Paramosi woman fix her keiza.

"None yet," Zenyra said, still deep in thought. "Although I believe I have figured out the connection between the white flash and how it relates to ascension. Correct me if I am wrong, Aina, but you said you remained in a blank space for a few good seconds?"

"I think so."

"Did you see a torana anywhere in the space?"

"A torana?" Aina cried. "No! But I wasn't especially looking. Why would there be a torana?"

"How familiar are you with the Second Principle of Chitronic Equilibrium?"

"Not very," Aina said, bemused. "Aranel might have mentioned it a couple times, but nobody listens when he starts showing off."

"Listen carefully to me, then," Zenyra said. "The Second Principle of Chitronic Equilibrium states that souls can only exist in realms with a chitronic rotational speed equal to or less than their own."

She looked at Aina expectantly. Aina stared back, fidgeting with her bedsheets.

"Take the example of a Mayani soul," Zenyra said, "with an average positive chitronic spin of say, one hundred forward rotations per second. Now, this soul can exist in any of the lower realms, since the spins of these realms are backward and thus negative. But it cannot exist in Paramos, for which the required minimum chitronic spin is somewhere around one million forward rotations per second.

"Similarly, a Malini soul with a backward spin cannot ascend to Mayana, where the required minimum spin is a positive one rotation per second. But it can descend freely to Narakh, which has no requirements. Am I making sense?"

Aina nodded slowly. "Kind of?"

"The Aria of Ascension puts it nicely," Zenyra continued. " 'In realms which spin lower, a soul may exist; but realms which spin higher shall that soul resist.' "

"Which means that a soul can only enter a realm if its spin passes a certain lower limit," Aina said, catching on. "Wait, isn't that essentially Toranic Law?"

"In a manner of speaking." Zenyra beamed at her. "The Second Principle is what governs the workings of the torana, enforcing upon the realms the ultimate and unbreakable order of the universe. So while some may consider it all religious, the reality is nothing more than chitronic science."

"Right," Aina muttered. Even if the bleeding law was science, it didn't make her resent it any less. "So it really is absolute. Guess there's no chance of Kaldrav's army breaking it down, then."

"Breaking it down?" Zenyra's brow creased. "Wherever did you hear that?"

"In Kaufgar. A couple of soldiers were talking about it. They said the king has a plan to break Toranic Law so they can invade the upper realms. I couldn't tell whether they were being serious. In any case, they didn't seem to think he'd succeed."

"Would it please you if he did?"

"You mean he can?" Aina exclaimed. "Is that Kaldrav's grand plan, to attack the torana? Is there some scientific way his soldiers can break in and enter?"

"The sun will sooner diminish before Toranic Law falls to the likes of mere soldiers," Zenyra said disdainfully. "No Malini army, however large, could pose a threat."

"I see." Aina tried to ignore the shred of disappointment she felt at Zenyra's statement.

A part of her had hoped that without Toranic Law, Kanna might ascend. That in Mayana she might treat Aina with kindness. But it seemed there was no chance for her after all.

"Coming back to the Second Principle," Zenyra reminded her. "Descension from Mayana to Malin occurs when a soul changes spin—from positive to negative, forward to backward, whichever term you prefer. When this happens, that soul is dragged through a nearby torana by force. Or, if there is no torana in the vicinity, a temporary one materializes.

"On the contrary, when a soul's spin changes from negative to positive, they are not forced through the torana from Malin into Mayana. Because the Second Principle still allows souls to exist in realms with spins lesser than their own. However, they become able to ascend if they so wish."

"That's what happened to me," Aina confirmed. "I never even realized I could ascend till I slipped through the torana. But what does that have to do with the blank space or white flash?"

"There is a moment in ascension and descension between Malin and Mayana," Zenyra said, "when the soul stops spinning altogether. It is an infinitesimal moment before the soul's spin changes direction. In that instant, the soul has a spin of zero."

"A soul with no spin." It made sense mathematically, though Aina still didn't see why it was important.

"During that split second of zero spin," Zenyra said, "the soul passes through another place. The Universal Void. Some call it the fifth realm."

"There's a fifth realm?" Aina asked, sitting upright.

"The Void is not a habitable realm like the others, just a blank space of nothingness. It is not governed by Toranic Law, which means any can enter it. However, the Preservation destroyed nearly all the torana leading to the Void centuries ago.

"The only remaining way to access it is to open a torana by force. This happens naturally when a soul's spin becomes zero, although the torana disappears once the soul starts spinning again. For most souls, the transition is so fast that the Void remains open for a split second, registered in the brain as no more than a flash of white.

"But in your case . . ." Zenyra paused. "Since your chitrons change their spin more gradually than most, your transition through the Void lasts a few full seconds. The torana you open ought to remain usable for that time, before it disappears."

Her eyes sparkled, but Aina still did not understand the appeal. "What's in the Void?"

"Nothing, supposedly," Zenyra said. "It is called the Universal Void for that reason, and its function remains a mystery."

"Then why did the Preservation destroy all the torana leading to it?"

"Do not ask me why the Preservation do anything, Aina. The actions of those sanctimonious fools oft defy logic."

"Right." Aina sighed. "So I can open a door to a nowhere realm with nothing in it."

Did Zenyra think this tidbit of information would cheer her up? It was oddly intriguing, but Aina could find no use for it. Besides, she did not think her soul would change spin again soon, given the state of her keiza. She had spent half a day flying around

Malin with her chitrons bared, after all, and her keiza still shone bright.

"Is my defect the only reason I'm not like her?" Aina asked, alarmed by the revelation. "You said it yourself. My soul changes spin slower than others. If my keiza was normal, does that mean I would have descended by now?"

Much as Aina had wanted to descend to Malin before, four moons with the Balancers had made her realize being Mayani was not so bad after all. She didn't want to become like Kaldrav's soldiers, who harmed innocent children without a care. She didn't want to become like Kanna, who destroyed everything around her each time she channeled.

Aina looked at Zenyra desperately, her voice small. "I don't want to turn into a monster."

"Oh, Aina," Zenyra said softly. "You sweet child." She took Aina's hands in hers. "You could never be a monster. Not when you have such a good, kind heart."

"How do you know that?" Aina asked. "I've done bad things too. Not as bad as my—as Kanna. But up in Mayana, I stole, and I injured, and I did things that would be punishable by Toranic Law. I wish I hadn't done them, but I already have."

"Toranic Law does not judge solely by action, Aina. Your intention, and that you deeply regret what you did, does not undo your sins. But it may lessen their severity."

Aina nodded, and Zenyra's eyes crinkled as she stood. "I did not tell you about your keiza to make you doubt yourself, Aina. I wanted you to know you are special . . . in more ways than one."

ONCE SHE WAS feeling sufficiently calm, Aina left her room in search of Meizan.

She wasn't sure what had prompted his return, but he had

known Kanna in the year Aina had been in Mayana. Despite what Aina had told Zenyra—what she believed—she needed to hear it from him. Hear that Kanna really had not cared.

Meizan wasn't in his room, by the lake, or under the banyan tree. Aina climbed the crater to search the thicket. There was no sign of him, but Aina did come across Aranel seated under a tree and lost in thought as he poked absently at the dirt with a branch.

Right. Today was Aranel's turn for lookout.

Aina took a step forward, trying to calm her nerves. She didn't know what was wrong with her. She had spoken to Aranel alone before. More often than not, he ended up pissing her off with his various obsessions—Toranic Law, his brother, ascension.

He's just a soul-obsessed freak, Aina told herself as she wiped sweaty palms on her trousers. A soul-obsessed freak who had risked his soul coming to a battlefield to find *her.*

Aina took another step forward. Then she turned on her heel and made to leave the clearing.

"Aina?"

Her heart stumbled at his voice, and Aina wanted to punch something. Was there a defect in her heart as well? She turned back around, avoiding Aranel's eyes.

"How are you feeling?" he asked. Something about his careful, gentle tone made Aina want to cry all over again.

Instead, she forced herself to look up at him despite the wild fluttering in her heart.

"I learned about the Second Principle," Aina said. "And I can open a door to nowhere."

"You're in a strange mood."

"Where's Meizan? I need to talk to Meizan."

"He left for the springs a few minutes ago." Aranel stepped toward her. She could count the flecks of gold in his eyes. "Is it about your mother, Aina? Are you doing all right?"

Aina looked away. She didn't think she could handle a conversation about Kanna with Aranel of all people right now.

"Forgive me for asking. Of course you're not." Aranel rested a hand on Aina's shoulder, and the fluttering increased tenfold. "Just . . . take care of yourself, all right?"

As they stood there, Aina found herself wishing against her better judgment that he'd step closer. Stroke her hair. Take her hand in his. Her fingers twitched, but before she could reach out, Aranel released her with a sad smile and returned to his spot by the tree.

Heart galloping, Aina squeaked out a thank-you and bolted from the clearing.

Stupid defective heart, Aina thought, speeding down the crater. *You're worse than my keiza!*

She stopped by the lake near the entrance to the hot springs, hoping Meizan would be in a good mood once he got out. The springs tended to do that. Aina needed a visit herself.

Meizan emerged a few minutes later and sat by her side on the ground. Neither of them spoke. When Aina pulled off her boots to dip her feet into the lake, Meizan did the same.

"I didn't think you'd come back," Aina finally said. "Did Kanna discard you too?"

Meizan stiffened, exhaling through his nose. "Sort of. Are you going to be okay?"

"You know what she's like. That woman was never one for kindness, and . . ." Aina bit her lip. "Did she ever speak about me? Did you know who I was? Or that I existed?" Meizan shook his head, and Aina's shoulders sagged.

"I know now." Meizan offered her a half-smile. "We're clanmates, Aina."

"Clanmates," Aina repeated. "I don't think of myself as part of Kanjallen."

"You'd be lucky to be," Meizan said fiercely. "Kanjallen is the last free clan and the only one brave enough to stand against Kaldrav."

Even now, his eyes glinted when he spoke of his clan. Kanna might have discarded him as she had Aina, but Meizan was still loyal to Kanjallen.

Aina watched as Meizan unbuckled the scabbard at his waist and held it out to her wordlessly.

"Is that . . . ?" Aina peered closer. It was not the sword Meizan usually wielded, but a thicker blade, its hilt set with glittering blue gems.

"Stones from the shell of a manikai," Meizan said. "They amplify the power of any channeling."

"That's useful. A better replacement for what I lost."

"It's a relic from Kal Ekana. Won by our first chief, Akanen, from an enemy clan in battle. It's been passed down through chiefs since, and last belonged to your mother. She gave it to me. But you should have it."

Aina pushed the scabbard away with a shake of her head. "She meant it for you, Meizan. Keep it."

Meizan said nothing as he refastened the weapon to his belt.

Aina leaned back on her elbows and watched the banyan. Its blossoms swayed in the cold breeze that whistled through the crater. She was reminded of the feast from about a moon ago, the night Hiraval and the other Balancers had left. They'd met Taralei since, but not the other two.

"I wonder how they're doing," Aina said. "Hiraval and Reimi. Incaraz feels empty without them." Especially Hiraval, who had been more involved in her training than even Zenyra had.

The Balancers must gather on occasion. Visit one another in the villages.

Aina would very much like to meet them again. Aranel and

Meizan would be there too, and Zenyra, of course. They could drink Amaratisian wine and play Spin of Our Souls, placing bets upon the results.

"I don't know what being in a clan is like." Aina turned to Meizan. "But do you think—do you think the Balancers could be our clan too?"

Meizan's lips curled, and Aina wasn't sure if he was smiling or mocking her.

WHEN AINA RETURNED to her room, she stopped in front of her dresser. Kanna's rock figurines stood in a neat row, as Aina had placed them a few weeks ago. It had seemed a waste keeping them inside a dusty pouch, especially once Aranel had fixed them.

Aina swiped her forehead. A blast of chitrons raged from her hands and ground the figurines to dust. She swept the particles off her dresser and out the window, watching as they floated across the crater, then disappeared into the darkness like the mother she no longer had.

CHAPTER TWENTY

@

Divine Logic

URING MOMENTS LIKE this, Aranel longed for his golden wolf helm; while stifling to wear, it did a tremendous job of concealing emotion. He struggled to keep his expression blank as he sat cross-legged atop his pole in the lake. Meizan and Aina balanced on their own poles, deep in conversation.

And as with every blessed conversation of the past week since they'd returned from Kaufgar, this one, too, had converged on one topic: the history and customs of clan Kanjallen.

"It was during the golden age of Kal Ekana," Meizan was saying, "when the clans were at war. The other side had the gazarou. Flaming wolves could snap a man in half with one bite."

"The gazarou are gentle beasts," began Aranel, but both Meizan and Aina ignored him.

"We needed something to balance the fight," continued Meizan, "but the megarya were elusive, and the last clan who dared approach a vandraghor was eaten alive. So we had no choice but to seek the nagamor's alliance in the great war."

"We?" Aranel interrupted. "The One Realm Era ended centuries before *you* were born. And I'd hardly call it a golden age. It was full of bloodshed and destruction, and the 'great' war you speak of threatened to shatter the universe and—" He stopped himself, wishing he could retract his words.

While the Great Toranic Separation brought peace to the upper realms, Aranel had witnessed firsthand the war that continued to rage across Malin. He remembered Meizan's comments about death, how many Malini wished for it.

The situation during Kal Ekana might have been preferable to their current reality.

"We, as in clan Kanjallen," Meizan deigned to reply, before returning to his story as if Aranel didn't exist.

Aranel's guilt gave way to irritation, along with an urge to shove Meizan off his pole. It wasn't as if this training exercise required much concentration anymore, given their progress with precision channeling. Every time Aranel had tried to make conversation, Meizan and Aina either made fun of him or sniped at him to shut up.

"Our chief, Akanen, approached one of the nagamor," said Meizan to Aina. "He held its gaze for a full day, and in that time lived through lifetimes of suffering. But Akanen endured the pain and didn't look away. And with that, he gained the nagamor's blessing and an agreement they would fight alongside his clan in the war."

"You've got the timeline all wrong," said Aranel irritably. "According to the Song of Salvation, the alliances between human and beast happened *before* the war started—"

"Akanen never fully recovered from the trauma." Meizan went on, as if he hadn't heard him. "Even as he fought through the war, his tears never stopped flowing. Eternal tears shed in eternal pain, to gain us the alliance of the nagamor."

"That didn't last, did it?" asked Aina. "Why did the alliance crumble?"

Aranel narrowed his eyes. What was her problem?

Aina had never cared for Malini politics. But ever since her mother had been revealed as Meizan's clan chief, Aina had become unusually interested in everything he said. And Meizan was encouraging it, regaling her with tales about Kanjallen's past. Tales that—historically inaccurate depictions of Kal Ekana aside—he'd never bothered sharing with Aranel, much as Aranel had asked.

If he has so much spare time, he ought to practice projection instead of being Aina's personal storyteller.

Aranel turned to his clan-obsessed teammate, an admonition at the tip of his tongue. Meizan was recounting one of Kanjallen's battles as he twirled an index finger above the lake. With the slightest of movements, Meizan summoned looping fountains and tiny hurricanes, bending the water to his will.

Aranel watched in fascination as a little nagamor, thick as his forearm, materialized in front of them. It arced through the air and circled overhead, showering them with droplets.

His competitive side spurred, Aranel flicked his fingers. His chitrons threaded through the dirt and molded from it a small figurine. The dirtman dashed up Aranel's arm to perch on his shoulder. He equipped it with a grass bow and sharpened twigs, which it began shooting at the nagamor in earnest.

Meizan gave a huff, and his watery creation shot upward to dodge the barrage.

They dueled like that for a while, Aranel raising a tiny regiment of dirtmen to battle the nagamor. Their chitronic creations clashed furiously until Meizan's nagamor opened its watery beak and dove toward the army of dirtmen, who raised their bows in response.

The nagamor swerved at the last moment. It splashed against Aranel's face, drenching him in frigid water.

"What was that for?" demanded Aranel with a glare.

Shoulders shaking, Meizan covered his mouth and didn't respond. His dark eyes curved into crescents, and Aranel's embarrassment turned to wonder.

He'd never seen Meizan laugh. He hadn't thought him capable.

"You'd know, if you'd fought in a real battle before," said Meizan, fighting to keep a straight face. "The best tactic is to take out the commander."

"Fine," relented Aranel, wringing his hair. "You took out the commander. But given your nagamor has dissipated and most of my army is still intact"—he motioned at his dirtmen—"I win this round. Which brings us back to a tie this week."

Meizan's scowl returned. "I'm still at four wins to your three. Yesterday's spar was a stalemate."

"How was that a stalemate? You collapsed three seconds before I did."

"And you count that as a win?"

"A full three seconds," said Aranel.

"Fine." Meizan rolled his eyes. "Take what you can. It's the only way you stand a chance."

Aranel cursed at him, and Meizan's lips quirked. "Such hatred, Aranel. Careful it doesn't weigh down your soul."

"My soul puts up with you every waking hour, Toranic Law will understand," retorted Aranel, suppressing a smile of his own.

Meizan hopped off his pole ten minutes later and announced he was headed to the hot springs.

"Do you have to go now?" Aina sounded panicked. "I—um—I wanted to spar!"

"I'll spar with you," said Aranel.

"No!" Aina leaped off her pole and refused to meet Aranel's eyes. "N-not you. Meizan. He's been teaching me the Kanjallen fighting style."

"What?" Aranel bristled. "Why? What's wrong with how you fight now?"

Aina didn't respond, and Aranel felt another spike of annoyance. He was convinced more than ever now that she was avoiding him. Aranel didn't know what he'd done to offend her, but she'd spent the past few days refusing to speak with him, while clinging to Meizan like ivy.

And receiving private sparring lessons, apparently.

Am I not one who's suffered the brunt of his flashy, dizzying fight style ever since we got here? So why is he teaching it to her?

Aranel hoped Meizan would refuse Aina's invitation. But he agreed, much to Aranel's dismay, and followed Aina across the lake.

"I'm getting the hang of it," Aina was saying. "I think I'll match you with more training."

"It's centuries too soon for that," replied Meizan.

As Aranel watched them leave, his chest tightened at the half smile that played across Meizan's lips. Seeing it directed at Aina made him sick to the stomach.

It's the chitrons, Aranel told himself firmly, tearing his eyes away from the pair. *It's the chitrons of Malin, finally taking their toll on me.*

ARANEL'S FOUL MOOD persisted when he met Seirem that night by the torana.

"I would ask for your report." Seirem frowned as he took in Aranel's stormy demeanor and lack of proper greeting. "But it seems you have something to say first."

"I visited one of the Balancer villages a week ago," said Aranel without preamble, and Seirem leaned forward expectantly. "Taralei was there, with a group of Malini children. They'd been injured in the war, and we healed them."

"That is the Balancers' stated goal, after all. You did a good thing, Aranel."

"But had they been born to Mayana, I wouldn't have needed to. Had they been born to a peaceful life, as I was."

"But they were not, unfortunate as that is," said Seirem. "What are you implying, Aranel?"

"I respect Toranic Law." Aranel's thumbs drew rapid circles against his thighs. "And I believe its judgment to be just for those born to Mayana who commit wrongdoings and fall to Malin as a result. But I don't see how it's fair to babies and children. To those born to Malin. Or to N-Narakh."

"The Narakhi cannot bear children. Their bodies are far too twisted."

"But the Malini can! Those children I healed were so young, Lord Seirem. Some could hardly even speak or walk." Aranel's voice quaked as he thought of the wailing toddler at the Balancer village. What fate would have awaited them, had Zenyra not found them in time? "It seems unjust that they're condemned to a life of eternal suffering before they ever commit any sin."

"They are not condemned for eternity," said Seirem. "If they remain on the right path, their suffering will allow them to ascend in time."

"But why must they suffer in the first place? What wrong could a baby possibly do? Why was he born to a lower realm, judged before he even had a chance to think or act for himself?"

"Some say those born to Malini are inherently evil by nature, and that evil only reveals itself as they grow—"

"They're not!" Aranel burst out. "I know someone, my age,

who grew up in Malin. He's a jerk, but he's not *evil*. He never was. It was just the influence of the chitrons and everything else plaguing that infernal realm!"

"Even so, it is not your burden to bear, but his parents'. The Malini are at fault for bringing children into such a world. That sin rests upon them."

Aranel stared at the Preserver, aghast. "What are you saying? That the Malini should never bear children? That those children should have never been born at all?" As he thought of Meizan and Aina, a wave of anger overtook him. "They deserve to be in this world, Lord Seirem. What they don't deserve is the suffering that's been thrust upon them."

"That may be so, but I did not make the rules, Aranel," said Seirem, a hint of weariness in his voice. "Are you doubting Toranic Law?"

"I—I'm not doubting it," stuttered Aranel.

Except he was. He'd been hoping Seirem would have an answer for him, some divine logic that justified Meizan and Aina being born to Malin. But the Preserver had nothing, and Aranel felt empty.

"Aina was right," whispered Aranel. "It *is* flawed."

No, it's more than flawed. The entire system . . . it's twisted. Wrong. Our lives are shaped by the realm of our birth, and our births are determined by luck.

"Aranel." Seirem's voice was stern. "Even if Toranic Law has its flaws, it is absolute and not something to be questioned. You need to shift your focus to Zenyra if you want to ascend. During your time in the village, did you discover anything that could be linked to the erasures we spoke of earlier?"

"Nothing." Aranel crossed his arms. "The Balancers' mission is full of good intention. If anything, their presence in the villages will reduce the likelihood of a soul voluntarily erasing."

"So you say, Aranel. But I recorded two disturbances in the chitronic system last moon, in the days after your cousin's mission was dispatched. I cannot ignore the timing nor the overlap with the Advisory. Why would Zenyra go so far if she truly has nothing to hide?"

"It might be a coincidence. Or perhaps she doesn't want to risk the Preservation interfering. It is no secret that you disapprove of her activities, and the missions *are* important. For her and for the realm."

"There was a third disturbance last week," said Seirem. "Around the time you say you visited the village."

"There was a war going on then!" Aranel snapped, losing patience. "With village raids, and a nagamor torturing hundreds of soldiers with its glare! Respectfully, Lord Seirem, but have you not considered that the war could be the linking factor between the missions and the erasures? That Zenyra only dispatches missions when the needs of the realm are dire? Dire enough to result in souls destroying themselves otherwise?"

Seirem closed his eyes and massaged his temples. "I pray to Sorken that is the case," he said at last. "But I entreat you, Aranel. Delve deeper into the erasures. And please keep an eye on Zenyra."

ARANEL'S THOUGHTS WERE in turmoil as he returned to Incaraz. He crept past Aina, who was practicing stun beams by the thicket, and made his way around the still lake.

A voice punctured the silence. "How fared your meeting with the Preservation, Aranel?"

"My—my what?" Aranel's mind went blank at the sight of Zenyra, a small spyglass in hand, leaning against the banyan. "You're mistaken, I—I was only—"

"I know you are their spy." Zenyra waved him off. She glided across the lake to stop in front of him. "Do not lie, Aranel. It is unbecoming of you, and you are quite bad at it."

Aranel stared at her, numb. "You were watching me?" he managed, nodding at her spyglass.

"Oh, this?" Zenyra twirled the spyglass in her fingers before stowing it away. "No, this is for stargazing. A favored pastime of mine."

"Then did Meizan tell you?" Was this what his teammate had meant by loyalty?

"Meizan knew?" asked Zenyra. "If so, he never said a word. But I suspected it the day you walked into this crater. I had never seen you at any of our recruitment meetings, and I knew from Taralei that your family had connections to the Preservation. My suspicions were confirmed when I saw you sneak out of Incaraz while you were supposed to be on lookout duty."

Aranel gulped, looking anywhere but at the Paramosi woman. "If you knew, why did you not stop me?"

"Because I have nothing to hide," said Zenyra. "I do not know what the Preservation suspect, but my mission here is clear: to provide equal opportunity to all, regardless of soul-spin. Even if you revealed the location of Incaraz, those fools are too terrified to enter Malin. There is no information you could give them that would get in my way. So I thought it best to let you continue freely and learn the truth for yourself."

"Learn what truth?"

"That the Preservation are the problem, not the Balancers." Zenyra fixed him with a shrewd stare. "You are not convinced. I sense you have begun to doubt yourself, but you doubt me as well. Out with it, then."

"Out with what?"

"Your questions, your suspicions. Lay it all out, Aranel. I will tell you everything you wish to know."

Aranel was taken aback. He had not expected that, but Zenyra's face was frank, her keiza burning brightly. He had nothing to lose. This woman would never harm him, and the conversation with Seirem had left Aranel more confused than ever. Some clarity would be welcome.

"When you saved us from Kaufgar, why did you attack Kanjallen?" he asked. "I don't know how much Aina told you, but you've been in this realm for years. You must have known Kaldrav's soldiers were the real threat."

"Aina did not tell me anything, and I only received a vague message through Taralei," answered Zenyra. "As for why I attacked Kanjallen—I try to keep the Balancers as removed from realm politics as possible. When I reached Kaufgar, the chaos made it difficult to differentiate friend from foe, and my priority was breaking you three out. If you recall, it was Aina's mother who attacked me first. I only did what was necessary to defend myself."

"And what of the other Balancers? I met Taralei, but are Hiraval and Reimi well? And what about the ones who came before?"

"You could have met several others," said Zenyra dryly, "had you and your dear teammates not disobeyed my instructions and gotten yourselves captured. I planned to have you assist another village or two, but you can understand why I am less enthusiastic to do so now."

Aranel hung his head. When she put it that way, he felt foolish for even asking.

"It is all right, Aranel," said Zenyra. "I know you only wanted to help your friends. Now, do not hold back from telling me what is truly bothering you."

"The hot springs." Aranel raised his eyes to meet Zenyra's. "The water does strange things to my chitrons. It's not natural.

And I know about the second barrier too, the one beneath the lake. Are you hiding something, Zenyra? What is it, exactly, that flows through the springs?"

Zenyra's countenance darkened at his question, and for a moment, Aranel felt more terrified for his soul than he ever had since coming to Malin. But then she relaxed, and his fear passed, for Zenyra looked nothing more than a weary woman.

"It is a question I should never have put you in a position to ask," she said gravely. "I only hope you can understand my motives, Aranel, and that I did what I thought best."

"What did you do? What is that liquid?"

"Water. Infused with megarya blood."

Aranel staggered back. "But that's—that's illegal!"

"In Mayana, and for good reason. Do you know why?"

"Because it's blood! Of a megarya, the noblest and purest creature to exist in the realms. You'd have to be utterly barbaric to spill one's blood!"

Aranel's gaze flickered to her keiza in horror. Incaraz's springs were large, far too large to be sustained by the blood of a single megarya. Had she butchered an entire horde?

"It was a gift!" Zenyra's eyes flashed. "The megarya possess the ability to heal themselves, and I was given this blood as a gift. From my dear friend Fei, whom I have known since long before you were born."

"Why did you not tell us about the springs, then? And is that what you're keeping under the lake? A vat of your *friend's* blood?" Aranel shuddered in disgust. "Why in Sherka's name did you have us *bathe* in it?"

"Aranel," said Zenyra, "what I am about to reveal is something you must keep strictly to yourself. Knowledge that none other, outside the Preservation, is privy to."

"And what is that?"

"The secret property of megarya blood." Zenyra lowered her voice. "It can temporarily increase the positive rotational speed of a soul's chitrons."

Aranel's jaw dropped. "You mean . . ."

"It can boost the forward spin of one's soul." Zenyra sighed. "I admit, I have been drinking some regularly myself. That is part of the reason my keiza remains so bright and why I could still ascend to Paramos if I wished, although that is far from the reason I drink it."

"Then why?" Aranel was shaking. "Why do you parade around as a Paramosi, deceiving us all? How dark is your soul, really?"

"Not once have I claimed to be a Paramosi."

"All the same, your keiza—"

"I drink because I am afraid. Being in Malin puts me and my chitrons at risk. And I am worried that if my soul reverses its spin, that could derail the Balancers' entire mission and destroy everything I have built here."

"That is no justification. You're cheating! You're circumventing Toranic Law!"

Aranel thought of Seirem by the golden torana, the shimmering droplets that had spilled from the Preserver's flask. *Youth tonic, my foot! He quotes the Aria of Ascension every damn chance he gets, but he's nothing more than a hypocrite! Sam was right in warning me about him.*

At that, an even more horrifying thought arose: Was that how his brother had ascended? And his parents? Aranel touched his own keiza. Taralei had once told him it had gotten brighter. Was that also an effect of the megarya blood?

I could ascend too. If I drank the blood, I could join Sam in Paramos.

Aranel felt sickened with himself a moment after. That would not be true ascension. He could not partake in such trickery. *But I already have . . .*

"You shouldn't have kept it from us, Zenyra. Every second I spent in those springs, I—" Aranel brought a hand to his mouth and swallowed down bile.

He'd been bathing in megarya blood. It was no small wonder he'd felt so light after, his chitrons so viscerally affected.

"Forgive me, Aranel." Zenyra pressed a fist to her forehead. "I should have never used it on you without your knowledge or consent. But I feared for your soul and all the Balancers'. Even with the shield around Incaraz, being in Malin takes its toll. While the effects of bathing in megarya blood are nowhere near as potent as drinking it, they are enough to neutralize the taint of Malin's chitrons, which I believe is necessary for us to stay in this realm for a prolonged period."

"You still ought to have told us. Given us the choice."

"I did not want to tempt any of the Balancers," said Zenyra, her gaze boring into him. "Drinking it yourselves would be immoral. I think you, more than anyone, can understand why I felt it prudent to withhold the knowledge."

Aranel gave a grudging nod. He wasn't happy with her, but her reasoning made sense.

"By keeping you unaware, I was shouldering the burden of wrongdoing myself. I felt it only fair, and besides . . ." Zenyra gave a mirthless laugh. "I can always drink more blood to ease my soul."

Aranel considered this. "So if a Malini were to drink the blood. One of the children from the villages, or . . . or if Meizan—"

"Do not entertain that thought, Aranel. While it is safe for those of us whose souls spin forward, for a Malini, pure megarya blood can have disastrous consequences if consumed in the wrong quantities." At his enraged expression, Zenyra added, "The blood in the springs is extremely dilute. Even if Meizan swallowed some by accident, he would be in no danger."

"Right," said Aranel, somewhat mollified. "What would happen? If a Malini drank undiluted blood in the wrong quantity?"

"That knowledge would terrify you."

Aranel couldn't tell whether she was telling the truth or trying to dissuade him from trying to find some for Meizan.

"You were right to hide it," he admitted. "I would've been the first fool to try and drink it, if I'd known back then. But not anymore. I swear on Sherka."

"I believe you, Aranel. I would not have told you otherwise. So." Zenyra folded her hands. "Any more questions?"

Aranel inhaled deeply and slid his palms across his face. Despite the outrageousness of it all, he understood Zenyra's logic. She had used the blood for a benevolent purpose—so she could stay pure and continue helping the Malini. She had not used it for her own benefit.

Unlike the wretched Preservation. Aranel balled his fists. Seirem would have lived a plentiful life in Mayana. There was no reason for someone like him to drink the blood unless he wanted to stay in power and remain in Paramos.

And how many other Preservers had done the same thing? How much of their wisdom and purity was nothing but a farce?

And if the Preservation were frauds, it called into question their ideology, their teachings, and Aranel's whole mission. What did they truly want with Zenyra? Were they simply terrified of her because she knew about the megarya blood?

"It seems I have given you plenty to think about," said Zenyra delicately. "Come find me when you have made a decision."

"A decision?"

Zenyra gave him an enigmatic smile. "A decision on where your loyalties lie."

ARANEL STRODE THROUGH Incaraz in search of Aina, but the dratted girl was either at the hot springs or avoiding him again.

You were right, Aranel wanted to tell her. *All along. About everything.* Because Toranic Law was flawed, the Preservation's purity but a charade, and Zenyra the only one worth following.

When he reached their usual training spot by the thicket, Aranel found Meizan, alone, practicing with his new sword. His teammate's presence evoked a confusing rush of emotions that Aranel was not prepared to face, especially when his entire belief system was on the verge of shattering.

But Meizan had noticed him, and Aranel couldn't keep himself from approaching.

Aranel ground out the first thing that came to his mind. "Spar with me."

He was seldom the one to initiate their spars, but Meizan nodded and tossed him a practice sword.

With the rhythmic clashing of metal, Aranel let the muddled thoughts fade from his mind, focusing solely on the whirling of Meizan's sword and the taut muscles of his arms . . . the sharp jut of his cheekbones and the droplets of sweat that clung to his dark lashes . . .

Aranel's breath caught, and he looked away at once.

No, he told himself, horrified by the dawning revelation. The strange fire that Meizan's presence sparked, so unlike anything he'd felt before. *Not him. Anyone but him.*

"What's wrong with you?" asked Meizan as Aranel spun away in retreat. "You're acting weirder than usual."

"It's none of your concern," said Aranel primly. He leaped up to avoid the kick that came flying toward his shin before slamming his sword down with all the strength he could muster.

"You can tell me." Meizan blocked him with ease and shoved him back.

"I don't want to. And it's not as if you've been especially open sharing your past with anyone but Aina."

"If you knew my past," countered Meizan, sending Aranel stumbling back with a flurry of successive blows, "you would cry. And throw up. Then cry some more."

"I would *not*!" Aranel regained his balance and swiped at Meizan's left, then spun around to hit his right. Both times, Meizan twisted away just in time. "You've gotten rather close to Aina lately."

"I have to look after her."

Aranel couldn't believe what he was hearing. Aina was a tiny hooligan and an excellent fighter. She could project her soul with more skill than the both of them combined, and Zenyra doted on her as if she were her own daughter.

"Aina can look after herself," he bit out.

"I know," said Meizan. "But I promised my chief."

Aranel froze at the admission, hardly taking notice of the blade Meizan held to his neck. "What?"

"It was her final command. To look after her daughter." Meizan sheathed his sword with more force than necessary. "If you breathe a word of this to Aina, I'll chop your hair off."

"So when you said loyalty . . ."

Of course. Meizan's loyalties had never shifted. He was still loyal to his Kanjallen chief, and everything he did was as per her command. While a part of Aranel filled with relief, another part felt stung by the discovery.

"Is that the only reason you're here?" asked Aranel. "For her?"

Meizan shrugged. His bangs fell over his eyes, and Aranel was overcome by an urge to push them away. He dared not try, in case Meizan broke his fingers.

"Aina's my clanmate," said Meizan.

"I suppose she is." Aranel swallowed, uncomfortably aware of the thundering in his heart. "But then what am I?"

He regretted the words the moment he said them. Meizan was looking at him as if he'd sprouted scales and a beak. Aranel struggled to come up with an excuse for the question.

He was saved from having to when a loud screech rent the air. A shockwave surged through the thicket. It bent the trees and stripped them of their branches, forcing Aranel and Meizan to the ground so they didn't get swept away.

"The shield," said Meizan. His shock faded to grim resignation. "Kaldrav."

He stood and bolted, with Aranel close behind. They stopped at the eastern rim of the crater that overlooked the rest of Malin. Here, the air around Incaraz was wrinkled like a translucent tissue. It appeared ripped in parts where the chitronic shield unraveled in a cascade of sparks.

And through the largest tear marched a regiment of ironclad soldiers carrying black banners emblazoned with rings of white.

CHAPTER TWENTY-ONE

❂

Enemies Unmade

A SPLIT SECOND OF rumbling was all the warning Meizan had before the crater blasted apart beneath his feet. Kaldrav's regiment either had proficient channelers with them or a bunch of explosives. Meizan hoped like hell for the latter.

"Flaming maggots," he growled, a familiar animosity creeping up within him as he hurtled toward the ground.

Meizan reached for his sword as he landed in front of the incoming soldiers. Aranel dropped gracefully beside him, hands glowing with green light.

"I'll hold them off," Meizan said. "You warn Aina and Zenyra."

"I'd consider that explosion warning enough," Aranel said, shooting off a stun beam.

He had a point. Meizan whipped out his blade, then rammed it through the nearest soldier's helm. It gave a satisfying squelch, and the soldier fell screaming. Meizan drew a thumb across his keiza, Balancer techniques all but forgotten.

The chitrons of Malin oozed forth in response. They brought with them a slick power that engulfed his soul. An acrid taste arose in Meizan's mouth. His sword began to vibrate as the stones set into its pommel amplified the hateful energy.

Meizan raised the sword with a grin, channeling the air into razor-sharp streams that wrapped around the advancing soldiers. He squeezed the pommel and the soldiers fell, their torn flesh dribbling through the cracks in their armor.

Weak, Meizan thought contemptuously. *Pitiful and weak.*

With a rush of adrenaline, he raised his sword again, the wind swirling and swerving at his command. Another four soldiers exploded under the pressure, and the air grew bloody with mist. Aranel was shouting something, his words buzzing at Meizan's ears like flies.

Meizan ignored his teammate in favor of flinging one of his knives at a line of soldiers. He manipulated the air currents so the blade spun across the sky like a boomerang. It sliced off four heads in rapid succession before swinging back to Meizan.

So easy, he thought, laughter bubbling in his throat. Hot blood streamed down his skin, but none of it was his, and Meizan made to throw his blade again when a hand gripped his wrist.

He turned to see Aranel, face white with horror. "What?" Meizan snarled. "We're under attack, don't tell me to—"

Aranel shook his head and pointed wordlessly behind him. A swarm of soldiers had scaled the top of Incaraz. They poured down the northern wall, right near the living quarters.

"Aina." Meizan swore, then turned and sprinted back into the crater, Kaldrav's men in pursuit.

A burst of his chitrons sent another wave of soldiers flying. Out of the corner of his eye, he could see Aranel, long hair whipping around him as he fired off stun beams along with needlelike silver objects.

Kapizer spines, he realized, as a line of soldiers keeled over, yawning. Aranel must have procured them back in Merumarth. The upper fired another round, his expression almost comical when they had no effect on the second wave.

"Manglers," Meizan grunted. He mowed the advancing soldiers down with his blade. "Your trick won't work on them. They inject themselves with kapizer venom from birth, the freaks."

Aranel looked devastated by the realization he was actually going to have to fight properly, but Meizan didn't give a shit. No soldier could build an immunity to chitrons, and he had the power of the realm at his call.

Despite their best efforts, Meizan and Aranel found themselves surrounded by the time they reached the islet at the center of Incaraz. There was still no sign of Aina or Zenyra. Kaldrav's men charged toward the edge of the lake and crowded its banks. With a collective shout, they released a barrage of weapons that flew at the islet from all directions.

Throwing up his arms, Meizan emptied the lake to raise a wall of water that caught the incoming weapons. He spun his hands in a circle, turning the wall into an airborne whirlpool.

Cries and curses rent the air as the whirlpool spat the weapons back at their owners with twice the force. A ring of soldiers toppled over in a spurt of blood. Meizan dropped his arms as a wave of exhaustion washed over him. He doubled over, catching his breath.

Where the *hell* was Zenyra?

"You're channeling too much," Aranel said. His eyes flitted between Meizan's forehead and the jeweled pommel of his sword. "You need a break."

"If I stop, they'll crush us," Meizan panted.

"They won't," Aranel said, face set in determination.

He swiped a thumb across his keiza. The banyan tree behind them gave a groan, its prop roots shooting out of the ground to batter away a volley of arrows. Its branches twisted through the air and wrapped around a dozen soldiers.

The branches squeezed, and Aranel halted the channeling with a cry. But the banyan kept moving, crushing the trapped soldiers until they burst into a pile of flesh, bone, and blood.

Aranel dropped his arm, ashen-faced. "That wasn't supposed to happen!" He turned to Meizan in distress. "I only meant to bind them!"

"I know," Meizan said as Aranel vomited onto the ground. Sighing, Meizan raised his arms again and shaped the water into a swarm of nagamor. "That's why you should've left the channeling to me, idiot."

"No." Aranel swayed on his feet as he stood. Meizan caught him, noting his labored breathing. Aranel wasn't used to such extensive channeling in this realm. It was taking a toll on him, body and soul. "Your control over the chitrons. It's even worse than mine."

"I control them just fine!" Meizan said, incensed.

"You don't." Aranel fired off more kapizer spines with a shocking precision for someone who looked ready to pass out. "You let them control you."

Burn that, Meizan thought. What did Aranel know?

He stepped away from his teammate and bonded his own chitrons to the banyan. Its branches whipped through the air and tossed several soldiers over the edge of the crater.

A glistening, tar-like substance trickled across the golden bark. Meizan felt an inexplicable sadness well up inside him as he channeled, watching the wilting blue flowers and how their light faded rapidly under the taint of Malin.

What did you expect? Nothing stays pure here.

"Zenyra's likely at one of the villages," Aranel said with a cough. He leaned heavily against the rotting banyan. A spear had broken past their defenses and was embedded in his thigh, pooling blood onto the ground. Aranel reached for the weapon with trembling hands and wrenched it out with a grimace.

"We need to find Aina and get out of here," Meizan muttered, scanning the crater.

Kaldrav's forces had breached the eastern and northern sides of Incaraz. He could only hope that Aina had the good sense to get out of the way or hide herself. Chunks of Zenyra's broken shield hailed down in sparkling fragments that exploded as they hit the ground.

Hit by inspiration, Meizan channeled the surrounding air to redirect the fragments as they fell. A series of small explosions ripped across Kaldrav's army, opening a path through the throng of soldiers and toward the southern wall of the crater where the shield was still intact. An escape route, unless Kaldrav's soldiers had flanked that side of Incaraz too.

"Come on!" Meizan grabbed Aranel and dragged him through the mess.

Weapons and chunks of the broken shield rained overhead. Meizan blasted out his chitrons to create a shield of his own. But a triad of soldiers leaped at them before he could complete the channeling. Meizan's sword sliced through the air, but he was too late. The soldier's blade came slashing down—

Only for its wielder to topple over midslash, an arrow sprouting from his forehead. A moment later, the soldier's two companions joined him on the ground.

Meizan looked up to see a small figure crouched atop the side of the crater, shooting arrows in a fury.

There you are! Relieved, Meizan completed the chitronic

shield. The shimmering dome blocked them from further attacks as he and Aranel raced toward the southern side of the crater. Aina followed their route from the cliffs and shot down any soldiers that dared cross their path.

They were going to make it. They were going to escape.

All they had to do was climb the southern wall and flee Incaraz. Whatever soldiers pursued them across Malin could be easily outrun with the Balancer techniques.

The crater exploded inward just as Meizan started to climb. His shield trembled under the ensuing rockslide. A stone broke past and smashed his head, sending waves of pain through his skull. Meizan's eyes watered. As he clutched his head, his fingers brushed against a deep gash. Hot blood—his own now—dribbled down the side of his face.

He scrambled out of the pile of rock, head spinning as he tried to find Aina. The explosion had created a gaping chasm where she'd been standing, had she—

"There." Aranel pointed. A copper-haired figure sprinted across the rim of the crater—whatever parts of it that were still intact. Zenyra carried a limp body in her arms.

"Aina," Meizan croaked.

He staggered to his feet, only for Aranel to tackle him to the ground. The broken rock split Meizan's chin as a flurry of arrows whizzed overhead. When Meizan looked back up at the crater, Zenyra was gone, taking Aina with her.

"That bleeding bitch," Meizan swore as cold realization dawned upon him.

Zenyra had fled, leaving Meizan and Aranel to deal with the rest of Kaldrav's soldiers alone. So much for her upper realm morals. Chief Kanna would have never abandoned him.

Meizan exchanged a horrified look with Aranel. They stood shakily and drew their weapons.

We're going to lose . . . we're going to be captured again . . .

Both Meizan and Aranel were exhausted from their earlier channeling. Aranel could barely stand, his left leg gushing copious amounts of blood. Meizan was still lightheaded from the wound on his forehead. More soldiers had broken through the southern wall and sealed off their escape route.

Footsteps reverberated behind them. Meizan turned toward the destroyed perimeter of Incaraz with a heavy heart.

Only it was not Kaldrav's ironclad army that poured in through the fissure, but another, whose armor bore those achingly familiar twin blue stripes.

"Kanjallen," Meizan gasped. He gripped his still-reeling head and collapsed against Aranel.

They were saved.

He watched with giddy relief as lines of his clansmen marched into the crater. From the looks of it, almost a quarter of Kanjallen's troops had arrived.

Aranel dragged Meizan behind a pile of broken rock. They crouched there, watching as the two armies clashed by the lake and darkened its clear water with blood.

Bright green light warmed the side of Meizan's head, and he jerked away.

Aranel lowered his hands with a frown. "I'm trained in healing. Trust me."

"It's not you." Meizan nodded at the withered banyan.

"Fine, then." Aranel reached into his pocket before pressing something lightly against Meizan's head. He recognized the gazarou fur from its earthy scent. In a few seconds the pain receded to a slight stinging. Meizan allowed Aranel to wrap his head with a strip torn from his tunic. The upper's own leg had already been packed and wrapped.

"Don't get injured again," Aranel said. He held Meizan's

eyes for a long moment, then stood abruptly. "Time to go."

"Go where?" Meizan asked. "Kanjallen is here. We can win."

"Meizan! You bleeding brat! I'll skin you alive next time you ditch us like that."

At the familiar rasp, Meizan turned to see three members of Kanjallen running toward them. The stockiest of the three raised an arm. Meizan winced at the sight of blackened skin covered in blistering pustules.

"Taezur," he greeted. "You look a bit . . . burned."

"Not the time, you little shit." Meizan could almost see Taezur's scowl through his helm.

"Where's the girl?" asked the tallest of the three. Meizan vaguely recognized him as Renjan, the outspoken son of Kanjallen's former chief. The burning ices of Agakor had peeled off half his face, and his arms were wrapped in cloth bandages. "Chief Kanna commanded us to find a sixteen-year-old girl. Where is she?"

"The Balancer leader escaped with her," Meizan replied. "How did you get here so soon?"

"Chief had a bunch of us stationed nearby," Taezur said. "She had a feeling those roaches would attack your hideout, and we've been waiting to crush them since Kaufgar."

"Then let's crush them." Meizan spun his sword in a circle. "Our enemies unmade."

"Our enemies unmade," Taezur grunted.

"Enough of that," Renjan ordered. "Meizan, make yourself useful and join the battle. Taezur, Einez, bind the upper and stick his keiza. We'll leave him as a consolation prize for Kaldrav's men."

Aranel stiffened as Taezur and Einez advanced. Before Meizan fully realized what he was doing, he had stepped in front of Aranel to point his sword at his clanmates.

"Touch him, and I swear on Azyaka I'll make you wish you were still buried in that lava," Meizan growled.

"Have the Balancers scrambled your brains, Meizan?" Taezur barked. "He's an outsider. And an upper."

"Is this insubordination?" Renjan unsheathed his own sword. "The chief isn't here, Meizan. I could hand you to the enemy and let them drag you back to Kaufgar. It'd be a waste, after all the trouble it took to break you out."

"I am Chief Kanna's second-in-command," Meizan said. "Any insubordination will be yours."

Renjan gave a gurgling laugh. "Lower your head, you ass. The chief may favor you, but I take no orders from—" He stopped when Meizan shoved his blade forward, the manikai stones on full display. "Why the blazes do *you* have that?"

"You will not harm Aranel." Meizan pressed the tip into his clanmate's neck. "You will treat him as one of our own."

"Put that sword down, Meizan," Renjan hissed. "You've no right to wield it."

Before Meizan could reply, a series of explosions rocked the Kanjallen troops. Kaldrav's army pressed forward and broke through their ranks. Meizan and Aranel took advantage of the commotion to slip away from his clanmates.

"We need to find Aina," Meizan said as Renjan and the others raised their weapons and leaped into the fray.

"Aina's with Zenyra. She'll keep her safe," Aranel replied, his face unreadable. "And you ought to stay with Kanjallen. They'll keep you safe."

Meizan raised his sword to block an incoming arrow, blasting chitrons toward the charging soldiers. He was swept into the melee, the next few minutes a maelstrom of chaos.

"They'll keep you safe too," Meizan yelled over the ruckus. "I'll—"

His words died on his tongue when he registered Aranel was no longer beside him. Meizan pushed through the ranks of Kanjallen soldiers, searching for the bright golden head. Even covered in blood and grime, Aranel would stand out in Malin.

He sighted him at the edge of the army. Fleeing the battle.

Not just the battle. The revelation felt like he'd been doused in ice. *That bleeding traitor.*

Aranel was fleeing the realm. Meizan was sure of it.

Because with Incaraz broken and Zenyra gone, there was no reason for Aranel to stick around. He would take one of those silver torana and return to Mayana for good.

Meizan gripped the chief's blade, its sharp gemstones cutting into his skin. He should have expected this. Aranel had his own loyalties, and they were never with the Balancers.

For a moment, Meizan considered running after Aranel. Beating him senseless and forcing him to reveal exactly what the Preservation had sent him to do. A second later, Meizan wondered why he even cared.

What am I? Aranel had nervously asked him less than an hour ago.

In truth, Meizan wasn't sure how the hell to answer that. It would have been easier if Aina had been the one asking. Aina fit into his life. She was the closest thing left that connected him to his chief—to the one person in the realm Meizan would do anything for. Even before he'd known she was the chief's daughter, Aina had felt familiar. Comfortable.

Aranel felt neither familiar nor comfortable. He didn't fit into Meizan's life at all. Yet Meizan had grown accustomed to having him there, a constant annoyance, a splinter in his side that stung even worse when you tried to wrench it out.

Well, it's out now.

This was no time for bleeding sentimentality. Meizan needed to find Aina.

MORE OF KALDRAV'S troops arrived as backup an hour later, forcing Kanjallen to retreat from Incaraz. Meizan watched from a distance as Kaldrav's soldiers desecrated the crater. They smashed the stone, burned the banyan tree, and flooded the lake with filth.

It hurt to watch.

Much as Meizan loathed to admit it, the Balancer hideout had become something of a home. It had kept him safe and well fed, and given him a warm bed to sleep in—comforts he'd never enjoyed even before Kanjallen's capture. As Meizan watched Incaraz break and burn, he felt as if someone had twisted a blade into his heart.

The shrill cry of the nagamor announced the chief's arrival. The beast circled Kanjallen once, then shot down like a blue arrow.

Kanna dismounted midair and landed in front of Meizan. "You're all right." She gripped his shoulders, her gaze darting about. "Where's Aina? Why isn't she with you?"

"I'm sorry," Meizan said. The chief's sword slid from his grasp and hit the rocks with a clatter. "Zenyra took her and fled."

Kanna's grip loosened a fraction. "Then she's safe for now. But I still need you to find her."

Meizan rubbed his eyes. The exhaustion—from the fighting, the channeling, and everything else—crashed on him in one draining wave. "Incaraz is gone, Chief."

"Yes, but there are still the Balancer villages," Kanna said impatiently. "Zenyra must have taken her to one of those. Find them, Meizan. I command it. Once you do, I'll send the troops over. If Kaldrav means to destroy the Balancers, he won't stop at just one hideout."

Meizan nodded, not voicing the thought that had plagued his mind ever since he'd spied Kaldrav's soldiers skulking around the crater: the Balancers, even with Zenyra on their side, were not strong enough to resist Kaldrav's army. They could either stay in Malin and be wiped out. Or flee through the torana like Aranel had.

PART IV

The megarya breathed the stars and skies,
kindled the sun, and sculpted the moon.

The nagamor belched forth fire and ice,
stirring up seas deep blue as its plume.

The gazarou coaxed trees and plants to rise,
seeded the earth and set it abloom.

The vandraghor wove, of its own device,
dark to brighten the stars with its gloom.

In the new realm, the seitarius then
birthed lesser beasts and two-legged men.

Their powers now drained, they chose to retreat
and sought out slumber, their great work complete.

–CHORUS OF CREATION–
Verse III: The Making of the Universe

CHAPTER TWENTY-TWO

◎

The Shadowed Sea

*A*INA AWOKE TO a throbbing headache with her cheek pressed against rough wood. She rubbed her eyes and sat upright to find herself in a dinghy surrounded by choppy water. A line of jagged cliffs rose in the distance.

Why the stinking hell, Aina thought, scrunching her nose at the stench of salt mingled with a sulfurous rot, *am I on a boat?*

Across from her, Zenyra sat at the bow, a brass spyglass held up to the sky. "Soon," the Balancer leader muttered under her breath. "Soon as I get it, I will try again. It will work this time. It must. All shall be worth it once we are reunited. Soon."

Aina pressed a hand to her head to find a blood-caked swelling. Courtesy of Kaldrav's soldiers, no doubt. Zenyra must have rescued her and brought her . . . onto this boat?

From the ragged gray waters, Aina guessed they were in Mir Tamasa, the Shadowed Sea. But it made little sense for them to be here, and Aina's mind was a haze as she struggled to gather her thoughts.

"Kyrian, that bleeding hypocrite," Zenyra rambled on, and Aina languidly noted how odd it was to hear her swear. "Spreading lies, preaching falsehoods. As if he were not there. As if he were never a part of us."

Who's Kyrian? Aina wondered. Zenyra seemed upset with him. *An old lover?* She suppressed a giggle at the notion. *Kyrian. Kyrian . . .*

She had heard the name before, and it stirred something in her. A vague memory, of someone mentioning it in passing, maybe Aranel—

"Aranel!" Aina croaked, panic piercing through her stupor. "Meizan!"

Last she remembered, they had been fighting Kaldrav's troops in Incaraz. But there had been some sort of explosion, and Aina couldn't recall any of what happened after.

"You are awake." Zenyra pocketed the spyglass and leaned forward, pushing back Aina's bangs to peer at her keiza. "How do you feel?"

"My teammates." Aina licked her parched lips. "What happened? Where are they?"

"They are safe. Kanjallen arrived at Incaraz shortly after the invasion. I am sure Meizan has been happily reunited."

"And Aranel? Do you know where he is?" Zenyra said nothing, and Aina's panic swelled. "We need to find him!"

She stood, and the boat gave a wild lurch, forcing her back to her seat.

"I would keep your voice down," Zenyra said, "and avoid sudden movement. Lest you attract their attention more than we already have."

She motioned toward the water, where large triangular shapes circled the boat. Not choppy waves, as Aina had first assumed, but fins. Dozens of fins, metal-gray and sharp as blades.

Aina's breath froze in her throat, all thoughts of her teammates evaporating.

"Saberfin sharks," Zenyra said casually. "I placed a chitronic shield around the boat so they cannot get to us. But I would rather not test it out just yet."

"Why—" Aina gulped, trying to keep her voice steady. "Why are there so *many*?"

"They migrated to Mir Tamasa following Merumarth's explosion. It warmed the water to their liking, and Kaldrav's men breed them for their fins. They make excellent blades, you see. Can cut through bone with a single slice." At Aina's shiver, Zenyra added, "Worry not, for they will not penetrate my shield. If anything, their presence ensures we will remain undisturbed, for few would dare traverse these waters."

Their presence is what keeps us trapped on this blasted boat, Aina wanted to yell. But words failed her as she stared at the chitronic shield, a translucent dome of shimmering air. A pale, tubular something extended from the waves and slithered up the boundary, poking and prodding but unable to break through.

"Tentacles," Zenyra continued, sounding freakishly calm about the entire situation. "You know, I always have felt the saberfins were poorly named. While their fins are fearful, the tentacles are their deadliest weapon. They would ensnare you, rendering you immobile and at a hungry shark's mercy." She gave a wry laugh. "In any case, you realize why it might be foolish to leave this boat."

"Then why did you bring us here?" Aina burst out. A second and third tentacle joined the first, creeping up the dome of air. "Why would you abandon Aranel and Meizan?"

"Everything I did was to keep you safe, Aina," Zenyra said.

Her unflinching calmness was beginning to grate at Aina's nerves. "You do not appreciate the peril we were in. Incaraz has fallen, and if I cannot get things under control, the other villages will follow. Over a decade of work and planning reduced to dust. I did what I could, but—" She broke off and brought a hand to Aina's forehead, tracing her keiza. "It is enough that you are safe, Aina. I cannot lose you."

Aina felt a strange mix of flattery and annoyance. "You won't lose me." She gave Zenyra a weak smile. "Although your definition of *safe* is a bit skewed." Several more tentacles had slid across the shield. "How long do you plan to keep us here?"

"Not long," Zenyra murmured. "Not long now."

Aina tried very hard not to stare at the writhing tentacles and the enormous underwater shadows that circled their boat with increasing speed. "So I can't swim to shore and search for Aranel, but I could project my soul—"

"No!" Zenyra's eyes flashed. "Absolutely not, Aina! You will *not* project your soul and expose yourself to the taint of Malin!"

"But my keiza stops me from—"

"I forbid it!" Zenyra's eyes were wild, her fingers gripping Aina's arms like claws. "You swore to me, Aina! After you ran away from the Balancer village and I risked my soul to save you, you swore that you would listen to every word I say!"

"I did," Aina said, taken aback by her ferocity. She had never seen Zenyra look this fanatic. She was reminding Aina of Kanna. "But I need to find Aranel, because I . . . *I* don't want to lose *him*."

"Aranel will be fine," Zenyra dismissed. "Men like him always are. He cares for his own soul above all else and will go to any lengths to preserve it."

"Aranel isn't like that! At least not anymore. He risked his soul for me when I ran away! He even descended from Mayana and joined the Balancers because *I* inspired him!"

"Is that what he told you?" Zenyra shook her head. "You are a fool to believe him, Aina. And an even greater fool if you think Aranel could ever love you."

"I—I don't—" Aina sputtered, reddening. "I mean— I barely even—"

"He was a spy for the Preservation. He was lying to you the whole time, and any feigned kindness was merely an attempt to get information about me through you."

The words felt like repeated blows to her chest.

It couldn't be true.

Aranel might have been selfish and spoiled before, but he had changed. He'd helped her train and tried to fix her figurines. He'd looked her in the eye and said the sweetest things.

But he also interrogated you about Zenyra and the Balancer villages, a snarky voice chimed in her mind. *And while he did come running into a war zone to look for you, he seemed even more upset by the prospect of Meizan leaving the Balancers. Who's to say he hadn't followed Meizan and run into you by chance? Or that he only worried about your safety since you were his key to Zenyra?*

"Are you sure he's a spy?" Aina's voice wavered. "How did you find out?"

"Aranel admitted it to me himself, the day Incaraz fell," Zenyra said. "Meizan knew as well but chose not to reveal it."

"Meizan *knew?*"

Another blow, and Aina's eyes stung. If Meizan had known, why hadn't he said anything? Hadn't he called her his clanmate? What of the fabled Kanjallen loyalty? Why would Meizan keep secrets for Aranel, an upper whom he barely tolerated, from *her?*

"There are plenty more young men in the realms, Aina," Zenyra said, eyes softening. "Just as handsome, but far kinder and worthier of your love."

"It was just a feeling," Aina mumbled, admitting it aloud for the first time. "A feeling so small it was hardly there. Far from love. But I am a blasted fool, letting myself think . . ."

She wiped her eyes on her sleeve. Had Aranel even considered her a friend, or had that been a lie too?

"Aranel was the first person your age to treat you with kindness." Zenyra patted her head. "Given the life you had, it is natural you would grow to feel something for him. But I expect he returned to Mayana three days ago. You would do best to not waste your thoughts on him, nor your tears. Especially when we have far more pressing concerns at hand. What matters is that you are safe, Aina. As long as I have you, it will all work out."

The Balancer leader lapsed back into silence, holding up a fist. Aina caught a glint of something that piqued her curiosity—a tiny amulet made of cloth.

"What's that?" Aina asked.

"A good-luck charm, made by one dear to my heart."

Zenyra opened her palm to display a small silk pouch tied to a white ribbon. It was embroidered with the same six-petaled flower as Zenyra's tunic, each petal in a different-colored thread.

"What's going to happen to the Balancers?" Aina asked in a small voice. "Hiraval, Taralei, Reimi, and all the rest?"

"Some may return to Mayana," Zenyra said, grasping her charm. "Some may remain. It matters not. My work as their leader is over. The Balancers are finished."

Aina stared at the sharks that circled their boat, her fear overridden by a tight, crushing regret. As if the tentacles wrapped around the shield were squeezing her heart and snuffing out any hope she dared hold on to. Meizan was with Kanjallen and Aranel back in Mayana. The others would follow suit, leaving her all alone.

And I was stupid to hope for any better. The universe would not be so kind, to allow her to enjoy such comforts as the Balancers for long.

At least I have Zenyra. Her former leader sat hunched over her charm and was rambling feverishly to herself again. *Though the shock of losing Incaraz appears to be making her lose her mind.*

"It will work this time," Zenyra muttered. "It has to work. Soon, you will break free of that horrible prison. It will all break down and you will be free."

"What will break down?" Aina asked, confused. "Are you talking about Toranic Law?"

Zenyra stared at her, then seemed to realize that she'd been speaking to herself. "Toranic Law cannot break, Aina. I have told you this. It is more powerful than the Preservation, who swear by it."

The Preservation. Aina felt a shiver of disgust at the name.

And to think Aranel was a spy for them!

She wished she could confront Aranel, maybe break a bone or two while she was at it. But as Zenyra said, he'd already returned to Mayana three days ago.

Wait. Aina narrowed her eyes. *Three days?*

It felt like yesterday when Kaldrav's forces had invaded Incaraz.

How long have I been asleep? Her eyes flicked back to the shield, the circling shadows and slicing fins, and a flicker of doubt crossed her mind. It was the kind of thing Kanna had done on occasion—when Aina asleep was more conducive to her plans than her awake.

"Have you been drugging me?" she asked Zenyra. "To keep me on this boat?"

"With kapizer venom," Zenyra said without missing a beat. "I have lost enough and cannot afford any more risks. You are all I have left, Aina. My only hope."

"That doesn't mean you can drug me for days on end," Aina exclaimed. "None of what you're saying makes any sense! What are you planning? You mentioned freeing someone, and something breaking down, but I don't understand any—"

She stopped when the boat began to move, drifting through the water with the chitronic shield. Aina wondered if Zenyra had changed her mind and decided to seek out the remaining Balancers after all.

But they were not headed ashore, but rather in the opposite direction.

As they sailed, a craggy island materialized in the murk. On it stood a single shabby torana with columns black as night.

"No," Aina gasped. Terror wracked her bones. "No! That leads to— We can't go there—"

Golden threads shot from Zenyra's palm, gagging Aina and binding her limbs. She thrashed and struggled, but to no avail.

"Soon," Zenyra whispered over Aina's muffled curses. A tear rolled down the Paramosi woman's cheek, and she pressed the amulet to her breast. "Soon, all will be righted."

Aina caught a flicker of movement behind the black pillars as the island grew closer. A cloaked figure stepped out of Narakh and raised an arm.

CHAPTER TWENTY-THREE

@

Unbreakable

L *ESS THAN A* day had passed since Aranel's return to Mayana. He had fled Incaraz and the bedlam of battle to trudge through the desolation of Martharan. It had taken him hours of stumbling through its woods—tripping at least a dozen times over gnarled tree roots and folds of hardened lava—before he'd found the torana through which he'd originally entered. Its pillars were a bright, burnished silver when viewed from the other side.

Now, back in his hut in Kirnos, Aranel mended his injuries with ease. And how clean the chitrons felt! How he'd missed being able to channel without fear or worry!

Once mended, Aranel grabbed a spare sword, a sack of healing supplies, and his old armor—reshaping the breastplate so the decorative holes were fully covered—and left his hut in a rush. He intended to cloudsurf his way back to the Meruhirs so he could reenter Malin.

But at the first touch of his foot against the blade, Aranel froze in place. His chitronic flows snapped with his resolve, and he fell flat on his back.

What in Sherka's name was he thinking, going back? Malin held nothing for him anymore. He could try to find Taralei, warn her about Kaldrav's soldiers—but he was more likely to get himself captured before he made it near her village. He could only trust that his cousin and the other Balancers had managed to flee in time.

Aina was safe with Zenyra, and Meizan . . . Meizan had his clan.

Aranel stood, dusted himself off, and picked up his fallen sword. He tightened his grip on the pommel, its emeralds digging into his skin.

Meizan had stood up for him. Threatened his own clan members to keep Aranel safe.

Aranel's heart soared at the memory. He'd been tempted to stay with Kanjallen. By his teammate's side. But then what?

Meizan's clanmates were warriors. Meizan was a warrior.

Aranel had seen firsthand how Meizan had fought in Incaraz. The gruesome ways in which he'd cut down his enemies. The way Meizan had *laughed* through it all, eyes wild with joy and face splattered with gore.

Aranel had convinced himself it was the influence of the chitrons, but Zenyra had never looked that way when she channeled.

Much as Aranel had tried to repaint them to suit his preferences, he'd seen Meizan's true colors since the day they met.

I wanted to believe he could be different. Believe he could be someone I . . .

Aranel released the pommel of his sword and started across

the field. There was no place for him in Meizan's life, or even Aina's. His business was with the upper realms.

He ought to have felt relief. The nightmare had ended. He could now live a safe and peaceful life in Mayana. Yet, as Aranel hiked up the familiar path that led to the palace gardens, all he felt was regret.

Because things could not continue like this. The thousands of children who dwelled within Malin could not be allowed to suffer the injustice of Toranic Law. Zenyra's mission and the Balancers' purpose could not be allowed to dissolve to nothingness. The Preservation could not be allowed to perpetuate their illusions of purity.

Aranel stopped in front of the torana that led to Paramos. In the moonless night of Kirnos, its columns shone like molten gold. Behind it, the uppermost realm was quiet and shrouded in darkness. He tossed through the round pebble they'd used to communicate, then waited for Seirem's arrival. The Preserver came within the hour, his expression one of polite puzzlement.

"I did not expect you to contact me from Mayana," said Seirem, handing Aranel the pebble. "Is everything all right?"

"No." Aranel ground his teeth together and flung the stone back through the torana. "I quit."

Seirem's expression remained unruffled. "I am sorry you feel that way. I know it is difficult, Aranel, but the Balancers are—"

"The Balancers are destroyed. Incaraz was attacked. Zenyra is no longer a threat. Although she was never the real threat, was she?"

"Pardon me?"

"I know about the megarya blood! I know you and the Preservation have been drinking it to inflate your chitronic spin and stay in Paramos! To stay in power so you could control the realms!"

Seirem took a step back, raising a hand to his forehead. "Aranel, whatever poison that woman is feeding you—"

"I saw you," seethed Aranel. "I saw you drinking it from that flask you always carry around. How dare you stand there and look down upon me, down upon *her*, when all she's trying to do is help those less fortunate! The very thing that the Preservation ought to be doing but isn't, since you're a bunch of corrupt geezers who care about nothing but your own twisted souls!"

"Aranel, please." Seirem stepped through the torana into Mayana. "Let me explain."

"Is that why you sent me on this forsaken mission? Why the Preservation are so terrified of Zenyra? Because you're afraid she'll reveal the truth and shatter the illusion you've built around yourselves?"

"It is not the Preservation's illusion I am worried about her shattering," boomed Seirem, "but the realms themselves!"

Suddenly, Aranel found himself unable to move, the air solidifying around him to hold him in place. When had Seirem channeled? He'd been so quick, Aranel hardly had time to react.

"I regret having to bind you like this, Aranel," said Seirem. "But I entreat you to give me the chance to explain myself. Then you can make an informed judgment based on both sides."

"Not much to your side beyond lies and powermongering."

"It is true that certain members of the Preservation, myself included, drink megarya blood on occasion," said Seirem. "Not all, but near a third, although I can assure you that His Supremacy Lord Kyrian has never needed it."

"Why would I believe your assurances?"

"Please, Aranel. Allow me to admit to my actions and apologize for misleading you. My true realm, if I am honest with you, is likely closer to Mayana than Paramos. The same could be said about the other dozen or so Preservers who drink the blood—

which is common knowledge amongst the Preservation. It is also why we have two factions."

Seirem raised his sleeve to show a ring of silver around the hem. "The blooded, including myself, are marked by this ring. We possess neither the power nor the authority of the unblooded faction, for our purity is sustained by the blood, whereas theirs is true."

"So that's what Sam meant," muttered Aranel. "I should've listened when he tried warning me about you."

"You've had contact with your brother?" asked Seirem sharply. "When? Does he know of your mission?"

"It's not your place to be interrogating me!" snapped Aranel. "Why even have a blooded faction? Why not let those of you too impure for Paramos reside in Mayana?"

"An excellent question." Seirem looked relieved that Aranel had asked. "There are several reasons, one being that we are able to govern the upper realms so peacefully and without contest precisely because the Mayani believe in our purity and wisdom. The brightness of our keiza and our Paramosi status are proof of this purity, and it uplifts the morale of our subjects, who strive to become better people in order to follow our example and ascend.

"This is why ascension ceremonies are so popular with Mayani royalty, for they indisputably prove the worth of those in charge and inspire those around them. Were Preservers allowed to fall back to Mayana, this belief in us would be weakened. Why would a Mayani trust a Preserver if they suspected he or she might fall the next day? Why would they follow an organization filled with those whom they viewed as equals, rather than their superiors?"

"That's nothing but an excuse to stay in power," said Aranel in disgust. "Mayana is a peaceful realm, full of good people. It would function well even without the Preservation's interference."

"Perhaps it would," said Seirem. "But there is one more reason Preservers cannot be allowed to fall: we know far too many secrets about the origin of the universe and the chitronic system that governs the realms . . . secrets that would become deadly were one of us to fall to Malin and decide to use them for evil."

"What secrets? What could *you* possibly know that would endanger the realms? Everything runs on Toranic Law, and it's not as if you can control . . ." Aranel trailed off, blood going cold. "Can you?"

"Of course not. Toranic Law is absolute, as unbreakable and unchangeable as gravity. The Preservation can neither affect nor control it. We can only safeguard."

"What's there to safeguard? You just said Toranic Law is unbreakable and unchangeable."

"Come with me," said Seirem, his tone somber. "It is time I show you the truth. The whole truth about the universe."

ARANEL SCRUTINIZED THE white limestone walls and their four statued columns. The musky scent of marigold pervaded the room, bringing with it a strange sense of nostalgia.

He was familiar with the temple of Kirnos. He'd visited weekly, in addition to all the times he'd escorted Aina here so she could serve penance for her various crimes.

Am I being locked up too? wondered Aranel. Aina would never let him hear the end of it if she found out.

Seirem nodded to Aro, the high priest, who swept out of the shrine without a word, leaving Aranel alone with the Preserver.

"Look at this room, Aranel," said Seirem. "Tell me what you see."

"A shrine. And the statues symbolize the four Planetary Beasts, the seitarius."

"Yes. Now look closer. What else is there?"

Aranel frowned, not quite understanding where Seirem was going with this. "The inscription on the ceiling, about the Great Toranic Separation—"

"What else?"

"There's nothing else!" exploded Aranel. "What are you getting at? Speak plainly!"

"Observe the color of the walls," said Seirem. "Pure white, with not a single carving or inscription. Every single shrine, in this realm and in Paramos, has blank walls of pure white."

"So?" Aranel scowled. "Did you bring me here to talk about temple design?"

"If the statues symbolize the seitarius, what do you think the blank walls symbolize?"

"That whoever built them clearly lacked inspiration . . ."

"The Universal Void, Aranel," said Seirem with a sigh. "The Chorus of Creation, verse one. The universe started out as but a blank emptiness from which the seitarius created our world."

"So it's the Void," said Aranel impatiently. "What does that have to do with anything?"

"Look down."

Aranel did, noting the fine carvings that ran across the white marble floor: four rings, one encircling each statue. Extending from each ring were three fine lines connecting to the other rings.

It was a fairly simple design, neat and geometric. Aranel didn't understand what he was supposed to find so fascinating about this.

"This shrine represents the Void," said Seirem, "and the chitronic system that lies within."

"You mean the system you've been monitoring?" Aranel blinked several times. "That's in the *Void*?"

"It is the only place in the universe stable enough to hold it," answered Seirem. "You are well-versed in the Second Principle of Chitronic Equilibrium and its implications, I presume?"

"Souls can only exist in realms with a chitronic rotational speed equal to or less than their own. In essence, it's Toranic Law."

"Answered wonderfully, as expected. Now, Aranel, a trick question: How were the realms made? What are they, really?"

"They were made by the seitarius, who split the original realm into four overlapping ones during the Great Toranic Separation."

"Ah!" Seirem's eyes gleamed. "See, that is where you are missing the nuance. The seitarius did create the realms, so to speak. But a more precise definition would be that the seitarius *are* the realms. Their slumbering bodies lie within the depths of the earth. And their souls—which have been projected outside their bodies—make up the chitrons of the realms."

"I've heard that before," said Aranel, remembering Hiraval's explanation the day they had entered Incaraz. "From one of the Balancers who was training to be a priest in Ashkator."

"Yes, the priesthood of Ashkator is particularly devoted toward studying the seitarius," said Seirem. "Now here is the part your priest friend will *not* have told you. The barriers between the realms that limit ascension are nothing more than a set of giant, unbreakable chitronic shields . . . made from a portion of the seitarius' souls. These shields are designed to operate under the Second Principle, protecting our realms."

For the love of Sherka!

Aranel forced his mouth shut and leaned against the temple wall for support. *Chitronic shields? That's all it is?*

Aranel had never given much thought as to exactly *what* separated the realms, maintaining the absolute order of Toranic Law. He'd assumed it to be something sophisticated and mystical that transcended the boundaries of human understanding.

But chitronic shields were the most rudimentary of techniques. Most Mayani children learned to make them by the age of ten. The power of the seitarius would be immeasurable in comparison. Yet to think it was nothing but a set of shields that stood between Mayana and Malin. Between Mayana and Narakh . . .

Images flashed through Aranel's mind, of Kaldrav's soldiers bursting into Incaraz, pieces of Zenyra's shield raining down. He pressed his fingers to his temples as the disturbing revelation sank in: that any chitronic shield, no matter how powerful, could be broken if subjected to enough force.

"Is that . . ." Aranel found his voice. "Is that what Kaldrav's soldiers meant when they spoke of breaking Toranic Law? When I asked you about it, you claimed it could never break."

"It was no mere claim but the truth." Seirem tapped his chin. "There is a fine distinction between Toranic Law—and the chitronic shields and torana that operate under it. Most people do not know or care for this difference, and the two are often treated and spoken of interchangeably."

"And that's wrong?"

"Wrong indeed," said Seirem. "Toranic Law has existed since the beginning of time, dictating the spin of one's soul. It is what causes chitrons to spin a certain direction and speed based on one's intentions, thoughts, actions, and emotions. Beyond that, on its own, Toranic Law has no practical effect."

"But what about ascension and descension?"

"A soul's movement between realms, while wholly dependent on spin, is not controlled by Toranic Law itself," explained Seirem. "Rather, it is regulated by the chitronic shields and the torana, both of which were created by the seitarius during the Great Toranic Separation as a means to stop the war that almost broke the universe. But this was done centuries *after* Toranic Law came into being."

Aranel narrowed his eyes. He, too, had assumed Toranic Law

and the torana were one and the same. None of the scriptures bothered to make clear the distinction, something he'd begun to think was deliberate.

"So if one spoke of breaking Toranic Law," said Aranel, "what they'd actually mean is—"

"Breaking the shields between the realms," answered Seirem. "But I would not worry about some army, Aranel. They cannot break anything from within Malin, and they have no access to the chitronic system. That this king believes physical strength is necessary proves he knows nothing about how the universe works." Seirem shook back his sleeves and clapped his hands. "Returning to the matter at hand. The realms, and the seitarius themselves."

"What about them?" asked Aranel. "The realms are made from the seitarius, and the chitrons from their souls." He crossed his arms. "I know the Chorus of Creation refers to the Planetary Beasts as our creators and benefactors, but I expected something more conceptual."

"Religion is more literal than you would expect. That is why it is so easy to have faith. Our deities exist, Aranel, in both physical form and spirit. We walk across their backs and channel their souls."

"Must be annoying. I certainly wouldn't want a bunch of tiny humans walking all over me and using my chitrons for their trivial purposes. Or my blood, for that matter."

Seirem ignored the jibe. "Our deities are tolerant and benevolent," said the Preserver. "It also helps that they are asleep. Their chitrons may be vaguely aware of what is happening, but the Beasts themselves are in a near-comatose state. Or they had been, until recently."

"The disturbances." Aranel caught on. "You mentioned there

were explosions in the chitronic system, caused by erasures. Are they somehow awakening the Beasts?"

"There is a risk they might," said Seirem. "You see, right after the Great Toranic Separation, the seitarius had a part of their souls—namely their chitronic cores—stored in the Universal Void for safekeeping." He gestured to the white temple walls and the seitarius statues, then pointed at the floor with its geometric web of lines. "The design represents the chitronic system that upholds our realms, with the seitarius cores at its foundation. Think of it as a control unit for the shields and the torana."

"And this control unit, this entire system, is inside the Void?" Aranel's voice rose a fraction. "The Void that the Preservation have *access* to?"

"Now you see why we must drink megarya blood and remain in Paramos," said Seirem. "There is a single torana that leads to the Void. It is located in Ashkator, guarded day and night by one of the Preservation. But imagine what could happen if the wrong person with the wrong intentions knew of the Void and what lay within. They could recalibrate the soul-spin limits on the chitronic shields, for example, allowing more Mayani to enter Paramos. Worse, they could dismantle the shields altogether, which would throw the realms into chaos."

"When you recruited me, you mentioned Zenyra was sighted near Ashkator," said Aranel. "Do you think she plans to do something in the Void?"

Such as change the limits on the shields? he wondered but dared not say in front of Seirem.

"Regardless of her plans, the Preservation will never permit her near the Void," said Seirem. "Even so, we cannot stop whatever it is she is doing in Malin that is causing the erasures."

"We have no proof that it's her."

"Call it an old man's intuition, Aranel. I have seen with my own eyes how those explosions are reverberating through the chitronic system and shaking the seitarius cores. If Zenyra is allowed to continue, whether she intends it or not, she could end up awakening one of the seitarius—Azyaka, the planetary naga-mor, to be precise."

"And what happens if Azyaka awakens?" asked Aranel, voice trembling.

Seirem's face turned grim. "The shield around Malin will crumble. And the universe will break."

They left the temple soon after and walked through the empty marketplace. Aranel hardly registered where they were headed as he tried, with a profound effort, to process everything he had just learned.

"You could've mentioned some of this when you recruited me," he said.

Even if Seirem's suspicion of Zenyra turned out to be wrong, someone—or something—was causing erasures in Malin. Erasures that might awaken Azyaka and doom the universe. Yet even after spending over four moons in the lower realm, Aranel had no clear answers.

Have I been completely useless all this time? Have I achieved nothing?

"The Preservation are not perfect, Aranel," said Seirem as they reached the golden torana to Paramos. He stepped between the pillars and reached into his pocket. "But we are doing the best we can to protect the realms. Same as you."

Seirem pulled out a familiar-looking flask and held it through the torana.

Aranel took a step back. "Is that . . ."

"You did well, Aranel. But if the Balancers have been destroyed, as you say they have, there is no reason to prolong your mission and continue risking your soul."

"But—"

"When you took this mission, I promised you that your soul would spin swifter for it and you would be permitted into Paramos." Seirem pressed the flask into Aranel's palm. "Drink this, and ascend."

Pulse racing, Aranel stared at the flask, then back at Seirem.

The Preserver's eyes crinkled as he gave Aranel a warm smile. "Your parents are waiting for you atop Ashkator, as is your brother. He joined our number recently, and there may be a place for you as well."

A place for me? In spite of himself, Aranel felt a thrill at those words and the future they promised. *I'd be the youngest Preserver ever. I'd beat Sam's record.*

"What about the erasures in Malin?" he forced himself to ask. "Are you not worried about Zenyra, and the planetary nagamor?"

"I am," said Seirem. "But with the Balancers gone, there is nothing more to expect of you. We can hope that with the Balancers' disappearance, the erasures will stop too."

"And if they don't?"

"Then I, or another Preserver, will handle it. You have provided us with more than enough information, for which I am greatly obliged. But you can relax now, Aranel. Leave the rest to me and enjoy your life in Paramos. You have earned it."

Earned it? Aranel bit back a retort, closing his fingers around the flask of megarya blood. He could see through Seirem's generosity. Aranel now knew far too much about the Void and what lay within it. *They're offering me a seat to keep an eye on me. They're trying to buy my silence with megarya blood.*

"This is a wonderful opportunity, Aranel," said Seirem. While the man's countenance remained pleasant, there was a slight tightness to his jaw. "You have proven your merit, and the Preservation could do with a righteous young man like you. Given your experience in Malin, you might even make some suggestions to improve the way we govern the realms."

It was a tempting offer. If Aranel joined the Preservation, he could change things. Perhaps he could reinstate the Balancers in some capacity. A few moons ago, he would have taken it in a heartbeat.

And why not, piped a voice in his mind. *I've done my part, it's only fair I reap the reward. I'd no longer need to slum around in Malin to be helpful. I'd never have to visit that forsaken realm again . . .*

Aranel pocketed the flask and bowed deeply before straightening. "Words cannot express my gratitude, Lord Seirem," he said, a smile at his lips. "For so many years, I have yearned for this exact thing. Allow me some time to set things in order here, and I will join you shortly. Could you tell my parents to expect me for dinner tomorrow night?"

"Excellent!" Seirem patted Aranel's shoulder, beaming. "The Preservation are honored to have you, Aranel."

"No, sir." Aranel's smile widened. "The honor is all mine."

CHAPTER TWENTY-FOUR

⊚

Blood and the Beast

ZENYRA WAS WRONG, Meizan thought as he stared at the ruined banyan. He ran a hand along the blackened bark. A single blossom remained, its graying petals crumbling at his touch. *Beautiful things can't thrive in this realm. Nothing can, except misery.*

Around him, the crater of Incaraz was a pile of shattered rock, with pools of murky water where the lake had once stood.

Even after Kanjallen's withdrawal, Kaldrav's troops had given chase. It was only thanks to the chief and her nagamor that they had escaped, taking refuge deep underground. But Chief Kanna hadn't let them stay there for long.

Barely half a day's rest, and she'd sent off search parties to look for Aina. Meizan himself had scoured the ruins of Martharan, but there had been no sign of Aina or Zenyra. At Kanna's command, he'd doubled back to the now-empty Incaraz in the hope the pair would show up. He'd already spent one night camping out in the desolation of the crater. Tomorrow he would return empty-handed and face the chief's disappointment.

Meizan traipsed back to his campsite—little more than a thin blanket next to a pile of smoking firewood, since his old room had been crushed to pieces—and flumped onto the dirt.

He picked up Chief Kanna's sword, its manikai stones glimmering in the dim light. His earlier attempt to kindle flames had blown a giant fireball into the ground, and Meizan had quickly learned not to rely on it for small-scale channeling.

A tug on one of his chitronic trip wires had Meizan back on his feet.

He sprinted over the broken rock, blade poised to strike. The trip wire gave another tug, then snapped, and Meizan ducked to avoid being smacked in the face.

Something bright gold landed in his field of vision and the scrape of a sword broke the silence. The next few moments were a blur of clashing blades. Meizan whirled around and slammed his sword down to meet a pair of familiar hazel eyes.

Aranel backed away, arms falling to his sides.

"Look who's come crawling back from Mayana," Meizan sneered.

He lowered his sword and took in Aranel's appearance. He was shinier than Meizan remembered him being a few days ago, and wearing the most obscene golden breastplate inlaid with green stones. He seemed *new*, almost as if he'd been reborn, and completely healed of all the bruises and scratches he'd accumulated in Malin.

"Didn't think I'd see you here after you ditched the realm." Meizan couldn't resist adding, "Nice armor."

Aranel flushed. "It was worse before. There were these decorative holes, and Aina stabbed me through one a while back, so

I covered them up. More practical this way." Meizan rolled his eyes, and Aranel continued. "I came here to look for her and Zenyra. Have you seen them?"

"No."

"What about you? And your clan, is everything all right with them?"

"Don't pretend like you care," Meizan said, stalking back to his campsite.

He could hear Aranel's frantic clanking as he followed. His armor really was bleeding ridiculous. Did Mayani not understand the importance of stealth?

"I had no choice," Aranel insisted. "I had nowhere else to go! Zenyra took Aina, and you had Kanjallen. What the hell was I supposed to do? Besides, you left too, back at Kaufgar! The only reason you came back was because of your so-called loyalty to Aina's mo—"

Aranel broke off when Meizan swung around to point his sword at his neck.

"You'd dare talk to me about loyalty," Meizan growled, "as if you know what it means. I've always been loyal to my chief. But you? You've been vacillating between the Balancers and the Preservation."

"I'm not—"

"Just pick a damn side, Aranel. And if you don't want to, then stay the hell out of this realm."

"My mission was to investigate Zenyra," Aranel said finally, pushing Meizan's blade away. "The Preservation think she's doing something that might endanger the realms. Something that might awaken Azyaka."

"The planetary nagamor?" Meizan asked dubiously.

Aranel launched into an explanation about the Planetary

Beasts and their chitronic cores, all part of some control system stored in the Universal Void. It made no sense to Meizan, beyond the disturbing claim that there really was a massive flaming snake underground . . . and on the verge of waking up.

"Erasures," Meizan said, once Aranel had finished. "Surprised your Preservation even know those exist."

"They've seen them in the Void. Disturbances that appear to be erasures and coincide with the timing of the Balancer missions."

"How do they even know the timing of the—" Meizan broke off. "You. You slimy little—"

"Stop looking at me like I betrayed Incaraz!" Aranel snapped. "I told Seirem that Zenyra's innocent, but he refuses to believe me. Besides, the Preservation haven't done anything to harm the Balancers with the information I provided."

"And they think these erasures will wake Azyaka?" Meizan asked. "Who will proceed to destroy the realms?" Aranel nodded. "And they sent *you*, a soft-souled coward who can't properly hold a sword, on this critical mission that could break our universe?"

Aranel drew back, offended. "I'm not the one who insists on gripping his sword in reverse, as if that's any more useful in a fight! And I'll have you know I came of my own accord this time. Seirem thinks I'm in Mayana, but *I* snuck away."

"How depraved of you. Do you want a medal?"

Aranel's brow twitched. "If what Seirem said is true, then now's as good a time as any to search Incaraz. At the least, I could find a clue as to Zenyra's whereabouts."

"Search away. I won't stop you."

"You could help," Aranel said hopefully. "Not as if you have anything better to do."

Seeing no reason to refuse, Meizan sighed, then followed Aranel as he set about poking through the rubble.

"Zenyra had a hidden chamber," Aranel said. "There was a chitronic shield under the lake, but it must have broken during the invasion. It's where she kept her supply of megarya blood."

"Her supply of *what*?"

"Megarya blood," Aranel said. He began yet another explanation that sounded even stupider than his first, and Meizan regretted every bath he'd taken upon entering Incaraz.

"Why are you telling me all this?" Meizan asked, flicking aside a large boulder with a blast of chitrons. "About the blood and the Beasts? Isn't it classified information, reserved for the Preservation?"

"It is." Aranel's face went red, and he turned away. "But I—I trust you. Even though I know I shouldn't, and I know you don't trust me. And since your realm will be affected worst by all this, I think you have a right to know."

Aranel refused to meet his gaze, and Meizan grabbed the upper's shoulder. "You're hiding something."

Aranel jerked away as if burned. "I'm not! I've already told you *far* more than I ought to have."

That was true, Meizan reasoned. But then why the hell was the idiot acting so shifty?

Aranel leaned over, sweeping away a mound of debris. "I wanted to stay," he mumbled. "You'll never believe me, but when Kanjallen arrived, a part of me wanted to stay."

"Good you didn't," Meizan said.

Threatening Taezur and the others for Aranel's sake had been a boneheaded move. Meizan wasn't sure what had possessed him to do it, but the chief had given him an earful when she'd found out. Aranel didn't belong in this realm. He most definitely didn't belong with Kanjallen.

"There." Aranel pointed to a deep hole he'd unearthed.

He jumped in, and Meizan followed into an underground grotto filled ankle-deep with a silvery liquid. It was like the water in the springs, only thicker.

"Undiluted megarya blood," Aranel said faintly, looking as if he wanted to vomit. "So much . . . how did she . . ." His expression turned panicked as Meizan waded toward him. "Don't touch it, Meizan! It's dangerous! Here. I—I'll carry you."

Aranel bent over to offer his back, and Meizan stared at him, incredulous.

"Like hell you will," Meizan said, streaming chitrons to his feet so he was walking atop the blood instead.

"I suppose that works too." Aranel straightened, then looked away. "Just be careful. And whatever you do, don't drink it."

"I'm not going to drink it!"

"Good. And you never drank from the hot springs either?"

"The springs that everyone *bathed* in? What kind of sick freak do you think I am?"

"I only meant because Zenyra said—" Aranel quieted at the sound of a feeble whimper that echoed through the grotto.

Meizan turned to find a trembling creature with glossy black fur thrashing at the edge of the pool. Its curved body was lithe and powerful, but punctured by several thin tubes that were draining its blood into the pool. Its fins unfurled into a feathery plumage as it strained against the chains that bound it to the rock, letting out a series of pitiful cheeps.

Meizan had never seen anything so beautiful—or pathetic. And he hadn't expected to see a winged dolphin, the legendary megarya of Paramos, in this realm.

Meizan took a step toward the beast and extended a hand. The megarya cowered as he neared, whimpering softly.

"Wait," Aranel began, but Meizan ignored him. He stared into the creature's large, dark eyes and waited.

The megarya blinked, fat tears staining its fur with salt.

Meizan's chest constricted as he gazed at the trembling beast. How long had it stayed here, dripping blood into the pool? How long had it cried, alone and in pain, waiting for someone to find it?

The megarya wouldn't die of physical injury, since it possessed miraculous regenerative healing powers. During Kal Ekana, the megarya were said to have been invincible. But this creature had been suffering a fate worse than death, shackled to a cave and milked for its blood.

Something soft bumped against Meizan's fingers. The megarya nuzzled his palm with a long, rounded snout. Meizan let out a shaky breath and moved a hand along the creature's neck. Carefully, he pulled out one of the tubes. The megarya's fur glowed as the wound knitted itself back together.

"It let you touch it," Aranel murmured. "Do you think I . . ."

Meizan moved aside as Aranel extended a hand toward the megarya. The creature stared at him, liquid eyes unblinking, before nudging his palm and letting out another soft cheep.

Wordlessly, Meizan and Aranel removed the rest of the tubes, then waited for the megarya to finish healing itself.

"You're Fei," Aranel addressed the beast. "You're Zenyra's friend."

At Zenyra's name, the megarya raised its head, eyes darting around the grotto as it strained against its chains. Meizan slashed them with his sword, and the creature soared forth at once. It leaped across the pool in graceful arcs and sniffed the walls frantically with its snout.

"It's looking for her," Meizan said in disbelief. "After she kept it imprisoned for all these years, it still wants to be with her."

"The megarya are intelligent creatures, and Zenyra stated the blood was a gift," Aranel said. "I expect the shields around

Incaraz were also maintained with the help of Fei's chitrons. Do you think it's possible that it willingly—"

"Let her enslave it for years and suck its blood dry?" Meizan crossed his arms.

"But the megarya are said to be the noblest of all beasts."

"Nothing is *that* noble."

"But if it were for a greater cause—"

"She took advantage of it, Aranel!" Meizan glowered at him. "She abused its loyalty. How don't *you* of all people realize how twisted that is? You think Toranic Law would reward this kind of thing?"

"I don't give a damn what Toranic Law would or wouldn't reward."

"Did you hit your head on the torana? You sound like Aina."

"Because Aina was right," Aranel said. "The Preservation, the torana, the chitronic shields—it's all stacked against the lower realms, Meizan. Stacked against *you*. And the only ones with the power to win the game are already at the top!"

"Chitronic shields?"

"Never mind," Aranel said, wading through the megarya blood. "I'll take Fei back with me when I return to Mayana."

He reached a passageway at the end of the grotto and disappeared into the darkness. Meizan was about to return aboveground when a terrified cry echoed through the cavern.

"Aranel?" Drawing his sword, Meizan rushed into the passageway. Broken stone littered the narrow tunnel, where parts of the ceiling had caved in after the invasion. A rotting stench, more potent than the fumes of Merumarth, assaulted Meizan's nostrils. "What's wrong?"

Aranel bumped into him and grasped Meizan's arm. He pointed a single shaking finger at the floor.

Meizan looked down, his sword clattering to the ground. "No . . . that can't be . . ."

The ground beneath them had split open to reveal a decaying body half-buried in the stone. Blank, soulless eyes stared at them from beneath an unmarked forehead, no keiza in sight.

Bones could be seen where the corpse's skin was sloughing off. Its bloated face would have made it unrecognizable, if not for the faded patterns inked across the moldering skin, the coral beads threaded into its lank silver hair.

"Hiraval." Meizan struggled to breathe. Aranel had gone still, his grip viselike on Meizan's arm. "What—what happened to him?"

"He's dead," Aranel whispered. "Hiraval's *dead*."

"How can he be dead?" Meizan turned to meet Aranel's petrified gaze. "Death doesn't exist!"

"But his soul's gone," Aranel croaked. He pointed at Hiraval's eerily blank forehead. "And his body's still here."

Meizan tore his gaze away from the corpse. Shock coursed through his veins. It didn't make sense. No matter how gruesome the injury, souls stayed in their bodies. Unless . . .

"He's not dead," Meizan said. "His soul erased."

"What? But his body's still—" Aranel's fingers dug into Meizan's forearm. "Of course. Projection."

Erasure only destroyed a soul and its chitrons, but due to the sheer amount of energy released, it usually ended up obliterating the original body too. But if Hiraval's soul had projected far enough during the moment of his erasure, it was possible that his body had escaped the explosion intact.

"He couldn't have." Aranel's voice cracked. "He was a *good* person, Meizan! And kind! Why would this happen to him? How?"

"I don't know."

A block of square-cut stone caught Meizan's eye, and he leaned down to pull it out of the rubble near the corpse's head. It measured the length of his arm and was engraved with slanting letters:

HIRAVAL OF AMARATIR
KC 373–394

They were dates. Year 373 of Kal Charana marked the birth of Hiraval's soul and year 394 its erasure.

"Zenyra must have buried him," Meizan said. He set the stone down. "This is her hidden chamber, right? Come on. We may find an answer to whatever your Preservation suspect."

They stumbled upon two more bodies, half unearthed by the fallen rubble and in worse states of decay than Hiraval's. Next to each body was a brick of stone engraved with the dates of their soul's birth and erasure.

NAMYRA OF AMARATIR
KC 376–393

SORANIL OF SAMARAS
KC 374–392

Several more bricks stood in a neat line with no trace of a body nearby.

"They're Balancers." Aranel's voice trembled. "They're all previous Balancers. I recognize the names from the Preservation's list."

"What happened to their bodies?" Meizan tore his eye away from the third corpse. "And why the burning hell was Zenyra hiding all this down here?"

The passageway led to a small circular room containing a stone desk and a large shelf stacked with empty vials and syringes. A crate next to the desk was filled with junk—torn blankets, twigs, and a single moldy boot.

Meizan picked up one of the syringes as Aranel began rummaging through the desk. The syringe was empty but for a single drop of shimmering megarya blood. Most of the others were in a similar state. A couple had remnants of another liquid, black as night.

"Do you know what this is?" Meizan held up the syringe with the dark liquid.

Aranel looked over his shoulder and shook his head, then turned back to the stack of notes he was flipping through. A few moments later, he swore loudly.

"What?" Meizan asked. Aranel rarely swore, and never with such malice.

The upper held a crumpled piece of parchment in trembling fingers. Meizan peered over his shoulder to read the contents. Lines of elegant script described instructions for some sort of experiment.

SCENARIO 0: *Natural ascension, observation only*
SCENARIO 1A: *Inject keiza with concentrated megarya blood*
   to trigger ascension
SCENARIO 1B: *Inject keiza with concentrated vandraghor blood*
   to trigger descension
SCENARIO 2: *Inject keiza with dilute vandraghor blood and have*
   soul project out of body to trigger descension through mixed
   action of blood and taint of Malin

Meizan narrowed his eyes and scanned farther down the parchment. It listed several names he'd heard in passing, of former

Balancers, along with details of their experiments. A certain name caught his eye, and Meizan inhaled sharply.

NAME: *Reimi*
AGE: 18 years
TORANIC CLASSIFICATION: *Mayana*
SCENARIO: 1*B*
VOLUME INJECTED: *Seven-tenths of a syringe*
RESULT: *Erasure*

And below:

NAME: *Hiraval*
AGE: 20 years
TORANIC CLASSIFICATION: *Paramos*
SCENARIO: 2
VOLUME INJECTED: *One-tenth of a syringe*
RESULT: *Erasure (out of body)*

The list went on, with at least a hundred names, Taralei's notably absent. Most of the experiments stated their result as erasure. Over two-thirds of the test subjects were aged between one and twelve years old with their Toranic classification stated as Malin.

Children from the Balancer villages, Meizan realized in horror. Almost all the children had been subject to injection with megarya blood. Those who ascended were a rare few. The majority of them had ended in erasure.

Meizan stared at a line of script stating that an unnamed two-year-old baby had met the same grisly fate. Hot rage flared within him.

"That bitch," he snarled. "Why the hell— For what purpose?"

"Seirem was right," Aranel said hollowly. He picked up the

boot from the crate of junk and squeezed it so hard his knuckles whitened. "It was never the war. It was her. Zenyra's the one triggering erasures." He strode to the shelf with the syringes and held up the one Meizan had been investigating earlier. "She's been experimenting with ascension and descension, and it's been causing the erasures, although I can't imagine *why* anyone would do such a heinous—"

He stopped abruptly, then slammed the parchment onto the table.

"This." Aranel pointed at a line of script. "This bit about the white flash. Do you know what it is? I've heard Aina mention it, but I can't seem to remember what she was talking about."

Next to some of the experiments—those few that had resulted in ascension or descension—Zenyra had scrawled a single phrase in the margin: *Duration of white flash negligible.*

"It's just something that happens during ascension between Malin and Mayana," Meizan said.

"Yes, but what does it signify? It must have some importance if Zenyra is so concerned with its duration!"

"It happens when the chitronic spin of a soul reverses. I've never seen it myself, but Aina told me about hers. She said it was less of a flash and more like she was floating in a sea of white."

"A sea of white . . ." Aranel repeated. "Aina did mention something . . . an irregularity in her keiza . . . a door to nowhere . . ." He froze, eyes growing wide. "Of course."

"Of course what? What do you know?"

Aranel began to pace around the cave, muttering under his breath. "Equal opportunity to all, regardless of soul-spin. So when she said that, what she meant was—"

"Who said that?" Meizan chased after him. "Zenyra? Why is she causing erasures? Is she trying to wake Azyaka?"

"No." Aranel stopped in his tracks, a strange gleam in his eye.

"The erasures were accidents. Failed attempts. What she's actually trying to do is open a torana to the Universal Void. So she can break the shields between the realms."

"Break the *what*?"

"The chitronic shields. They're part of the system in the Void. They're what keep the realms separated, and Zenyra wants to break them."

Meizan couldn't make much sense of Aranel's words, but the upper didn't seem in the mood to answer any more questions. Grabbing a syringe and a vial, Aranel sped out of the room. Meizan followed him through the passageway into the grotto.

The megarya had fled, but its blood remained. Aranel knelt down, filled a vial with the hellforsaken stuff, and screwed it shut.

"Oi." Meizan yanked him up. "What are you doing with that?"

"I'm going to Ashkator."

"In Paramos?" Meizan stared at him. "You can ascend?" Aranel swished the vial of megarya blood before pocketing it. "You're not serious? After all the moralizing shit you—"

"There's a torana there that leads to the Void," Aranel interrupted. "Zenyra plans to enter it and break the shields between the realms! Don't you understand what that means?"

"War and bloodshed," Meizan said slowly. "Kaldrav has an army that will be more than happy to annihilate your pretty little kingdoms."

"It'll be like Kal Ekana all over again." Aranel's face drained of color. "Everyone in one realm . . . constant fighting . . . all but a fraction of humanity wiped out."

"You're forgetting that Zenyra has Aina!" Cold fear slithered up Meizan's spine as he remembered Hiraval's soulless body. "What if she erases her too?"

"She won't." Aranel sounded unsure. "She wouldn't— She didn't mean to—" He cursed again and seized Meizan by the shoulders. "Find her. You have her mother and Kanjallen on your side. You'll be able to do it far quicker than I would."

"We've been trying. The past couple days, I've been—"

"I really must leave," Aranel said. Then he spun around and dashed out of the grotto without another word.

Meizan swore as he watched him go. He had no flaming idea what the loser was up to. He didn't think he understood what Aranel thought Zenyra was up to either.

But amidst all the uncertainty, one thing was clear: Zenyra was dangerous, and she had Aina. There were few people in the realm Meizan would risk his own safety for, but Aina had somehow become one of them. He would not let her soul end in erasure.

But how the bleeding hell do I locate her?

Soul projection was the obvious answer, but Meizan had not mastered it as Aina had. It still took him over an hour to push his chitrons out of his body. But it was the only way. Anything else and he might be too late. He was going to have to force a quick projection by leaving himself with no other choice.

Unsheathing his sword, Meizan took a deep breath, then shoved the blade into his forehead. Pain ripped through his skull as Meizan squeezed his eyes shut and *pushed.*

CHAPTER TWENTY-FIVE

❧

Fallen Warrior

ENYRA MOORED THEIR boat to an outcrop of rock. Leaving a gagged Aina bound inside, she stepped onto the island and swept toward the cloaked figure, who waved an arm in greeting. Aina couldn't make out much beyond a hulking frame and a mane of wild hair. Behind the torana the figure had emerged from, Narakh was pitch black.

"The things I do for you, woman," said a male voice. "Blasted roach almost bit my arm off!" He handed Zenyra a syringe filled with dark liquid. "Never again am I descending to that cursed realm voluntarily."

"I never asked you to," Zenyra said, examining the syringe and pocketing it. "You could have sent one of your men. Based on our last count, you seem to have quite a few."

"Those cowering clods?" The man gave a guttural laugh. "Very few are decent channelers, and I've already lost dozens trying to bleed the damned beast. My soldiers are more useful to me here than stewing in a vandraghor's belly."

Soldiers? A vandraghor?

Who was this man? And why was he giving Zenyra what sounded like vandraghor blood?

"So you decided to go yourself?" Zenyra did not sound amused. "Rash heroics aside, it seems you still have a certain affinity for the roach."

"Some bonds never fully break." Another gruff laugh as the man shook back his hair. Aina suppressed a gasp at the sight of his face, a gruesome patchwork of reddened skin and angry, raised scars. "Anyhow, this better be the last of it. You've wasted enough blood on your failed experiments."

"I will not fail this time," Zenyra said. "You know, while you were off hunting roaches in Narakh the past two weeks, your troops nearly jeopardized the whole plan. You were told to keep your soldiers *away* from Incaraz and the Balancer villages. You failed me, Kaldrav."

Kaldrav? The name sent shockwaves down Aina's spine. *What the blazing hell is the king of Malin doing with Zenyra?*

Aina had never seen Kaldrav in person, but his existence had cast a shadow upon her life for as long as she could remember. She and Kanna had spent fourteen years fleeing his soldiers as he methodically absorbed the warring clans, destroyed their villages, and sometimes tortured those too weak to fight.

Kaldrav the Cruel. Kaldrav the Conqueror.

That man—that *monster*—was here, a few feet in front of her, speaking to Zenyra with casual familiarity.

"I'll have every chump who was involved in the attack flayed and sent to Agakor for a week," Kaldrav said. "Longer, if you want. Would two weeks be enough? Two moons?"

"I want you to control your army," Zenyra replied in a voice like ice. "It would do you well to remember, Kaldrav, that torture and fear do not beget control."

"On the contrary, fear of torture is *exactly* what keeps my soldiers in check."

"Spoken as a true mangler. There are kinder ways to gain a person's loyalty."

"Spare me the lecture," the king of Malin scoffed. "You use your methods, Zenyra, and leave me to mine. My soldiers left your hideout alone for years. But they've grown bored of razing shitty little villages, full of fleas that can't put up a fight. They're craving proper violence. And war. The war that *we* promised them."

"And they will get it," Zenyra said. "But first, they must learn discipline if this war is to have minimum casualties."

"Minimum casualties." Kaldrav snorted. "Stop pretending you care about those children. Anyone my men hurt only served as fodder for your villages. A bloodless war would never satiate my soldiers, nor the demons of Narakh."

Zenyra remained silent for a long moment. "The Narakhi," she finally said. "That is the first you have spoken of them in years."

"So?"

"I thought you no longer . . . I thought they were a thing of your past . . ."

"How optimistic of you." Kaldrav gave a caustic chuckle. "Those demons are my past, my present, and my future. I can hear them in my head even now, thirsting for bloodshed, clamoring for violence—"

"Pay them no heed," Zenyra interrupted. "It is the Malini soldiers you must focus on. They can be restrained with ease, for they are not gifted channelers."

"No, but they're delightfully vicious."

"Because you have not disciplined them as per our agreement," Zenyra said heatedly. "You have only bred their bloodlust and allowed them to run amok. If not for Kanjallen's timely intervention, I would have lost my key to the Void during the breach of Incaraz."

"Stinking weepers! If it weren't for that nagamor, I'd *crush* Kanjallen. Capture their worm-worshipping runt of a chief and skin her to her bones."

"You will do no such thing." Zenyra gave a frustrated sigh. "You are missing the point, Kaldrav. This obsession with inflicting needless suffering will be the end of you."

"How dare you," Kaldrav retorted. "*You* are the one who triggered all those erasures! It is *your* plan to break the realms that will cause more suffering than anything I have ever done!"

Erasures? Break the realms? Aina felt another wave of shock. *What is he talking about?*

"I create suffering for a reason," Zenyra said. "As a means to an end. You, however, have no end. You are a fallen warrior, bereft of his strength. You let yourself be ruled by bloodlust, and it has wrought a fool of you."

"Oh, I have an end." The king gave a dark chuckle, taking a step forward. "Several ends. You think I'm going to hand you my army for nothing?"

"Without the army, the Preservation will simply remake the shields after we break them, and all will have been for naught. You wish to topple Kyrian's empire as much as I."

"Oh, I do." Kaldrav took another step. "I've wanted to crush that sententious sycophant for centuries. I've wanted to hear him scream, feel his warm, *pure* Paramosi blood on my fingers. But there is something I've wanted even longer."

The king lunged at Zenyra, smashing his face to hers.

A resounding slap sounded over the waves. Kaldrav flew backward and crashed against the torana.

"Devious bitch," he snarled. Ropes of dark energy snaked from his palm.

Zenyra raised her arms, and Kaldrav let out a strangled yell as stippled golden light wrapped around him and bound him to the black pillar.

"I raised you an army, you tramp!" Kaldrav roared. "Kept the realm safe for you and your Balancer scum! I did more for you in the past decade than that sobbing pile of shit will ever do in his lifetime! The least you could do is—"

"Speak no more," Zenyra cut in, her voice dangerously soft. "I owe you nothing. I tolerated your foolery out of deference to our old bonds. But I no longer need you. The attack on Incaraz has made me realize how unreliable you have become."

"Unreliable?" The king growled. "How am *I* the unreliable one, when that son of a worm hasn't been seen for bleeding centuries! I've seen you with that eyeglass of yours, staring at the skies. You're stupid to wait for him, Zenyra! He's never going to show up! You'll dry up and wither before you ever come close to—"

Kaldrav swore as his neck snapped back, head slamming against the pillar.

"I will find him," Zenyra said, walking toward the bound king. "I will find them both. I will break the barriers and overthrow Kyrian's Preservation. It is unfortunate that you will not bear witness to any of it."

She reached into her pocket and pulled out a syringe. Not the one he had given her, but another, filled with a shimmering silver substance. Kaldrav went rigid at the sight.

"Zenyra," he croaked. "Is that . . . no . . . you can't . . . you wouldn't."

"Concentrated megarya blood," Zenyra said as Kaldrav began thrashing against the ropes. "The purest substance in the universe. You know the First Principle of Chitronic Equilibrium.

We learned it together back at Ashkator." The syringe glinted as Zenyra raised it to eye level. "The transfer of chitronic energy as per the First Principle is a gradual process over the course of a soul's existence. A sudden clash of chitrons with opposing spins would never occur within one's soul."

She shook back her sleeves, swirling the contents of her syringe. "Not naturally, that is."

"You conniving wench," Kaldrav moaned. "I raised you an army . . . two hundred thousand soldiers to fight for your cause . . ."

The king was weeping now. Aina watched in transfixed horror. She hadn't the slightest idea as to what Zenyra was doing and why Kaldrav seemed so terrified of that syringe.

"This megarya blood could scour your soul and help you ascend," Zenyra said, almost gentle as she brushed the king's matted hair from his forehead. "Or, if the clashing chitrons are too extreme, they could destroy you altogether."

"Don't do this, Zenyra . . . think of your sister . . . she would never condone it . . . even *he* would never . . ."

"It is not their judgment you must face, but mine. You hold too much of the darkness in this universe, and now *I* must protect the balance." Zenyra twirled the syringe in her fingers. "So which will it be, Kaldrav? Ascension or erasure?"

Erasure? Aina couldn't believe what she was hearing. Kaldrav went slack, his voice a broken whisper.

"Zen . . . please . . . release me . . ."

In one swift movement, Zenyra plunged the syringe into the king's forehead.

A brutal convulsion wracked through Kaldrav's form and he let loose a soul-curdling scream. Beams of light shot out of his keiza, illuminating the island and sending large cracks splintering through the rock.

"I pray you suffer for this!" Kaldrav screamed. "I pray the

Beasts wake! I pray the comet strikes and the torana shatter and death reigns once again! I pray every moment of your life is spent in absolute, unbearable agony while Kyrian's—lies—unravel—across—the—"

A deafening roar shook the sky, ripping the fabric of the universe. It rattled Aina's bones and squeezed the air from her lungs. With a great burst of light like a supernova, Kaldrav the Cruel's body exploded into nothingness—his screams, his soul, and his existence wiped from the universe for eternity.

"And so the blight was purged," Zenyra murmured. She tossed the empty syringe into the Shadowed Sea. "As expected, you were too far gone for it to work."

Aina stared ahead, open-mouthed, still trying to process what she had just witnessed. The island gave a menacing rumble, and the cracks upon its surface widened. Only the torana to Narakh remained unbroken.

Zenyra leaped nimbly across the rock and joined Aina in the boat. They sped away from the island just as it split to pieces. With a great splash, it sank, torana and all, swallowed by the murky waters of Mir Tamasa.

Desperate to distance themselves from the submerged torana, every saberfin shark in the vicinity fled at once. They wouldn't return. Nothing would—not with this new monstrosity lurking beneath the surface.

"YOU HAVE A lot of explaining to do," Aina spat, once they made it ashore and Zenyra removed her binds. Zenyra offered a hand to help her out of the boat, but Aina slapped it away. "Don't touch me!"

She stumbled onto the gravel beach, of half a mind to run away. But her desire for answers outweighed all else.

Aina followed Zenyra up the cliff, bombarding her with questions. "Since when were you aligned with Kaldrav? And why erase him now? And what was that about triggering erasures?"

"Aina, listen to me—"

"And the war! He said you promised his army a war, what was that all about? How could you lie to me?"

"I did not lie to you, Aina. Not as much as you think. I merely omitted certain aspects of the truth that I felt unsuitable for your ears at the time."

"Cut the shit! What was your plan with Kaldrav? What was the point of the Balancers if you were on *his* side the whole time?"

"I established the Balancers a decade ago, out of a genuine desire to help the lower realms," Zenyra said. "Our initial aim was to improve the Malini's standard of living and help them ascend. My focus was on babies, young children—those who had not yet accumulated dark deeds during the course of their lifetimes. But the more I stayed in this realm and studied those who lived within it, the more I realized this was a fruitless task. For how could one ascend when Malin's chitrons themselves are fickle, twisting even the most basic of channeling into a sin?

"You were a rare case, Aina, due to the irregularity in your keiza slowing their influence on your soul. But for a majority of the Malini born into this realm, there is no chance of escape. The barriers and the torana are the problem."

"You mean Toranic Law," Aina said.

"Not quite," Zenyra replied. "Toranic Law existed for centuries before the torana were created. I suspect the Preservation named the torana after it to strengthen the perception that the two are one and the same. In reality, Toranic Law only dictates soul-spin. It is the torana and the shields that prevent ascension."

Aina blinked. "So when you said Toranic Law could never fall . . ."

351

"It cannot. But the barriers between the realms—chitronic shields, to be precise—can. Breaking them would create one realm, not unlike that of Kal Ekana."

One realm.

It was a tempting thought but far too abstract to be real. How could Zenyra possibly bring about something like that?

"Breaking the shields became my new goal," Zenyra said. "To do so, I needed access to the Universal Void. Unfortunately, the Preservation destroyed the torana leading to it. All but one, located in Ashkator and guarded closely by their own. I sought to break in several times, but despite my best efforts, my best disguises and illusions . . ." Zenyra threaded her fingers together with a sigh. "They thwarted my every attempt, until it became impossible for me to set foot within a mile of Ashkator without alerting them to my presence. So I had to look for another method. Another way to enter the Void."

"That's why you became so interested in ascension and descension," Aina said, the realization hitting her like the blunt end of a sword. *That's why you were interested in me.*

"Once I began studying the white flash, I discovered that the moment a soul changes spin could open a temporary torana into the Void," Zenyra said. "I experimented with some of the Balancers, as well as children from the villages, to try and make that torana appear. I used varying quantities of megarya and vandraghor blood to stimulate their ascension and descension. Sometimes, I even had them project into Malin to see if separation from the body made a difference to the duration of the torana. Despite my best efforts, the torana only ever materialized momentarily, and a way into the Void eluded me."

"What happened to them?" Aina asked. "The children and the Balancers you experimented on?" Panic seized her. "That little girl, Ummi? What happened to Hiraval, Taralei, and Reimi? They were already from Mayana, which means they couldn't have ascended!"

"I never experimented on Taralei, for I needed her to look after the village. But the others . . ." Zenyra dropped her head, gaze hooded. "The most common outcome, by far, was erasure."

"Erasure?" Aina's voice cracked. She sat down to steady herself. Tears pricked her eyes as she thought of Hiraval and his unflagging patience as he taught her chitronic control. Reimi with her moon-eyed smile, always so full of laughter. "Y-you *monster*! How could you?"

"I did not mean for it to happen!" Zenyra's head snapped up. "I cared about them too, Aina! But the spin of a soul is a tricky and volatile thing. Even a slight miscalculation, a slight error in the quantity of blood—"

"That's no excuse!" Aina shouted, shock giving way to rage. "You knew the risk, yet you continued—"

"They were necessary sacrifices!" Zenyra stood, pupils dilated, and loomed over Aina. "I am trying to change the future of the realms! Achieve equality for all, regardless of their birth! A few erasures along the way are regrettable but unavoidable!"

"What future? You'll break the chitronic shields—then what? Have Kaldrav's army march upon Mayana? What good will another war do?"

"It will force the Preservation to change the status quo. Prevent them from reestablishing the existing shields."

Zenyra sank to her knees and grabbed Aina's face. "You must want this too, Aina. You said yourself that you care not for a natural order that blesses some and curses others. This is our opportunity to change things. If we break the shields between the realms, the resulting war will be no worse than that which already ravages Malin. But it will end one day. And once the violence abates, people like your mother will have a chance at a peaceful, plentiful life. Is that not what you want?"

"I don't have a mother anymore. She threw me away, and *you* were all I had left." Aina wrenched her face from Zenyra's hands. "I would've been happy, living here with you. You, Meizan, Aranel, the Balancers."

Zenyra's eyes softened. "Aina. Dear child."

Aina stood, turning her back to Zenyra as they resumed their climb. "You could've told me about your plan. You could've trusted me. But instead you told me I was *special.* You made me believe that I actually meant something to you! When all you wanted was to use me as your key to open the Void!"

"I did not want to burden you with the knowledge of what I was doing." Zenyra paused. "I know you do not want to hear this from me. But your mother does care for you, Aina. In a better world, she may even be in a position to show it."

She doesn't care, Aina wanted to scream. Yet at Zenyra's words, she felt a glimmer of hope. That in a better world, Kanna might look at her as she once had—not with love, but at least with concern.

"What if nothing changes?" Aina asked in a small voice. "What if she doesn't?"

"She will." Zenyra placed a hand upon Aina's. They had reached the top of the cliff. In the distance stood a line of barren trees, marking the edge of Martharan.

When Zenyra removed her hand, a single syringe rested on Aina's palm—the one Kaldrav had procured, filled with an inky black liquid.

"Vandraghor blood," Zenyra said. "Three-quarters to the brim, fully concentrated. I ran the calculations dozens of times.

Given your unique keiza and the stubborn nature of your soul, the risk of erasure is negligible."

"Why—why are you giving this to me?"

"The torana to the Void will appear at your descension." Zenyra smiled, sweeping Aina's bangs from her forehead. "I could stab you myself, but we can both agree I have subjected you to enough manipulation to last a lifetime. This time, the choice is yours."

Aina stared at the syringe, her reflection warped in the dark blood.

If she smashed this now, Zenyra would have no way into the Void. There would be no war. She and Kanna would live separate lives. Aina could return to Mayana. The Balancer's memory would fade over time and become another old bruise to join her collection.

But if she injected . . . Aina's eyes smarted at the possibility, too surreal to imagine. The cycle of imbalance, finally broken. Kanna, living in peace once the war subsided: well fed, meat on her bones, lines of worry smoothed away. Maybe it would smooth her temper too. Maybe she'd *thank* Aina for it. Take back the cruel words and soften her slaps to caresses.

The syringe trembled in her grasp, and Aina squeezed her eyes shut. *Don't make me choose,* she wanted to scream at Zenyra. *Don't make me decide the fate of the universe. It's too much. It's not fair.*

The universe is not fair, Kanna's words echoed in her mind.

And for the first time in her bitter, miserable life, Aina had the power to change it. Steadying her hand, she raised the syringe to eye level.

CHAPTER TWENTY-SIX

@

The Chitronic Prodigy

ARANEL SURVEYED THE maelstrom at the base of Ashkator. The chitrons of Paramos crashed over his senses and seemed to stir a song within his soul—a melody of such unfiltered splendor it made him feel both brave and overwhelmed at once. They poured down the mountainside in a rustling avalanche of colored light, whipping up whirlpools around its base. As Aranel neared, the rustling grew to a roar like the cries of a thousand beasts melding into one crescendo.

Such chitronic turbulence, he thought, his awe edged with terror. Even the Aurora Rapids of Mayana seemed but a trickle in comparison.

Aranel's own chitronic flows felt weak, almost negligible, as they ebbed within him. But he could conceive no way to scale Ashkator with his current level of control. The chitrons were too fast and unruly to bond with. Even the smallest misstep would fling him against the rocks.

The Preservation had no need to defend the torana to the Void. Ashkator and its chitronic waterfall were as good a natural defense as ever.

Fei the megarya bumped against Aranel's arm and burrowed its snout into the crook of his elbow. Aranel patted the sleek head, his fingers curling against the rich downiness.

"You're free now," he said. "You're back in your realm."

He had found Fei just outside Incaraz, sniffing around for Zenyra. Aranel had somehow convinced the creature to follow him into Paramos. Feeling intensely vile, he had chugged a flask of its blood as the megarya watched him with wide, liquid eyes.

Fei bumped him again, harder this time.

"I'm not sure I know what I'm doing here. Or what I'm supposed to do." Aranel sighed as he stroked the luxuriant fur. "I don't even know how to get up this mountain."

The megarya gave a cheep and lowered its head.

"Are you giving me permission to ride you?" asked Aranel. "Truly? You can get me up?"

The megarya resembled a water-dwelling dolphin but for its wings, fur, and the striking fin on its forehead. Its muscular body was twice Aranel's size—yet he couldn't imagine how it could possibly navigate the thrashing currents above them, especially after it had been imprisoned for years.

Then again, the megarya are miraculous healers. Aranel scanned Fei's form. Not a wound in sight, no sign of the trauma it had endured. And the megarya were known as masters of the skies and seas for a reason.

"Very well, then." Aranel inclined his head. "I will be eternally grateful."

He clambered onto the megarya and leaned forward to wrap his arms around its neck. He supposed this was Fei's way of thanking him for setting it free, though he couldn't help but feel rather unworthy of his mount.

Muscles tensing, Fei emitted a high-pitched whistle before shooting into the currents like an arrow. Aranel held on tightly and wrapped his own chitrons around the beast's girth so he didn't fly off while it climbed.

The megarya's body rippled as it gained momentum. It crashed out of the currents and vaulted into the sky, then spread its wings to soar through the air. Fei scaled the treacherous slopes of Ashkator in great, leaping arcs, finding safe paths amidst the raging lights.

Aranel reached out with his own chitrons in an attempt to assist the climb. The moment he did so, he was nearly torn off Fei's back from the intensity of it all. The chitronic forces around Ashkator were destabilizing. It was all Aranel could do to cling to the megarya without slipping off.

As they neared Ashkator's flattened summit, the forces lulled to a mist that flowed in languid swathes toward the mountain's rim. Rising from the mist were the slender forms of buildings, sinuous and fluid as if they'd been carved by the chitronic currents themselves. Wrought of diamond and glass, they bore spires of filigreed silver, their moats spanned by gossamer-thin bridges.

Aranel stared at the Preservation's headquarters in wonder. For years, he had longed to see this very sight and set foot atop Ashkator.

My parents are somewhere around. And Sam . . .

But Aranel had no time for familial visits. He slid off Fei's back and stroked the megarya's glossy mane.

"I cannot thank you enough," said Aranel. Fei nuzzled his cheek before letting out a short whistle and shooting into the sky.

"When I invited you to Paramos, I did not expect you to arrive on the back of a megarya. You continue to impress me, my boy."

Aranel whirled around at the voice. "How did you—"

"The chitronic currents around Ashkator," said Seirem with a smile. "None can set foot near this crater without the Preservation's knowledge. The currents have helped us keep Zenyra at bay for years, although your presence is far more welcome."

"Glad to know," said Aranel. "So the Void is safe? And the torana?"

"We have our finest guarding it. Although I detected yet another disturbance—an erasure—but an hour ago."

Aranel's heart plummeted. *Not Aina. For the love of Sherka, please, not Aina.*

"Might I see it?" he asked. "The Void and the chitronic system? I am still trying to wrap my head around it all. Seeing it in person might help."

"Soon," promised Seirem. "But not today. I am sure you are weary from travel and eager to meet your parents. I also have several Preservers I would like to introduce you to when the time is right."

"That would be nice." Aranel's eyes flitted around the crater as he took a step toward Seirem. The headquarters were at least a mile away. They were alone in the eddying mists.

Aranel took another step and slid his hand into his pocket. His fingers curled around the syringe swiped from Zenyra's secret chamber earlier.

"Perhaps the introductions could wait." Seirem observed Aranel in concern. "You look unwell. Is everything—"

He reeled as Aranel struck in one swift motion, ramming the syringe into his forehead.

"Vandraghor blood," said Aranel viciously as Seirem's face screwed up in pain. There had been only a drop left in the syringe.

He prayed it would be enough. "You have stayed here too long, enjoying the undeserved bliss of a realm too pure for your soul. It is time you descend and return to where you belong."

"I had high hopes for you, Aranel," lamented Seirem, his keiza dimming. "It was not your place to punish me."

Aranel watched in satisfaction as the air around Seirem rippled, then peeled apart to reveal the lotus of Kirnos amidst a field of cloud. With a flicker, a silver torana materialized in front of the tear.

"'Vengeance and rancor doth make a soul weep,'" recited Seirem as the torana sucked him toward it. "'That which thou hast sown, one day thou shalt reap.'"

"'To unheed a crime, in itself, is a sin,'" said Aranel. "'Intervention, if just, shall not slow a soul's spin.'" He pulled out the vial of megarya blood he'd taken from Incaraz. "You're not the only one who can quote the Aria of Ascension when convenient, *Lord* Seirem. And even if my soul does slow from this deed . . ."

Aranel dumped the blood down his throat, his chitrons singing in delight. "How blessed I am you taught me how to counteract it."

Seirem's eyes bulged as the torana dragged him through its pillars. "How do you have more of that? Did you bleed the megarya yourself? Or is it from that infernal woman's supply? What do you intend to do, foolish boy? Are you helping her?"

His shrieks turned to silence as the archway disappeared and the universe sealed itself.

Good riddance, thought Aranel, glancing around the billowing mists.

There was no one in sight, but he was pressed for time. He didn't know how much megarya blood Seirem carried on his person, but Aranel was certain he would try to reascend through the nearest torana—likely the one in Kirnos, which led to a spot a mile west of Ashkator's base.

Assuming he's able to scale Ashkator himself, I have a few hours at best before he informs the Preservation. Even less if these chitronic mists somehow alert them of his descension.

Aranel raced through the river of mist in search of the torana to the Void. The currents grew faster around him, pulling at his ankles. He realized that he'd reached the inner rim of the mountain. Here, the ground slanted down like Incaraz had—giving way to a vast caldera into which the chitronic lights spilled in a dizzying drop.

Aranel could not see what lay within the swirling vortex. There would be no better location for a torana than at the bottom, hidden from sight. And for him, falling down would be far easier than climbing up.

Drawing a deep breath, Aranel swiped his keiza and dove. He thought his soul would be ripped from his body as he hurtled down. The colored lights pounded upon him, inexorable, inescapable, snapping his chitronic flows before he could properly wield them.

Seconds later, the intense pressure lifted. Aranel steadied himself and tumbled onto soft grass.

He looked up to be greeted by the sight of multihued heavens, the sky a kaleidoscope of spiraling light. Beneath it, Aranel found himself in a meadow of such exquisite beauty that the palace gardens of Kirnos seemed but faded wastelands in comparison.

In the distance stood a lone hill ringed by fruit trees. And atop it was a stark white torana, its columns unadorned. Aranel had jumped to his feet when a velvety voice stopped him in his tracks.

"Ran? Is that you?"

Samarel strode across the meadow with a grin, his expression devoid of any wariness or hurt from their last encounter. Aranel noted he wore his Kirnosi breastplate over his Preserver robes.

Seirem, that old stone-soul! He must have assigned him today on purpose.

"It *is* you." Samarel swept toward him and placed his hands on Aranel's shoulders. "I heard from Lord Seirem that you'd be arriving today. Have you been well?"

"Well enough," muttered Aranel. He wasn't prepared to see his brother here in front of the torana. "You . . . were right, Sam. About Seirem, I mean. He tricked me." He traced the unadorned sleeves of Samarel's robes with a rush of relief. "You're in the unblooded faction, then? So you didn't drink to ascend?"

"No one drinks to ascend," said Samarel, scandalized. "Only to remain. I'm glad to see you are well, and finished with that forsaken mission." He ruffled Aranel's hair, something he hadn't done in years. "Mother's been keeping your room ready. I thought you'd visit home first. What are you doing here?"

Aranel bit the inside of his cheek. Would Samarel not understand if he knew the whole truth? Would he not agree to help and come up with some sort of miraculous solution that had evaded Aranel?

"I want to enter the Void," said Aranel, meeting his brother's eyes. "I want to see the chitronic system that governs the realms and recalibrate the limits on the chitronic shields."

He proceeded to pour out every detail of what had transpired over the past few moons, from his first meeting with Seirem and his interactions with his teammates to what he and Meizan had discovered in Zenyra's secret chamber.

Samarel pressed his hands to his temples. "You are in over your head, Ran," he said, once Aranel had finished. "Go home and get some rest. Mother's made all your favorites for dinner."

"Don't just tell me to go home!" cried Aranel, stung. "Were you not listening to what I said? The universe is unbalanced, Sam. Everyone says it is the judgment of Toranic Law, but really, it's just the chitronic shields!"

"And what do you intend to do about that?" asked Samarel. "We don't know if it's possible for the shields to be remade or recalibrated."

"It *is*! Seirem let it slip that one could change the limits on them."

"The current limits were set by the seitarius, the very beings that founded our realms. What makes you think that you, a seventeen-year-old child—"

"Eighteen! I can't believe you'd forget my birthday."

"You're still a child," said Samarel. "Once my shift ends, I'm going to have a word with Lords Kyrian and Seirem both to ensure you stay out of this."

"It's too late for that!" Aranel grabbed his brother's arms, glowering up at him. "You can't expect me to simply forget about everything! The Malini deserve a better life, Sam! They deserve more chances at happiness!"

"Your attachment to this Meizan is stopping you from thinking clearly."

"It's not only about Meizan! You didn't see those children, Sam! There was a two-year-old boy, and he was all alone, and—"

Aranel broke off, at a loss for words. His brother was supposed to be kind and generous. How could Samarel of all people be so narrow-minded?

I was like that once as well, Aranel reminded himself. *I thought the Malini were devils who deserved to suffer. Sam hasn't seen what I have.*

"The current chitronic system was made by the seitarius," said Samarel. "By the gods. By doubting the system, you are doubting the gods."

"Of course *you'd* say that!" Aranel ground his teeth together. "The current system favors you, after all. It's favored you since birth. Even amongst the Mayani, you were always considered flawless. *Perfect.*"

"I'm not—"

"But it's a broken system! A corrupt system that should have never been allowed to exist. You're too brainwashed by the Preservation to see it."

"Ran, even if the system were less than ideal, there's no way you could fix it by yourself. What do you wish to do upon storming into the Void?" Samarel raked a hand through his hair. "Do you think you can change things merely out of sheer will? Even if the shields could, in theory, be recalibrated, the amount of energy and skill that would require is far beyond your ability or mine."

"I'm sure Zenyra can find a way to—"

"That woman is dangerous!" Samarel's eyes flashed, and Aranel took a step back. His brother seldom raised his voice. "You said it yourself! How many of her own so-called comrades has she sacrificed? How many erasures has she caused?"

"I don't agree with her methods," said Aranel. "But Zenyra's intentions are honorable, and the Preservation are just as unforgivable for perpetuating an unfair system. If I can convince her to recalibrate the shields instead of breaking them down—"

"You will not be convincing Zenyra of anything," thundered Samarel. "You will stay far away from her."

"But the chitronic system!"

"I do not care! You are my brother, Aranel. I will not let you endanger your soul by partaking in that woman's unhinged plans. And I certainly will not let you near the Void."

Samarel slid into a defensive position, and Aranel wanted to scream.

In all these years, Aranel had never come close to defeating his brother in a spar—and that was with Samarel going easy on him. If his brother went all out, Aranel was certain the chitronic prodigy would decimate him in moments.

But Samarel wouldn't go all out. Not against him. And that was Aranel's one advantage.

"Go home, Ran," said Samarel, an edge to his velvety voice. "Don't force my hand."

"Make me," retorted Aranel, reaching for his sword.

But Samarel was faster. Golden energy shot from his palms to rope around Aranel.

"Must we do this?" asked his brother with resignation. "A spar between us will only ever end in one outcome."

"Don't be so sure." Aranel wrested an arm free of the binds. "We haven't faced off in a while, and I've learned some new tricks."

He swiped his keiza and loosened a blast of chitrons, breaking himself free. Aranel leaped three paces back as Samarel watched, unbothered. Almost lazily, his brother flicked a finger.

Aranel cursed as the meadow erupted beneath his feet. Samarel lifted his arms to draw forth the ground and raise hills to entrap him.

Streaming chitronic energy to his sword, Aranel mounted the blade and took to the sky. He skirted over the hills and fired a volley of stun beams at his brother. Samarel wove through them deftly, his movements swift and precise, as the grass around him exploded in flames.

"Is that a Balancer technique?" asked Samarel. He molded a shield from the dirt and sprung aboard, riding the wind until he was directly above Aranel.

They darted through the air like a pair of dueling hawks and exchanged blows whenever the other swooped close.

Samarel leaped off his shield to swing down with a foot. Aranel raised an arm to counter, but his brother changed direction midswing, and rotated to hit him square in the chest.

Pain wracked Aranel's bones as Samarel unleashed a barrage of kicks with infuriating speed—impossible to dodge, much less retaliate.

Even the Balancer techniques are no good against him, realized Aranel, as he was knocked off his sword and sent crashing into the ground. His brother was simply too fast.

A lattice of tree roots wrapped around Aranel like a shroud. Samarel glided in front of him, back on his shield, with not a strand of hair out of place.

Aranel felt a mixture of admiration, annoyance, and embarrassment. Just how much had Samarel held back all these years? And how much was he restraining himself still?

Aranel spent the next few minutes trying to land a hit on his brother, his every effort nullified. Samarel read Aranel's pattern of attacks and manipulated the chitrons before Aranel had a chance.

"Give it up, Ran," he said, sending the branches Aranel had summoned whipping back at him. "I taught you all of that."

Samarel was right. Aranel's usual attacks may have worked against enemy soldiers, even Meizan and Aina—but they would never fool his brother. He needed to do something different. Unpredictable.

Aranel drew upon his chitrons once more, gathering heat from the still-flickering flames kindled by his missed stunners. The tree roots around him withered to ash, and Aranel broke free of his prison. The river behind Samarel reared up in fury, then shaped itself into a hundred watery swords.

Samarel snapped his fingers. The swords merged to form a

giant watery gazarou that doused the flames and sped toward Aranel, its gaping maw large enough to swallow him whole. Aranel's chitrons reared, and the gazarou melted into a nagamor that twisted around to dive at his brother.

"Learn that in Malin?" Samarel leaped aside as the nagamor crashed to the earth with a great splash.

Aranel did not answer, focused solely on his channeling. The chitrons here were more malleable than those of Mayana. Aranel conjured a fireball three times the size of any he would have been able to create in his own realm.

But with a flick of his fingers, Samarel turned the fireball into a flurry of fireworks. The grassy walls Aranel raised around him disintegrated into storms of flower petals.

"You cannot win against me, Ran. You have a decade's worth of training ahead before you come close."

Samarel's voice held no disdain, yet it infuriated Aranel further. "We'll see about that," he said. "You're not always right, you know. Certainly not about this."

So far, Samarel had relied primarily on hand-to-hand combat when dealing damage. While his attacks had been effective, they had caused minimal harm to Aranel. Samarel's pure chitronic moves—while impressive—had focused on blocking, trapping, and neutralizing.

What Aranel needed was for his brother to unleash one of his hard-hitters. A chitronic move so devastating it would drain his reserves and knock Aranel out in one blow.

I'll have to go all out myself then . . .

Aranel's chitrons gushed out of him in torrents until he was left reeling with dizziness. He hadn't attempted this type of mass channeling before. He'd limited his use of chitronic energy in Malin and had never needed to in Mayana.

Noticing the buildup of chitrons, Samarel took a step back and swiped his keiza once more. "Shall we end it, then?" he asked. "I am sorry it has come to this."

"Don't hold back on me."

"But you'll miss dinner."

"And stop treating me like a damned child!" Aranel slammed his hand onto the dirt.

The chitrons of Paramos surged forth, the meadow rippling around him. A humanoid mass burst from the earth to crash through the grove and lunge at Samarel.

"Sorken almighty, please lend me your strength," murmured his brother, eyes closed and palms aglow with bright energy.

The heavens above gave a roar, and the vortex of colored light twisted into a tornado. It swelled in size by the second, siphoning the lights of Ashkator into its funnel, until it had grown powerful enough to suck Aranel's creation into its depths.

Gritting his teeth, Aranel sank his chitrons into the ground to keep from being swept away.

Then the tornado spun into the form of an enormous beast with four heads, each shaped like one of the seitarius. Glowing golden threads extended from Samarel's hands, linking him to the creature. Samarel flicked his fingers, and the threads went taut. The shimmering beast bounded forth with a roar that set every chitron of Aranel's soul atremble with an awestruck fear.

Just how strong are you, Sam? wondered Aranel, as the beast crashed down in a deluge of light.

This attack would knock him out with a single hit. It would suck him dry of his energy and leave him exhausted for days. Unless, somehow, Aranel escaped the brunt of it.

There was only one way to dodge something so vast. Aranel squeezed his eyes shut and projected out of his body as the world exploded in colored light.

ARANEL WATCHED SAMAREL sink to the ground. His brother's breaths came hoarse and ragged. Controlling the chitrons of Ashkator had taken a toll on Samarel. Aranel had never seen him look so spent.

He felt a flicker of pride that he'd come out of the encounter conscious—if his soul being outside his body counted as consciousness.

Semantics aside, I endured it.

Aranel's own form lay battered in the depression Samarel's attack had made, but he hadn't lost any chitronic energy trying to withstand it.

Aranel returned to his body and hissed in pain. Even though Samarel had stopped his chitrons from causing serious physical injury, Aranel felt as though his muscles had been shredded. But the pain was fading rapidly.

Aranel cracked an eye open to see his brother kneeling beside him, hands glowing with energy. He almost smiled at the absurdity of it all. Of course the first thing Samarel would do after nearly destroying him was heal his every bruise.

Aranel lay there and allowed his brother to fuss over his various injuries. Samarel's hands began to shake. The previous attack had taken a lot out of him, and this healing even more. He was on the brink of exhaustion, just as Aranel had hoped.

Once his body felt sufficiently recovered, Aranel opened both eyes to meet Samarel's worried ones. "Thank Sorken," said his brother, sending chitrons to bind Aranel's arms to his side.

The sly jerk. He thinks I'm drained of energy but still doesn't trust me.

"I overdid it, Ran," said Samarel. "Will you forgive me?"

"Sam—" Aranel coughed. "My ribs—"

Immediately, the binds lessened in pressure. Aranel surged upright in one fluid motion, grabbed a kapizer spine from his pocket, and shoved it through the gap in Samarel's breastplate.

His brother wheezed, eyes fluttering. "What . . . why . . ."

"Don't worry about me, Sam," said Aranel as his brother struggled to stay awake. "I can take care of myself."

He laid Samarel's head on the ground before leaping to his feet and dashing toward the white torana.

CHAPTER TWENTY-SEVEN

☉

The Four Realms

*F*OUND HER." *MEIZAN* collapsed at the chief's feet, gasping for air. "Boat—Mir Tamasa—southeast of Martharan—"

Kanna knelt beside him and patted him on the back.

"M'fine," Meizan heaved. "Just tired."

It wasn't a lie. He was exhausted to the bone but fine otherwise. Not like the times he'd channeled and felt the depravity of Malin wrap around his soul. His mind remained clear despite the projection.

Waking up with his foot submerged in a pool of megarya blood probably had something to do with it. Meizan had bolted away from the cursed liquid and dragged himself back to the nearby cavern Kanjallen was using as a hideout. He'd vomited thrice along the way.

How had Aina projected so easily? Meizan felt miserable. At

least his chitronic abilities had returned, though he didn't feel ready to channel yet.

Luckily, Chief Kanna did not expect him to. She pulled Meizan to his feet and led him outside the cavern, where her nagamor lay in a tightly curled mass.

She climbed its neck and ordered, "Get on."

Meizan followed, careful to stay clear of the beast's sharp beak. The nagamor paid him no more heed than a fly as Meizan settled a couple feet behind the chief. Its vivid scales were hard as armor and chafed his thighs as the nagamor uncoiled itself.

"Hold tight," Kanna said.

Meizan had a brief moment to prepare before the nagamor shot upward. It wove across the sky in a rough rhythm, its body rippling, wavelike, with each beat of its feathered tail. Below, Malin blurred into a muted shadowscape. As they flew, Meizan filled the chief in on what he'd learned about Zenyra's true plans.

"Break the chitronic shields separating the realms?" Kanna turned over her shoulder to look at him. "You're sure that's what she means to do?"

"That's what Aranel said. But he was being annoyingly vague about it all."

"Kal Ekana." The chief frowned. "But if she means to restore the One Realm Era, then Kaldrav's army will attack the first chance they get. The Narakhi too . . ."

Meizan's gut churned at the mention of the demonic souls who dwelled in Narakh. They were a distant, almost intangible threat. Yet it was the knowledge of their foul existence that kept most Malini in check and stopped many from committing a crime evil enough to get them thrown into Narakh. Meizan shuddered to think what would happen if the Narakhi were loosed from their realm.

"What will Kanjallen do?" Meizan asked. "If the shields break and a war starts?"

"There will be no war," the chief said tightly. "There will be no breaking of any shields. We will stop Zenyra, and Kanjallen will stay in Malin. As will Kaldrav's army and every other filthy creature that inhabits this realm and the one below."

"You don't want the chitronic shields to break? Why not?"

"I would have wanted them to once," Kanna admitted. "For years I cursed at the torana, wishing they would crumble."

"What changed?"

Kanna's shoulders tensed as if in preparation for an attack. When she spoke, Meizan had to strain to hear her over the wind and the nagamor's tailbeats.

"Aina was a sickly baby," the chief said. "I could never feed her enough. We were alone in the frostlands, always on the run. The snow kept most enemies away, but it was no place for a newborn. Each night, I would swaddle her shaking little body and hold her to my chest. She could not die, but she could suffer, and feeling her tiny toes and fingers turn cold as ice . . . hearing her pitiful voice, those little gasps as she fought to survive . . ."

Kanna's voice grew thick, a tone Meizan had never heard from her. "I prayed one night, the first and last time I ever did. I prayed to Azyaka, if she existed, to make me suffer in Aina's place. I prayed any sickness or pain that was to come her way come to me instead. I prayed fate take pity on this innocent creature, who was doing everything in her power to thrive, and give her the life it had denied me.

"Azyaka did not answer my prayers. Not then. I tried shoving Aina through the torana as a baby, to no avail. Fourteen years later, a nagamor attacked us and Aina ended up in the realm she should have been born to from the beginning. And the torana and the shields are what will keep her safe there." Kanna wiped her eyes with a short laugh. "They may condemn me to endless suffering, but they will allow my daughter to live a peaceful, healthy life. The life she deserves."

Meizan remained silent for a long while, and Kanna whipped her head around to face him. "What about you?" she asked, reverting to her brusque self. "What do you want to do?"

"Whatever my chief commands."

"Blast your chief's commands. Meizan, what do *you* want?"

Meizan pondered this, conflicted. The idea of ascension was tempting, even for him. Except it wouldn't be ascension since there would be no upper realms left.

There would only be war. Whatever goodness and beauty existed in Mayana and Paramos would fall before the armies of Kaldrav and the Narakhi. The universe would burn, and the fires of war, now confined to two realms, would spread to all four.

Double the violence, Meizan thought. *Double the bloodshed.*

Innocent Mayani children would suffer as innocent Malini children did now. Soft-hearted idiots like Aranel would be captured and tortured, and their idiotic flowery kingdoms would burn. There was no way the Mayani would be able to fight back. They may be skilled channelers, but their soul-fearing tendencies would make them weak in battle.

If Zenyra did break the realms, it would not lead to balance or equality. It would only drag the entire universe into darkness.

When he voiced all this to the chief, she gave a satisfied nod. "You could live in Mayana too," she said. "If you drank megarya blood to ascend. I'm sure there's a way of ingesting it gradually so as not to risk erasure."

"I wouldn't last long. I'd fall within a week."

"You won't fall," Kanna said, sounding more confident in Meizan than he ever had in himself.

He *had* considered drinking the blood after learning what it could do. He'd even entertained the idea of ascending and living in—Kirnos? Nishaki? Amaratir? Meizan had heard plenty about the Mayani kingdoms from the other Balancers, but he could never picture himself living in one. His loyalties were with Kanjallen, after all. His home was the clan, not the realm. And after seeing the outcome of Zenyra's experiments . . .

There's no way in hell I'm ever drinking that shit.

It took an hour of skimming over the fume-laden wasteland of Malin before Mir Tamasa, a leaden expanse edged by ragged cliffs, appeared on the horizon.

The nagamor sailed low over its slate-gray waters, but there was no sign of Zenyra's boat or the small island Meizan had spied during his projection.

"There!" Kanna motioned toward the shore.

By the top of the escarpment stood two figures, one taller than the other.

The nagamor veered toward them. Meizan streamed chitrons to his eyes so he could see the figures clearly: Zenyra and Aina, the latter no longer bound. She clutched something in her shaking hands. Meizan squinted to get a better look.

Is that a syringe?

"Faster." The chief kicked the nagamor's side, urging it forth.

They were close enough for Aina to see them if she just looked up at the sky.

Meizan was about to call out when Aina raised the syringe and slammed it into her forehead. She crumpled to the ground, her scream muffled by the roaring wind.

The nagamor dipped down. Meizan and Kanna leaped off its back to land heavily on the gravel.

"Aina!" Meizan shouted. He drew his sword and rushed toward her writhing form.

The chief was a step ahead, energy crackling at her fingertips. Kanna fell to her knees beside Aina and slapped her daughter's cheek. "What have you done? Answer me, stupid girl!"

Dark veins snaked across Aina's face and her keiza grew duller by the second. The syringe dripped black liquid down her nose.

"Vandraghor blood . . ." Meizan stared at the syringe, then at Zenyra, who was watching Aina with an air of detached interest. "What did you do to her?"

"Nothing at all," Zenyra said, tossing her braid over her back. "Aina did that to herself."

"You treasonous bitch," Kanna hissed. "You were supposed to keep her safe!"

Before Zenyra could reply, the air around them shifted. Meizan glimpsed a torana. Aina's body lay just beyond it, surrounded by a blank whiteness.

The Universal Void.

Stumbling, the chief caught Aina's body. She set her down with a curse, then dashed into the Void after Zenyra. Sparing a glance at Aina, Meizan followed Kanna just as the universe sealed itself around them.

The Void was an empty, all-encompassing nothingness. There was no up or down. No perception of space or direction. Somewhere in the distance—Meizan couldn't tell if it was ten feet away or thousands—floated four spheres of colored light.

Meizan and Kanna raced after Zenyra. It was unsettling, running through the Void. There was nothing below him, yet Meizan could move as if he were on solid ground. As the spheres grew closer, Meizan saw them for what they really were: masses of chitronic energy trapped within spherical cocoons of rock, each large enough to fit a mountain the size of Merumarth.

Are those the chitronic cores of the seitarius?

Aranel had said something of the sort, but Meizan hadn't

been able to decipher much of his frantic explanation. Meizan ran toward the spheres, noticing the carvings upon each rock: peaks and ridges and craters, tiny stone forests, and cracks that resembled rivers.

It's the realms.

The rocky spheres of the seitarius cores represented each of the four realms. Which meant that the threads of pulsing light between them—three extending from each sphere and connecting to the others in a web—must be controlling the chitronic shields somehow.

"Chief." Meizan lowered his voice as he came up to Kanna. "Whatever happens, those threads of light can't be disturbed."

She nodded, and Meizan streamed chitrons to his feet, attempting to latch onto those of the Void so he could propel himself faster. But he was met with a resounding emptiness.

There were no ambient chitrons in the vast blankness of the Void. Even the chitronic cores of the seitarius seemed to be sealed within their rocks, their chitrons inaccessible.

"We won't be able to channel the environment here," Kanna said, as she tried and failed to do the same. "We're limited to our own chitrons and not a drop more. Use yours wisely, Meizan. I can't be waiting around for you to recharge while I fight this madwoman."

Zenyra reached the sphere and threw her arms back. In her palm roiled a bolt of squirming chitrons, saturated with the filth of her soul.

"No!" With a wild cry, the chief unleashed her own bolt and pushed it toward Zenyra's.

The two bolts collided with a sizzle. While Zenyra's was stronger, the chief's was enough to alter its trajectory so that it curved away from the web and exploded in the distance.

"Witless woman," Zenyra hissed. "Even your own daughter

wanted this! Why would *you* of all people stand against me?"

"Because Aina is a brat who doesn't know what's good for her," Kanna snarled. Her chitrons formed a crackling whip in her hand.

She lunged, and Meizan followed her lead. They attacked Zenyra in a fury, whip sizzling and sword flashing as they wove around one another in a seamless onslaught, focusing their strikes on her keiza. But even without chitrons, Zenyra was a force to reckon with. She danced out of reach, pressing one hand to her forehead and fending them off with the other.

Meizan had fought many battles alongside the chief. Yet Zenyra saw through their every attack pattern, not faltering even once as they whirled around her like twin hurricanes.

We can't keep this up.

Meizan swerved to avoid an elbow to his face. But the exhaustion of projection hadn't worn off, and his body wasn't moving as he was accustomed. Pain bloomed across his eye and he reeled back, vision swimming. Kanna swooped into his place. Her whip lashed at Zenyra's feet, then her forehead, but both attacks missed narrowly.

After what felt like an hour, the chief's whip scorched a trail across Zenyra's cheek while Meizan opened a shallow gash across her shoulder. But Zenyra's keiza remained untouched. Losing patience, she summoned a pair of chitronic whips thicker and stronger than Kanna's.

Meizan cursed as one of the whips curled around his waist and bound his arms to his sides. The chief was caught in a similar position, her own whip fizzling away.

"Stand down," Zenyra ordered Kanna. "I do not wish to harm a member of Kanjallen. But if you continue your attempts to thwart me, I may be left with no choice."

The chief strained against her binds and met Meizan's eye. *Keep fighting,* she seemed to say.

They had forced Zenyra to rely on her chitrons to subdue them. The more they struggled and the longer Zenyra held them, the quicker her energy would deplete.

But Zenyra was not willing to wait. Gripping both whips in her left hand, she lowered her right, palm glowing, from her forehead.

"No!" Kanna cried, as Zenyra loosened a bolt of chitrons that streaked toward the seitarius cores.

Green light burst through the Void and knocked away Zenyra's bolt a second time. A new figure leaped in front of her, pointing his sword at her keiza before she could react.

"Perfect timing, you idiot," Meizan exclaimed with relief.

Aranel's gaze flickered to him, then returned to Zenyra.

"Aranel," Zenyra said in greeting, unbothered by the blade resting against her keiza. "How good of you to join us. It seems the Preservation are having you do all their dirty work nowadays."

"I'm here by choice." Aranel's blade trembled. "I saw your chamber under Incaraz, Zenyra, and the results of your experiments. Tell me, what's your great cause for which you've sacrificed over a hundred innocent souls?"

"Stab her already!" Meizan shouted.

The whip around him tightened. A stream of chitrons rose from its end to bind his mouth and muffle his voice. *You already know she wants to break the shields! Stop being dramatic and stab her!*

"My cause?" Zenyra gave a sharp smile, eyes gleaming in the whiteness of the Void. "Why, I plan to destroy the chitronic shields and restore the universe to its former glory. To bring back Kal Ekana, a single realm where good and evil intermingle at will."

"Is that truly necessary?" Aranel asked. "If your goal is to help the Malini children, what if you recalibrate the shields instead of breaking them? Make it so innocent children cannot be born to Malin in the first place?"

"You naive child." Zenyra sighed. "Even if I were to recalibrate them now, the Preservation would reinstate the original limits in a matter of weeks. You underestimate what they are capable of. This imbalance with the shields is but the tip of their treachery, and their leader, Kyrian, has a vested interest in maintaining the system as it was first created. It was his idea to hide it away in the Void and destroy all the torana leading to it."

"The Preservation *put* the chitronic system in the Void?" Aranel asked, aghast. "I thought that was done by the seitarius!"

"So they would have us believe," Zenyra said. "That particular detail is omitted from the Song of Salvation, and I suspect few of the current Preservation are privy to it. Kyrian will go to great lengths to preserve this inequality, which is why breaking it down is the only option. The first step to an egalitarian universe."

"But if you break it, you'll spark a war," Aranel said, and if Meizan wasn't tied up, he would have bashed his stupid, shiny head in for stating the obvious.

Have you learned nothing living in Malin, Aranel? Attack first, talk later!

"War is a necessary evil," Zenyra said. "The four realms were only created when the peace of Kal Ekana was shattered by a war that threatened to break the universe."

"But—"

"All I am doing is destroying an already broken reality so that from its pieces we might create our universe anew."

"But Kaldrav's army will tear the upper realms apart!" Aranel's sword nicked Zenyra's forehead, drawing a single droplet of blood. "The war during Kal Ekana killed nearly all of humanity—"

"Which is no longer a risk, since we are immortal," Zenyra said. "And I will control the army, Aranel. Contain their violence."

"How? How will you control the king of Malin and his army?"

"Kaldrav has already been . . . disposed of."

Disposed of? Meizan almost choked on his own tongue. *Did she erase him too?*

Zenyra gave a chuckle at Meizan's and Kanna's shocked expressions. "He was no longer fit to lead, and his army now belongs to me. The two of you ought to be thanking me rather than standing in my way."

Kanna let out a muffled string of curses, and Zenyra turned to Aranel. "Your fool of a teammate may not comprehend it, but surely *you* can. Without Kaldrav instigating violence and away from the taint of Malin's chitrons, the soldiers will soon lose their desire to fight. Especially once they realize their opponents wish them no harm. I expect several will desert after a few days breathing the sweet air of Paramos."

Even with half of Kanna's face obscured by the binds, her disbelief mirrored Meizan's own. *That's the most absurd logic I have ever heard,* Meizan thought. He recalled his encounters with Kaldrav's men. While some had been forced into fighting, twice as many had relished the bloodshed and torture.

Zenyra had only dealt with Malini children. She severely underestimated the hatred and resentment that brewed within the older generation. Amongst clans like Chiren and Razamir that had volunteered themselves to Kaldrav's cause.

And the bloodlust of the most sadistic of Malini would not hold a candle to the demons of Narakh.

Lose the desire to fight? Even an idealist like Aranel wouldn't fall for such shit.

"The war will be short-lived," Zenyra continued. "A series of targeted attacks upon the Preservation and their most powerful allies. It will end once I have overthrown Kyrian, enabling the creation of a new order with everyone returned to their rightful realm."

Zenyra prattled on, and Aranel listened in silence, shoulders shaking as he held his sword to her keiza. Meizan didn't know what the hell he was waiting for. A few feet away, the chief gave an experimental wriggle. Had she managed to break free?

With a blast of dark energy, the binds around Meizan snapped. *Nicely done, Chief!*

He slid into position by Kanna's side, sword poised to attack. A few feet away, Zenyra took advantage of the commotion to twist away from Aranel's blade. She unsheathed a knife and drew it to Aranel's throat.

The chief made to pounce. Meizan threw an arm out to stop her.

"Wait," he said under his breath. "If we don't time this right, she'll slit his throat!" Kanna shot him a livid look, but Meizan held his ground. "We need him conscious. We can't defeat her two to one."

"Fine," Kanna grunted. "But whatever you're planning, make it quick."

Aranel's eyes met his across the Void. Meizan held his gaze, waiting for a signal so he and Kanna could charge. All Aranel had to do was not get himself stabbed. Sending chitrons to harden the air around his neck would do it.

Aranel's jaw tightened, sword shuddering in his hand. "I'm sorry," he mouthed.

Then Aranel swung his blade around to point at Meizan's chief.

"What do you think you're doing?" Meizan growled.

"Picking a side," Aranel said, his face unreadable.

"Like hell you are."

Meizan tossed the sword to Kanna—it was hers to begin with, and she needed it more—before drawing a pair of serrated knives and pouncing on Aranel.

The upper seemed just as exhausted as he was. Aranel's movements were slow and heavy as they traded blows. Out of the corner of his eye, Meizan could see the chief bearing down upon Zenyra, blade whirling rapidly.

"Meizan," Aranel grunted between strikes. "Why are you resisting? Her vision—one realm—do you not want that as well?"

"What makes you think that?" Meizan flipped back so he was out of reach of Aranel's blade and released a throwing star.

"The shields are unfair, as is the current separation!" Aranel caught the throwing star on the tip of his sword and whipped it back at Meizan. "This is for the better for Malin."

"You're in no place to decide that!" Meizan yelled, ducking the throwing star to swipe his knife at Aranel's chest. "How can you trust a flaming word she says, after what she did to those children? After what she did to Aina?"

"Her methods were unforgivable, I admit!" Aranel's face was pained as he parried Meizan's strikes. "But all that's done now! If she doesn't succeed, those erasures will have been for nothing, and innocent children will continue to suffer! Zenyra's trying to make the realms more equitable, the universe a better place."

"Better how, you self-righteous pile of shit?" Meizan shouted. "Once the shields break, there'll be nothing but a giant, burning war! Do you really believe Zenyra's going to be able to curb the violence? End centuries of hatred with a few sugary words and breaths of fresh air?"

"Even so, the war will be temporary."

"Burn you, Aranel!" Meizan aimed a punch at his face,

reveling in the satisfying crack as his fist met its mark. Aranel tottered back, clutching at his jaw, and Meizan lunged at him in a fury. "You've never been in a damn war! You have no bleeding clue what it entails!"

"I've read about Kal Ekana," Aranel insisted. He brought an arm up to shield himself from Meizan's next punch. "Did you not hear what Zenyra said? Since there's no death this time—"

"That'll only make it worse, you maggot-brained moron! War only ends when one side dies! Without death, it'll be an endless cycle of violence, more brutal than anything you could imagine!"

"Even more brutal than what plagues Malin now?" Aranel blocked Meizan's next punch and used the momentum to spin into a kick. "You think I *want* a Malini army invading my realm? You think I *want* Mayana to suffer because of the Preservation's selfishness? But I've seen the lengths those frauds will go to conserve their authority. A war is not ideal, but if it's the only way to force the Preservation out of power and change things for good, then so be it!"

"Not *ideal?*" Meizan's shin slammed against Aranel's, and he pivoted away. "Those battles by the Muzireni and at Incaraz were nothing, Aranel! Nothing compared to the hell that will break loose if those shields come undone! If all of Malin and Narakh are unleashed upon your stupid, soft upper realms. Your Preservation may be liars and frauds, but the Narakhi are much, much more dangerous. And once your realm is destroyed, they'll turn on mine!"

He leaned over, panting. Across from him, Aranel struggled to stay on his feet. Meizan couldn't tell which of them was worse for wear. He'd broken Aranel's jaw, from the look of it. But in addition to the black eye Meizan had received from Zenyra, Aranel had cut him in several places.

"You've outdone yourself with your stupidity," Meizan said, wiping the sweat from his brow. "You think you're helping those children, but you're going to make everything worse."

"I'm doing it for you too!" Aranel stumbled toward him, fist raised. "You, and Aina—"

Meizan blocked Aranel's punch and aimed a kick at his head. "You don't get it, Aranel. You never will."

There had been a time, not long ago, when Meizan had reveled in the fighting. Felt alive amidst the excitement of it all. But he'd spent his whole life fighting, and it had gotten exhausting. The last thing Meizan wanted was to get himself and Kanjallen embroiled in another war, especially one that included the Narakhi.

Some souls were so twisted, so cruel, they *needed* to remain separate from the rest.

The chitronic shields around the realms could not break. Zenyra and Aranel could not win. Drawing upon his last reserves of strength, Meizan gripped his knife and charged.

CHAPTER TWENTY-EIGHT

⊚

Mother

*A*INA WATCHED IN horror as Kanna and Zenyra clashed in the Void. Not far from them, Meizan and Aranel exchanged blows.

What were they even doing in here? Aina wanted to shout out and break up their fights—but she was nothing more than a disembodied soul, her body left behind in Malin.

The white flash had lasted five whole seconds, and Aina had seen the torana materialize. She'd expected Zenyra to run in, but she hadn't expected Meizan and Kanna to jump from the sky and follow. But they had, leaving Aina thrashing alone on the ground after Zenyra had tossed her back into Malin. Unable to move her body in time, Aina had projected her soul into the Void just before it sealed itself.

What had shocked her the most was Aranel—pious, soul-fearing Aranel—siding with Zenyra. Aina watched him fight Meizan until both were on the brink of collapse. She watched

Zenyra batter Kanna's body until she had exhausted her physically and chitronically.

Why are you fighting? Aina wanted to yell at Kanna. *Zenyra's plan will only help you! Help us!*

But with each passing moment, Aina grew unsure. And Meizan's arguments, shouted across the Void, grew more and more convincing.

What if Zenyra's war never ended? The upper realms would be dragged into the same darkness and violence that plagued Malin, or one even worse once the demons of Narakh were unleashed.

And Kanna doesn't even want that, Aina realized, ashamed. *Once again, I thought I was saving her, when she never wanted to be saved.*

Her shame boiled to a seething anger because, once again, Zenyra had manipulated her. Aina had *let* Zenyra manipulate her. She had foolishly believed in Zenyra's vision of a world where she and Kanna could live together in peace.

Had Aina been in her body, she would have torn her own hair out.

How could I let her talk me into this?

She watched, helpless, as Zenyra knocked Kanna back and snatched the jeweled sword from her grasp.

"You will not wield that weapon against me," Zenyra snarled. She strode toward the chitronic system with its glowing webs of light. Once again, her hands crackled with energy, this time amplified by the stones in the sword. "And you will not stop me. Not when I have come this far. Not when I am so close."

Aina watched in horror as a bolt of energy shot toward the center of the chitronic web. She watched as Meizan shoved Aranel away from him and ran toward the beam of light, but he was too slow, he wouldn't make it in time—

A shattering explosion rocked through the Void. Aina's soul was whipped through the whiteness.

What happened? Did it hit?

Aina flew back toward the chitronic system, relieved to find it still intact. Meizan, Aranel, and Zenyra had all been knocked back by the force of the explosion, and Kanna . . .

Kanna collapsed midair in front of the webs of light, her face soaked with blood. Her legs had been utterly shattered and dangled uselessly from her waist.

But she had blocked it. Kanna had blocked Zenyra's chitronic attack with her own body.

"You meddlesome worm!" Zenyra's face contorted in fury. "Why are you so hellbent on stopping me? Even if there is a war, in the long run, my actions will benefit the realms! All four of them!"

Kanna coughed, splattering the front of her torn tunic crimson. Beneath lank, blood-drenched curls, her eyes glowed bright.

"I don't care about any of that," Kanna rasped. "Not when Aina's future is worth more to me than the entire universe."

Aina's soul seemed to lighten at her words. Painful memories she'd kept buried resurfaced in an instant. And as Aina stared at Kanna's haggard face in the Void, the memories shifted, revealing the loneliness and fear her mother had kept locked underneath a mask of fury.

The way Kanna had pushed Aina into Mayana, veiling the tremor in her voice with curses and threats.

The way she had scolded her daughter once Aina revealed her reason for descending.

The way her mother's palm shook even as she slapped her.

Mama, you bleeding liar . . .

Aina took in her mother's graying hair and premature wrinkles. The circles that ringed her eyes, a testament to sleepless nights guarding their hideout while Aina rested. The frail arms and bony frame, from years of skipping meals so Aina could eat another morsel.

Her mother would have lied to the very end if it meant keeping her safe. And Aina was stupid, oh so stupid, for not seeing through it all. For taking her mother's words at face value and not fighting harder to remain by her side.

But not anymore, she thought, chitrons abuzz with elation despite the taint of the vandraghor blood. *Once we get out of here, Mama, I'm going to stick to you like a leech. You can hit me and curse me all you want, and I'll take it with a smile.*

Whether or not the realms broke, whether they ended up in Malin or Mayana, there had to be some corner of the universe where Aina and her mother could find a new home. Nothing large or decadent. Just a small hut made of stone, by a stream filled with fish.

Zenyra had gotten to her feet, tucking a wayward strand of hair behind her ear. "Someone worth more than the universe?" she said to Kanna, her whisper carrying across the Void. "I can understand that. In which case, I am truly sorry it has come to this."

"There's nothing you can do." Kanna coughed again, as Zenyra walked toward her. "That last attack drained your chitronic reserves, and it will be hours before they recharge. There is nothing in this Void you can channel. You have no way to break the shields."

"It would seem that way," Zenyra said. Her deathly calm sent fear jolting through Aina. "It would seem you did a commendable job stopping me, Kanna. I require a vast amount of energy to break the shields . . . energy that, as you said, I no longer possess."

Zenyra's voice morphed into a growl, and she reached into her pocket. "But you do, Kanna of Kanjallen! And so you shall pay for this with the chitrons of your soul!"

Zenyra lunged forward, swinging her arm. Aina's mother made to dodge the blow, but her broken body was unable to react in time, and Zenyra rammed a syringe—filled with a shining, pearlescent liquid—straight into Kanna's keiza.

Aina watched in terror as her mother's keiza began to flash. A strange light seeped through Kanna's veins and mottled her skin. Violent convulsions tore through her form.

Mama! Mama? What's happening to you?

Aina sped toward her as Meizan tore across the Void.

"Chief!" Meizan yelled, catching Kanna as she fell. "Chief, get ahold of yourself!"

"Meizan . . ." Kanna whispered as her convulsions increased in intensity. "Tell Aina . . . tell Aina I'm sorry . . . and that I lo—"

Her mother's words melded into a pained shriek, her forehead splitting open. Beams of light tore through her flesh, dazzling, like rays of the sun.

No.

"Get back!" Aranel shouted. He grabbed Meizan by the arms and pulled him away.

No, no, no, please, someone, do something, no—

Aina could only watch in numb shock as the crushing realization speared through her soul.

In a few moments, her mother would no longer be in this universe.

In a few moments, Kanna would be gone for eternity.

Sorken, Sherka, Azyaka, Andraken, if you exist, please stop this, please, I beg of you—

An earsplitting roar shattered through the Void as her mother burst into nothingness; her body, her being, her chitrons, all utterly erased from existence.

NO! Aina screamed.

She had no mouth, no voice, but she screamed, despair ravaging her being and threatening to rip her apart.

Out of the corner of her eye, she spied Zenyra channeling the last of her mother's chitrons toward the glowing web. But Aina didn't care because none of that mattered. Nothing mattered anymore.

Please, Mama, Aina sobbed. *Don't do this! Don't leave me here all alone!*

The last thing Aina saw before her soul was whipped away from the chaos was the pulsing threads of the chitronic system. They were taut and shuddering, but whole and unbroken.

Then the web gave a ripple. One of the threads snapped.

CHAPTER TWENTY-NINE

@

A Shift in the Air

*T*HE VOID HEAVED* and shuddered.

The force of the explosion ejected Aranel and Meizan through the white torana and sent them sprawling onto soft grass. They were in Paramos, in the meadow at the heart of Ashkator, but for only a split second.

A silver torana materialized before Aranel. The air thickened and tightened around him as an unseen force dragged him through its pillars.

Descension, he realized morbidly. The megarya blood had worn off and his actions had caught up with him. He was falling back to Mayana.

A copper torana appeared a foot away and sucked Meizan into Malin. Aranel tried calling out to him, but Paramos sealed itself before he could get out a word.

He found himself in Kirnos, in the depths of Aran Kirenkar. Sunlight filtered through the gilded canopy and filled the forest with a warm, buttery light. As Aranel lay there, gasping for breath, he tried to wrap his head around what had just transpired.

Zenyra had attempted to harness the energy from an erasure to break the chitronic system. Not just any erasure, but that of Meizan's clan chief. Aina's *mother*, who she'd spent over a year trying to find.

Aranel sat up and promptly spilled the contents of his stomach onto the grass. It did little to quell the guilt that was festering within him.

Never had he meant for such an odious thing to happen. Never had he imagined Zenyra would go to such lengths.

But he'd known what she was capable of, and Meizan had warned him in the Void. Aranel doubted either of his teammates would be willing to listen to his excuses or apologies.

I as good as betrayed them both. Bile rose in his throat once more.

Yet despite the fact that Meizan—and Aina, once she found out—might be inclined to attack him on sight, Aranel wanted nothing more than to find them.

Meizan can break every bone in my body, but the least I can do is apologize. And figure out what we're going to do next.

Because it was done now. Zenyra hadn't destroyed the entire chitronic system as she'd intended, but a single thread connecting two seitarius cores had snapped. Aranel didn't know the technicalities of how the system worked, but surely it would have some effect on at least one of the chitronic shields.

The question remained whether it would be enough to overthrow the Preservation and build a new, more equitable world. Or whether all the sacrifices, all the erasures, had amounted to nothing.

Aranel rolled to his feet and sprinted through the forest, careful to conserve his chitrons. The fights with Samarel and Meizan had exhausted him. He needed his remaining energy so he could cloudsurf to the torana and unseal it using the method Seirem had taught him.

As he ran, he glimpsed sweeping white robes between the slender tree trunks. Aranel ducked behind a patch of bracken and peeked through its golden fronds.

That damned stone-soul!

Seirem paced in the nearby clearing, accompanied by three Preservers. They spoke in urgent, hurried tones. Aranel was tempted to eavesdrop but dared not draw near. In his current state of exhaustion, with blood dripping onto the grass—curse Meizan and his nasty right hook—he didn't think he could manage a chitronic concealment powerful enough to elude a Preserver.

Sticking to the shadows, he slunk past the clearing. He left Kirnos in haste and mounted his sword to scud across the sky.

Aranel brushed aside his fatigue and forced himself to fly more swiftly than he had during any of his races. He reached the Meruhirs before dusk and found the torana he'd used twice now to enter Malin, wedged between the glittering peaks.

Aranel had dismounted and taken a step toward it when he felt a faint twitch.

It was nothing but a shift in the air. A subtle heaviness. A hint of decay amongst the freshness of Mayana.

With a grinding scream, the earth gave a spasm and the heavens convulsed in fury.

A massive quake ripped through the mountain. It rattled the ground and sundered the rock, sending new peaks bursting skyward.

Aranel would have been swallowed into the chasm if he hadn't latched on with his chitrons, scarcely managing to hang on as the world unraveled around him.

Pieces of the sky rained down, enormous chunks that smashed against the earth, opened new craters, and sent up fountains of bright sparks.

Not the sky, realized Aranel, staring at the chunks. *The chitronic shield. It's coming undone.*

Zenyra had succeeded, at least in part. The shield around Mayana was breaking.

Chunks hailed from the sky for minutes, then hours, until Aranel lost track of time. All he could do was cling onto the bit of mountain that remained and pray to Sherka he didn't get crushed.

And then it stopped. Aranel looked up, lungs seizing and breaths coming short.

The torana in front of him had disappeared, leaving a gaping wound on the horizon, a blemish of red that stained the magnificent golden sunset.

A grating screech shook the air again. The hole grew bigger as the fabric of the universe ripped apart by its seams. The smell of ruin, sharp as a knife, splintered through the honeyed air of Mayana.

Then Aranel felt it in his soul and through his chitronic bond with the rock—a creeping unease that swelled to a miasma of despair as new chitrons poured into the realm. Aranel released the bond in dismay and clambered onto the cliff.

The redness of Malin swallowed half the sky. Zenyra's actions had opened up a giant rift in the chitronic shield. Around the rift, Mayana appeared intact, with its chitronic shield ruptured but not fully undone. But here, the sky and earth opened into Malin, connecting the two realms as one.

In the distance Aranel heard the rumbling of thousands of footsteps. A dark wave converged upon the horizon.

Kaldrav's—no, Zenyra's army.

Aranel's spot on the mountain afforded him a good view of

the forces as they poured through the rift into Mayana: a never-ending river of dark armor and tattered black flags, all marked with a single white circle.

There were thousands of them. Tens of thousands, perhaps hundreds.

Far more than Aranel had envisioned.

Fear wracked him as he watched them pass.

Meizan was right.

The forces at Kaufgar and Incaraz had been but a fraction of this monstrosity. Kirnos would have a day's notice at best, the other Mayani kingdoms a couple days or weeks more. That might be enough to hold off an army of ten or even fifty thousand. But this?

They would be destroyed.

The villages and towns would fall first. Then the smaller kingdoms, Nishaki and Samaras and Amaratir. Eventually, the great kingdoms of Kirnos and Tahamur would fall as well. They had skilled channelers, but they would be outnumbered by an army of such scale.

Not all the soldiers will attack, Aranel tried to reassure himself. *Zenyra said several will desert. For those who remain, surely she can curb their violence and direct their attacks toward the Preservation. But as far as I know, the chitronic shield around Paramos is still intact, which means she has no way to march directly upon Ashkator.*

"My soldiers!"

A familiar voice rolled through the air like thunder. Zenyra stood silhouetted against the blazing sky. She balanced atop a floating chunk of rock, copper hair rippling like a cloak of flame. Fragments of the chitronic shield rained around her, but Zenyra redirected them with a swish of her fingers to send them exploding in the distance.

"Over a decade ago, we made you a promise—myself and the man who called himself your king. Today, that promise has been delivered upon." Zenyra's magnified voice echoed through the heavens. "I have broken a portion of the barrier that separated Malin and Mayana, my soldiers. I have given you the war you desire."

Dissatisfied mutters broke through the ranks, and several soldiers shouted their discontent.

"You were supposed to break all the barriers, you bitch!"

"We're not *your* soldiers, you blood-haired tramp!"

Zenyra raised her voice, drowning the shouts. "Keep your focus, my soldiers! This is but the first step in restoring Kal Ekana. As you say, only one set of barriers is broken. But that presents us with an opportunity. To march upon Mayana and sow chaos. To smoke the Preservation out of Paramos like roaches before a flame. To distract and incapacitate them before they have a chance to repair this barrier and reseparate the realms!"

"Screw incapacitation!" screamed a soldier. "Let us annihilate them!"

"Exterminate them!" added another. "Smash their bones and crush their hearts!"

"Stop wasting our time with bleeding speeches! We're here to fight!"

"We will not win this war with aimless violence," said Zenyra. "We cannot defeat the Mayani with the sharpness of our blades and the savagery in our hearts. They are a disciplined folk and excellent channelers. So I ask you, my soldiers, to trust my word and follow my command in battle. I ask you to refrain from indiscriminate slaughter and the harming of innocents."

"Why the hell should we follow you, upper-born wench?" came a shout.

"What do you know of the savagery in our hearts? You've never known a day of pain!"

"I say burn this soft-soul and give us our maggoty king!"

It's not working! Cold fear gripped Aranel. *There's no way she'll be able to control an entire army!*

When Zenyra spoke again, her voice took a sharper tone, edged with a cynicism Aranel had never heard from her.

"Give you your king?" She let out a cold laugh. "Oh, how I wish I could . . . give you a taste of how he begged and groveled, like the broken warrior he was. Give you a glimpse of Kaldrav's tear-soaked face in the moment before I erased his soul."

The soldiers' yells died down, and Aranel's mouth went dry. He'd suspected Zenyra had erased Kaldrav herself, but the way she spoke of it now sounded more like a premeditated attack rather than the result of a failed experiment.

"You think I cannot understand your pain?" She chuckled. "I have walked these realms since Kal Ekana. I have nurtured centuries of pain, and my hatred runs deeper than yours. I have no greater desire than to see the Preservation crumble. Shatter like this very barrier I have broken before your eyes."

There was a round of raucous laughter at this, and Zenyra continued. "Follow my lead, my soldiers, and you will have your moment of justice. Your moment of revenge."

The laughter faded, and Zenyra's voice grew louder, shaking the skies. "For centuries, you have lived under the dominion of Toranic Law, your lives bound within its shackles. You have festered in corruption and darkness while they basked in the light. You have known pain and famine while they knew comfort and abundance.

"You have been told you deserved this torment, that you fomented it with your sins. Yet it is not sin that birthed you into Malin, but the rotten hand of chance. It is not the spin of your soul that begot your suffering, but a hapless spin of fate.

"And it is time to reverse that spin." Zenyra spread her arms.

"Time to even the score. Balance the imbalance. In our new world there shall be equality! Equal fortune, equal merriment . . . and also equal suffering!"

"Damn right!" yelled a soldier, and several others hooted and clapped.

"Embrace your hatred, my soldiers," cried Zenyra. "Embrace every bit of agony and misery, and let it burn within you. Channel the flames upon those who would keep the realms split unjustly. Those who would preserve past inequalities for their own benefit."

Aranel shrank against the rock. *She doesn't mean it,* he told himself. *She's only trying to speak to their savagery so she can get them on her side.*

Zenyra's terrible voice rang through Malin, heavy with rage. The soldiers grew louder, the air thick with jeers and curses that had never before been uttered in Mayana.

But they were cursing now not at Zenyra, but at the Mayani and the Preservation.

Zenyra drew herself up and pounded the sky with her fist. "Their minds shall break!"

"THEIR MINDS SHALL BREAK!" The soldiers chorused her vicious promise while thousands of weapons beat the ground in unison.

"Their hearts shall wither!"

"THEIR HEARTS SHALL WITHER!"

"Their souls shall tarnish!" screamed Zenyra, her beautiful face twisted in fury.

"THEIR SOULS SHALL TARNISH!"

She doesn't mean it, repeated Aranel like a mantra. *She's only doing it to earn their respect. To ensure they obey her in battle and don't slaughter indiscriminately.*

Except how much would Zenyra be able to control once the fighting started? And how much of the coming violence would be worth it in the end?

Aranel dug his nails into his palm, carving circles into the flesh. He couldn't afford to be dragged into Meizan's pessimistic outlook. Zenyra had already garnered the support of her army with one blistering speech. She would control their chaos. It was the only way to bring down the Preservation and restore the chitronic shields to a more equitable state.

"Today is the birth of a new universe!" declared Zenyra. "Our first target is the kingdom of Kirnos, where the hand of the Preservation holds most sway."

Aranel's breath faltered. *It's a necessary sacrifice,* he told himself. *Better Kirnos than one of the smaller kingdoms or, worse, the villages. The Kirnosi are healers. Excellent channelers. No matter what she throws at them, they will survive.*

"Charge, my soldiers!" ordered Zenyra. "Attack Kirnos and destroy the kingdom! Burn their great lotus until there is nothing left but ash and withered petals! Ravage their temples and palaces until there is nothing left for the Preservation to restore!"

With an answering roar, the army charged across Mayana, crashing through soft grass and sweet air in a wave of dread.

CHAPTER THIRTY

☉

Splintering Sky Above

MEIZAN JOLTED AWAKE to the chilling shrieks of the kapizer. He found himself sprawled on his back with the cadaverous trees of Martharan looming above. He leaped up and reached for his sword, only to find his scabbard empty.

He'd given the sword back to his chief. And his chief had—

Meizan buried the memory and kicked himself for falling asleep. He was supposed to be looking for Aina.

After the explosion had thrown him out of the Void and back into Malin, he'd spent close to a day tracking her through the charred woods of Martharan. He'd been too exhausted for another soul projection, but with Kaldrav's army blocking off a large part of the forest, there was only one way she could have gone.

Bones aching, Meizan dashed in the direction of the shrieks. The kapizer only screamed for a reason. Sure enough, Meizan found half a dozen monkeys in a clearing, hellbent on attacking something—or rather, someone.

Meizan rushed forward as he recognized the mop of tangled hair, but Aina didn't need his help. The kapizer were flung back in a blast of dark turquoise. The attack seared the air and left a smoldering crater around its channeler.

Was that a stun beam? Meizan eyed the smoking bodies. Somehow, Aina's chitronic control had gotten worse.

He took a step toward his teammate. Aina's cheeks were sunken and her gaunt face smeared with dried blood. Her right side was marred by a large wound with ribbons of flesh dangling around its edges. It seemed the kapizer had gotten a few swipes in before Aina had defended herself.

At the sight of Meizan, Aina let out a growl like a cornered animal. Her keiza had dulled. The direction of its swirl had flipped to match his.

"Aina." Meizan's voice faltered.

What could he say? How could he tell her about her mother?

"You." Aina's hands curled into fists. "You were there. And you let it happen."

"What?"

"I saw it!" Aina screamed, face contorting in rage. "I projected into the Void and I saw everything! And you were there, you were with her, so how could you let it—"

She jumped at him. Meizan stumbled back, catching her fists as she pounded his chest.

"You were supposed to protect her!" Aina's eyes were bloodshot, and tears poured down her cheeks. "You were supposed to stop it from happening!"

"I didn't expect—"

"You were her second-in-command!" Aina shoved him, and Meizan let her. Mostly because he was too stunned to react, and also because Aina was right. He should have found a way. He should have stopped the chief from taking Zenyra's hit.

"She trusted you!" Aina shrieked. "If you couldn't have stopped it, you should've taken her place!"

Meizan hung his head. His fingers ghosted over the empty scabbard at his waist.

"Say something!" Aina grabbed his collar and shook him. "Say something, damn you!"

"You're right," Meizan whispered. "I failed her . . ."

Aina punched him, hard, and Meizan didn't bother to tilt his head away. Pain tore across his jaw, but it was nothing, *nothing* compared to the agony in his heart.

In the time he'd known her, Kanna had been more than a chief. She had rescued him from a lifetime of bitterness. Taken him under her wing, guided him, and given him a purpose. They shared no bloodline—no bond beyond clan alliance—and yet Kanna had risked Kanjallen's troops to rescue him from Kaufgar.

And now she was gone, and Meizan was left with her daughter. A girl who wished him erased from the universe.

But it's not all my fault, Meizan told himself as Aina slammed a fist into his gut. *Aina's the flaming idiot who stabbed herself to open the Void. She's the bleeding fool who got carried away by Zenyra's lies.*

Meizan dodged Aina's next blow and kicked her across the clearing.

"None of it would've happened if you weren't so damn gullible!" he shouted. "We were coming to save you, Aina! From the start, your mother was trying to prote—"

"You think I don't know that?"

Aina let out another blast of energy, darker and more powerful than anything Meizan had ever felt from her. She wasn't channeling but only unleashing her own chitrons. They washed over

Meizan in a torrent of anger and grief, amplifying his own misery. Unable to withstand the raw anguish of Aina's soul a moment longer, Meizan erected a chitronic shield.

She was Malini again. But she carried more hatred and pain than most in the realm.

Another scream ripped from Aina's throat as she pounced on him in a fury. Meizan dodged swiftly, his shield chipping away under her continued assault.

He didn't recognize this Aina. There was no telling what she'd do. He should attack outright and get it over with, and yet Meizan found it impossible to raise a fist against her.

Because even if Aina was dangerous, she was the last of Kanna's blood. The girl Meizan had promised—and failed—to protect.

Meizan dodged a barrage of punches, then sent his chitrons to wrap around Aina like a shroud. She thrashed against the shield as it encapsulated her and contained her attacks. Aina's chitrons rubbed against his, malicious and clamoring for revenge.

Meizan heard approaching footsteps behind him, and Aina gave a furious yell. The shield shattered and she dove forward. A dark claw of energy extended from her palm.

Aina flew past Meizan to pin Aranel against a tree.

"You!" Aina snarled. "You bleeding traitor! You self-serving son of a bitch! I can't believe I ever—" She let out an enraged cry, and her chitrons tightened around his throat.

Aranel coughed, and blood spilled from his lips, but he made no move to fight back or break free. "Aina . . . I'm so . . . sorry."

"I'll erase you for what you did! I'll wipe out every chitron in your soul!"

"Aina . . . wait . . . this isn't you."

"There's nothing left of me!" Aina's voice broke as more tears leaked from her eyes. The claw squeezed tighter. Aranel's breaths grew erratic, his fingers scraping at his neck. "Everything I was, everything I did, was all so I could be with her again! And you destroyed her! You and that manipulative witch!"

Choked sobs wracked Aina's thin shoulders as the chitrons around Aranel's neck tightened.

Was the idiot just going to let her choke him until he passed out?

Swearing, Meizan tackled Aina from behind, and the binds around Aranel flickered. He broke free as Meizan and Aina rolled on the ground, both struggling to get the upper hand.

Meizan scrambled to his feet as Aranel reached into his pocket. There was a flash of silver, and Aina's eyes drooped shut, the kapizer spine embedded in her shoulder. Aranel caught her and laid her on the ground. He bound her side with a strip of his tunic before turning to Meizan.

"Meizan, I'm sor—"

"Save it."

"But I never meant—"

"It doesn't matter what you meant," Meizan said. "She came prepared with the blood. Regardless of your intervention, she would've done what she set out to do. I was stupid to think we could stop her."

Aranel was silent, and Meizan stared at the sky above. The chitronic shield had disintegrated in parts, giving way to patches of golden light where Mayana seeped through. The chitrons were disrupted too; their frenzied flows clashed like lightning overhead.

"I saw the army," Aranel said, his tone desperate, pleading. "It's bigger than I thought it would be. They're attacking Kirnos first. They're going to destroy it."

I warned you, Meizan almost said. In the Void, he'd been shocked by the ease with which Aranel fell for Zenyra's illogical claims of a short-lived war with minimal destruction. *Then again, it's just like him to believe her.* Meizan remembered their first encounter in Martharan and Aranel's thickheaded refusal to injure the kapizer. *He's always been idealistic to the point of idiocy. And now it's come to bite him in the ass.*

"I betrayed my kingdom," Aranel said, pained. "I betrayed my realm, and Aina . . . and you." His voice quivered. "I suppose I've made you hate me even more than you did before."

"I never hated you." Meizan met his eyes for a brief moment, then lowered his gaze. "And you didn't betray me. We were never on the same side to begin with."

"We could be now," Aranel implored. "What happened in the Void can't be reversed, but we *can* fight for what comes next. If Zenyra can overthrow the Preservation, everything will change. We could rebuild the chitronic shields and make them more balanced. Make them so innocent children don't have to suffer or be born to violence and hunger."

Can you really?

Aranel talked as if he knew all about how the shields worked. Meizan doubted that was the case. It was all hypothetical and theoretical and far in the future. Their present reality was the war. A war that Zenyra herself had sparked.

"I know her methods are extreme, but so is the system the Preservation are trying to protect," Aranel said. "You could fight with us and help topple them." He reached toward Meizan but seemed too afraid to touch him. "You and your clan. Zenyra will need all the help she can get if she's to mitigate the violence in the upcoming war. Kanjallen can help keep discipline amongst the soldiers, and I had this idea about coating all the weapons with kapizer venom to—"

"There are a couple hundred thousand soldiers in that army,"

Meizan cut him off. "Even with Kanjallen on her side, Zenyra has no chance of controlling them all."

"What if some of the Mayani kingdoms were to ally with us? We could start by convincing Kirnos and Tahamur. If they agree, the others are likely to follow."

"You think you and Zenyra can convince a bunch of uppers to join a Malini army and rebel against their precious Preservation? I don't know about your realm's politics, Aranel, but what you're saying sounds delusional."

"But it's our only chance!" Aranel withdrew his hand. "To change things. To make them right. You're going to be embroiled in the war, whether you like it or not, so you may as well—"

He clamped his mouth shut as Aina stirred. She stood with a groan and pressed a hand to her waist, then tore off the strip of cloth Aranel had wrapped it with.

"Where are you going?" Meizan asked as Aina tossed the bloodied cloth aside.

"To find the Preservation," Aina grunted. "There's nothing stopping me from entering Mayana, and they're the only ones with the power to stand against Zenyra."

"Why would you—" Aranel fell silent at Aina's glare.

"I'm going to erase her," she whispered harshly. "I'm going to obliterate every chitron of her being from this universe, no matter what it takes. And I'll do the same to you, Aranel, if you dare cross paths with me again."

She opened her palm to display a syringe containing a single drop of dark blood. Aranel stumbled back, stricken.

"What about the war?" Meizan asked. "And the chitronic shields?"

"To hell with the war and the shields," Aina spat. "None of it matters anymore."

Meizan watched her go and felt half compelled to follow. He had promised his chief he'd protect her. In her current state of mind, Aina was bound to do something foolish.

"So she's aligning with the Preservation." Aranel shook his head. "Never would I have imagined . . ."

"She's aligning with the Preservation," Meizan repeated. "And you're aligning with Zenyra."

"What about you?" Aranel asked. "Will you . . . go with Aina?"

Meizan glanced down at his scabbard. Despite his promise to Kanna, there wasn't much he could do if Aina chose to seek out the Preservation. Zenyra was the greater threat, but there wasn't much he could do about her, either, given she was surrounded by an army and headed for war.

Meizan's life had been miserable living under the chitronic system, but he couldn't see how Zenyra would make things better. She would overthrow the Preservation, and then what? Seat herself upon their throne in Paramos? The woman was cunning and vile and ready to erase souls. In Meizan's book, she was worse than Kaldrav, who at least had made no false pretenses about his morality.

There was no point overthrowing a system if there was nothing to replace it with. Meizan wasn't convinced by Zenyra's methods or Aranel's naive plan.

And the Narakhi, Meizan thought with a chill. The chitronic shields around Narakh seemed to have remained intact for the time being. But there was no telling what Zenyra would do next. For both sides of the war, releasing the demons of Narakh from their realm would be the worst outcome.

"I'm returning to Kanjallen," Meizan said. He had to tell them about the chief, along with everything else that had transpired. Whatever decision he made next would be contingent on his clan.

Meizan spared Aranel a final glance, then turned on his heel and strode from the clearing.

The splintering sky above was split in an eerie dichotomy, half golden sunset and half murky red. Sparks lined the edges where the two realms opened into one another.

When he looked over his shoulder, Aranel had disappeared. Fingers curling around his empty scabbard, Meizan trudged through the woods in search of his clan.

EPILOGUE

A Sliver of Flame

*I*T *BEGAN WITH* a groan. Then a great rumbling that split the ground asunder and ripped through the sky, crumbling mountains to dust and stirring up waves that swallowed entire villages.

It came from the deepest, darkest crevice of Malin—a realm near emptied as its armies marched upon Mayana. But those Malini who remained shuddered at the sound. At the promise of an inescapable doom yet to come.

She is waking, they whispered, fear slicing through their hearts. *The end has begun.*

Miles below, the darkness parted to reveal a sliver of flame, wide as a lake. The eye blinked, then vanished.

OF LANGUAGE
AND
NOMENCLATURE

THE LANGUAGE SPOKEN in the realms has remained largely unchanged since Kal Ekana and employs a logographic writing system where words and morphemes are designated with unique symbols. While each symbol carries a particular meaning, when combined into words—especially proper nouns—the overall meaning is oft subject to interpretation. Below is a list of key nouns and some common interpretations.

Agakor
Fiery ices
Combines **aga** (fire, fiery) with **kora** (ice, icy)
A vast network of caves in southern Malin, location of Kaldrav's torture chambers[1]; contain pools filled with ice so cold it burns

Aina
Girl of love, girl who is loved, girl who seeks to be loved
Combines the characters for **ai** (love, loved) with **-na** (common name ending meaning "girl of")

Akanen
Of red eyes, red eyed
Combines **aka** (red) with **nen** (eyes)
The founder and first chief of clan Kanjallen

Amaleni
River of purity
Combines **amala** (pure, purity) with **eni** (river)
A river in eastern Mayana; drinking or bathing in its waters can heal weariness and uplift spirits

---

1 While the surface caves are filled with Kaldrav's soldiers and their victims, the subterranean ones miles below—where no men dare trespass—serve as the nagamor's favored breeding grounds.

Amaratir   Isle of honey
Combines **amarata** (honey) with **-ir** (Amaratiri variant of place ending meaning "isle of" or "island of")
An underwater[2] kingdom in central Mayana, located in Mir Amaratis; sculpted entirely from a vast coral reef, it houses a thriving ecosystem of sea life

Andraken   King of darkness, darkened king
Combines **andra** (darkness, night) with **ken** (king)
The name given to the planetary vandraghor of Narakh

Aranel   Son of the forest
Combines **aran** (forest) with **-el** (Kirnosi variant of a name ending meaning "son of")

Aran Kirenkar   Forest of broken tree light (colloquial: Dappled Forest)
Combines **aran** (forest) with **ki** (tree), **ren** (break, broken), and **kara** (beam or ray of light)
A forest at the heart of Kirnos, named for the way sunlight filters through the trees

Aro   Ascent
The head priest of the temple of Kirnos

Ashkator   Blessing of knowledge, blessed by knowledge
Combines **ashka** (blessing) with **tora** (knowledge, knowing)
A crater in Paramos, home of the Preservation headquarters; the chitronic flows pouring down its slope make it impossible to scale for any but the most proficient of channelers

Athanken   Eighth king
Combines **athan** (eighth) with **ken** (king)
The current king and elected ruler of Kirnos, father to Princess Himalia

Azyaka   Queen of torture, queen who tortures, tortured queen
Combines **azya** (pain, torture) with **ka** (queen)
The name given to the planetary nagamor of Malin

Chiren   Broken blood, breakers of blood, those who break and bleed
Combines **chi** (blood) with **ren** (break, broken)

---

2 Mayani seawater is breathable for humans.

A Malini clan, the first to declare their allegiance to Kaldrav; thus named for their mutilation rituals wherein members receive multiple cuts with the branch of a bloodreaper bush[3]

Chitron   Conscious particle, particle of consciousness
Combines **chita** (consciousness) with **ron** (particle)
Subatomic spinning particles that make up human souls; created by thoughts, intentions, emotions, and actions, and accumulated throughout a soul's lifetime; while individual chitrons are invisible to the human eye, they appear as colored light when channeled en masse

Einaz   Sharp spear
Combines **ei** (sharp, sharpness) with **naza** (spear)
A member of clan Kanjallen

Eniya   Son of the river
Combines **eni** (river) with **-ya** (Tahamuri variant of a name ending meaning "son of")
A Balancer hailing from Tahamur

Fei   Loyalty
The name of a megarya that befriended Zenyra

Feragaz   Irongrass
Combines **fera** (iron) with **gaza** (grass)
A prairie in southern Malin, home to clan Kanjallen until they migrated north to Raitani; sharp enough to cut skin, the individual blades of grass are often harvested to make weaponry

Gazarou   Grass wolf
Combines **gaza** (grass) with **rou** (wolf)
Great beast native to Mayana; has the form of a wolf with grassy fur, which can be used to relieve pain and heal any nature of injury

Himalia   Moonflower
Combines **hima** (moon) with **lia** (flower)
The current princess of Kirnos, named after a species of lily native to the region

---

3 Starting from a member's first birthday, a number of new cuts are made each year, corresponding to age.

Hiraval
Of diamond hair, diamond haired
Combines **hira** (diamond) with **vala** (hair)
A Balancer hailing from Amaratir

Ibaran
Thorn Forest
Combines **ibara** (thorn) with **aran** (forest)
*A forest in eastern Malin, location of clan Chiren's villages;
    known for its distinct crimson soil and prickly, bone-white
    vegetation*

Incaraz
Secret revolution, revolutionary secret
Combines **incara** (revolution) with **raza** (secret, clandestine)
Name of the main Balancer hideout in Malin

Ish'shai
Gloomstone
Combines **ish** (stone) with **shai** (gloom)
*A towering rock formation in northern Malin; a nearby rift
    houses one of the Balancer villages*

Kal Charana
Four Realm Era
Combines **kala** (era, age) with **chara** (four) and **na** (realm)
*The age after the Great Toranic Separation with four realms
    segregated by soul-spin; at the onset of this period, human-
    kind gained immortality, although other living beings
    remained mortal*

Kaldrav
Warrior of the ages
Combines **kala** (era, age) with **drava** (warrior)
The tyrannical king of Malin

Kal Ekana
One Realm Era
Combines **kala** (era, age) with **eka** (one) and **na** (realm)
*The age before the Great Toranic Separation with one realm for
    all soul-spins; during this period, humans, like other living
    beings, were mortal*

Kamaltani
Lotus vale
Combines **kamal** (lotus) with **tani** (vale, valley)
*A valley in western Mayana; lotuses of all sizes bloom in its
    ponds, some large enough to build a house on*

Kanjallen
Eternal sad water (colloquial: eternal tears)
Combines **kan** (sad, sadness) and **jalla** (water) with **en** (eternity)
*A Malini clan, the only one to successfully avoid absorption by
    Kaldrav; consists of an alliance wherein several smaller*

clans assimilated under Kanjallen's banners and adopted
their name; said to carry the ancient "blessing of the nagamor," members of the original bloodline are both chitronically and physically gifted[4]

Kanna   Girl of sadness, girl who is sad
                   Combines the characters for **kan** (sad, sadness) with **-na** (com-
                   mon name ending meaning "girl of")
                   The current chief of clan Kanjallen

Kapizer   Poison monkey
                   Combines **kapi** (monkey) with **zera** (poison)
                   *Beast native to Malin; has the form of a horned monkey, with
                   needlelike spines containing a poison that induces sleep*

Karaeni   River of light (colloquial: Aurora Rapids)
                   Combines **kara** (beam or ray of light) with **eni** (river)
                   *A skybound river in Mayana known for the chitronic turbulence
                   of its luminescent waters; when viewed from the ground at
                   night, it resembles ribbons of dancing light*

Kaufgar   Home of fear, fearful home
                   Combines **kaufa** (fear) with **gara** (home)
                   *A fortress in northern Malin, location of Kaldrav's stronghold
                   and prisons*

Kazegir   Windhill
                   Combines **kaze** (wind) with **gir** (hill)
                   *A hill in eastern Mayana; known for the melody produced when
                   the wind blows through the surrounding bamboo forest*

Keiza   Seat of wisdom
                   Combines **kei** (wisdom) with **za** (seat)
                   *A swirl of raised skin on the forehead and the most important
                   of the nine spiritual receptors; stimulating it by swiping a
                   finger allows a human to access their chitrons for channel-
                   ing; while the keiza's brightness and direction corresponds to
                   an individual's soul-spin, its color is thought to be random[5]
                   and unique to each individual*

---

4 While members of the assimilated clans do not possess the same level of skill as those hailing
  from the original bloodline, decades of mentorship have transformed even their weakest—
  excluding young children and the infirm—into warriors considerably stronger than Kaldrav's.

5 Keiza colors are unrelated to ethnicity or soul-spin.

Kirnos   Provenance of enlightenment

Combines **kirana** (enlightenment) with **-os** (Kirnosi variant of place ending meaning "birthplace of" or "provenance of")

Named shortened from Kiranos; a kingdom in Mayana contained within a giant lotus that floats freely across the realm and thus has no fixed location; its unique ambulatory nature has attracted settlers from across the realm, giving it a far more heterogenous population than other parts of Mayana

Kurogir   Blackhill

Combines **kuro** (black) with **gir** (hill)

A hill in Malin with woods that are prone to wildfires, giving it a charred appearance

Kyrian   Prince of glory, glorious prince

Combines **kyra** (glory) with **-ian** (name ending meaning "prince of")

The leader of the Preservation

Malin   Filth

The lower realm between Narakh and Mayana

Manikai   Jewel shell

Combines **mani** (jewel) with **kai** (shell)

Beast native to Mayana; has the form of a sea tortoise; the gems encrusting its shell can be used to store and amplify chitronic energy

Martharan   Forest of death (colloquial: Dead Forest)

Combines **martha** (dead, death) with **aran** (forest)

A forest in Malin that encircles the volcano of Merumarth; named for its barren trees and toxic air, which make it unsuitable for most species, save the kapizer who are immune to the toxins

Mayana   Realm of illusions, magical realm

Combines **maya** (magic, illusion) with **na** (realm)

The upper realm between Malin and Paramos

Megarya   Master of the clouds

Combines **mega** (cloud) with **arya** (master, one who is skilled)

Great beast native to Paramos; has the form of a winged dolphin with a wide, round snout; the color of its fur varies, with most common hues being black, gray, and dark purple

Meizan   Unfortunate destiny, one destined to misfortune
Combines **mei** (destiny) with **zan** (unfortunate, misfortune)

Meruharis   Needle Mountains
Combines **meru** (mountain) with **hari** (needle)
A mountain range in eastern Malin; named after its unusually thin and pointed peaks

Meruhirs   Diamond Mountains
Combines **meru** (mountain) with **hira** (diamond)
A mountain range in western Mayana, composed entirely of diamond; it is believed that immense chitronic and geological pressure during the Great Toranic Separation transformed the rock

Merumarth   Dead Mountain
Combines **meru** (mountain) with **marth** (dead, death)
An active volcano in Malin whose fumes have made the surrounding forest of Martharan almost uninhabitable

Merunils   Blue Mountains
Combines **meru** (mountain) with **nila** (blue)
A mountain range in central Mayana, named for its high concentration of lazurite deposits

Meruten   Heavenly Mountain
Combines **meru** (mountain) with **ten** (heaven, heavenly)
A volcano in eastern Mayana, located in Nisharan; once a year, it erupts flowers that pour down its slopes and rain from the skies for three days; this is considered an auspicious period, during which surrounding villages host festivals that include feasting and dancing under the flowerfall

Meruxars   Rotting Mountains
Combines **meru** (mountain) with stem of verb **xaru** (to rot)
A mountain range in Malin, bordering Mir Muzira; while the eastern slopes remain dry, an acid rain blows from the sea and falls on the western slopes, causing the vegetation to decay

Mir Amaratis   Sea that births honey (colloquial: Honeyed Sea)
Combines **mira** (sea, ocean) with **amarata** (honey) and **-is** (Amaratisian variant of place ending meaning "birthplace of" or "provenance of")

A sea in central Mayana known for its sweet-tasting water; natural habitat of the manikai; a hydrothermal vent in the seabed pours forth holy nectar and is a popular pilgrimage destination

Mir Himamani   Sea of moon jewels (colloquial: Pearl Sea)

Combines **mira** (sea, ocean) with **hima** (moon) and **mani** (jewel)

A sea that spans across eastern and western Mayana; known for the nacreous sheen of its water caused by colonies of plankton; at night, their silvery bioluminescence creates the appearance of billions of tiny pearls floating under the surface

Mir Karasura   Sea of rays of sunlight (colloquial: Sunbeam Sea)

Combines **mira** (sea, ocean) with **kara** (beam or ray of light) and **sura** (sun)

A sea in southern Mayana known for its clear, glittering water; whirlpools and large waves are frequent occurrences and attract channelers who want to hone their skills surfing the water

Mir Muzira   Noxious Sea

Combines **mira** (sea, ocean) with **muzira** (noxious, harmful)

A sea that spans across eastern and western Malin; its corals release unusually high levels of toxins that rise to the surface and cause the water to steam and bubble; acid rains frequent the sea and its surrounding regions

Mir Renkora   Sea of broken ice (colloquial: Iceshard Sea)

Combines **mira** (sea, ocean) with **ren** (break, broken) and **kora** (ice)

A sea in southern Malin with a frozen surface; repeated crossings by Malini have caused the ice to break in several places

Mir Tamasa   Shadowed Sea

Combines **mira** (sea, ocean) with **tamasa** (shadow)

A sea in central Malin named for its tenebrous waters; the currents are difficult to navigate and stir up dark sand from the seabed, hampering visibility beyond a couple feet in any direction

Mirya   Son of the sea

Combines **mira** (sea, ocean) with **-ya** (Tahamuri variant of a name ending meaning "son of")

The current prince of Tahamur, childhood friend and rival of Aranel

Muzireni	Noxious River Combines **muzira** (noxious, harmful) with **eni** (river) *A river that cuts across western Malin; choked with toxins from Mir Muzira, its sludgy waters are guaranteed to cause debilitating disease if consumed*
Nagakost	Snakebone Combines **naga** (snake) with **kosta** (bone) *A group of islands in Malin, located in Mir Renkora; thus named for their resemblance to a snake skeleton*
Nagamor	Peacock snake Combines **naga** (snake) with **mora** (peacock) *Great beast native to Malin; has the form of a giant snake with blue scales, a beak, and a feathered tail; meeting its gaze triggers intense, hyperrealistic hallucinations that force the victim to relive their most painful memories*
Namyra	Daughter of waves Combines **nami** (waves) with **-yra** (Amaratisian variant of a name ending meaning "daughter of") *A Balancer hailing from Amaratir*
Narakh	Hell *The lowermost realm beneath Malin*
Nishaki	Dream tree Combines **nisha** (dream) with **ki** (tree) *A kingdom in eastern Mayana, located on the fringes of Nisharan; famous for its bathhouses and cloudmist springs[6]*
Nisharan	Forest of Dreams Combines **nisha** (dream) with **aran** (forest) *A floating jungle in eastern Mayana, suspended miles aboveground; natural habitat of the gazarou*
Ozoreni	Dread River Combines **ozora** (dread, despair) with **eni** (river) *A river that cuts across eastern Malin; stained by the red soils of Ibaran, its waters give the appearance of blood*
Paramos	Provenance of supremacy Combines **parama** (supremacy, the highest state of being)

---

6 The condensation from clouds collects on branches and drips down to form pools, which are then chitronically heated.

with -os (Kirnosi variant of place ending meaning "birth-place of" or "provenance of")

The uppermost realm above Mayana

Raitani   Lightning vale
Combines **rai** (lightning) with **tani** (vale, valley)
A valley in Malin, located within the eastern fringes of the Meruxars; so named due to the severe lack of moisture in the air that causes excessive perennial static; several clan Kanjallen villages populated this region but have since been razed by Kaldrav's army

Rangaran   Forest of Colors
Combines **ranga** (color) with **aran** (forest)
A forest in western Mayana known for its vibrant trees; their leaves change hue depending on season, cycling through all shades of the rainbow

Raxaz(i)   Fiend, demon(ess)
A brother and sister duo, both members of clan Chiren

Razamir   Clandestine sea, of the secret sea
Combines **raza** (secret, clandestine) with **mir** (sea)
A Malini clan allied with Kaldrav; once a band of seafaring pirates, they overbred saberfin sharks for their fins—until the unnaturally large shark population attacked and destroyed all their ships

Reimi   Daughter of ambition, ambitious daughter
Combines **rei** (ambition) with **-mi** (Nisharian variant of a name ending meaning "daughter of")
A Balancer hailing from Nisharan

Renjan   Broken human, human who breaks
Combines **ren** (break, broken) with **jana** (human)
A member of clan Kanjallen, son of the former chief

Samaras   Provenance of legend
Combines **samara** (legend) with **-as** (Samarasi variant of place ending meaning "birthplace of" or "provenance of")
A mountainous kingdom in western Mayana, nestled deep within the Meruhirs; little is known of their culture, for they prefer to remain secluded, although several Samarasi families of note have been settled in Kirnos for centuries

Samarel Son of legend, legendary son
Combines **samara** (legend) with **-el** (Kirnosi variant of a name
  ending meaning "son of")
Older brother to Aranel

Seirem Fortunate life, life of fortune
Combines **sei** (life, life force) with **rema** (fortune, prosperity)
A member of the Preservation

Seitarius Life star beast (colloquial: Planetary Beast)
Combines **sei** (life, life force) and **tara** (star) with **-ius** (ending
  meaning "beast")
*Cosmic beings who created the universe from the emptiness of
  the Void, worshipped as gods and goddesses throughout the
  realms*

Sherka Queen of kindness, kind queen
Combines **shera** (kindness) with **ka** (queen)
Name given to the planetary gazarou of Mayana

Soranil Blue sky
Combines **sora** (sky) with **nila** (blue)
A Balancer hailing from Samaras

Sorken King of the skies, sky king
Combines **sora** (sky) with **ken** (king)
Name given to the planetary megarya of Paramos

Taezur Enduring difficulties
Combines stem of verb taeru (to endure) with zura (difficulty)
A member of clan Kanjallen

Tahamur Island of bravery
Combines **tahama** (bravery) with **-ur** (Tahamuri variant of
  place ending meaning "isle of" or "island of")
*An island kingdom in southern Mayana, located in Mir Kara-
  sura; the greatest of the Mayani kingdoms, inventor of several
  chitronic arts,[7] and rivalled in might only by Kirnos[8]*

---

7 Including the art of walking across air and water and the discovery that exposure to sunlight
  can recharge chitrons quicker; Kirnos, however, is more advanced when it comes to chitronic
  healing.

8 Kirnos and Tahamur have a long-standing rivalry in cloudsurfing and other chitronic sports;
  while Kirnos has grown stronger in recent years, Tahamur holds nearly twice as many records
  historically.

Taralei

Daughter of stars

Combines **tara** (star) and **-lei** (Kirnosi variant of a name ending meaning "daughter of")

A Balancer hailing from Kirnos

Tareinjil

Star mirror lake (colloquial: Starglass Lake)

Combines **tara** (star) and **ein** (mirror) with **jila** (lake)

A lake with clear, still water, located south of the Meruhirs

Tenshir

White heaven

Combines **ten** (heaven, heavenly) with **shira** (white)

A Balancer hailing from Nisharan

Torana

Knowing gateway, gateway of knowledge

Combines **tora** (knowledge, knowing) with **ana** (opening, entry, gateway)

Gateways that connect the realms and operate on the basis of Toranic Law, created during the Great Toranic Separation

Torhan

Knowing judgment, knowledgeable judgment

Combines **tora** (knowledge, knowing) with **han** (judgment)

Refers to the omniscient knowledge and perfect judgment of the universe, that is, the force of nature that determines the spin of chitrons; the original spelling and pronunciation have been all but forgotten, and it goes more commonly now by the misnomer Toranic Law

Ummi

Hope

Derived from **umid** (hope)

A young girl born to Malin

Vandraghor

Evil roach, roach of sin

Combines **vandra** (roach) with **ghora** (evil, sin)

Great beast native to Narakh; has the form of a giant cockroach with multitudinous protruding eyeballs and countless legs

Virator

Strength and knowledge

Combines **vira** (strength) with **tora** (knowledge, knowing)

A Malini clan, one of the last to ally with Kaldrav

Zenyra

Daughter that is everything

Combines **zen** (all, everything) with **-yra** (Amaratisian variant of a name ending meaning "daughter of")

The founder and leader of the Balancers

Zerajil   Poison Lake

Combines **zera** (poison) with **jila** (lake)

A lake in Malin, south of the Meruxars; its shores were once a favored breeding ground for the kapizer until overhunting by Malini clans[9] led the surviving colonies to flee northward to Martharan; however, centuries of kapizer habitation poisoned the water, rendering it uninhabitable to aquatic plants and animals

---

9 The kapizer were hunted for their poisonous spines as well as their horns.

AUTHOR'S NOTE

FOR THOSE INTERESTED, I have provided a brief note on the inspiration behind *Spin of Fate*'s magic system.

TORANIC LAW AND KARMA YOGA

The Toranic[10] system is very loosely inspired by my understanding of Hinduism's karma yoga, that is, the theory of karma. This philosophy has fascinated me ever since my mother introduced me to the Bhagavad Gītā at a young age.

Often surrounded by misconception, karma yoga is an extremely nuanced spiritual way of thought—one that I am still learning more about every day. I have included some resources in the Further Reading section for anyone who would like to read up on it in more depth. However, for the purpose of this note, to provide a gross oversimplification of the concept of karma: It is a causative principle wherein a person's actions (and more specifically the intentions behind their actions) determine their future—including future births.

The idea of reincarnation is thus crucial in the context of karma's workings since the circumstances of one's birth and nature of their life are often determined by the deeds of their

---

10   The name Toranic Law echoes the name of the in-universe gateways, or torana, which in turn was taken from the Sanskrit word *torana* used to describe ceremonial gateways in Hindu architecture, and also the Japanese word *torii* for similar archways in Shinto shrines.

soul in previous lives. This presents a glaring disconnect with *Spin of Fate*'s universe, wherein humans are immortal . . . so how could Toranic Law possibly work as intended? This is an issue that will be explored through the course of the series.

Removed from the creative decisions and modified portrayal in my story, the law of karma itself is a beautiful thing, complex in its workings and—when one really delves into its nuances—convincing in its effects. In some ways, I might even consider it the closest thing we have to a real-life magic system.

OTHER INFLUENCES FROM HINDUISM

While *Spin of Fate* features a polytheistic religion, none of the imagined deities are based on any of those from Hinduism. Rather, I created them inspired in part by *Naruto*'s bijū, and also several legendary Pokémon. The idea of realms, however, was loosely influenced by the Hindu concept of lokas, which are planes or realms (the translation varies) of existence. You can read more on my blog at A2Vora.com.

FURTHER READING

The theory of karma was narrated by Lord Krishna, who explained it to the warrior Arjuna before the war of Kurukshetra. The story of the war is narrated in the epic Mahābhārata, while the scripture Bhagavad Gītā focuses on Lord Krishna's teachings. There are several translations of these ancient texts, as well as countless interpretations of karma yoga. I have included here a few that I personally found insightful.

1. *Theory of Karma* by Hirabhai Thakkar—an English translation of the same author's original Gujarati *Karmano Siddhant*—does a fantastic job of breaking down the multifaceted and complex concept of karma in a way that is very accessible.

2. While several versions of the Bhagavad Gītā exist, Professor Sarvepalli Radhakrishnan's translation and commentary is one that I enjoyed recently.

3. Regarding the epic tale of Mahābhārata, I grew up reading the Amar Chitra Katha graphic novels. My most recent read, however, was by the author Kamala Subramaniam.

ACKNOWLEDGMENTS

I'D LIKE TO express my gratitude to all the people without whom the world of *Spin of Fate* (or *SOF*, as some call it) would have remained but a figment of my imagination.

My literary agent and fellow *Naruto* fan, Jon Cobb—the one "yes" amongst hundreds of "nos". Thank you for giving my story a chance when no one else would. I owe so much to your tireless enthusiasm, prompt communication, and creative direction. Without you, Aranel wouldn't have been a spy, Aina wouldn't have been a key, and Meizan wouldn't have . . . existed, really, until book 2. I simply can't thank you enough (believe it). And a heartfelt thanks to your team at HG Literary, especially Soumeya Bendimerad Roberts and Ellen Goff, for working tirelessly to spread this book's message far and wide.

My editor, Polo Orozco—your keen editorial instinct made *SOF* more accessible and engaging, shaping it into the story it needed to be (because we know if I'd had it my way, there would have been far more exposition about historical details and magic system intricacies . . . and far less focus on character relationships; relationships that I now realize form the true heart of this novel). Your suggestion to include epigraphs and poetry also led to some of my favorite sentences ever written. I really hope to meet you and Jon in person one day.

The incredible teams at Penguin Young Readers and

G. P. Putnam's Sons for their unflagging dedication in taking *SOF* to completion and getting it out into the world, and for considering my (verbose and overly detailed) input in all aspects from artwork to tagline to map. My gratitude to Jen Klonsky for championing Team Spin since submissions and for enthusiastic remote celebrations (with cake, in sweatpants—yep, I remember). Copyeditors Kellie Hultgren, Cindy Howle, Lana Barnes, and Misha Kydd for their meticulous reads and for coaching me on archaic English usage, proper comma placement, and the rules of capitalization after em dashes. I promise that book 2 will be more polished! Cover designers Tony Sahara and Jessica Jenkins, whose artistic sensibilities led to the classic high fantasy cover of my dreams. Sidharth Chaturvedi, my ridiculously talented cover artist, for interpreting my amateur drawings and bringing the terror and beauty of the nagamor to life. Interior designer Suki Boynton for the stunning pages and for finding a way to incorporate my keiza scribbles at the start of each chapter. Map artist Sveta Dorosheva for taking my all-too-long PowerPoint presentation and transforming it into a gorgeously detailed rendering of my world, better than I could have ever imagined. Natalie Vielkind, Madison Penico, and Amanda Cranney, unsung heroes who worked tirelessly on the production front. In no particular order, I'd also like to thank Jen Loja, Debra Polansky, Shanta Newlin, Elyse Marshall, Emily Romero, Christina Colangelo, Alex Garber, Felicity Vallence, Shannon Spann, James Akinaka, Carmela Iaria, Helen Boomer, and Kim Ryan.

A huge thank-you to my fantastically talented beta readers, starting with Ali-chan: my old roomie and longtime *nakama*. You make me a better writer and a better person. Thank you for loving my characters possibly more than I do. You've nitpicked my story (in the *best* possible way) and given so many fabulous suggestions to tweak characterization and plot. Thank you for being Aranel's fiercest advocate when the rest of us were biased toward Meizan (except my mom, who obviously likes Aina best). Book-2 Aranel and I owe so much to you.

Donovan: my ex-engagement manager, fellow Sanderson fan, and dear friend. Your first critique on that one slide deck convinced me I needed the same for my book—thank the Valar we have the same interests. Your thorough and perfectly structured feedback certainly elevated my plot and magic system. And I did enjoy our book-3 PS sessions; that speakeasy in Omotesando is long overdue a visit!

Rosaria Munda: my first ever author friend. It's surreal I can call you my friend, since I was once just another Aurelian Cycle fangirl. Thank you for (digitally) holding my hand through the publishing process, and for your insightful notes on my draft. You pointed out plot conveniences and saved me from committing so many blunders—remember that time I wanted to use diacritics for every vowel in every proper noun? Glad we scrapped that. (Also, anyone who is reading this and hasn't already checked out her book *Fireborne*, do it now.)

Hedy: one of my favorite people to exist, the Sasuke to my Naruto, the Nozomi to my Eli. You've given me advice on my manuscript, my cover, my social media presence . . . and while I've still much to improve on the latter, your thoughtful comments have been invaluable throughout.

Thank you, Shagun, *mellon nin*, for essentially cultivating my taste in high fantasy when you introduced me to *The Wheel of Time* and *A Song of Ice and Fire* during that one MUN conference back in middle school. And for being the one friend who gets my *Silmarillion* references and Fëanor memes. Thank you, Ishani, for . . . well, you know what for; IB HL Chemistry was exponentially more fun with you there to fangirl with. Priyanka Khanna, for giving me my first—and only other—writing stint at *Vogue India* back in the day when I had no qualifications or experience otherwise. The wonderful folk at Manuscript Academy—Jessica, Julie, and Valentina—for helping me through the punishing querying process. Brent Taylor for giving me great feedback on one of my oldest (and messiest) drafts, even though you didn't have to.

To the colleagues and friends who supported me through this process—Kristie, Ellie, Nat, Ayumicchi, Kennosuke, Matt, Philipp, Steph, Aashna, and so many others. My teachers at Mitchell Elementary for instilling in me a love for writing through Treehouse; at Dhirubhai Ambani International for shaping me into the person I am and cheering me on years after graduation; and at Princeton and Cambridge, for teaching me so much about the world and helping spread the word about *SOF*. (Special shout-out to CJBS MBA class of 2019; you guys rock!)

Thank you, *Pappa*, for keeping me grounded and teaching me important life lessons. Thank you, always, to *Masi*, *Nani*, and both my *Dadas* for your support, blessings, and prayers. Thank you, *Mamma*, for—well, I don't know where to start. You have shaped my entire belief system and made me into the person capable of telling this story. You have done so much, sacrificed so much, for me; all I can do is try to carry it forward as best as I can.

To my family in Japan. お母さん、お父さん、お婆ちゃん、安那、ふぃふ、いつも応援ありがとう！最近、小説の仕事でずっと迷惑をかけてしまってごめんね。でもおかげで忙しい中でも書き終わらせることが出来たので、心の底から感謝しているよ。落ち着いたらまた皆で沖縄とか行こうね！そして、将太朗くん。あぁ〜なんか言葉が足りない気がするけど色々本当にありがとう。チットロンの話とか、カタツムリの話とか。あいつは少し登場したけど、気付いたのかなぁ？頼むからこれからは変なアイディアを出さないでね（笑）。そして、私が編集とかを出来るよう

に、家のことをしてくれたり、ご飯を作ってくれたりして、最高の旦那さん
でいてくれてありがとう！これが全部終わったらポケカやりまくろうぜ。
大好きな同期達、Aムロという完全生物、マイ弁護士　フレンズ、あゆみ
っち♢、南山国際の皆：応援本当にありがとう、！

    Thank you, Aina, Aranel, and Meizan, for coming to me during a part of my life when I really needed you and helping me through my own darkness. And lastly, to you, my reader. Thank you for giving me your precious time and letting me share my world with you. There's a lot more of this story to come, so please stay tuned if you're interested. May your soul spin straight and swift!